Peter Hayes was born in Leonia, New Jersey in 1948. Of Latin–Irish descent, he was educated at Phillips Exeter Academy and Harvard College. He is the author of *The Supreme Adventure* (1988), and his short fiction has appeared in *The Atlantic* and other magazines. Peter lives in New York State with his wife Uma and their young son.

PETER HAYES

The Feathered Serpent

An *Abacus* Book

First published in Great Britain by Little, Brown and Company 1993
This edition published by Abacus 1994

A CIP catalogue record for this book
is available from the British Library.

ISBN 0 349 10546 4

Printed in England by Clays Ltd, St Ives plc

Abacus
A Division of
Little, Brown and Company (UK) Limited
Brettenham House
Lancaster Place
London WC2E 7EN

To Gurumayi;

and for my wife
Uma

Author's Note

The Republic of Dorado is a product of the author's imagination. It was assembled piecemeal – a volcano here, a revolution there – from the geography and history of half a dozen states.

The novel's characters are similarly formed, and any resemblance to actual persons, living or dead, is purely coincidental.

Contents

Part IV: The Bliss of Liberation

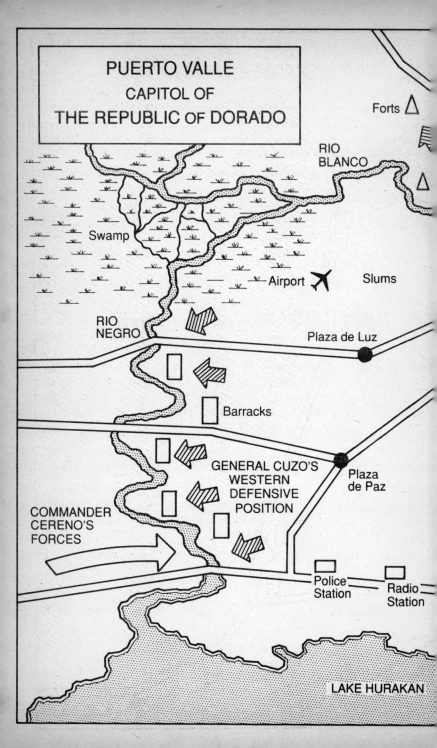

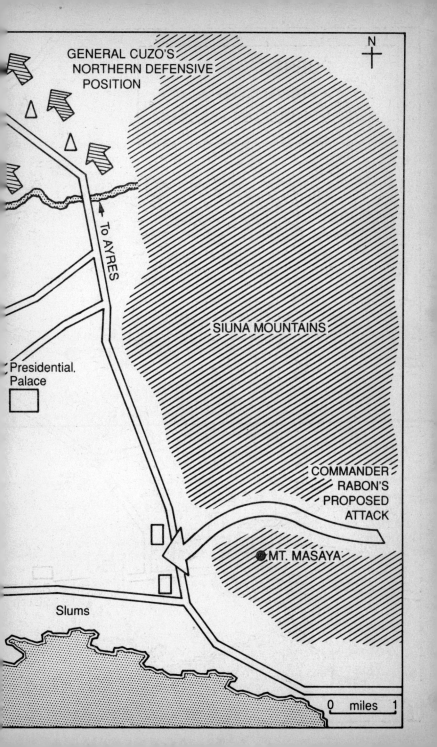

A Loss Of Nature

Part 1

Since Queen Ishtar went down into the underworld,
The Bull no longer mounts the cow . . .
                                    – Babylonian Myth

The Traitor

◆

Chapter 1

When Garcia finished reading his wife's letter, he replaced it carefully in its envelope, crossed the bedroom and sat down by the window. It was a spring evening: salmon clouds swam away in the west, while distance and a tarnished gold sunset made the tenements and the *barrio* streets below antique and toy. He had read that morning in *El Diario* an article on the neutron bomb. The story said its explosion killed all life but left the landscape intact and buildings standing. Though Garcia did not fully comprehend how a bomb could do this, he believed it had something to do with *rays*. And he remembered this now because this was how he felt: as though there had occurred, silently and invisibly, in the half-minute that had just passed, the detonation of this tremendous weapon and the secret release of its radioactivity – and the world was dead, and life was gone, though everything was still standing.

Garcia was very much in love with his wife and he had never imagined that she might forsake him. In their three months of wedded bliss, he had tried to be a loving husband: tender, faithful, hardworking and, though he was thirty years older than his bride, regular in the performance of his holy matrimonial duties. Why, only a week ago, they had spent many hours making love in their brass bed, the street lamp shining in their window like a private moon. It is true they had spent many hours because, in the midst of it all, Garcia

3

had 'lost his nature,' but these things, embarrassing as they are, happen to the best of men. It is true, too, that the next night and the night following, Garcia's manly nature had again failed him, and it is also true that his young wife had finally cried at his failure and with primitive emotion beat her black braids against the brass bedposts and asked him all those questions that an inexperienced girl will ask a man in such a situation: 'Am I not desirable?', 'Are you sick down there?', 'Do you not love me?'

But in the end, Garcia believed, he had persuaded both himself and her that it was nothing. He was tired. He had much on his mind. It was merely a temporary 'loss of nature,' nothing more.

And though a week had gone by and Garcia's nature had not been restored, still, this spring evening when he came home for supper and discovered her letter – '*Mi Corazon,*' it began – and learned she had left him – 'because, My Heart, what is Love without Love's passion?' – the pain of abandonment, so utterly unexpected, was like being blindsided by a blackjack.

Garcia sighed and bit his lip. For though he did not wish to admit it to himself, he knew the reason for this sudden apparition of heartache and loss. He knew it had arrived with the evil little fetish that had appeared on his doorstep one morning last week.

Why in the Name of the Virgin's Immaculate Womb had he touched the vile thing he couldn't say – except to plead he hadn't known what it was then, and that his name was printed on the front of it in a large, uncertain hand: *Capitán* Ambrosio Garcia. And so, naturally, he had stooped and picked the bundle up (he was still in his bathrobe; he had not yet scraped the silver burr from his jowls or tasted his espresso or morning cigar) and turned it over in his rough soldier's hands to examine it more closely.

It was a doll of sorts, but so crudely made it was almost fetal in its incompleteness: a sock stuffed with dried beans was cinched with string and on the bulb of white fabric thus created, an ugly, noseless face had been drawn in silver ink.

Arms and legs of yellow yarn dangled from the torso, like the limbs of a paraplegic. And then he felt a stinging pain, and noticed that his hand was bleeding.

He gave a cry and dropped the thing at once (as once in the mountains of Haiti he had liberated a viper mistaken for firewood) knowing even then it was too late, for a straight pin hidden in the evil idol had pricked him, drawing blood. And looking up, Garcia saw scrawled in chalk on the wall of his landing a single word which had not been there when he went to bed: '*Traidor!*' Traitor! To a military man, it was worse than a curse. And Garcia had made the Sign of the Cross and called upon the Holy Mother, for he knew then that someone had made a 'work' against him. Against *him*! *Capitán* Ambrosio Garcia-Reyes!

Remembering that evil morning now, Garcia shivered and gazed out at the deepening night. He was a handsome man of fifty-five or six, graying nicely, with broad shoulders, a barrel chest, and a silver moustache so minute, it might have been a pubic hair misplaced above his lip. He was dressed, as always, with a military neatness, from the ironed pleats of his white *guayabera* to the spotless tips of his white ventilated shoes.

Garcia tried to think of someone he had betrayed, someone who would want to hurt him, but he could think of no one, try as he might. He sighed. A drink, perhaps, might jog his memory; at least, he thought, it would assuage his pain. And so, tucking his wife's letter into his pocket, he went downstairs and, as was his habit each evening at about this hour, wandered into The World of Love.

The World of Love was quite deserted. There were only two other patrons seated at the bar – an old couple who were in their cups. Garcia was relieved the place was empty, for he wished to sit alone and ease his loss with a quiet rum – but the moment he raised the drink to his lips, his old *compañero* stuck his head in the doorway, looked about wildly, and made a beeline for his table.

Dr. Castellano

◆

Chapter 2

Garcia's comrade, Dr. Arsenio Castellano, was a tall, thin, fanatical *hombre* with sore red eyes and an overlarge moustache who carried with him everywhere the sour odors of sleeplessness, disinfectants, and overwork. He was the only private doctor in that corner of the *barrio*, every other doctor with brains (as he was fond of saying) having opened up a methadone clinic or fled to New Jersey – and he could not keep up with the endless afflictions of the poor.

Only an hour ago he had 'pronounced' a young child. The child – a little girl – had choked to death on a mango stone, and though the Doctor had been a doctor in the *barrio* for years, the sight of her clenched, purple face that afternoon had sickened and unnerved him.

Immediately afterwards, he had locked up his office and negotiated the three dark flights down to the street. The airless stairwell possessed that indescribable odor of poverty; it was an odor he knew by heart – not just dirt exactly, but something more hopeless and complex: some compound of rancid cooking oil and fried pork, marijuana fumes, tuberculosis germs, ruined dreams, the smoke of past arsons.

He crossed the slum street, assaulted by the blaring *salsa*, drunken arguments, the sound of drums, and watched by the old shawled *señoras* who sat, summer after summer, in the open windows of the ravaged brownstones, speechless,

6

dreaming with the heat – until one summer morning, he thought, you look and the window is empty – and went on along the broken sidewalk past piles of fruit and produce heaped in leaking cardboard crates that spilled out beyond the doors and ragged awnings of the poor *bodegas* in such a jumbled glut that, from afar, the tenements suggested silos that had burst at their bases.

On the corner, a band of drunken men were quarreling, as usual, over women and money. It was an argument that never ended, though the women and money were forever changing hands; while above their heads, fat drumstick arms and heaving, milkfilled bosoms threatened to spill into the street as large, cigarette-chomping mamas kept a watchful eye on their progeny below, screaming at them in a concert of voices which – the Doctor was absolutely certain – would have reopened the wounds of Christ.

Besmirched, the Doctor thought, was the English word that described the *barrio* best, that conveyed its air of disrepute, of penny miseries, nickel griefs, and buffaloheaded sorrows. Every inch of its sidewalks had been baptized with blood, due to the peculiar barbarism of the race. For the Spanish, the Doctor firmly believed, were a species of demon, or how else to account for the outrages he had witnessed over the years: the murder-rapes, the torture-executions?

Why, only last week there had been a nauseating tragedy. A young black man had robbed the *carniceria* on the corner and shot the butcher twice with a small-caliber revolver. But the butcher had simply absorbed the two slugs and chased the boy out the door and down the avenue, finally catching up with the unfortunate child and decapitating him with a stroke of his cleaver. Then the butcher had sat down and died himself. And by the time the Doctor had been called, the sunny street corner was a charnel house and dyed with blood. The chest wounds and headless child had bled like taps. Children and dogs had strayed in the crimson pools, tracking little red footprints up and down the block. Then, when the Doctor had arrived, people had expected him to do something. *Do* something? What could he do? His name was not

Jesus. He could not bring back the dead. He could not sew the boy's head back on or subtract the slugs from the wounds in the butcher's lungs, and, even if he could, what good would that have done? They only would have got back up and butchered each other all over again. Which was the way these people were, the Doctor told himself.

For the Doctor was not one of them. Of course, he *was* one of them, *really*, but he was like unto one who has been lifted up from his station far above the other dervishes by the hand of Allah – or, in the Doctor's case, by the hand of Harvard Medical School. This had been pleasant enough – the questionmark appearing when the Doctor had been set *down* by the hand.

For the Doctor had come to the *barrio* of *Nueva York* the autumn after medical school to intern at Harlem Hospital. From being an aristocrat's child in Cuba, a refugee kid in Miami, and a prince of the earth at Harvard, the Doctor had arrived in Manhattan and had been treated like any other two-bit spic, and this rude awakening had put a permanent crease in the Doctor's personality.

Of course, the Doctor's state was not helped by the facts that he had not been to sleep in thirty-six hours, that he had not eaten since breakfast and was extremely hungry, or that an hour ago his nieces had called to announce that Constanza Garcia had left her husband and sought refuge with them for the night – and he could hear the woman wailing in the background.

The Doctor was fond of Constanza Garcia. She was, in fact, a lovely woman. But with his mother-in-law and three young nieces to care for already and with his intense personality and easily exacerbated nerves, the thought of five distraught females crying out loud for days in his living-room was more than he could bear.

'I thought I will find you here,' the Doctor said to Garcia now in English which was almost perfect. He collapsed in a chair and ordered a rum from the bar with a wave of his hand. 'Now, please tell me, *amigo*, what in the name of hell is going on? Your wife is crying her eyes in my living-room.

My house is in an uproar. My mother-in-law is praying on her rosary. I am missing my supper. Ambrosio, my God, tell me, what did you do to her?'

'She is upset over nothing,' Garcia said morosely.

'She is not acting upset over nothing! She is crying her eyes! Meanwhile, I am missing my supper. You have no idea how long, all day, I look forward to my supper!'

'I tell you it is nothing,' Garcia insisted harshly. 'And that is the problem,' he admitted, '. . . this nothing.'

'What nothing?' the Doctor said, exasperated already, looking around the barroom hungrily for his rum. He turned back to Garcia. 'Ambrosio,' he sighed, anxiously pressing his fine, olive hands upon the wooden tabletop. 'Please speak to me. Is it money? I can help you.'

'You know it is not money,' Garcia said proudly.

'Please,' the Doctor said, 'do not be offended.'

'It is my nature,' Garcia groaned.

'Ambrosio,' the Doctor pleaded with him, still misunderstanding. 'You are a man. I am a doctor. There is nothing a man should not say to his doctor. Do you want my nieces crying their eyes? Do you want my mother-in-law praying on her rosary?' He looked around the barroom. 'Where is my rum?'

'I am trying to tell you, Arsenio,' Garcia said. 'But you will not listen. It is this *nothing* that is my problem. At night, when I take my wife in my arms, there is only this . . . nothing.'

'*Nada*?' the Doctor asked, momentarily forgetting his rum.

'*Nada*,' Garcia said, looking away in shame.

'Doctor,' came a drunken voice from the bar, 'may we ask your respected medical opinion?'

'No,' the Doctor said impatiently, waving the voice away. 'Cannot you see that I am busy?'

'Please, Doctor,' a second voice persisted. 'It will take but a moment of your most precious time.'

'*Hijo de puta*,' the Doctor cried, falling back in his chair and raising his eyes to heaven, as though he had given up upon this world but still hoped, through some miraculous intercession of the next, that peace, rum and supper might descend upon him from above. There was nothing, however, but the scaling paint on the flyspecked ceiling.

'Doctor, what is your opinion on the hard-cooked egg? Because, you see, when my *esposa* she eat of the hard-cooked egg, it make her nose so very hard and dry.'

'This is true,' the old woman informed them, nodding sagely and turning her drunken bloodshot eyes on Garcia and the Doctor. 'When I eat the hard-cooked egg my nose he become very hard and dry. Now, what is your professional opinion, Doctor?'

'My professional opinion,' the Doctor said, beginning slowly and calmly, but almost instantly losing control, 'is that you are two of the most drunken idiots who should be shot in the head for wasting my life with your stupid hard-cooked story of eggs and drying noses and I am sick and tired of you crazy people until I think I am going to cry!' He stood up from the table. 'Where is my r-r-um?' he demanded.

'But *Señor* Doctor . . . !'

'Please come with me,' the Doctor said to Garcia with that strange calm that precedes madness, 'or I am going to start to scream.'

The two men stepped out into the *barrio* evening and headed back the way the Doctor had just come. They passed *El Encanto* and *La Gran Parad*, two dismal *cantinas* which were neither grand nor enchanting, and continued on past El Dorado Travel, whose miserable storefront, the Doctor was aggrieved to see, no more resembled the legendary lost city of the Incas than the Olympus Cafe, a grizzled ginmill just beyond, suggested the home of the Greek gods.

The Doctor sighed, feeling his courage fail him. Tonight, he felt oppressed by even the beauty of the season. He regarded the pure spring sunshine falling through the rubbled lots upon the burned and ruined buildings all around him. The fine light made their dereliction seem all the more unbearable. And yet, the Doctor had seen such sights before; he had lived here nearly fifteen years. So why, he wondered now, did a white linen curtain, shredded by the wind and rain, flapping high up in an empty window, bring him this evening to the verge of tears?

'Where are we going?' Garcia asked.

'To your examination,' the Doctor answered, and a few moments later they turned off the crowded street, marching up a dark stairwell, up three rickety flights, to the steel door the Doctor had had installed after the pebbled glass with his name on it had been kicked in twice in one week, his office plundered, and his insurance cancelled.

Garcia gazed through the office windows. He could see the whole *barrio* laid out before them and, in the distance, silver bridges suturing the island to Queens.

'You will drop your trousers,' the Doctor ordered as he began washing his hands with the liquid disinfectant whose sour odor never left him. 'And now you must tell me. This loss of your nature. When did it first occur?'

'A week ago.'

'And since that time,' the Doctor asked, 'has you nature been restored at all?'

'How do you mean?'

'I mean, have you regained it after sleeping, perhaps, or when you see a young woman in the street bending over, let us say, in a certain way.'

'I am not a boy anymore,' Garcia said hotly. 'You know I have not the nature of a boy!'

'You will please answer me yes or no,' the Doctor said coolly.

'No.'

'I see,' the Doctor said whisking down Garcia's drawers and examining his genitals. 'Cough,' he said. 'Again. Sleeping? Appetite? How do you feel?'

'I am fine,' Garcia said.

'Turn around, bend over,' the Doctor said, slipping on a transparent plastic glove.

'Ay, *Dios mio*!' Garcia gasped.

'Be a man,' the Doctor said.

'I feel more like the woman,' Garcia tried desperately to jest.

11

'Quiet and cough,' the Doctor said. 'Your prostrate is enlarged.' He probed. 'One lobe.'

'Bad?' Garcia asked, alarmed.

'Normal,' the Doctor said, 'in a man of your old age.'

'I am not an old man,' Garcia said, angered by the remark, by the finger in his rectum, by the indignity of his problem and position. 'And you, you are an old woman!' he snapped petulantly, instantly regretting his remark since the Doctor was neither old nor a woman, though he did seem beyond his forty-one years.

The Doctor ignored him. 'You know what I should like to do?' he said happily, out of the blue. 'I should like to do some fishing. I especially like the bottom fishing. Do you know the bottom fishing, my friend?'

'*Si,*' Garcia said. 'It is what you are doing now!'

The Doctor laughed. 'How clever you are! No. In the bottom fishing, you place your bait upon the bottom and you wait to catch *la platija*. How do you call it?'

'Flounder,' Garcia grunted.

'Flounder, yes!' the Doctor went on happily. 'That is what you do. That is *all* you do. You wait for your flounder to eat your hook. Sometimes, your flounder . . . she is not hungry.' He shrugged. 'It is very restful. You worry about nothing. I enjoy it greatly.'

'And when was the last time you caught a flounder?'

'When? Ages ago. In Cuba. When I was a boy. There!' he declared removing his finger and stripping the glove from his hand. He depressed a pedal and neatly dropped the used prophylactic into a tin bin. He sighed. 'I can find no organic cause for your problem. I suspect it is in your mind. If you like, however, you can make an appointment and I will perform for you exhausting tests. I will try,' the Doctor went on, his English deteriorating slightly with fatigue, 'to be squeezing you inside of the next week. You may lift your trousers now.'

Garcia stooped, then froze. 'Arsenio,' he whispered.

In the doorway stood a boy with a pistol. He seemed to have materialized there out of nothing, out of the pure darkness of the *barrio* stairwell. The boy was shaking, his gun was shaking, and he was sweating, so that his light moustache resembled wisps of damp brown moss. Garcia instinctively reached for his trousers.

'Stop!' the boy cried in a voice that was rabid and out-of-control. He shook the gun at Garcia like some deadly metal finger.

The Doctor frowned, then said sharply, 'You will get out of my office. You will get out of it now!'

But the boy ignored him and, stepping in, shut the door behind him. His back protected, he grew braver. 'Shut up, you, and do not move!'

'Please,' Garcia pleaded. 'What is it you want?'

'He wants junk,' the Doctor sneered with undisguised contempt. 'He wants pills and junk. Don't you, my friend?'

'Shut up, you,' the boy said nervously, trading the gun to his other hand, then back again.

'Arsenio, please,' Garcia said. 'This boy is sick. He is crazy. Give him what he asks.'

'I will give him nothing!' the Doctor hissed. He was in a seizure of white and statuesque fury. 'He will get nothing!'

'I told you, shut up!' the boy said and began to sidle warily around the office towards the files and medicine chests, swinging the pistol back and forth between Garcia and the Doctor. He yanked open a drawer and clawed inside. Glass amphules shattered on the floor in a burst of sickening pops.

'Idiot!' the Doctor cried. 'You are breaking my medicines.'

'Shut up or I shoot you!' the boy screamed, enraged, and jerked another drawer from the metal cabinet and sent it flying across the room in a hail of glass, pills, and bouncing plastic bottles that, for what seemed like ages to Garcia, continued to rattle and roll around the office – the pills spinning dizzily and richocheting off the walls, while the plastic bottles tumbled and bounced at Garcia's feet with an absurd, *galumphing* sound.

'That is quite enough,' the Doctor said when the office was still again. 'You will stop it now. I will give you your pills. And then you will leave!' And with a cold, perfect calm, he drew a key chain from his pocket and crossed the office, the broken glass and scattered capsules cracking under his tread. He opened a second cabinet and began withdrawing bottles of pills and placing them on the examination table.

The boy watched him restlessly, glancing at Garcia now and then with wet rabid eyes. 'All right, you. Fat one,' he said. 'Bring them to me!' and he waved the gun at Garcia with a reckless abandon that Garcia felt in his bowels.

'Move!' the boy shrieked, and Garcia hurriedly gathered the bottles and began to shuffle toward him, praying the gun would not go off in his unprotected belly. He glanced at the Doctor, only to see a ghostfaced statue staring at nothing. '*Mira*,' the boy said, stretching out a nervous hand.

Garcia did not do it on purpose. He simply fumbled the hand-off. For a moment, the bottles threatened to spill and in that instant, Garcia saw the opening – the boy's confused hands – and without even thinking, he lunged for the gun and the two men fell backward into the cabinet with a horrific, glassy crash. And then Garcia was struggling on the floor, and his heart was pounding with a joy and fright he had not felt since combat. He knocked away the pistol and wrestled the boy's arms above his head, pinning them there fast.

'Ah ha!' the Doctor exclaimed, like a statue coming to life. 'How *brilliant*, my friend! Hold him!' he cried and snatched up the gun. 'All right,' he said to the boy. 'As you can see, my magnificent comrade has disarmed you. Do not struggle or you will cause yourself only injuries, I assure you!'

'But . . . I *know* this boy!' Garcia cried in surprise. He stared down at the sick, dark face. 'I *know* you!' he breathed, still panting from his heroic exertions. 'You are Juanita Solano's boy. Are you not? At first, I did not recognize you.'

'Solano?' the Doctor cried. 'Solano who? Solano the seam-stress?'

'The same! Her eldest, if I am not mistaken. What is your name?' Garcia said to the boy almost tenderly now, though he was still holding him down. 'It is Miguelito, is it not?' he asked, using the affectionate diminutive.

'Miguelito Solano?' the Doctor repeated in a daze.

'Please, *Señors*. Let me go.'

'Let you go?' the Doctor cried. 'Why, I should shoot you in the head for what you have done to me! Miguelito Solano,' he asked incredulously, 'do you know who I am? It is I . . . *I* who am your mother's doctor. It is I . . . *I* who delivered you into this world! Now tell me, my friend, do you think it is right that I should deliver you into this world so that you can take me *out* of it?' He slammed the gun down on the examination table. 'My God,' he said, 'what is wrong with you people?'

'Arsenio, control yourself,' Garcia said, rising to his feet. He took the Doctor by his shoulders in order to restrain him – and in that instant, the boy was up and gone and lost like a ghost in the darkness of the stairwell.

'Halt!' Garcia cried in dismay.

'Never mind,' the Doctor sighed in a voice suddenly careless with despair. The gun slipped in his hand, hung by its trigger guard from his finger for an instant, then clattered to the floor.

'I will call the police,' Garcia said.

'Police?' the Doctor repeated in a daze as his eyes vacantly scanned the ruined office. Then they fell upon Garcia and he smiled. 'My congratulations, *Señor*.'

'It was nothing,' Garcia said modestly. 'He was just a boy.'

'It is hardly nothing,' the Doctor insisted. 'Regard yourself!'

Garcia, still standing with his trousers down round his knees, regarded himself. '*Dios mio!*' he gasped in amazement.

'Ha, ha, ha, ha, ha,' the Doctor laughed.

'It was all the excitement,' Garcia explained.

'Ha, ha, ha, ha,' the Doctor laughed, tears beginning to stream from his eyes.

'It is nothing to laugh at,' Garcia said, hiking his trousers, red in the face.

'I am not laughing,' the Doctor said, laughing. 'I am just very happy. Cannot you see? Now you may remove your

15

wife from my living room. Now my nieces may stop crying their eyes. Ha, ha, ha, ha,' he said again.

'My wife! I must go to her,' Garcia said. For he could hardly wait to recount to her now the astonishing events of the disquieting spring evening, of his struggle with the intruder, and how afterwards his manly nature had been restored.

And it was then, quite suddenly, that the Doctor began to cry. His high, shrill laughter simply veered into tears and he began to weep bitterly into his hands. Garcia had never seen the Doctor cry before and it affected him deeply. He put his arm around his old *amigo* and held him close for quite some time. 'Arsenio,' he said sternly at last, staring over the Doctor's shoulder at the smashed glass cabinet and scattered pills, 'you must forget all this. To be a man, you must learn to . . . look beyond.'

'Beyond?' the Doctor repeated in a daze. But, lifting his eyes and looking beyond the office windows through the orange and violet dusk of the *barrio* evening, all the Doctor saw – as far as his eye could see – were row upon row of burned and ruined buildings, and beyond the burned and ruined buildings, clots of sick, drunken men, and beyond the sick, drunken men, there were more burned and ruined buildings, and beyond the burned and ruined buildings there was nothing but the failing spring twilight and the empty night sky.

The Middle Man

◆

Chapter 3

Two hundred miles north of the *barrio*, in a duplex apartment on Beacon Hill, Philip Higgins stood before a latticed window regarding the splendor of the same luminous June evening. He had worked quite well today – good, really, for the first time in quite a while. In fact, he had been so absorbed in his literary labors he had not seen the sun slide from the sky, burnishing the copper rooftops of Boston, and twilight fall; and when he had finally looked up from his pages, the room was dim and the light outside, a burning coral.

Higgins was a youngish-looking man of average height and a middling build kept that way with doses of *hatha yoga* and meditation. His blond hair, at thirty-four, still showed no signs of thinning. His face was ruddy, Celtic, and eminently forgettable – except for his eyes, whose sea-green depths held a certain calm Druidical beauty, a depth and intensity inherited from his mother which saved it from being just another wild Irish mug.

Higgins watched the sun set above the Charles, turning the river into a molten flow of gold which thinned in the distance into platinum filaments.

On impulse, he picked up the phone and dialed the number of a woman he had met at a dinner party the week before and toward whom, ever since, he had nursed a certain amorous intent. Her maid answered and, while Higgins waited, he turned his eyes from the gilded river to a book on the sill. It was a hardboard copy of *Men Without Women*. He had had it in college; on its flyleaf was written: 'Adams House 35.'

Higgins had always liked writing. At eighteen, when he was first beginning, he had even liked to type up other writers' stories. He remembered how, from this very book, he had typed the opening paragraphs of 'In Another Country' again and again, just to feel how it felt to write like that, so tellingly, with such a fine eye and such sure, clean strokes.

Curious to see if the story was as good as he remembered it, he opened the book up. And that was when his luminous mood, so carefully shored by work and hope, grew dim. For between the pages was a snapshot of *her* standing in the windy sunlight of some long-forgotten New England garden, squinting, holding a straw sun hat on her head. And at the unexpected sight of *her* beloved face, Higgins felt a pain like a sword in his heart.

'Yes?' A voice came over the line. 'Hello? Yes?'

Higgins quietly depressed the receiver. What else could he do? For beside *her* face, the voice on the phone held for him now no more value or attraction than a scrap of cardboard or the vomit of a crow.

Philip Higgins was a gentleman, a writer, a businessman, and a scholar, though not necessarily in that or in any given order. The income he received each month from a trust fund for doing nothing other than being his mother's son made him a gentleman, while the publication of several short stories and a slender volume of Indian poetry had earned him the dubious title of writer. Higgins' book, *Passionate Encounters*, (Harvard Press, 198—), a translation of the first seventy verses of the Sanskrit *Shatakatraya*, qualified him as a scholar, as well, and had actually brought him some small renown.

Unfortunately, neither the gentleman, the writer nor the scholar provided him with all the income he required. And so Higgins was also a businessman: a middleman, to be exact, bringing buyer and seller together. His commercial philosophy was simple: when a large load of goods and a sum of money is about to change hands, station yourself in-between. It was a strategy that revenue agents and claims lawyers had used for years with great profit.

Sometimes the goods in question were computer parts, sometimes raw steel. As for the money, if steel can be bought for a few pennies less a pound, well, you might say, no big deal. But when one is purchasing ten thousand tons, those pennies add up.

Most of the time, it was perfectly legal. Then again, there had been a few occasions when the two parties Higgins had brought together were forbidden by certain protectionist legislation from doing business with each other – or the item in question was taboo. Not drugs, or guns or anything so wicked, but other things: platinum, computer chips, once even sweaters from Peru – though nothing they could ever get him for, hopefully. For Higgins didn't *break* the law so much as bend, spindle, and mutilate it. Plus, he was careful. He did what he did with secrecy and circumspection, shielded by layers of shell corporations whose essence was as impenetrable, inscrutable, and arcane as portions of the Talmud.

But Higgins' questionable business practices were the last thing on his mind right now, as he packed his bags and got ready to depart. For he had to get out of there. He was going insane. If it wasn't *her* picture, then it was the junk mail which still arrived in *her* name. And once again, for the billionth time, Higgins found himself remembering *her*.

Her was Higgins' twenty-five-year-old wife who had died beside him in her sleep, so that in the morning when he'd reached for her she had already been cold. Cause of death? A blood clot which had broken from a vein in her thigh, traveling to her heart and 'gumming a valve,' the assistant medical examiner had confided in Higgins – as though her heart had been a car part.

After that nothing had ever been the same for him again. He remembered some lines by a poet he liked:

Though I have lanterns and the sun,
Fire, moon and stars to give me light,
Without you, it is night.

Higgins sat down on the edge of the bed – suddenly now, in the midst of his packing – like a man who doesn't know yet that he's just been shot. Where was his detachment? At the sight of her picture, his heart had cracked.

For like the Italian major in the story he had so admired, Higgins could not resign himself. This was Higgins' problem. Despite his wealth, his education and all his philosophy, he was utterly unable to resign himself to losing her.

Higgins contemplated this on the Amtrak to New York after calling the Doctor from a pay phone in South Station. The Doctor was Higgins' oldest and dearest friend and would welcome him fondly, Higgins knew. Higgins had not actually spoken to the Doctor, but to the Doctor's niece, Luisa. There were women sobbing on the other end of the line, but Higgins had long ago learned that such background noises were a constant in the over-circulated film of the Doctor's life and had tried not to let it faze him. He did check, to reassure himself, that the Doctor was not dead – the Doctor being one of those persons you worried about that way – but Luisa had assured him that her uncle was very much alive, even if he was late for supper.

Though Higgins had spoken to the Doctor often enough by phone, he had not seen his friend in the flesh for almost a year – since that time six weeks after the funeral when *her* death had finally boomeranged and Higgins had had what the Doctor referred to as 'your nervous breakdown.' Higgins disliked the term and insisted to this day it had been no such thing. It was only that his emotions, which he had buried with *her* corpse, had finally come back to him, and he had found himself crying over the silliest things: television commercials, tiny acts of kindness, baby animals, songs on the jukebox. It is true that for a week or so, he was as good as useless and that the Castellanos – the girls in particular – had

20

had to care for him like the family pet, feeding him at decent intervals, brushing his hair, petting and playing with him and taking him for regular handheld walks. But it was *not* a nervous breakdown, even if he had sometimes cried at those 'silly things' twenty, thirty times a day. The proof that it wasn't a nervous breakdown, but just the *opposite*, was that he had felt much better after that, and had gone back to Boston, picking up the pieces of his life. And that, Higgins told himself now – after a weekend in Manhattan – was exactly what he was going to do again.

Old Soldier

◆

Chapter 4

Garcia's native country had been named El Dorado, in memory of and longing for that mythic land whose streets are blown with powdered gold. Unfortunately, the only gold in Dorado was in the teeth of its leaders and in the yellow streak that ran down the spine of its generals who, in the century and a quarter since its inception, managed to lose to their neighbors half of Dorado's original territory, along with the El that preceded the Dor. It was the last of these losing battles which had prompted Dorado's great President and war hero, General Jose D'Aquila, to deliver that oft-quoted gem of political realism. When asked by a naive and idealistic minister 'what his country's true and proper borders were,' D'Aquila had replied, 'Whatever she can defend.'

Garcia was to learn this lesson firsthand. For at fifty, returning from a war abroad, he had been made a lieutenant in the élite Wild Boars. His first morning in command, he and his men had left their mountain fortress and almost at once encountered guerrillas, who led them on a dizzying chase, circling round and doubling back so many times in the unfamiliar hills, that by noon Garcia and his men were lost. Then, toward evening, the rebels were sighted once again and the mighty Boars gave chase. No sooner, however, was a hilltop crested than Garcia's men began taking heavy fire from an enemy complex hidden among the trees. Garcia ordered the Boars' lone plane to strafe and bomb the rebel stronghold – only to discover, when the bombing was over, he had just leveled his own fortress.

Garcia said his prayers that evenings, fully expecting, come sunrise, to be taken out and shot. But instead the Generalissimo was almost understanding, blaming the incident on the fortunes of war and closing his dispatch with a quote from the *I Ching*: 'An old man marries a young woman. No blame. But no praise either!' And adding: 'It furthers one to come to Puerto Valle.'

And so, Garcia had returned to the capitol where his talents might be put to better use. Two weeks later, at the age of fifty-one, he was promoted to the rank of *Capitán* and given command of the Palace Guard – even if, unbeknownst to Garcia, he was elevated to this position by the Generalissimo and his Senior Officers because of his big heart, his tiny brain, and his perfect willingness to believe whatever nonsense he was told.

And so, when Garcia discovered the Commander of the Air Force looting the officer's mess of chickens and beer, he'd been delighted to learn it was a secret, humanitarian operation engineered by the Generalissimo to help the Indians, a gesture that had so touched Garcia he had solemnly called the sweating Colonel aside and thrust into his palm ten *pesos* of his own.

But though he was laughed at behind his back, in the end, it was Garcia's simple, credulous nature that had saved his neck. For when the Generalissimo was subsequently heaved from the Palace roof and a junta composed of Junior Officers seized power, no one thought of reprisals against the harmless *Capitán* whose Palace Guard had slept through the coup – through the machine-gun and rocket fire – after an orgy of roast pig, yellow rice, rum, cigars and whores which the Junior Officers had thoughtfully provided that evening in their honor. They had even promoted Garcia and raised his salary.

But after the coup, it was not the same anymore. He did not like the Junior Officers who called him 'Pops,' and danced the Monkey and smoked American cigarettes instead of cigars. He did not like the nickname they gave him – *El Hombre*, The Man – though there was nothing actually insulting about it, except their intonation. Nor did he like seeing the naked body of his old friend, the Generalissimo, which hung in the street for the next two and a half weeks, twisting slowly in the tropic wind, the target of soldiers' bullets, children's stones, and women's jibes, its lower extremities eaten by dogs. And so Garcia, a man of sentiment and conviction, resigned.

'OK, Pops,' a Junior Officer in shirtsleeves croaked at the news, chainlighting another Winston and winging the letter of resignation, unread, across the desk into a box marked 'Out.' Garcia waited for more – something – but instead the Junior Officer went back to fiddling with a radio, trying to get the rumbas broadcast from Brazil. 'Hey, Pops,' the young man asked at last, when he saw that Garcia was still waiting. He grinned, displaying blackened canines. 'You like to *boogie*?' And two young lieutenants loitering by the radio burst out laughing. Garcia, a soldier to the end, gave a final salute and left the office, his tears cold on his old cheeks in the hot sun of the military compound. When he reached the dusty square and the body of the Generalissimo, he forced himself to raise his hand and bid his friend one last goodbye, though the Generalissimo, of course, did not respond, being little more now than a cross between a rack of mutton and a country ham, thickly studded and glazed with flies – the Generalissimo who had always been so well groomed, Garcia mused.

This minor irony was a profound one for Garcia and brought to mind his own mortality. Though he had planted a dozen children in the bellies of as many women, he had no real family, except for a very aged mother who lived – or rather *died* – in New York. Garcia's mother was ninety-three and at death's door, where she had set up shop some ten years earlier, refusing to budge an inch either way. Remarkably, the clarity her mind had lost had been transferred to her flesh, so that her skin was as clear and transparent as Lucite: in the

Polaroids her nurse had sent, he could have numbered each old bone and dear purple vein. Perhaps, he thought, someday soon I will be joining her.

In the meantime, Garcia retired to his farm outside the capitol. It was lovely and quite peaceful there. Sitting on the stoop at sunset, smoking a cigar, listening to his turkey cocks and the breeze rattling the coconut palms, Garcia wished his life could be this way forever. But alas, nothing pleasant lasts for long. Out of good, evil cometh; after a parade, there's shit on the ground.

And this is exactly what had happened in Dorado. For when the Junior Officers finally permitted elections to be held (good), the opposition leader, Rodolfo Benitez, was unexpectedly elected President (bad), the army panicked (worse), and the country which had seemed on the verge of a great expansion had suffered instead a sharp repression.

One morning the citizens of Dorado awoke to find the streets were filled with soldiers, and though there was resistance, some of it fierce, within a week of his election, Benitez's new government had fallen and the Junta was once again in control. A purge by the secret police had followed in which the new left and the old right – Benitez's people and the Generalissimo's men – were both declared to be enemies of the state. Garcia, in fact, had barely made it out of Dorado alive, escaping that very evening with a party that included the newly elected and exiled President himself. They had fled across Lake Hurakan in a leaky boat, disguised as Indians, and as the lights of the capitol dimmed in the distance, Garcia, who could feel Death's elbow in his ribs, had marveled at *El Presidente*'s courage and calm, at the way he sat proudly in the prow of the punt, undisguised and undefeated. They had rowed for hours; the night was rainy, and when the lights of the capitol were finally extinguished from view, Garcia had wept aloud and unashamed – for there are times when a man is permitted to cry, and the night that he loses his country is one of them.

On the lake's far shore, their boat was met by rebels, some of whom wanted to execute Garcia on the spot, but the President, happily, intervened. The past was forgotten; Garcia was now one of them, he declared. And there, beneath the hissing, dripping trees, Garcia had bent his knee to Benitez and kissed his wet, pink hands in the old feudal gesture of friendship and allegiance. By noon, they had crossed the border and were safe. A freighter later took him to a dockyard in Manhattan.

And so, like a soul returning to the Godhead, Garcia returned to his mother and to the frail, silvery body that had borne him, taking up residence in her *barrio* flat. He had managed to smuggle out with him a small quantity of gems and gold, but since it was all the wealth he possessed in the world, he husbanded it carefully, so that mother and son lived in genteel poverty.

Still, it was not a bad life: and recently Garcia had even taken a young bride, and now – *carumba!* – already she had left him!

Garcia headed home alone from the Doctor's office. The salmon in the west was gone; the sun had set long ago – and with it, his erection. He let himself in the door of their apartment and called out hopefully, but his wife had not returned. He sighed and entered his mother's bedroom.

His mother was staring at him with her one good eye from her cranked-up bed, her hair and flesh so bleached with age it was difficult to say where she ended and the sheets began. She seemed half-ghost, half-cadaver, save for that single living eye shining with an undimmed brilliance and will.

Tonight, Garcia saw that she was frightened, for the eye was bulging, wet, and scared. As soon as it saw him, it began to roll, and his mother printed on a pad by her bedside: 'Someone was here!'

'Constanza, Mama?'

She shook her head and began to sweat.

'Who?'

'Dark,' she scrawled. She didn't know.

Garcia's first reaction was disbelief. As his mother's mind and body weakened, her imagination was getting stronger.

Then he saw, tucked beside her pillow, another of those hateful dolls.

Snatching it up, he went through the apartment, but there was no one there now. Curiously, he found himself pawing at his torso – until he realized he was looking for the pistol he no longer owned. And yet, what good was a gun in such a situation? Bullets were useless against a curse. He paused and examined the fetish more closely. It was similar to the one he had received the other day, except that the twine around the neck of this one was black, and was frayed at its ends into the semblance of fingers. The face was barbaric, almost childish in its execution; its expression accusing. *Traidor!* it almost seemed to say.

But who, Garcia wondered, considered him a traitor, and if so, a traitor to what? Surely it couldn't be the Junta in Dorado for it was they, after all, who had betrayed Garcia! Or was it someone else? One of the Generalissimo's men; someone who, now that time and fortune had reordered loyalties, was taking things too personally?

What he needed now was information. Yes. He must discover who was here from his violent, checkered past. Perhaps a name, or a nickname even, would unlock a door behind which stood the shadow of some long-forgotten enmity.

The mere beginnings of a plan improved Garcia's mood. He went back to the bedroom and checked on his mother, but the eye was closed. Then he went into the kitchen, doused the doll with lighter fluid and burned it in the sink. The beans inside it jumped and squirmed like hatching worms. When the doll was reduced to gold-limned ashes, he opened the faucet, and rubbed with a sponge until there was nothing left but a gray smear on the white porcelain. But even then, he had the feeling he would not be rid of it so easily as that, as though its little black hands had already reached inside him, disturbing his heart.

Spanish Harlem

◆

Chapter 5

Higgins' cab driver's name was Philip Grovolney. It was printed on his medallion beneath the mug shot of an escaped sex-offender. Higgins gave Grovolney the Doctor's address and the cabbie took off, running a light. He scrutinized Higgins in the rear-view mirror. Uncomfortable under his prying glare, Higgins made the mistake of remarking on the fact that he and the cabbie shared the same name.

'Wha? Grovolney?'

'No. Philip,' Higgins said, sorry now he'd said anything at all.

Higgins looked out the window. He had no idea where they were. New York mystified him. The Battery, Queens; they were only names. He had left his new Lexus garaged in Boston. He would have only become lost driving in Manhattan, while the car would have certainly been stolen or trashed if parked outside the Doctor's office.

'Hey, yo,' the cabbie said, eyeing him in the glass. 'If you don't mind me saying so, pal, you don't look so hot. You aware of this?'

'No,' Higgins said.

'Yeah. You look a little peaked.'

'*Peaked?*'

'Yeah,' the cabbie went on, nodding smugly. 'Vitamin deficiency. That's what it is. See? I can spot it anywhere. Now take me,' he said, turning completely around. He smiled. 'I'm healthy as a horse.' He chuckled to himself. 'Why youse probably thought this was some kinda *candy* I was munchin' on.' He smirked at Higgins' foolishness even as he produced from the gloom of the front seat a little paper sack full of wet dark things. 'Seaweed,' he said. 'Full of iodine. Sure. I take all that stuff. Seaweed. Yeast. Desiccated liver. You name it. Ask my wife. Says I'll bury her!'

And suddenly, from out of the driver's words, spilled pieces of a dream from the night before. In it, someone had said to Higgins exactly that, *Bury her*. But who? Yes! He remembered now.

He'd been sitting at the feet of a sorceress, a seer – a girl with deer-colored skin and eyes like crystals. In the dream, his wife was beside him, but when he turned to speak to her, her chair was empty, and he wondered where she could have gone. Then, with a wretched freshness, he remembered that his wife was dead. The seeress had looked at him and said, 'We have work to do. You must bury her quickly.' And as the painful nightmare ended, Higgins had realized with a mounting horror that he could not remember what his wife looked like any longer! He shook his head. What a crazy dream!

' "Lolly," ' the cabbie was saying. 'That's British for dough. It was on the tube. Alexander Guinness. You aware of him?'

'Look,' Higgins said. 'I don't really feel like talking just now.'

The driver shrugged. 'Suit yourself.'

By now the cab had reached the outskirts of the *barrio* and they were hurtling down a side street past vast ruined lots. The area had been condemned and razed and what Higgins could glimpse of it in the moonlight was as desolate and surreal as a nuclear bombscape. Crumbling walls stood in the midst of great fields of shattered, moonbleached brick, while here and there water pooled and ran, or a cellarhole gaped like an entrance to the underworld.

Then they were in the *barrio* itself. Though it was eleven

o'clock on a Thursday evening, the streets were filled with cars and people, while the air was charged with smoke and *salsa*, tantalizing odors, Caribbean drums. Coming upon the Doctor's office, Higgins saw the lights were still burning, and he ordered the cabbie to halt beneath windows that read in flaking, peeling gilt:

Arsenio Castellano, MD
Consultas Medicas

'Hey, pal,' the driver said, looking around him queerly at the wild slum street. 'You sure you got the right address? I mean, you want me to wait for you or what?'

'Why?' Higgins said.

'Well, you know,' the cabbie sneered. 'This ain't exactly Park Avenya.'

Higgins paid Grovolney, who brightened at his tip and mumbled a warning about the evils of white sugar in farewell.

Then Higgins dragged his bag out of the cab and up into the tenement. He found the Doctor alone in his office, sweeping glass. 'So,' the Doctor said, smiling broadly, 'my nieces said you were expected. Hello, my old friend, and he put down the broom, crossed the office and embraced Higgins warmly in the Latin fashion.

'Hello, Arsenio,' Higgins said. 'Here I am again.'

'Of course! Of course! Welcome!' the Doctor said like the grand *seigneur* of some great hacienda.

Higgins sat down. He was glad to have arrived. It was pleasant in the Doctor's office. The rhythm of the drums floated through the night, while a pink tissuepaper moon was pasted above a toy bridge in the distance. For the moment, he was content to put himself in the Doctor's care.

'I am glad you have come,' the Doctor said, warmly. 'I have already found an apartment for you – and a job, if you want it.'

'Job?' Higgins laughed. 'I'm just here for the *weekend*, Arsenio.'

'Yes,' the Doctor continued as though deaf. 'I am thinking

of hiring you as my financial consultant. My affairs need . . .
looking into.'

'You couldn't afford me,' Higgins said, changing tack.

'What would you charge?'

'You? Discount. Five hundred a day. Plus expenses.'

The Doctor raised his eyebrows and considered this a
moment. 'I will give you ten dollars a week, an apartment,
and all the rice and beans you can eat. Take it or leave it.' He
smiled sternly.

'You old bastard,' Higgins laughed. It was as simple as
that. For if the Doctor really wanted his help why shouldn't
he stay on a few days extra? He had nothing – and no one –
to return to, really.

'All right,' the Doctor said, pulling up his chair. 'Now
please tell me what is going on.'

So Higgins told him. After he had told him, he realized
there wasn't much to tell. He was lonely. His wife was dead.
He had tried to forget her, but he couldn't. He knew that
many other men and women had lost the one they dearly
loved, but when it happened to someone else it didn't matter.
When it happened to you, well . . . you went a little crazy.

On the other hand, Higgins knew, he should be grateful.
He had plenty of money. He had his health, his freedom, and
a place to stay. He had the Doctor and the Doctor's family
who loved him, and indeed, the two men had already resumed
their friendship as though the past year had been a brief lull
in a lifelong conversation. And yet . . . and yet . . . he felt a
little sick inside, as if there was something smashed in there:
broken crockery, a pocket of rattling shards.

'Do not look so sad, *amigo*. It is a shock to the system, I
know, but it goes away in time. You must be a realist now.
You must forget her and . . . look beyond.'

But Higgins was already staring beyond at a skeleton by
the window, a little figure of lacquered yellow bones – until
he realized it was the skeleton of a child, and he looked away.
When he turned back to the Doctor, he had tears in his eyes.
He didn't know why.

'Forgive me,' the Doctor sighed, 'for such a stupid speech.

It was useless advice given me uselessly earlier in the evening. I don't know why I passed it along. Do you see what these idiots have done to my office?' He gestured with a bandaged finger at a murderous scimitar of glass still attached to a cabinet, the cause and effect relationship between the bandaged pointer and the bloodied shard painfully obvious.

'What idiots?' Higgins said, wiping his eyes, just now noticing the signs of violence that had not yet been swept away.

'Nothing,' the Doctor said. 'Just a boy. Who I brought into this world.' His face blazed. 'Ha! To think it is *you* who delivers your own murderer!'

'What are you talking about, Arsenio?'

'Nothing,' the Doctor said, rising briskly to his feet. He reached in his shirt. 'Take this,' he said, dispensing to both himself and Higgins a small yellow tablet.

'What is it?' Higgins asked.

'Medicine,' the Doctor said obscurely. 'Now bring your bag. And come with me.'

The Doctor locked up his office and the two men went down the stairs and out into the night. It had grown darker and quieter on the street except where groups of drunken men stood in the light outside of taverns, from out of which a rising voice or hand hailed the Doctor as they passed.

In front of one *cantina*, the Doctor stopped and addressed a short, muscular, middle-aged gentleman, built like a small bull. The man was fashionably dressed in the Spanish manner. A curvaceous crucifix adorned his neck along with several thousand dollars' worth of gold chains and platinum medallions.

'*Señor* Omar Maldonado. *Señor* Felipe Higgins,' the Doctor said, introducing the two men formally, with a slight bow. 'My new consultant and dearest personal friend. You will treat him accordingly, *amigo*, I am sure,' he said, looking directly into the man's black Spanish eyes.

There was the briefest of hesitations as the man flicked an invisible ash off the pocket of his freshly pressed linen trousers. The gesture was just enough to insinuate his irritation with the Doctor's imperious tone. The man turned to Higgins. 'Enchanted to meet you,' he said slowly in correct if heavily accented English. 'The Doctor is our . . . friend,' he said looking at the Doctor significantly.

'Thank you,' the Doctor replied. 'My respects to *El Duende*. And now we must be going.' And the Doctor rudely pulled Higgins away before he could even return the greeting.

'What's the matter with you, Arsenio?' Higgins said, annoyed.

The Doctor smiled. 'That was a necessary introduction. There will be a few more, but not many. Necessary introductions are one thing. But I warn you. Stay away from that man. I would trust him with nothing.'

'Why?' Higgins asked, recalling the dark, handsome face and the trousers creased as sharp as knives. 'He seemed like a perfectly nice guy to me.'

'Nice guy,' the Doctor sneered. 'I personally know two men he has shot.'

'Shot?' Higgins said, wanting to turn around to look at him again, but refraining. 'Who is he?'

'He is nothing,' the Doctor said. 'Just a thug. But at the moment, he is a good man to have on our side. Your introduction will be reported to *El Duende*. He's the *capo* around here. After that, I do not think that you will be troubled by anyone, for these barbaric people,' the Doctor said, 'still adhere to a certain code of honor.'

They walked on in a somber mood. Beyond the avenue, the streets grew darker and more deserted. But as the Doctor and Higgins turned the next corner, they surprised a group of teenage boys harassing a young *mestiza* girl. 'Stop it!' the Doctor said quietly but with such force in his voice that the boys abruptly froze. Then they laughed, and ran away.

The rescued girl lifted her head and gazed at Higgins through a set of startling gray eyes. Oddly, she seemed completely unperturbed; and what he could glimpse of her face in the lamplight was as gravely radiant, implacable, and serene as the gold mask of a Byzantine icon.

Higgins said hello, but the child did not answer and he

wondered now, in a whispered aside, if she was deaf or maybe blind.

'Mad,' the Doctor sighed. 'For years now. She will talk to no one. She will hear and see no one. Not even her friend, the Doctor, who once she would sing for,' he said squatting down and gently pressing the child's hands which she offered him as if they were not a part of her, as if they might come off in his own. The Doctor searched her dusky face. 'I look, but I do not see you,' he told her.

'Has she been to a hospital?' Higgins asked, stirred by the vague inspiration that hospitals were supposed to care for such people.

'Hospital? No. She just roams about . . . like some wandering spirit. Sometimes, you may see her laughing to herself. There are those who say she is touched by God. Not God, I think. Poor girl. Ah, but there are many like her here, I'm afraid.' The Doctor sighed and rose to his feet.

Just then the girl reached out and placed her hand on Higgins' cheek. She caressed it tenderly for a moment or two, and seemed as though about to speak. Then she laughed and drifted off into the night.

'How odd!' the Doctor said. 'She seems to know you. Have you two met?'

'Met her? What? Of course not, Arsenio.'

The two men resumed walking; Higgins found his suitcase growing heavier with every block. At last, they turned down a little back alleyway that ran into a cluttered yard sheltered by a tree of heaven. The Doctor sat down on a broken stoop which Higgins had not seen in the dark and quickly lit a joint, drawing it to a fiery point. Higgins exhausted, sat down on his suitcase.

'I feel I am fourteen about,' the Doctor said, 'but I cannot smoke this shit on the street because of my reputation, you will understand. And I cannot smoke it up there,' he said, gesturing at a high, shaded window, 'because of your roommate's paranoid mind, to whom, after this, I will introduce you. Go ahead,' the Doctor said, passing Higgins the joint. 'It is part of your treatment.'

A short while later when they were both stoned, the Doctor said, 'Stop it. You are thinking of *her*.'

'I can't help it,' Higgins said. 'I still do, you know. All the time. Next month, it'll be a year. Can you believe it, Arsenio?'

'Really?' the Doctor said dreamily. 'Has it been so long?'

'It seems like only yesterday,' Higgins said, knowing now it had been a mistake to smoke the joint, knowing he was going to start thinking about *her* all over again, and he didn't want to do that, he didn't want to even start.

'You do yourself a grave disservice,' the Doctor said. 'To keep dwelling on her, I mean. Because what you think is what you see, and what you see is what you get.'

'And what you've got is stoned, Arsenio,' Higgins laughed.

'No. I am being perfectly clear,' the Doctor insisted. 'The world is a Rorschach. You know? One of those inkblots on a piece of paper the doctor shows you when you are going crazy. One man sees a beautiful flower. Another? A tiger or a poisonous snake. We see what we want to see, hear what we want to hear.' The Doctor paused, 'All I ask of you, my friend, is that you look for the flower.'

Higgins glanced at the Doctor. He could not see him clearly in the shadows, but he could feel him there beside him in the darkness, and could almost hear the kind, ironical smile with which he twisted these last words. 'Thank you, *Señor*. I will tell you when I see it.'

'Excellent!' the Doctor laughed, flicking away the roach, and getting to his feet. 'And now bring your bag. I will show you your new hacienda.'

They went back out to the street and clamored up the front stairs of a rundown brownstone. One glance told Higgins there were rats in the cellar the size of pigs.

'You will like it,' the Doctor said, rattling his keys. 'It is wonderful. And so convenient. Kitchen . . . dining room . . . bedroom . . . study!' He looked at Higgins. 'All in one room!'

The two friends laughed and went on up the stairwell. But

when the Doctor got to the door, he paused and frowned. 'Damn,' he said. 'I have forgotten the password.'

'Password?'

'Your paranoid roommate,' the Doctor said. 'He requires a password to enter and, damn, if I haven't forgotten it again! Yesterday, it was "mad dog." This . . . ? It was some sort of *insect*,' he said, rubbing his brow. 'Let me think. *Caterpillar?* No. *Mosquito?* No,'

'Ant?' Higgins offered, beginning alphabetically 'Aphid?'

'No. Grasshopper? No. Espider. No.'

'Butterfly,' Higgins said, setting down his bag. 'Beetle. Bee.'

'That's it! How brilliant, my friend! Bomblebee!' the Doctor shouted. 'Bomblebee, bomblebee!' he screamed and began pounding on the door.

The Lovesongs Of Lucho Barrios

◆

Chapter 6

The person who opened the door – Higgins' new roommate – was a tall, lithe, handsome young man with a cleanly shaven olive face, the big, white teeth of a thoroughbred, and the insolent and reproachful eyes of a fallen lord. His name was Jorge Vazpana and he was a Doradoan freedom fighter, or so he confessed. He further declared that he greatly welcomed the presence of their new comrade, Higgins, and was prepared even now to defend Higgins' life with his own.

'I hope that won't be necessary,' Higgins smiled, disliking the boy at once.

'Why is it, whatever you say, you make it sound like a speech?' the Doctor asked. 'Why is it that when you say, "Pass the *azúcar*," I see it as a wall poster?'

'Which bed's mine?' Higgins asked, looking at the two identical bunks beneath two identical closed and shaded windows.

'Whichever is more comfortable,' the Doctor answered. 'I had my niece change the sheets this evening. What did you do all day?' he said to Jorge. 'Why don't you open some windows in here?' and he went to a bed, raised the shade, and opened the window. 'Since my friend is not yet a "political prisoner," ' he said sternly, 'I hope you will not make him feel like one.'

'But of course not,' Jorge said. 'It is only . . .'

'And I must warn you,' the Doctor said, 'not to talk too much politics in his ears. Philip's mind is of the capitalist persuasion and he is not "up" as we are on all the current political theories. In fact, Philip is so politically backward, he still thinks Castro is a convertible bed! Ha, ha, ha, ha!' the Doctor laughed.

Higgins put his suitcase down. He had finally landed. Nor was the animal in him displeased to be sheltered once again, to have a roof overhead and a bed to lie in – even a bed in a *barrio* garret.

'Well,' the Doctor said proudly, looking about him, 'what do you think?'

'It'll be just fine,' Higgins smiled. For it was, in fact, though a little cramped for two, a pleasant room: neat, comfortable and clean, with a fine, high rooftop view of the great, bright slum.

'Good!' the Doctor said. 'And if there are any *cucarachas*, it is not my fault. Our friend here would not permit the exterminator to enter.'

'Why's that?' Higgins asked.

'Why do you suppose?' the Doctor asked with a faint smile.

'He did not know the password,' Jorge explained apologetically. And they all laughed.

'Look,' Higgins said, 'maybe this sounds silly to the two of you – or maybe I missed something – but would someone please tell me *why* we have a password in the first place?'

'It is a matter of security,' his new roommate said earnestly. 'You see, it is important that we maintain the highest security.'

'Why?' Higgins asked.

'It is nothing,' the Doctor said. 'Our friend here is just . . . keeping a low profile.'

'Yes,' the young man explained to Higgins. 'I am keeping a low profile,' though the way he said it made it sound like an actual physical silhouette he had stashed away in his dresser drawer.

'For our friend . . .' the Doctor continued, 'has enemies. Or so he believes.'

'So I believe?' the young man cried. 'Why, you know yourself . . .'

'Please,' the Doctor said in Spanish, 'do not start. Or I will have another nervous attack!'

Higgins had seen the Doctor's *ataques de nerviosos* before. They were not 'nervous attacks' at all but fits of rage, and Vazpana had obviously seem them, too, for he bit his lip and looked away.

'And anyway,' the Doctor said, 'our friend here' – meaning Higgins, who had asked the question – 'is not interested in all these stupid things. He is tired. He is my new consultant. He has come all the way from Boston!' And he glared at Jorge as if he'd been *molesting* Higgins. It was plainly time for the Doctor to go.

'*Hasta mañana*,' Higgins said, embracing his friend in the Latin American fashion. 'When would you like me to look at your books?'

'When?' the Doctor said angrily. 'Tomorrow, of course. First thing in the morning. I will call you,' he said and stalked out the door.

A moment later, he stuck his head back in. He looked dazed. 'I am sorry,' he said. 'Good-night. I am thinking.' And this time he disappeared for good.

Jorge hurriedly relocked the door. Then he looked at the window as if its open lights were a grave threat.

'Don't comrade,' Higgins said, reading his roommate's mind. 'It's hot in here. No one can get in.'

'Yes, but a bullet . . .'

'A bullet?' Higgins said. 'You mean someone might try to *shoot* us through the window?'

'Well, no,' the young man admitted uneasily, 'I am only being nervous, I suppose.'

'Nervous?' Higgins laughed. 'I'll say you are!'

His roommate dropped the needle on the phonograph, sighed and sat down on the edge of the bed. Higgins went into the bathroom to wash up, unable to figure out what the young man's problem was. He wondered if perhaps he wasn't high on something. These days. everyone was on drugs – including, he remembered now, himself.

When he was finished with his ablutions, Higgins dried his face and hands and came back out. His roommate was sitting on the edge of his bed watching him intently.

'And what do you do all day?' Higgins asked. 'Do you work somewhere?'

The young man smiled. 'It is to the cause of freedom that I devote myself. To the liberation of my country.'

'I see,' Higgins said, dismayed by the boy's insufferable tone. Higgins stepped out of his pants and folded them neatly across the back of a chair.

'And you,' Jorge asked. 'To what do you devote yourself?'

Higgins thought about that one for a moment. It was a very good question. He remembered how once, as a child, he had been devoted to the Virgin. It had been a very pure, natural devotion. He had picked blooming weeds and placed them at her painted feet and lit a thousand candles in her honor, worshiping her naturally with flowers and fire, and the perfect certitude that she existed and would hear him.

Higgins had loved her. He would tell her all his problems, and say 'Hail Holy Queens' so fast the words blurred into an ecstatic circle of sound, piercing him with a pain so sweet it hurt his heart to feel it, and then when he cried, it was like the whole universe was roaring through his head.

Of course, later on he'd been devoted to *her*. Now there was nothing that he was truly devoted to any longer.

'Once, when I was a kid, I had this feeling in my heart . . . I had it later, too, with *her*. My wife. She's dead. I don't have it any more.' It was as close as he could come to an explanation.

'I'm sorry,' Vazpana said.

'That's all right. It'll be one year next month – since she died, I mean.' There he went again.

'Big wounds heal slow,' the young man enunciated, as though it was an English speech exercise.

'Yes,' Higgins said, 'big wounds heal slow.'

'Ah! Lucho Barrios knows!'

'Who's that?'

'*This* is Lucho Barrios,' his new roommate said, waving at the phonograph.

Lucho Barrios, Higgins now learned, was the Doradoan Perry Como and all his songs were high, sad plaints of abused and tortured love. Guitars in the background tinkled like mandolins. There were tinny strings and the peculiar sound of the *chuaranga*, which Higgins learned was made from armadillo shells and was the Doradoan national instrument. In every song, it sounded like Lucho Barrios was about to die – he wrung each note with such heartache and passion! And although he struck many notes with a wet, glistening sob, he was only awful when he assaulted the highest register – which he shouldn't have touched – and then it was a nightmare of high, squeaking shrieks, backed by the sound of the wretched *chuaranga*, like a dog's claws on glass.

But Jorge loved Lucho Barrios, and he asked Higgins now if he would mind their going to sleep to it.

'Yes,' Higgins said.

But Higgins didn't understand. Jorge promised to play it very low. And he confessed now that he did this every night, the sad music of his country helping him to sleep. Otherwise, he felt homesick and wide-awake. He paced the floor and smoked cigarettes, 'damaging' his lungs. Sometimes, when he could not sleep, he became very hungry, and he had to get up then and cook himself a meal which would create a huge disturbance to Higgins' rest – imagine the pots rattling and banging, the sound of frying meat, and the oven door slamming again and again!

'One side. Low,' Higgins said. 'I've had a long day.'

'Are you . . . on the run?' the young man asked.

'The run?'

'Yes. From the law?'

Higgins shook his head and laughed. 'What a question!'

Jorge put on Lucho Barrios – side two. They got into bed and turned out the lights. In the dark, very low, Lucho Barrios sounded beautiful now, like the voice of the *barrio* itself, very tinkly and sad, full of *centavo* miseries and tin-can sorrows.

'Good-night, comrade,' Jorge said.

'*Buenas noches*,' Higgins said. He lay in the dark. He was exhausted, and the bed felt good. He watched the headlights of passing cars crawl across the bedroom ceiling, and he thought of what the Doctor had said – about looking for the flower.

Then he thought of her. Love was magic all right, or was it merely sleight of hand? All those knots they had tied so carefully between them, those hundred strands he had thought were so skilfully cinched had been undone in an instant, like a trick with string.

He rolled over on his back, remembering the very first time he had kissed *her*. It had been in St. Botolph's, a little Catholic chapel in the Back Bay, where he had led her after having already made up his mind to seduce her there in the church's intimate, candlelit gloom. For she was truly beautiful, freckled, fair, and he was dying to get his hands on her. They had just left the Museum of Fine Arts where Higgins had approached her in front of Bellini's 'St. Francis in Ecstasy.' Higgins had had in mind Higgins in ecstasy. He was charming, if predatory. 'You mean you've never been to St. Botolph's?' he'd asked, as if St. Botolph's was a great wonder and not some cheesy parish shrine.

She wasn't a Catholic – her parents were from the North – and so Higgins had covered up his nervousness by elaborately explaining all about blessing yourself – only non-Catholics said 'crossing', he'd assured her – about the Holy Water, the Tabernacle, and why and when you genuflected, along with completely fictitious hagiographies of St. Botolph and the Holy Infant of Prague.

Then they had lit candles and dropped coins in the poor box. Finally, they had come to a statue of the Blessed Mother, and she had turned to him questioningly. He told her to bless herself – she remembered how, didn't she? – and then to close her eyes. 'That's right. Fine,' he had whispered. Then he had kissed her. 'You conniving Irish bastard,' she'd said into his mouth, but she had kissed him back. Higgins smiled, remembering.

But why was he thinking of the first day he had met *her*? It was getting lunatic, obsessive, the way he still dwelt on her and dragged her corpse into every conversation; how everything still reminded him of her, the way everything – an evening doorway, firelight, a young beggar girl glimpsed in the street – reminded the saints of God. The Doctor was right. Norman Vincent Peale was right. The seer in the dream was right. He had to stop thinking about her. He had to start thinking positively. He was becoming like that character in Dostoyevsky, the ridiculous man with a name like the noise a cricket makes, who shows up years after his wife's demise dressed in mourning, with a big, black, lugubrious ribbon tied around his hat and dangling idiotically in front of his eyes.

Higgins sighed, feeling the pill and sleep coming over him. Everything would be fine, he told himself. Just wait and see. He had plenty of time, plenty of money. Relax, he told himself. Just watch it all unroll – like a movie.

Then he said a prayer for the repose of her soul as he had every night for the past three hundred or so nights since the night she had died. And then, because he was still afraid and could think of nothing else to do, he closed his eyes, drew a breath, and threw himself upon the mercy of the Virgin.

Hello, Blackbird!

♦

Chapter 7

The Doctor's three nieces were his 'whore of a sister' Gilberta's, and each of the girls had a different father. His sister had left them sleeping on the Doctor's couch one morning six weeks before when she had taken TWA Flight 172 to Paris along with a band of long-haired musicians and $2,000 of the Doctor's savings. She had not told the Doctor she was leaving, though she did tell the children. And to extract the savings, she had simply posed as the Doctor's wife in a neat piece of work that even the Doctor had to admire. Along with the children, she had left a note that had amused the physician with its impertinent passion. 'I leave them in your charge; care for them well, Arsenio – they are the heartbeats of my soul! As for the money, I know you will appreciate, *muchacho*, that I desperately need it to finance my career, and I will pay you off at first chance when the band gets going good.' For the Doctor's sister was one of those musician types who believed she had a calling as a vocalist of Rock & Roll.

Gilberta had once been the Doctor's favorite sister. But having come to America when she was quite young, she had received a larger dose than the Doctor of the American nightmare, and at a more susceptible age. Evidently it had seeped into her marrow and softened her brain, like radiation. Whatever the reason, at nineteen she had changed radically into an alien creature that the Doctor did not like or understand. She had quit college and taken to dressing like a bandit and hanging around with various stoned-out characters, freaks, jazz-musicians and other lost souls. It is true that, at that time, in the early eighties, the fabric of civilization had torn and the underworld had debouched into the highest echelons of society, but still that was no reason, the Doctor felt, for his sister to adopt the color black. Because no sooner had she started wearing black and hanging out with these punk, musician, drug-dependent types than she was knocked up by one of them – or two or ten of them, who knows? Because you did not know anymore, did you, what your little sister did. Then, to complicate matters, she had insisted on keeping the child, and the two more that had soon followed, while at the same time refusing to marry any of the fathers! And it would not be an exaggeration, the Doctor thought, to say that her promiscuous habits and self-willed behavior had scandalized the Hispanic community to which they belonged and brought shame and dishonor upon the sacred family name of Castellano. Though when the Doctor had communicated this sentiment to his sister, she had only looked at him wearily and said, 'Sacred family name! Oh, cut the crap, will you, Arsenio?'

But what irritated the Doctor most about his sister's behavior was that she did not seem to suffer for it. Her children displayed no resentment toward their working mom, and the band had been so successful on its European tour that she had soon repaid much of the money she owed, while inundating the children with letters and gifts.

Even the Doctor had been a recipient of her gifts – and very beautiful ones, at that – toward which he felt torn. On the one hand, he didn't want to be beholden to his errant, wayward sister, while on the other, his heart was stirred by the fantastic boxes that arrived suddenly in mid-afternoon in the arms of puffing, bug-eyed postmen: a present! For you! First, a shaving mug of the best London bone china, then a cache of resinous and exotic spices, like the booty from some Spanish galleon.

And so it wasn't until the third gift – a matching set of

antique vases which the Doctor discovered this morning waiting for him as he sat down for breakfast – that it dawned upon the Doctor what his sister was doing: smuggling cocaine, and using her benighted and unsuspecting physician brother as her dupe!

This horrifying realization struck the Doctor with such clear force as he gazed upon the ancient vases that he picked one up and dashed it to the floor – only to discover that the certainty of a realization doesn't always make it so. Reality is iffy. It may be a delusion, as, alas, in the Doctor's case, it was. For the shattered vase was clearly empty.

The Doctor stared down at the scattered shards, horrified now by what he had done, at this stupid mutilation of human history (for the Doctor was a great believer in 'Man' and in 'the triumph of the human spirit,' as he phrased it when he'd been drinking.) The degree of sickness the Doctor felt only increased as he read the letter accompanying the gift, confirming the vases' extreme antiquity and identifying them as 'two fine examples of the Iznik ware of sixteenth century Turkey.'

The Doctor was still reading the letter when his mother-in-law appeared.

The Doctor's mother-in-law was not the Doctor's mother-in-law. She was in fact his sister's mother-in-law, or rather, since his Gypsy sister insisted on mating and reproducing 'without benefit of clergy,' as it was quaintly put in certain English books, she was the Doctor's mother-out-law, or rather, the Doctor's sister's mother-out-law, however it might be. Whoever she was, she had taken up residence in the Doctor's home the morning his sister had 'abandoned' her children, by a pre-arrangement between the two women to which the Doctor had not been privy. In essence, what she provided, he had decided – other than child care and surrogate maternity – was to inflict upon the Doctor the worst of two possible worlds – that is, he had the inconvenience and peculiar torture dependent upon a live-in mother-in-law without the solace of a wife and marriage.

Now the Doctor's mother-in-law looked at the Doctor and

concocted a wry, teasing smile. It reminded the Doctor of those gruesomely sweet drinks garnished with little paper parasols they serve at Hawaiian restaurants – to which generous dollops of fat and lipstick had been added. Even worse was the dim, but growing ardor visible in the depths of her eyes. For his mother-in-law, despite her age, had a certain romantic interest in the Doctor.

'You like?' she asked flashing her black eyes, and breaking into a shimmying *rumba*.

'No, I don't like,' the Doctor said.

She stopped short, pulling a face like a little girl. It was ludicrous, the Doctor thought. She was sixty, if a day. 'Here I am,' Rosita said, 'in my beautiful prime – a woo-man, so ripe, so matured like a great brandy ... and yet ... no one wishing to drink of it ...' She trailed off, her gaze wandering rather sadly and unsteadily, the Doctor thought. 'Arsenio!' she said hopefully, moving toward him again.

'Stay away from me! You randy old cow!'

'Oh! Old cow, am I!' she asked, with the hell-begotten fury of a woman scorned. And picking up the remaining vase, she brought it down upon the Doctor's cranium.

There is another country that exists wholly in the human imagination. To those brave or foolhardy souls who enter it, it appears as one high and mighty shivering white vibration of infinite stoned weirdness and demoniacal sensation. In this country, through which the Doctor was now traveling, windows drip and light curves with a Daliesque surrealism, flesh is the color of bone, time warps, things sing, black wings hover and flap just outside one's field of vision, and the music of Hell seems to be drifting lightly somewhere in the background. Entrance to this world is secured by a sharp whack to the head with almost any blunt instrument, after which the whackee explores many strange and fascinating states of consciousness. The Doctor, a tourist in this mental country, passed a big white duck displaying the silliest of grins, then saw the house he had lived in as a child or, rather, there was a dark interior, and then a smell and a line of sight, and the

Doctor was a child again back in the big Cuban *finca* by the sea with the clean yellow sealight and seasmell blowing through the rooms that smelled of damp sea-soaked plaster. Then, superimposed upon this idyllic vision, the Doctor saw the face of his mistress.

The Doctor's mistress was Señora Helena Olivia de Jesus; that is to say, *Mrs.* Helena de Jesus, for it was one of the great and central tragedies of the Doctor's life that his mistress was a married woman. Unfortunately, the affair had been stalled and going nowhere for months; and though, at first, there had been wild keening promises and rebellious oaths, plans to run away together, solemn vows of eternal love, bleary kisses in the adulterous light of midtown cocktail lounges, nothing had become of any of them and finally they had stopped talking that way. Helena de Jesus had remained a *señora* and a de Jesus, and the Doctor had remained a bachelor and alone.

In fact, the Doctor had not made love to his beloved in more than four months, due to a chronic complaint on Mrs. de Jesus' part which made intercourse extremely painful and limited their copulations to approximately once each fiscal quarter. And yet still their affair dragged on, month after month. For Helena had a hold on him. A professional violinist, she had a certain perfectionistic *pizzicato* tenor to her body, while her nerves were delicate strings which the world fretted and plucked with a willful cruelty. Because of this, she was often out of sorts, and the Doctor had to be careful so as not to make her annoyed.

It had not always been like this. Once there had been illicit embraces, and kisses sharper than a sip of gin. Once the fountains at Lincoln Center, lit against the incoming dusk, had shone in his eyes and his soul had felt polished by the sparkling Mozart which his beloved had just performed – accompanying an orchestra, of course. The Doctor remembered that evening so well. It was April in New York – O, tender was the night! The Doctor had looked superb, had moved like fluid, like fine machinery, had worn his white Planter's suit and his white, broad-brimmed Panama hat beneath which the black crescent of his moustache had gleamed as large and lustrous as some small fierce animal or luminous moon. And on the Doctor's arm, the perfect accoutrement and crest jewel of his Spanish manhood: Helena de Jesus, another man's wife, with whom he strutted through the adoring crowd, the envy of other men, the object of women's bedroom dreams; Helena de Jesus, through whom it appeared he might be entering at last into that mysterious 'better world' where perpetual fountains play in the night, where Mozart lives, and Love is True.

But, of course, nothing even remotely approaching this had occurred, and the magical world the Doctor had thought he'd been entering that evening had turned out to be founded on dexedrine, delusion, and too much champagne at inter-mission. While his delicate darling had further savaged the Doctor's dream with a most indelicate attack of diarrhea on the cab ride home.

Now, he realized, coming to, reality was once again impinging on his dreams. The Doctor had the unpleasant sensation of making love to a porpoise or to some big wet fish, then opened his eyes and saw it was his mother-in-law, covering his face with hot loud tears and cold wet kisses, and the Doctor screamed and pushed her away, the pain of the blow just beginning to register.

'Ooh, Arsenio,' she said, through real tears. 'I am so sorry. Did I hurt your poor *cabeza*, beloved?'

'Ay, yi yi!' the Doctor said, only now realizing what it was that had hit him, astounded and chagrinned that the two of them could have destroyed in five brief minutes so many years of human history.

'Clean it up, woman!' the Doctor barked. 'My God, you are a maniac. You might have killed me!' he added, trying to pretend that everything was all right and that the whole idi-otic little interlude had not occurred. For this is what the Doctor's life had become: a sequence wherein things looked promising at first, then suddenly and stupidly got out of hand, and finally ended with the Doctor attempting to recoup his losses – or this, at least, is how it had been of late.

But Rosita had picked up the accompanying card. She scanned it and cried, 'But why did you not tell me? My baby, Gilberta! She is coming home!'

'What!' the Doctor said, not having read that far, horrified by the idea, even though it was what he had been publicly begging for. 'Give me that! I am reading it,' he said, snatching back the letter, jealous of the fact that it hadn't been his news to tell.

It was true. His sister *was* coming home. There had been some sort of awful accident, though she herself, she wrote, was fine.

'Oh, my baby, my baby,' Rosita said, every square – or rather, round – inch of her oozing maternal concern and delight. 'And the children will be so happy!'

'Damn the children! And damn you, you old shrew! Look at the waste you've made,' the Doctor thundered, losing his temper, out of sorts with the news – at once envying, loving, and hating his sister with a persistent and unblunted-from-childhood pain.

'Oh, you don't mean that, Arsenio,' Rosita cried. 'Do not say it. You must take it back.'

'Eh?' the Doctor said absently, brooding on his sister's return.

'Damning the children the way you did.'

'Did I?' the Doctor asked, surprised, making a face . . . then remembering. 'Well, of course not,' he sputtered. 'Of course, you know, I did not mean . . .'

'Of course, you didn't,' Rosita soothed, superstitiously. 'Of course, you did not mean it,' she agreed, attacking with her naturally maternal air the Doctor's errant collar and cravat which were affixed to one side of his neck like the makeshift noose of a lynching or a suicide. 'Mother of Love, Mother Above,' Rosita clucked. 'Damning the children! Who would ever do such a thing?'

Identify the Enemy

◆

Chapter 8

The telephone woke Higgins and, disoriented, he stared at the clamorous instrument wondering if he should answer it; wondering also who and where on earth he was, for in his dream he had been a doctor in Liverpool making his way through a poor and cut-throat part of town. A frozen river, which he somehow knew to be the Mersey, lay motionless in the distance, appearing in the twilight like liquid nickel spilled, run, and then re-hardened. Curiously, he was dressed in an antique manner: he wore a top hat, knee boots, and a thick wool cape. The silver-headed cane he wielded doubled as a cudgel for, in the dream, the slums were dangerous at that hour, Higgins was returning from the arms of his mistress, and it was clearly the winter of 1859.

Higgins had been born with a slight turn in his right foot; for a year, as a child, he had worn a corrective shoe. But though he had not thought of this in years, he awoke now with the bizarre conviction that the dream doctor's limp was an earlier and more afflicted version of this same disability – or, to put it another way, that the crippled English doctor limping through the slums of Liverpool had been Higgins himself, one hundred and twenty-some-odd years ago!

But the Doctor's voice on the telephone hauled him back to reality: the dream dissolved, and the strange room, like a spacecraft adrift in an alien dimension, made a subtle but

51

abrupt metaphysical adjustment back into the present time and place, and Higgins remembered where he was: the *barrio*.

It was difficult, however, to make out what the Doctor was saying. The noise-level in his apartment was absurd: a radio was blaring *salsa* and a tea-kettle singing above the general din of the Castellano family rising from their slumber like some wild herd. '. . . burnt bread. This is what they feed me. As if I was a toad . . .' the Doctor concluded gloomily, evidently referring to what he considered to be an inadequate breakfast. 'At any rate, we will meet at my office. Ten-thirty sharp. Stop it!' he screamed at something or someone, and hung up.

Higgins lay back down in bed. His roommate was snoring and he could hear the cooing of the pigeons on the sill. A movie he'd once seen had called them 'flying rats.' He didn't understand how anyone could feel that way about such shy, tender doves.

Higgins assumed the *shavasana* now – the corpse pose – which only meant that he continued to lie on his back with his legs slightly parted and his hands at his sides. Then he tried to empty his mind but, instead, Higgins found himself remembering now a forgotten fragment of the morning's dream. For as the dream had ended, the little mad *mestiza* he had met last night with the Doctor stepped from behind a ruined building and beckoned with her eyes.

How weird, Higgins thought, that he should dream of her again. Again? But when had he dreamt of her before? Why the night before last – in the dream of his wife and the deer-skinned seer.

A cold bolt went up Higgins' spine and he sat up in bed – for he knew now his mind was on the verge of understanding something that he did not want it to understand. There was something the matter here. The chronology was wrong. It was not the fact that he had dreamt of the child this morning. After their encounter the night before, it was almost to be expected. No, the inexplicable thing was that he had dreamt of her *the night before that* – twenty-four hours before he had met her! That's why her face had been so familiar!

But that was crazy! He must be wrong. You could not dream of someone you didn't yet know.

Look, he told himself, it's very simple. You dreamt of a gray-eyed, doe-skinned seer, and then the next evening on the streets of Manhattan, you came upon a young woman who closely resembled the figure in your dream. Forget it.

Urged by a full bladder, Higgins forsook his would-be meditations, got out of bed, and slipped into the bathroom. The shower was nothing like his own at home with its Automatic Massager Nozzle and hot, lavish spray. The plastic curtain was mildewed and crawling with silverfish, the porcelain tub discolored with turquoise stains, while the spigot was a metal pancake through which water percolated and dripped in arctic cold and searing hot rivulets that simultaneously scalded and froze different parts of your body – until the hot water gave out entirely and it was too freezing to endure.

Finished with his shower, he flossed his teeth and carefully shaved. Then he went back out to the bedroom–living-room–kitchen–study. His roommate was awake, performing calisthenics.

'*Buenos días*,' Higgins said, resurrecting his prep school Spanish. '*¿Cómo está?*'

'*A-MEE-go*,' Jorge grunted, doing sit-ups. 'I am so very – GLAD! – that you arrived. I sleep so very – WELL! – last night, feeling so much more pro-TECT-ed, ugh!' He quit the exercises and punched his flat, brown belly while Higgins rubbed his wet hair dry with a balding towel.

'I'm sorry,' Higgins said, 'but I think I used up all the hot water. I don't see how. I was only under it a minute.'

'Friend,' Jorge interrupted him, holding up a traffic cop's palm, 'do not reprove yourself. For this, you see, is not your fault, but the responsibility of the fascist landlord who does not provide his tenants with the proper amount of hot water. And yet you will notice how effective his technique. For it is not he against whom your anger rages. No! You reprove *yourself* for this absence of water, and toward me, your comrade, you feel very, very guilty!'

'I see,' Higgins said, who wasn't feeling guilty in the least.

'Identify the enemy,' Jorge said, starting a series of deep knee bends. 'This is the first rule.'

'And what's the second?' Higgins idly asked.

'Kill him. And get away.'

Higgins stopped and looked at his roommate. What the boy obviously didn't know was that the Doctor owned the building.

'What are you doing today?' Higgins inquired.

'Today? I will be visiting my comrades.'

'Oh, really? And where do your comrades live?' Higgins asked, trying to make light conversation.

'In Brooklyn. Quite near the water. You can see from their window the Statue of Liberation.'

'Of Liberty, you mean.'

The boy shrugged with a diffident air, unimpressed by the subtleties of English expression. Suddenly, he stopped and looked suspicious. 'Why do you ask?'

'No reason,' Higgins said, slipping on his shoes, a pair of well-worn Cole-Haans.

'If you want to learn more, you ought to join us.'

'Thanks, but no,' Higgins said.

'Why not? Don't you believe the world needs reform? Aren't you in favour of liberation?'

'Sure. It's just that . . . I look at it this way. You want to reform somebody? Reform yourself. You want to liberate someone. Fine. Liberate the bastard who's screaming inside you.'

The young man did not blink. 'Selfish,' he said.

Higgins sighed. Perhaps he was. He didn't know. He only knew it was the only thing that had ever interested him, based as it was on the intuition that the Revolution was within you, and that Liberation, like the Second Coming, wasn't something you would see on the 6 o'clock news.

But it was too early in the morning for such a discussion.

'What's today's password?' Higgins asked, once again tactfully changing the subject.

'Aha! The password! You remembered!'

'But of course.'

'Since you are my guest,' Jorge said generously, 'it will be today whatever you wish.'

'How's "Rorschach?"'

'I do not know,' the young man said frowning. 'I have not seen him in some time.'

'As a *password*.' Higgins smiled. 'Don't tell me you actually *know* someone by that name.'

'Yes,' Jorge smiled. 'And it was he to whom I thought you were referring. Caspar Rorschach Ramos. He was our dear comrade.'

'Was?'

'He was arrested the second day of the coup.'

'Coup?'

'In Dorado.'

'I see . . . I'm sorry,' Higgins added, noticing the way the boy's face fell at the memory.

But Jorge's spirits instantly revived. 'As a password, however, it is an excellent choice. *Inspired*, one might even say. Not only does it recall to mind our lost comrade, but it is not a word that one might say easily by mistake. "Hello", for instance, makes a very poor password. "Are you there?" and "Anyone home?" are also bad choices for reasons obvious.'

Higgins just smiled. Finished dressing, he tried to open the door. It took a while; it was sealed like a pharaoh's tomb. 'Rorschach,' he said in farewell as he sprung the last lock.

'That is very good,' the young man nodded. 'However, with a password, my friend, you have only to pronounce it at the time you are entering!'

Higgins had breakfast across the street in a little flyblown luncheonette that flew sad flags of flypaper in the hot wind of table fans. The air was thick with fry and even the portrait of the Virgin was greasy. Higgins felt self-conscious when he first entered, but the sensation quickly vanished. After the first cursory glances in which his *gringo*hood was duly noted and received, he was treated like anyone else – a trifle more courteously, if anything. Even in *el barrio*, a white male had privileges, it appeared, and Higgins hoped it would stay that way.

Leery of the greasy grill, Higgins ordered a buttered muffin and a cup of *café con leche*. The bun was served on one of those heavy oval porcelain platters with hairline fractures in its shattered lacquer and one green line circulating its chipped circumference they save expressly for little corner Spanish luncheonettes to supplement their air of rinky-dink sadness and dopey third-rate loss don't ask who they is just eat your breakfast. What's the matter with you? Higgins asked himself. C'mon now. Shake it off.

For there was no good reason for Higgins to feel bad. His wife was dead; this was true. Still, there were many worse tragedies in life. Like what? Offhand, he couldn't think of any.

Higgins tried to imagine how Bhartrihari would have behaved had he been sitting here right now, for sometimes it helped Higgins, when he saw his life sliding straight for Hell, to imagine how someone much better and braver would have handled himself in the same situation, and the poet-saint, Bhartrihari, author of the *Shatakatraya*, was the one who always came to Higgins' mind.

Bhartrihari's sainthood was not like some. He was no goody two-shoes. He had been a man of the world and a great *maharaj* until a wandering sage had given him nectar, the elixir of immortal life, which Bhartrihari in his selfless love had passed along, untasted, to his Queen. She, in turn, had given it to her lover, who had presented it to his mistress who, in love with Bhartrihari, had returned it to the King. Thus was the great poet-saint-to-be apprised of his Queen's infidelity and, sick in heart and soul, he had renounced his kingdom and retired to the jungle.

But there in the wilderness, he had met a great master, and the King's bitter exile had turned unexpectedly to joy. Poetry had flowered on his lips, truth had taken root in him, a divine seed had blossomed in his depths, as though the hurt of the world and the silence of the wilderness had conspired not to harm him but to heal him by degrees. Higgins often prayed to the cuckold saint who knew what it was like to love a woman too much, who knew the sick taste in your mouth of losing her and the rotten stomach that accompanies a broken heart – for as Bhartrihari had written and Higgins had translated:

> *Gentlemen: Be serious. You know as well as I*
> *There are but two pursuits that truly call us;*
> *Young girls (with breasts so big they weary us)*
> *– Or the Wilderness!*

Higgins had already completed the first two parts of Bhartrihari's opus and was working on the third. His agent envisioned a large, coffee table-sized book, with erotic illustrations by an illustrious illustrator friend of hers.

Higgins' agent also envisioned him writing a novel. The novel she envisioned would make them both rich. What Higgins' agent didn't envision (and what Higgins hadn't brought himself to tell her yet) was that he *couldn't* write a novel. He had tried many times, and they had always turned into short stories. In fact, he had written his best short story that way: trying to write a novel, which, in the middle of a paragraph, toward the end of Chapter Two, had suddenly closed – self-willed and inevitable – like the lid of some ancient and enchanted box.

He remembered how happy he had been that day. He had read the story over again and realized it was very good; or at least, better than anything he had ever written. Then, afterward, he had gone shopping with *her* in Haymarket Square. It was fall, and there is no place more lovely than Boston in the fall. The army-greens and summer heat give way to cool, gold days. The light is blinding and the smell of the sea is like a spell. The wind spills leaves in the streets, hawkers cry on corners, women trail perfume in the air. At Haymarket Square, the harvest was in in profusion. Wooden carts and trucks loaded with produce from Lexington and Concord, Lincoln and Harvard – pumpkins and lettuce, apples and corn – clogged the streets, while beside them, freshly dredged from the sea, were dripping mounds of bearded black mussels, white clams, and pink boiled crabs.

Had that been the happiest day of his life? One of them, surely. And afterward, coming home through the autumn twilight, he had felt peculiarly whole and clear. He had *her* beside him, supper in his arms, and on his desk at home the very fine, freshly finished short story which was better than any novel he would never write.

Gunshots &
Triquitraques

◆

Chapter 9

The Doctor was at work when Higgins arrived at the office.
He looked fresh and rested, his large moustache on his over-
thin face was sleek and lustrous, and his pale Castilian eyes
were extremely clear. When the Doctor was not refreshed
and rested, his over-large moustache grew even larger, suggesting dry wire bristles, while his eyes became sores.

'Rorschach,' Higgins said in greeting as he entered. 'That's
today's password. I thought you'd like to know.'

'I never remember,' the Doctor sighed. 'Every day it
changes.'

'That's the whole point,' Higgins said. 'To keep you on
your toes.'

'And how was our friend this morning?'

'Our friend was wonderful. He gave me a lecture on the
political implications of my shower. I *like* that, Arsenio. I
don't get that every morning.'

'And has he told you that someone is trying to kill him?'
the Doctor asked.

'No,' Higgins said. 'But I got that impression. He has the
door locked like a bank vault. Is there?'

'Of course not. Would I be having you stay there if I
thought there was?'

'Of course not,' Higgins said. He thought for a moment.
'But what if you're wrong?'

'I am *not* wrong!' the Doctor said. 'He's been here six days and no one has laid a finger on him. If he wasn't my grandfather's uncle's son's child – or whoever it is he claims to be – I would not be playing this outrageous charade, I assure you. Charade,' the Doctor said smiling. 'That is a word that you yourself taught me the very first day I met you.'

Higgins remembered that day. It had been sixteen years ago, at Harvard, at the beginning of Higgins' freshman year. The Doctor – who was not a doctor then but a medical student – had taken Higgins to dinner at The Wursthaus in the Square. Higgins had noted the restaurant's outlandish Teutonic decor – the huge tubes of plastic sausages hanging from the wooden rafters, the titanic ceramic steins that adorned the walls – and pronounced it 'a charade,' a word which, when Higgins had defined it as 'a hollow or empty spectacle or game, often in questionable taste,' the Doctor had immediately seized upon with glee and commandeered for the rest of the evening to describe every possible aspect of his impossible life – from his relationship with his Vassar girlfriend to the ostentatious icing on the Bavarian cream pie.

It was later that same evening, over Mexican pot, French brandy, and Higgins' first Havana cigars, that Higgins and the Doctor had taken LSD. It was Higgins' first and only trip. Under the drug, Harvard Yard looked like some Moorish camp lit by grilled amber lanterns, and Higgins had gaped at his subconscious mind plastered all over the street, Square, dorms, and sky – it was weird. Allen Ginsberg floated by the moon; the Doctor glowed as though he was atomic, while the sweetest, deepest feelings coursed through Higgins' soul as he listened to 'The Four Seasons' trumpeting ecstatically at dawn on the Doctor's stereo – with which the Doctor was, that hallucinogenic moment, threatening to merge.

Afterwards, he was neither the befuddled wreck nor the enlightened wonder they had assured him he would be. He did know one thing, however. He knew that the Doctor was the grandest and most elaborate personality that had ever lived.

'But what if someone *is* trying to kill him?' Higgins asked now, beginning to consider the personal implications of a contract on his roommate.

'I tell you, nobody is trying to kill him! It is all his imagination. Look, I would understand if it was three years ago, if President Benitez had just fallen from power, and our friend was some big honcho in MIRA, opposed to the new government. In those days, even if you fled the country, they would come after you and kill you, like they murdered Stratton and Courvoisier. But our friend, who is he? Just an exile, a boy. He probably slept with some General's daughter – the wrong General, the wrong daughter. Maybe he *is* in hot water. But . . . marked for execution? By who? Ridiculous! You see, these exiles,' the Doctor concluded in disgust, 'they have lost their country and now they have nothing to lose but their minds!'

Though Higgins did not perfectly follow the Doctor's explanation – he had heard of Courvoisier, he thought, but not of Stratton, and who the 'they' was that had murdered them both was still a mystery – he was impressed and reassured. It did seem unlikely that his young roommate, zealot that he was, should be marked for extermination by the powers that be. And he remembered a man he had sat next to on a bus trip to New Hampshire who had offered him a corner of his peanut butter sandwich, then confided in a whisper that the Greyhound was being followed by Japanese spies.

'But what if you're wrong,' Higgins persisted, not quite convinced.

'I am not wrong!'

'But who is it then that murdered Courvoisier and . . . ?'

'AES,' the Doctor said.

'Ace?'

'A-E-S. *Aparato del Estado Securidad* – the Dorado secret police.'

Higgins sighed – at his own ignorance.

'Look, tell me what happened in Dorado. From the beginning, Arsenio. I still don't get it.'

'Get? What is there to get? Three years ago, for the first

61

time in its long and lamentable history, a democratically elected government took power, headed by President Rodolfo Benitez. And then because this government didn't crush its enemies and seize control of the army and police, it was brutally subverted and overthrown.'

The Doctor paused for breath. Like many Central Americans, he would have rather talked politics than make love to a beautiful woman; though, in the Doctor's case, the former activity produced the same physical after-effects as the latter, and left the physician gloriously exhausted, shining-eyed, and breathless.

'But how could Benitez have done such a thing?' Higgins asked, finding himself annoyed by the Doctor's imperious and know-it-all tone. 'You can't be a democracy and then go around *crushing your enemies*, as you so blithely put it. And anyway,' Higgins said, 'what the hell should he have done?'

But Higgins was instantly sorry he'd asked, for in the imaginary country of which the Doctor was imaginary President, treachery and sedition were rigorously expunged; saboteurs and curfew-breakers shot on sight. Though Higgins had known the Doctor in college to carry a hurt bird around in the sleeve of his overcoat until it had died there, in his political rantings he ordered the Chiefs of Police and Heads of the Army shot in the head with an alarming frequency and dispatch.

Partly, it was because he was a Latin, Higgins thought, and this was his ruthless history. Partly, it was because the Doctor was a realist, who knew what happened to presidents like Benitez who did not control the armed forces – 'Without which elections and constitutions and solemn vows of eternal brotherhood mean nothing. He could have controlled the Army,' the Doctor said now, 'but he demurred, and in the end he left "the People in uniform," as he called it, in the hands of the Generals – who crushed him with it.'

The Doctor forgave Benitez this fatal misjudgment, attributing it to his 'exalted vision of Humankind,' but to Higgins it seemed more like some lethal naivete, as though Benitez had truly believed he inhabited a world where men were honorable, wives faithful, troops loyal, children obedient, and in which the family dog has no designs upon the Sunday roast. For, as the Doctor said, 'though the boot was in his face and he could taste it, he continued to believe, like that poor little Jewish girl – what was her name? – that people were essentially "good at heart."

'Oh, there was resistance, of course, some of it fierce. And this is where MIRA comes in. MIRA was one of those political alliances which supported Benitez and resisted the coup – but they were hopelessly outgunned. For the first few days there was sniper fire and sabotage around the capital of Puerto Valle. But in the end, it was stupid. In the end, it was all like that sad Hungarian picture.'

'What sad Hungarian picture?'

'You know. In *Life* Magazine. The one of boys throwing rocks at tanks.'

The Doctor got up from the table, went to the sink and drew himself a glass of tap water which he drank greedily. 'I wish they would not play down there,' he said, gazing out the window at the children in the lot below. 'It is full of rodents.'

'And then what happened?' Higgins asked.

The Doctor shrugged. 'The usual. Reprisals. Torture. Exile for many. The first few weeks the secret police would come to your door and shoot you as they found you, making love to your wife, combing your daughter's hair, eating your breakfast, it did not matter. Other prisoners they brought to the *Estadio Nacional*, a soccer stadium they had turned into a torture chamber. The women, I understand, were especially abused.'

There was a brief, painful silence.

'And who did all this?' Higgins asked at last. 'To Benitez. To Dorado. To the women in the stadium.'

'I've told you,' the Doctor said. 'The Junior Officers. And their secret police force, AES. Apparatus For State Security.'

'And Jorge?' Higgins asked. 'Are the same guys trying to kill him?'

'No one is trying to kill anyone!' the Doctor shouted.

'I'm glad to hear that, Arsenio,' Higgins said, 'because I'd sure hate to have my meditations interrupted by a . . . bullet in the head.'

The Doctor sighed. 'There is one more story I would like to tell you. Only last year AES arrested a colleague of mine, Doctor Enrique Lopez, a fine and brilliant physician. He was not even from Dorado – he had just gone there to attend a medical conference! When next he appeared, four weeks later, he had lost his reason. He kept repeating, "I am Quinnones. I am Quinnones, the Bull," and then he would sob and sob. One can only imagine what they had done to this excellent man. For he was a friend of my father's and it was he who first interested me in medicine when I was young. Later, he was executed. With rifle butts, I understand.'

Higgins winced. And yet he somehow knew how dying like that would feel. He knew the scorpion-ridden cell and the sick taste of copper coins in your mouth that comes when your life is in mortal danger. He knew the thirst, the horse-flies, the listless jibes of the bored guards, and then the torture: the beatings, the fire and knives, the fearful interrogations.

Then one summer morning, they would come for you and push you into the dusty compound. The dawn courtyard exudes that magnificent reality that only death reveals: purple flowers growing by a trench – *your grave, Señor* – have a freshness you have only dreamed of, while the silence of the South American dawn, and the pure blueness of the eastern sky against the black crenelations of the stone fort, the guilty cough of the young soldier who avoids your eyes – even the pain of your open wounds – have a truth and a beauty you had not known existed. Then, they would shoot you.

'I'm sorry, Arsenio,' Higgins said at last.

The Doctor clucked. 'It is nothing,' he said. 'It happened to thousands. Perhaps, someday, who knows?' He laughed. 'It will happen to us.'

'Where are your books, Arsenio?' Higgins asked now, looking around the room for a filing cabinet.

'There,' the Doctor grunted, 'you will find everything.' And he waved at a squat, iron safe in a corner that Higgins had somehow overlooked.

Higgins knelt before the unlocked box, and retrieved from it (beside a rubber-banded wad of twenties and a pistol) a ledger book and an accordion folder stuffed with papers. Then he sat down at the Doctor's desk to begin his new job as the Doctor's consultant.

The Doctor's records were in order – up to a point: they stopped two years ago. After that, they deteriorated into a mass of canceled checks, receipts, undated invoices, bank books, loan applications, telephone bills, birthday greetings and snapshots of the Doctor at Jones Beach in swimming trunks and goggles eating a foot-long wiener. There were also two years of income tax returns which appeared never to have been filed. When Higgins brought this to his friend's attention, the Doctor looked relieved and said with genuine pride, 'And to think you will fix it! What luck you are here!'

For the next hour or so, Higgins struggled with the 'books,' trying to establish a rough idea of what the Doctor earned and spent. Though it appeared his friend was making over $70,000 a year between his private practice and his work at the hospital, he was heavily – unreasonably – in debt. To be sure, he was still paying off medical school, various bank loans, a car that had been stolen a year ago, his niece's braces, and his mother-in-law's bridge, but still, even at a glance, there appeared to be large sums of money missing and unaccounted for.

At 10:45, the Doctor's first patient arrived: a machine operator named Herman Gonzalez who had lost his fingers in a punch press some weeks before. Though Gonzalez had severed his thumb and forefinger, the hand was healing well and the Doctor seemed pleased when he undid the bandages.

But Gonzalez was not pleased. He held the hand with an injured air and looked at the Doctor through wounded, gloomy eyes. Gonzalez had had hopes of becoming a major league ballplayer – hopes he had left behind one day in the paperdust haze of a Queens bindery in the form of two bloody digits on a sunlit cutting table.

The Doctor had seen Gonzalez pitch in the Puerto Rican league. 'You had such a fastball that afternoon. It was so madly fast.'

'It used to hop,' Gonzalez said in a sweet, high-pitched voice, turning his sad, brown gaze on Higgins. 'When it got to the plate, it used to hop. I swear.'

'It was too fast to hit!' the Doctor assured them both. 'They clocked it once at ninety-five miles per hour!'

'Ninety-six point three,' Gonzalez moaned. 'Earned Run Average: One point eight nine.'

'And it used to hop,' the Doctor said. 'Our friend is right. When it got to the plate, it used to hop.'

The pitcher sighed. 'Like a little rabbit.'

Then Gonzalez expressed the hope that, someday, his fingers might grow back in. Higgins choked on his coffee, and looked up from the books in honor of such a monumental piece of wishful thinking. But the Doctor took the remark in stride as though this was a common misapprehension. 'My dear friend,' he began patiently, 'you must think of your hand as a world made up of living, breathing cells. Your accident destroyed that world. And what it didn't actually cut away, it shattered with its concussion and impact of force.' The Doctor paused. 'Now, the recuperative powers of the human body are marvelous, amazing, even miraculous, one might say, but they are not . . .' He struggled for the word.

'Resurrective,' Higgins offered.

'Exactly!' the Doctor said. 'Dead nerves do not feel again. Dead tissue does not return to life. We are not salamanders or starfish, my friend. We cannot grow new tails, or hands . . .'

'Or hearts,' Higgins said.

The Doctor looked at him intently. 'Or hearts,' he admitted. 'Quite correct!'

When Gonzalez had gone, the Doctor said, 'You will please to write "condition improving." And also, "no charge." He is a friend of my sister's.'

Higgins had been afraid of something like this. 'Look,

Arsenio, as your financial consultant, it is my duty to inform you that this is no way to do business. You owe two years' back taxes. You are greatly in debt!'

'See?' the Doctor said unfazed. 'You are helping already! Next!'

Just then there was a sharp retort from the street, and Higgins started, wondering nervously aloud if it wasn't a shot.'

'Firecracker,' Higgins said, unconcerned. '*El triquitraque.*'

A moment later, there was another report. '*El triquitraque,*' Higgins repeated intrigued by the word. But this time the Doctor rushed to the window, and Higgins followed right behind him.

Across the street, in the sunlight outside a *bodega*, a body was lying on the pavement, bleeding much too freely for Higgins' stomach and he turned away, suddenly re-tasting the morning's coffee.

The Doctor cursed and rushed out the door. Higgins used the opportunity to call his office and tell his secretary he would not be coming in. A minute later, the Doctor re-entered, accompanied by a vigorous, barrel-chested old man – though the man looked rather glum and cowed.

'You are incredible!' the Doctor hissed through clenched teeth. The Doctor was pouring sweat and was mopping ineffectively at his brow with a glistening forearm.

'What happened, Arsenio?' Higgins asked. But the Doctor did not answer. He went to the tap and drank off a glass of water, some of which dribbled down his chin. 'I will tell you what happened!' he gulped. 'Our . . . our . . . *compañero*,' he said, gesturing extravagantly in the old man's direction, 'will drive me to madness before he is through!'

Higgins looked at the man, but he only shrugged. 'What happened?' he asked again.

'All right,' the Doctor said attempting to regain his composure. 'I am *trying* to tell you. Our . . . our . . . comrade here, Ambrosio Garcia . . . do you two know each other? . . . Philip Higgins, my consultant and friend . . . goes to the *bodega* to buy himself a bottle of beer. In the *bodega*,' the Doctor said carefully as if he was trying to get a confusing story perfectly straight, 'he hears a gunshot and runs to the door.' He glanced at Garcia for confirmation.

'So he opens the door and steps out into the street. There he sees a man with a gun in his hand running away from the scene of the shooting. As the man comes near him, our friend raises his bottle and hits him as hard as he can on his head. The man falls to the ground and our friend jumps on top of him very proud to be such a great hero!' The Doctor stopped.

The old man said nothing.

Higgins glanced back and forth between the two of them, puzzled. 'Well,' he said, 'wasn't he?'

The Doctor tendered his weariest smile. 'Tell him, my friend.'

Garcia squirmed. 'The man who I hit . . . was the man who'd been shot.'

Higgins laughed, despite himself. He shook his head. 'That's wonderful.'

'Isn't it?' the Doctor asked. 'But that is not all! The man who was shot, and that our friend here hit, is Omar Maldonado – *El Duende*'s lieutenant!'

'What do I care?' Garcia said defiantly. 'I do not care if it was *El Duende* himself!'

'You don't care?' the Doctor shrieked. 'No! You won't care at all, I can assure you, my friend, when they drag your body from the East River!'

'I am not afraid,' the ex-soldier said with proud disdain, 'of *El Duende* or of anyone. They are dogs. They are no better than bandits with their numbers and drugs. I spit,' he said, 'between the legs of their sisters!'

'See?' the Doctor asked, with the calmest of smiles. 'See?' he said, turning to Higgins.

'But why did they shoot him?' Higgins asked.

'Why? Because they are afraid to shoot *El Duende*. Last week they shot two of his runners. One in the stomach, one in the leg. Now they shoot his first lieutenant. Clearly someone is trying to speak to the Goblin.'

'Who?' Higgins asked.

'Who? The Italians,' the Doctor said curtly. 'Or so I am told.'

But someone was coming. There were footsteps on the stairwell, and Jorge Vazpana appeared in the doorway. His eyes were wide. 'I heard the shots!' he said.

'Oh, yes? So what are you doing here then? Aren't you afraid they'll shoot you, too?' The Doctor was clearly fed up with the boy.

Vazpana gave a thin, ironic smile. 'According to the first lesson of the Doradoan revolution—'

'No lectures, please!' the Doctor interrupted, glancing at his watch. 'My God, what are they waiting for? If they don't bring him up here soon . . .' He turned to Garcia, 'Please come see me this evening. And as for him,' he said, pointing at Jorge, but speaking to Higgins, 'take him away from here. Will you do that for me? Take him away somewhere nice and undangerous. Somewhere where he won't get shot.'

The young man tensed at the Doctor's tone. 'I am not your dog,' he said, 'who you may order about in any way that suits you!'

'Oh, *no*?' the Doctor said.

'No!' the boy replied.

'Gentlemen, gentlemen,' Garcia soothed.

Just then, the office door flew open and a beautiful young woman entered the room. She resembled the Doctor a little, Higgins thought, with her long, clean lines, chestnut hair and light complexion, though there, mercifully, the resemblance ended. More than the Doctor, she reminded Higgins of a hawk he'd encountered on a rain-soaked branch one Maine dawn, for her manner wasn't shy, ingratiating, or gay, as beautiful women are taught to be. She was simply present – *there*. And she looked at Higgins now, deadpan and unsmiling – the way the hawk's gold eyes had looked at him that morning, neither accepting nor rejecting him, and equally oblivious as to whether he approved of her or not.

Higgins opened his mouth to speak, then foolishly shut it, wondering what it was he'd been about to say.

'Hello, Arsenio. There's someone to see you,' and she indicated with a graceful wave the bashed and bleeding gangster who two big goons were bringing in through the door.

For a moment, there was confusion. Then the Doctor rushed to his patient's side, as the group of men sheepishly departed – like quarrelsome brothers silenced and sent packing by a more sensible older sister.

The Beginning Of The End

◆

Chapter 10

'I thought you were keeping a low profile, *Señor*.' Higgins chided his roommate now as the two men, evicted from the Doctor's office, descended to the street.

'I did nothing improper,' his roommate contended. 'I was minding my own business when all the shooting began.'

'And where are you going now?' Higgins asked, hoping the answer was neither back to their room nor anywhere near the Doctor. But his roommate didn't answer. He walked on and Higgins followed. The summer day was turning chill. A cold breeze blew through the morning, silvering the leaves of the trees of heaven. Several times Jorge glanced behind him as though he was afraid they were being tailed.

'Okay,' Higgins said at last, unable to contain his curiosity any longer. 'What's going on? C'mon. Is someone really out to get you?''

The boy exhibited the cheesiest of grins. 'Who told you that?'

'No one,' Higgins lied. 'It's perfectly obvious, isn't it? All the locks on our door. And that silly password. The only thing I don't know is what we're supposed to be afraid of?'

'We are not afraid!' the young man shouted angrily. Then he quickly lowered his voice and said in an agitated whisper, 'However, it is true. There *are* people out to kill me.'

71

'What people?'

'Ha! That I cannot divulge!'

'Why not?' Higgins pressed, attempting to maintain his cool, but only barely succeeding. For he was, in fact, beginning to appreciate how the boy had got under the Doctor's skin. He had the arrogance of a god, the self-esteem of royalty. Nor had the young man answered Higgins' question. Higgins was getting very tired of it all. He considered the situation again in an objective light. Someone, it seemed, might be trying to kill his roommate, but his roommate wasn't going to tell Higgins why or who it was – Higgins, whose heart was full of unrequited cravings, whose throat was still so soft and young, and who slept at night not three dark feet from the intended victim. Was Higgins going to stand for that? He most certainly was not. To forget about it would be like asking for it. 'Who is trying to kill you, *Señor*?' Higgins repeated with an admirable calm.

'I can't tell you. And anyway, you have never heard of them.'

'Try me.'

Jorge hesitated. 'They are called AES.'

'Apparatus For State Security.'

'You know them?' He seemed surprised, then frowned and looked around him. 'Yes. I am sure it is them.'

'And why would they want to do a nasty thing like that? Kill you, I mean.'

'Because that's how they operate. They kill their enemies. I can't say I blame them. I would do the same if I could.'

'And how do you know this? Has anyone tried?'

'Well, no . . .' the young man admitted uneasily. 'Not yet.'

'Then how do you know?'

'I can just . . . feel it . . . coming.'

'Oh, for crying out loud!' Higgins said, disgusted. 'Let's start over again, shall we? Why would anybody want to kill *you*?'

The young man sighed and threw Higgins a pained, almost plaintive look. He paused. 'All right,' he said nervously. 'I will tell you. I was going to *have* to tell you anyway.' He drew Higgins closer with a curling finger until they had both assumed a properly conspiratorial air. 'You see, my friend, I am . . . a confidential agent.'

Higgins just stared at him. 'May I ask you something?'

'Certainly.'

'A confidential agent for whom?' Higgins said, remembering the man who'd been followed by Japanese spies, and figuring that maybe – just maybe – the young man was a confidential agent for *himself* – in which case, it didn't really count.

'Normally,' the young man went on, ignoring the question, 'I would not be speaking like this. But we need your help. There will be shipments arriving shortly.'

'Shipments?'

'Of plastic explosives.'

'Shipments arriving where?'

'To the room. But do not worry.' The young man grinned at his own cleverness. 'They know the password.'

'What room? Not *our* room,' Higgins asked, dismayed.

The boy appeared not to have heard him.

'Look,' Higgins said slowly, 'don't tell me you're thinking of filling our room up with explosives. Don't tell me you'd do a silly thing like that.'

'It will only be for a day or two at the most. It will all fit in the closet nicely with the rest. You will not even notice it.'

'Yeah,' Higgins said sadly, almost wistfully. 'But, you see, I'll *know* that it's there.' He stopped, and looked at the boy, harder now. 'What do you mean, "with the rest"?'

But the young man only blinked and swallowed.

'Don't tell me we have explosives there now.'

'Just a little dynamite.'

'Jesus H. Christ!'

'I have some on me, too,' the boy confessed.

'Mother of God!' Higgins said. The thought of dynamite completely unnerved him. And Higgins had the unpleasant sensation then that his pants were unraveling from around his knees, that he was sinking in quicksand, that someone was about to trip him up from behind.

'May I ask you something? What the hell for?'

'We have an organization. You will see.'

'No, I won't see,' Higgins said. 'I won't see a thing. Just tell me this, *Señor*. Exactly when are you getting rid of it? The dynamite, I mean. When will you be getting it out of our room?' He could hear the fear in his voice and he stifled its rising inflection and tried again. 'When?' he said, more calmly now. 'You see . . .' he explained reasonably, '. . . I happen to live there.'

'Couple of days.'

'Unacceptable,' Higgins said. 'You get rid of it now. Today. Before beddy-bye. You *read* me, *amigo*? And no deliveries!' For the information had put a major dent in Higgins' state of mind. He sighed. 'Do you really have some on you?'

'Very little.'

'How much?'

'Three sticks.'

'My God! What *for*?'

'I am delivering it to a comrade. In Brooklyn Heights. I was on my way when all the shooting began.' He made it sound so reasonable.

'Where is it? Don't touch it. Just tell me.'

'Taped to my chest.'

'Mother McCree!' Higgins said, reaching all the way back to childhood for the expression. Things were getting rather dangerous, fast. 'You mentioned a delivery. A delivery for whom?'

'The Doradoan underground.'

'Be specific.'

'The Aim-Taking Arm of the Independent Movement For Revolutionary Action.'

'Come again?'

'MIRA.'

'And they've sent you here to buy munitions?'

'Precisely. And you are going to help us get them.'

Higgins started, then stared. Then he laughed. It was beginning to get funny. 'Me? And to what do I owe this dubious honor?'

'We have done some research on you. You are just the man.'

'Excuse me,' Higgins said. 'But you must have me confused with somebody else. I'm Philip Higgins. I'm a writer. I translate books of Sanskrit poetry.'

'Yes, we know. *Passionate Encounters.*' The young man smiled. 'However, you also run a small consulting firm out of Boston. Trident Associates. Last month, your company helped arrange delivery of 400,000 micro-chips to Hansei of Japan.'

Higgins was astonished. 'And how the hell do you know that?'

Jorge smiled. 'We have our ways.'

Higgins studied him. He was impressed. Whoever he was, it seemed impossible that he could know about the deal with Hansei without the help of some intelligence agency. Not that the deal had been secret or illegal. Far from it. Everything was above board. Only that he had found out about it so fast! Higgins had only met the man last night and had not even known he was coming to New York until yesterday evening, less than fifteen or sixteen hours ago. And *Passionate Encounters*? It had sold six hundred copies. It was even *more* obscure. He must have procured the information sometime between eleven last night and eleven this morning. He looked at Vazpana in a new light. 'And so . . . you really are a foreign intelligence agent?'

'Oh, yes,' the young man said earnestly. 'And there are people out to kill me.'

'That's right,' Higgins said. 'He'd forgotten about that. There was that, too. 'Well, well,' Higgins said, looking around him at the wet slum street. And though he only half believed it, everything looked different now – smaller, harder. 'That changes things, doesn't it?' And they started walking again.

It had started to rain. Amazingly, Higgins felt high as a kite. Nothing like a shot of adrenalin to lift one's spirits.

Then it struck Higgins that the boy was lying through his teeth. Of course, the only way to know for sure would be to check him out. Higgins had his sources, too. And when he got back to the room, he would look in the closet. You could be sure of that. Higgins had suddenly a lot of unpleasant things to do, and an uncomfortable feeling that this was only the beginning. Of what? The end? And he wondered now, if looking back on it all – from his grave, perhaps – he would say, yes, this is where it had all begun to go wrong; where the fabric of his life had started to shred and so had begun the great and unfortunate unraveling.

But there he went again. Why was Higgins thinking of death? For the world seemed very peaceable now, the way it can only after a bit of a shock on a warm, hazy, rainy summer afternoon. They passed an unattended aluminum pushcart blaring strange Arabian music off into the rain: the cry of a *mullah* and stringed desert gourds ringing from a singing transistor beneath its drizzly canopy. And at that moment, it was impossible to feel afraid or to take Jorge's death fears too seriously. The city, or this rainy piece of it, at least, was quiet and at rest, and the attitudes of two old women hunched beneath a dripping awning were immemorial: the picture of creatures poised in the mouth of a cave. All around them, children played in the rain. Tired merchants leaned on their doorjambs. Dogs slept. Cats yawned. In short, it was that benign and peaceful hour that comes to the world once in a month of Sundays when fat men lean back with a satisfied groan and pick their teeth with toothpicks, and sighing sales-girls in failing boutiques place their chafed elbows on counter tops of finger-smeared glass and stare – through rheumy eyes – out the rainy window.

'But now,' the Doradoan said, halting abruptly. 'I must be living.'

'What?'

'Living,' he translated, 'to *go*. I have an important meeting to attend. You will excuse me,' he said, lurching off without Higgins.

'Hey, wait a minute,' Higgins said, not liking being ditched in this way, while half admiring the air of self-confidence and mysterious self-esteem that his roommate brought to the least of his endeavors. 'What meeting?'

'Please, I can only say that the liberation of my country may depend on it.' He paused a moment. 'Would you like to come?'

'Uh . . . no, thank you,' Higgins said, almost taken in again. 'And remember, no deliveries, partner.'

The young man burned him with his eyes. 'A pity,' he said, at last. 'Such a person as yourself could be of great use to us.'

But Higgins felt secretly relieved they were parting. He wanted to get away from his roommate, the human bomb. While the meeting, he was certain, had nothing to do with the liberation of Dorado. In college, he had attended a few such meetings and found them tedious exercises in futility and loss. Pasted to a wall was the inevitable map of the beloved country, its corners brown and curling, and beside it, the flag, and beside it, a rebel or a patriot – depending upon your politics – delivering hour after hour a humorless and strident harangue, while the atmosphere was thick with cigarette smoke, sweat, paranoia, rhetoric and hatred – the great concentrated pain and hatred of a homeless and defeated people, the bitter fruit of exile. Factions. Hysteria. Towards the end there'd be a fistfight. No, thank you.

But, by now they had reached what appeared to be an entrance to the underworld, since surely no subway station built by human hands was as miserable and hellish as this, and the two men descended into the noxious catacomb, Vazpana on his way to Brooklyn and Higgins back to the *barrio*.

'You are certain that you will not join us?'

'Hmm, no, thank you,' Higgins said, pretending to misunderstand the question. 'Work,' he insisted, trying to sound proletarian.

They shook hands and Higgins left the young man, crossing via a short filthy tunnel to the uptown side where he could see Vazpana across the tracks staring moodily down the long black tunnel. Higgins took the station in. The subway's walls were expertly spray-painted with the names and addresses of a hundred thousand citizens, like some colossal petition that had gotten completely out of hand.

The approaching train was announced by a tickling vibration that Higgins felt first in the skin of his shins, and by an indistinct murmur that might have been a nearby sea. And it was then that Higgins saw the slight, hurrying shape heading for Jorge in a perfect beeline across the station. Afterwards, he would insist that the peculiar hell of it all had been the fact that he had known exactly what was going to happen, but could do nothing to prevent it – like the inevitable outcome of a fixed equation. For as the train approached point A, the streaking figure, B, attained point C, and pushed Jorge Vazpana, D, over the edge of the platform – A. He flew through the air, landing on the tracks with a bone-shuddering jolt which registered in the depths of Higgins' bowels as well.

Vazpana had barely managed to rise when the train arrived. In the driver's defense, there was no question of his stopping in time, even if he had not panicked and hit the horn instead of the brake, a useless move but one which, Higgins later would declare, had added immeasurably to the moment's horror – the electric wail reaching him as what is called the Doppler Effect twisted it into a painful, veering scream. Then point A was passed and the equation was satisfied. Higgins closed his eyes and turned away, waiting for the detonation.

But when he looked again a moment later, everything was still standing. A ragged flat of sunlight fluttered down upon the tops of the cars from a metal grating in the ceiling, and it might have been any downtown Number Three train rolling into the station on a hot, steamy New York afternoon.

The Ensorcelled
Physician

◆

Chapter 11

At first, it had not been very much money that the Doctor
owed, a paltry sum, really: $10,000, which he had hastily
borrowed as part of the down payment on the building he
had bought, and had meant to repay at the end of the very
first week. Then the Doctor had taken ill with the Hong
Kong flu and complications, and for more than five and a
half weeks had foolishly ignored the debt, rising at last from
his sickbed only to discover that the amount he now owed,
like some drastic cancer, had nearly doubled in the short time
he had been ill, and that the interest alone – the *vigorish* as it
was called on the street – was already more than $7000, pay-
able on demand.

For a few minutes, five and a half weeks too late, the
Doctor had picked up a pen and made some hurried mathematical calculations, sickening all over again as he saw the
astonishing way the unpaid 'vig' compounded the debt, doubling, then quadrupling it within a matter of months with the
unstoppable logic and accelerating mathematical velocity of
an equation.

For two years now, it was this equation that had ruled the
Doctor's life. The weekly payments had once climbed to four

thousand dollars on a principal of forty grand, meaning that the Doctor was repaying the loan at a rate of ten percent a week and being driven by this confounded formula, inexorably, to ruin.

'A dime a week? Why that's five hundred and twenty percent a year!' the Doctor had screamed when he'd come to his senses. 'Why didn't you tell me those were the terms?'

But the shylock had only looked stupid. 'You didn't ask us, Doc.'

Of course, the Doctor could always stop making the payments. But since he could not stop the *equation*, he did not think that this would be the wisest course. Though the bleeding was conducted with a snide decorum, the Doctor had no illusions. He would be hurt – or worse – if he did not continue to pay. Not by the men he owed money to, exactly – it didn't work that way – but by someone they would send, someone who did not know that the Doctor was a respectable physician and had gone to Harvard, who had never even *heard* of Harvard probably, the Doctor thought, and for the thousandth time he cursed his creditors.

'In a decent society, this sort of abuse would never exist,' the Doctor told no one in particular, as he closed up his office for the evening and negotiated the three dark flights down to the street. 'Leeches, bloodsuckers, fiends!' For the Doctor, in the course of two years, had spent more than $40,000 attempting to repay the original $10,000 loan, and yet he still owed more than he had originally borrowed! It was infuriating. It was madness. No, it was merely extortion; or rather, he thought, it was like some virulent disease, or even more precisely, like a plague. For as in all successful epidemics, the parasites had taken pains not to debilitate totally the host whose blood they leeched and life they stole. After all, the Doctor was not completely broke! He slapped his wallet; it held seventeen dollars.

Who this 'they' was to whom the Doctor owed money was more difficult to say; Omar, the shylock, was only their agent. 'They' might be described as a powerful business and fraternal organization which existed in the *barrio* – the *barrio*, hell, the Doctor thought, in every major city in the world – and this 'organization', as the Doctor liked to think of it (it somehow seemed safer) existed as a kind of tertiary government that was as real and as felt as the municipal and federal ones. The organization's local franchise happened to be Latin and was chairmanned by *El Duende*, though the Doctor was aware that its leadership and ethnic profile could change at any time since there was a rival organization, an Italian concern – the industry giant, one might say – that had been actively seeking a takeover of the Spanish company for years. To bring about this end, the Italian concern had lately taken to shooting employees of the *Latino* firm in the stomach. A couple of times a month. Like today. This had been going on since Christmas and, frankly, was becoming sickening, the Doctor thought – reminding himself for the thousandth time that the sickening was his business.

And yet, it hadn't always been like this. Once life had been a joy and healing a miracle. He remembered the tumor he had removed from the neck of an Indian in the mountains of Dorado while vacationing there the summer after medical school. The Doctor had performed the surgery with a finely honed pen-knife and a topical anesthetic, operating on the man as he sat on a bench in the sun with the Indian's whole family watching and the entire barefoot, bluejeaned village arriving when it was over to gape at the monstrous white cancer – the size and shape of a cantaloupe – which, licked by flies and ticked and threaded with blood, was resting harmlessly now in a battered tin tub. Yes, those were the days!

But though the Doctor had tried since then to uphold the highest standards, the slum had seeped in all around. Take his office, for instance. Everything about it seemed jerry-built, rigged, propped up with sticks. If this was not so, then why did things he touched break in his hands, why did door knobs come off with a surprising socket-jarring lurch, and why, every time he adjusted the television set, did yet another small brown dial appear in his palm? Was it life? Or was it just the Doctor? Was it the *barrio*? Or was it just the world?

And then there was *El Duende*. Just wait. He would show him! Someday he would make him pay for his extortion; someday he would be free!

But though the Doctor railed, nothing happened. He was like an enchanted hunter in an old Germanic fable, paralyzed and suspended in the wood, the dead Odin hung from the windy Tree. His feet thrashed but he moved not, while with every passing night the debt grew and the noose tightened, and the sweetest sexo-horrific feeling of hanging tickled his blood. And it struck the Doctor then that even if he did pay off the whole outrageous sum, they would not let him go. For he was their *vaca* now, their cow, and they would continue to milk him until they had suckled him dry.

But though the Doctor knew this in his heart of hearts, still he said nothing, paid the money, ate the bread of tyranny washed down with the wine of his tears, and raised not a hand against his oppressors – because he was afraid. Paralyzed. Spellbound.

It was for this very reason, to shatter the spell, that the Doctor had shown his books to Higgins. In fact, Higgins' appearance had already given the Doctor new life. It was not simply that Higgins was smart and audacious and would help the Doctor, which, of course, he would, but rather that the Doctor was incapable of acting like the coward he was in front of his friend, and so had to appear to be taking positive steps which, once taken, made his freedom seem suddenly plausible and real – and something he should have thought about ages ago when the bleeding had first begun.

For the Doctor had not come to the *barrio* to be robbed by thugs, but in order to observe life fully and at first hand (and at the behest, too, of a strenuous social conscience which had given the Doctor no peace for years). And yet, the Doctor thought now, perhaps the real reason was so much simpler and less noble than he had been giving himself credit for all these years. Perhaps he had come and stayed out of a sadomasochistic fascination with suffering and pain; other people's preferably, but his own included. Maybe he had stayed not to heal so much as to gape at the carnage, the lunacy and despair that visited the lives of his patients with such a sickening regularity and deadly effect. And perhaps, after all was said and done, the Doctor's much-vaunted social conscience was nothing more noble than the impulse that attracts a crowd to a hanging, or the eye to a particularly gruesome sore.

Whatever the reason, the Doctor was tired of it: of his life, of his social conscience, of his mistress, of his practice, of the debt he owed. More and more often now – like tonight – instead of a glass of rum before supper, he found himself slipping into the children's bedroom and lying down across their beds with a whole menagerie of stuffed animals around him, and a bolt or a nut or a chicken bone or something invariably sticking into his back.

There was an odor to the children's bedding which the Doctor loved. He believed it to be the odor of innocence and, lying there in the curtained dark, he entertained the silly but delicious notion that he was perfectly safe and could not be found; that here, amidst the children's sweet pink inexplicable odor, he owed no one anything and no one owed him, and there was finally some measure of safety and repose, finally some end and quit to it all.

Often at that hour, the telephone rang, and the Doctor would listen with a guilty joy as his mother-in-law answered and called his name, waited, sighed, then declared in an annoyed and aggravated whisper that, though she would swear on the Neck of Jesus she had heard the good doctor enter their home, she couldn't for the life of her put her hands on him now.

Love At A Distance

◆

Chapter 12

'Absolutely no! I will not have it! You will only be hurt again. And then you will fall to pieces in front of my eyes and have another one of your nervous breakdowns!'

'Damn it, Arsenio! I didn't have a nervous breakdown!'

'What did you have then? A little mental vacation? I would come in the room and there you would be – tears streaming from your very eyes. And I would say to you "What is wrong, my friend?" and you would tell me it was nothing – only that you had watched a dog drinking water and that it was so beautiful you could cry!'

'I'm going to tell you again, Arsenio. For the thousandth time. 'I didn't have a nervous breakdown!'

'Oh, you've told me!' the Doctor said. 'I know what you think. You think it was some kind of *spiritual* experience. Yes! Everything seemed very ancient to you, and old, and emblazoned with a terrible significance – things you had never noticed before – the way light strikes a teacup, a human ear, a child's voice, the way a dog drinks water.'

'And what the hell's the matter with her?' Higgins protested, getting back to the original subject – for this was how the attack had begun, with Higgins merely asking the Doctor who the woman was they had met that morning at his office.

'But don't you see,'' the Doctor went on unfazed, 'that's exactly what it's like to be mad! Ho! The significance of things! The letter aitch in your name is also on the sign above the butcher's shop. What can that *mean*? And the sunlight looks so beautiful! More beautiful than it has ever looked to you before! However, when a man believes he is Napoleon, we do not refer to it as a *political* experience. We say that man is *loco*. And when this craziness comes upon him as quickly as it did you, lasts for a while, then goes away, we call it a nervous breakdown. I am a doctor!'

If the shouter of this harangue had been a North American, Higgins would have been insulted. But as it was, it was not only a different language that was spoken in the *barrio* – Yorka Rican, a deformity of Spanish – but the tone, volume, pitch and physical gestures that accompanied it were foreign as well. Two shrieking women who, from afar, appeared ready to claw each other's eyes out, turned out, when in earshot, to be discussing a rain date for the Holy Name Parade.

It is true, however, that the Doctor was in rare form this evening. He was emotional. He looked bonier than usual. His eyes were glittery and red and his moustache was so big and black and bristling it looked fake.

'Look, Arsenio,' Higgins said, 'let's just forget it, okay? Whatever it is, it's not something I want to argue about. Just tell me why you don't want me to get involved with her.'

'Because, are you crazy? Don't you know what she is?'

'One hell of a good-looking woman,' Higgins said. 'And besides,' he added, remembering the black fire in her eyes, 'she seemed to have . . . real character.'

'Character!' the Doctor smirked, clapping shut the book that was open on his lap. 'Since when do you look for *character* in your women? You have got it backwards, my friend. You look for women who are characters! Remember that girl you liked from Bronx? The one who entertained us all evening with imitations of unusual animals?'

'*The* Bronx, Arsenio!' Higgins corrected, resenting the Doctor's belittling tone. 'You always forget the article.'

'That is because I come from *the* Cuba. Don't you see?

No, no, no. She is beautiful, all right. I grant you that. But she is not for you. She is not for any man. She is . . . a *maricon*!'

'*Maricon*?''

The Doctor paused, clearly savoring his position as a linguistic authority. 'A sissy,' he hissed.

'A dyke?' Higgins asked in shock, his heart sinking. 'You're kidding me, Arsenio.'

'I wish I was. Didn't you know? In fact, I thought that was why you intended to get involved with her.'

'What are you talking about? Why would I do a thing like that?'

'Why?' the Doctor said. 'To make things more difficult for yourself. The way you like them.'

This remark stung Higgins – perhaps because it was true. But even if it was correct, Higgins did not appreciate the way the Doctor, like some grand *caballero*, ran roughshod over the course of his life, pointing out at every turn its pitfalls and its failings.

'Forgive me,' the Doctor sighed. 'I am just excited. But you worry me sometimes, Philip. You really do. And I do not wish to see you hurt again.'

They were seated in the Doctor's office. The Doctor put down the book he had been waving, went to a humidor, and extracted a Montecristo cigar. Higgins looked at the oversized paperback's cover. It was called *Dead, Dying, and Dismembered Gods*. It was the sort of fatally boring book the Doctor always read. 'I'm amazed you find time to read anymore, Arsenio,' Higgins said, hoping to change the subject.

'I don't. But still I enjoy it greatly when I do. Ah, the intellectual life – it is a wonderful thing! Books, I love. They are not like people. They change as you do – good ones for the better, bad ones for the worse. And yet they never really change at all – not one word, not one comma! I put down a story and everything stops! The sun rising, the lover's kiss, the bullet in mid-air. When I pick it back up – a day, a week, even years later – the lovers are still kissing, the morning is still fresh, and the whistling bullet is still only halfway to its mark.

'With human beings, you never know. A beautiful woman may have developed a wart on her nose, nasty habits, or a cyst on her pancreas. There is something wonderful, I think in anything that does not change. But I express myself poorly.'

'Not at all,' Higgins said sincerely.

Pleased by the compliment, the Doctor smiled and struck a match.

'Someone tried to kill our friend this afternoon,' Higgins said quietly at last.

The Doctor froze, like a character in one of his interrupted novels, a fly poised upon his shoulder. Then the book was reopened, the Doctor said, 'Who?' and the fly flew away.

'I don't know who. Some Spanish guy, I think. I didn't get a very good look at him. He pushed our friend in front of a train.'

'What train?'

'*What* train? The Number Three train! What the hell does it matter, Arsenio?'

'It doesn't!' the Doctor said. 'I was not thinking. Our friend – he is, of course, all right.'

'What do you mean, "of course"? It was a bonafide miracle. He somehow managed to squeeze into the crawl space between the track and platform. Don't ask me *how*. It can't be more than two feet deep. Then when the train pulled out, there he was, scared to death, but otherwise intact. He just banged up his hands and knees. They wanted to take him to the hospital but he wouldn't go. He was afraid they'd discover the dynamite he was carrying.'

'Understandable,' the Doctor concurred. Then once again, he froze. 'Dynamite?' the Doctor asked, smiling stupidly. 'And what was he doing with dynamite?'

'Walking around town with it. Delivering it to a friend.' Higgins smiled back.

'But why didn't it go off?'

'Because, evidently, dynamite's not like that. It needs a blasting cap or something. It doesn't matter if you drop it. Or so I am told.'

'I see,' the Doctor said.

'Yeah,' Higgins said. 'That's why I'm not concerned in the least that at night while I'm lying in bed I'm surrounded by all those . . . high explosives.' Higgins looked at the Doctor hard. 'Because you see, Arsenio, it seems he not only delivers the stuff, but he *collects* it, too. And you know where he keeps it? *In our room.* That's why we have a password.'

Higgins grinned. 'Isn't it wonderful? The way it's all beginning finally to make sense? Because our friend, you see, really is a secret agent.'

The Doctor raised an eyebrow. Then he scowled. 'Bah! I don't believe it.'

'You don't believe it? Don't you *know*? He's *your* relation, after all.'

'Maybe so, but I'd never met him until he appeared at my door one evening last week. He brought a letter from some uncle of mine in Dorado who I haven't seen in fifteen years. What could I do? Blood is thicker than water. I fed him some supper and gave him a bed. And since then he has been nothing but a pain, hinting darkly at conspiracies and that he is being hunted. By whom, I don't know.'

'The Dorado secret police.'

'AES? Certainly!' the Doctor said. 'And don't forget the Friends of Jesus, the Transit Authority, and the CIA.'

'I'm just telling you what he told me, Arsenio,' Higgins persisted. 'And you wouldn't be so cavalier about this whole damned business if you were in my shoes, either. You don't have to sleep in the same room with the guy. You didn't have to watch him get pushed in front of a train. *I* did. And it made me rather ill, I can assure *you*.'

'But it doesn't make sense,' the Doctor objected. 'If he really was a secret agent, why would he tell us?'

'I don't know,' Higgins said. He did not tell the Doctor that the boy wanted him to procure munitions, or that he knew things about Higgins that even Higgins' lawyer didn't know. Nor did he tell him how the door to their closet had been locked, and afraid of what was in it, Higgins had not been about to break it down. Instead he said, 'Maybe if he *is* a spy, he's not a very good one. People have this overblown, romantic notion about these guys, but spy, I suppose, is just like any other profession. Half of them are incompetents, fuckups and crazies. Who's MIRA?'

'MIRA is one of the factions in Dorado opposed to the Junta. They are, of necessity, an underground organization.'

'And could he really be working for them?'

'I don't know. I suppose he could.'

'I think we should find out, Arsenio.'

'Hokay, hokay,' the Doctor said, 'I will look into it. Hokay?'

'All right,' Higgins said. 'And so will I. Which brings us to another most unpleasant matter.'

'Which is . . . ?' the Doctor asked, surprised.

'Your finances, Arsenio. Or shall we say, your lack of them?'

'Look,' the Doctor said defensively, 'perhaps now is not the proper time . . .'

Just then Garcia entered.

'Ah, there you are, my friend!' the Doctor cried, seizing on the interruption. 'Come in. Come in. How are you feeling?'

Garcia smiled bravely, but to Higgins, at least, the answer was plain. His eyes were sad, while his pencil-thin moustache was already blurred with a day's growth of beard. Perhaps it was only the salt and pepper stubble, but to Higgins he looked at least twenty years older than he had that morning. Higgins nodded in greeting to the old *Capitán*.

'Gentlemen,' Garcia said, 'I see you are busy. Don't let me interrupt.'

'Nonsense . . .' the Doctor said.

'Very well,' Higgins agreed. 'Then I'll continue. I've looked at your "books," Arsenio, as you jokingly call them. And as your financial consultant, it is my duty to inform you—'

'Look, can't this wait till morning?' the Doctor said, beginning to exude little pinheads of sweat.

'—there are holes,' Higgins said, 'in what they call your "financial picture" big enough to put your hand inside and wave around a flag. In other words, there are large sums of money missing and unaccounted for on a regular basis – not to mention the fact that you're two years in arrears on your federal, state, and city income tax.'

'Tell him, Arsenio,' Garcia crooned. 'Go ahead.'

'Tell me what?'

'All right, all right,' the Doctor sighed at last, sitting down suddenly, and losing a hand in the great black bush that grew on his head and passed for his hair. And he described to the two men his predicament: the initial loan and the debt which had quickly grown, so that he had all he could do now to pay the weekly *vigorish*, never mind the principal itself. Higgins had heard such tales before. Suddenly, one morning, your freedom was gone – you awoke to find yourself another man's slave.

'And you asked the banks for a loan, of course. To pay off the debt.'

'Of course I asked the banks,' the Doctor growled. 'I even tried to re-mortgage the apartments. And you know what they did? Turned me down. Eight of them. In a row! I am still in shock!'

'You shouldn't be,' Higgins said. 'They don't like to lend money in this type of neighborhood.'

'But I am a doctor. And that is discrimination!'

'Most likely,' Higgins said. 'But let's get back to the business at hand. As your fiduciary consultant, I hereby order you to stop making payments. Immediately. Do you hear me, Arsenio?'

'Thank you,' the Doctor exclaimed, tears in his eyes, greatly relieved by his long-held confession, and feeling eternally grateful to his two friends for their wise and purifying counsel. Of course, that is what he would do. He would stop making payments. 'Except, my friends, you do not understand,' the Doctor remembered, writhing slightly with a cheesy smile. 'If I do not pay these *hombres*, they will kill me.'

'What *hombres*?' Higgins asked.

'*El Duende* and Omar,' Garcia said.

90

'Omar?' Higgins repeated, remembering the man he had met the night before and who he had seen again that morning, lying in a pool of blood. He laughed in dismay. 'Jesus H. Christ, Arsenio. Hell of bunch to pick for your bankers!'

There was a long, dismal silence as the truth of this observation sunk in. Both the Doctor and Garcia looked unhappy and glum.

Nor was Higgins particularly happy himself. He didn't like the heat which at 9 p.m. was equatorial. He didn't like the way the day had gone, the fact that his roommate was a human bomb, or that his vacation had been run over by a train.

He liked the girl he had met that morning; this was true. But then again, the Doctor wouldn't tell him who she was and insisted on playing his obnoxious and irritating game.

Higgins turned to Garcia. 'Who was the young lady we met here this morning?'

'Young lady?' Garcia repeated, straining dimly as though morning had been several centuries ago. 'Now let me see . . .' He brightened. 'Ah, why that would have been the Doctor's sister, Gilberta.'

'The Doctor's *what*?' Higgins exploded. He threw the Doctor a dirty look, while the Doctor, as though stabbed, cried and danced away on tiptoes.

'I was about to tell you who she was. But you never gave me the chance.'

'Your *sister*?' Higgins repeated, stunned. 'But how is that possible? Why haven't I ever met her before?'

'Only because of your extreme good fortune, I assure you!'

'The family does not speak of her,' Garcia volunteered. 'Ever since . . . they disowned the poor child.'

'Disowned her? Why?'

'Because she shamed them,' Garcia replied. 'By giving birth to three little *niñas*. With no husband.'

'What?' Higgins asked, incredulous. He threw the Doctor a long, searching look. 'And don't tell me that you went along with this . . . this medieval madness, Arsenio?'

'Damnit,' the Doctor cried. 'I will not have our behavior

criticized by you. This is a family affair. It is none of your stupid *Anglo* business!'

Higgins smiled bitterly. 'Oh, now I'm an *Anglo*, am I? And is that why you wouldn't tell me who she was? Afraid there might be some . . . mixing of the races?'

'What? No!' the Doctor cried aghast. 'My God! This is insane! You know that's not what I meant at all. I love you, Philip.'

'Sure, Arsenio,' Higgins said. 'You love my white *Anglo* ass.'

'My God,' the Doctor said. 'To accuse me of such a thing.'

'*You* said it, Arsenio,' Higgins insisted, rubbing it in.

'All right!' the Doctor said, throwing up his hands. 'Go ahead! Marry her!' Higgins looked up – but the Doctor's abrupt reversal did not appear to faze the Doctor in the least. 'Take her, *panito*. Take her, my friend, and may you both be happy. Till the end of your days.'

'What are you talking about, Arsenio?' Higgins said, becoming annoyed all over again. 'What do you mean, "take her"? I don't want to "take her." I just want to talk to her. I haven't even met the girl, and you've already got us married for life! What an idiot you are!' Clearly, the Doctor had been watching too many Mexican westerns.

But the Doctor now could not be stopped. 'Yes,' he said, 'take her, my friend! Be good to her though. Hold her as you would . . .'

'. . . a flower,' Garcia said, clearly having seen the same movie and starting now to water with emotion.

'For crying out loud,' Higgins said, disgusted by the evening's unexpectedly sentimental turn. 'Will you two idiots cut it out?'

But the Doctor could not be provoked any longer, for he had reached some place inside himself where taunts and names did not approach. His eyes were red and hot as cinders, his moustache as big as the wings of a grackle, while his face shone with an almost mystical light. 'Because the Spanish have a saying which is sad as it is true!'

'Spare me it, please.'

'*Amor de lejos, amor de tendejos.*'
'Say it in *Anglo*, Arsenio.'
'Love at a distance . . . is fool's love.'

The Last Sixty Years

◆

Chapter 13

Garcia left the Doctor's office and padded through the cracked and crowded boulevard toward home. He moved through the warm, rainy night with an air of expectation, hoping to find Constanza waiting for him when he arrived. They would embrace and kiss each other's tear-streaked faces, swearing they would never leave each other again!

But the apartment was dark and empty when he entered it, save for his ancient mother asleep upon her bed. There was no sign of Constanza – not a note, not a whisper. He had not heard from her now in over twenty-four hours. He had gone to the Doctor's house earlier to collect her, but Rosita had informed him she was no longer there. And standing in the night- and rain-darkened foyer, Garcia knew for certain then that she was never coming home. It was over with, done. In a week or two, one of her sisters would arrive to collect her possessions – and some months after that he would receive a letter announcing the annulment of their vows.

An old man had married a young woman. But the lines had changed. And the woman had left him.

Something choked him. Pressure filled his throat. Then the pressure broke, and he sank upon the horsehair sofa and wept bitterly, like a woman or a child. And yet even as he cried Garcia seemed to see himself from afar, an old barrel-shaped *hombre* with enormous arms and a tiny moustache sobbing to himself in a dark, rainy room.

He cried for several minutes. When he was finished, he wiped his eyes, sighed and sat back up. He felt quiescent, spent, like he did after making love. And Garcia knew then that although he would continue to miss his wife, he would not cry for her again. For in that moment, he had accepted her loss, accepted it with the same peasant grace with which he had accepted the loss of his country, or the blow to his head and the theft of his money – six months wages and a gold medallion – in a Princetown brothel when he was twenty-one.

Garcia drew a rag from his pocket and blew his nose, honking sadly. Yes, he accepted these things. What he could not accept was the brand of '*traidor*,' and the evil curse which accompanied the name.

Whom had he betrayed, and what punishment did they intend for him? This had become his constant meditation. For the dozenth time in as many days, he went back over the faces of all the officers and soldiers he had known in forty years of war, but he could think of no one who he had betrayed. No one except women, that is. For Garcia had betrayed many women in his day – though women didn't try to kill you for it, usually.

Standing by the window in the dark apartment, Garcia tried to conjure up the faces of all the women he had loved, but he had loved so many in so many different places that the women's faces bled into each other and the places he had lain with them blurred into a single whitewashed room.

For though Garcia and his cronies liked to brag about their military prowess, most of their conquests had been considerably more tender. Country girls were fatally attracted to their uniforms, and love affairs between the girls and the soldiers had blossomed with a tropical speed and fecundity – fertilized by the sight, perhaps, of so much death and gore. It did not seem to matter whose side they were on. Sometimes they were the liberators and the women threw themselves upon them with a patriotic fervor, frenzied with gratitude, faint with joy. Other times they were the enemy, and defiant young women slipped through the lines, oblivious to the bitter reproaches of their families, to rendezvous with their beloved *Capitán* – as though to prove, for the billionth time, that love is deaf as well as blind.

Garcia smiled, remembering. But why was he smiling? Now such memories only brought him pain. And anyway, he had paid for his conceit – the momentary restoration of his nature at the Doctor's notwithstanding; Garcia, who had always reveled in his manhood, and in the sound of a voice so profoundly low it could make your cup of morning java slither off the kitchen table. *O to be a guitar without a song, O to be a beast without a horn*! It was a popular ditty the children were singing. This was Garcia, a beast without a horn.

But Garcia had no time now to waste on the past or self-pity. It was the future he had to think of and the problem at hand.

Rising from the sofa, he unearthed his mother's fountain pen and a box of flowered stationery. Then he sat down at the kitchen table to compose a note. It was evident from the awkward way Garcia held the pen, and the extreme slowness with which he formed and rounded each letter, that writing was an activity which he practiced only rarely. He wrote with intense concentration, the pink tip of his tongue visible between his teeth. When he was finished, he read the note over, then sat back in his chair with a sigh of satisfaction. The letter was to an old friend, Manuel Gomez. It requested intelligence; namely, who was here from Dorado who might wish to do Garcia harm.

Garcia got up and went into his bedroom in search of the FAX number Gomez had sent. What he found instead was another little doll. It was waiting for him on his pillow, a tiny bone tied about its throat: the bone of a rodent, perhaps – or a child!

A tendril of nausea arose in his throat, like a gagging finger. Someone was attempting to drive him crazy. Someone was attempting to make him ill – but who? He felt a chill. The Virgin protect him! Garcia didn't want to die.

Why hadn't he recognized how precious life was! Sixty years had passed like a day! And though on the outside he was a gray-haired old man, on the inside he felt like the littlest boy.

Garcia listened to the cool spring rain, and heard the voice of his death speaking within it. And this is what Death said to him: Light on things; the shine on fruit, on children's skin, the frivolous song of coins flung across a worn formica counter, the most common phenomena of this physical world are become in your sight oh, so beloved and sweet – now you are about to lose them forever.

Glands

◆

Chapter 14

Higgins was aware his ex-shrink would have said that his sudden attraction to the Doctor's sister was a delayed reaction to the loss of his wife, and that he had seized upon Gilberta as a 'substitute' on which to act out his dreams of masculine conquest, thereby assuaging the recent blow to his ego (brought about by his wife's demise), though actually, on a deeper level, what he was *really* doing by picking a dyke was choosing another 'dead-end relationship' guaranteed to self-destruct and burn, thus re-enacting the central trauma of his childhood: his mother's rejection of him – all of which sounded okay, except that Higgins knew it had nothing to do with this at all.

It had to do with the fact that her face haunted him, singularly. It was at once familiar and unplaceable, like the content of a dream. When she had entered the Doctor's office, he had half wanted to rise and embrace her as he would an old friend returning home after a long journey. And when he had looked in her eyes, a mental dial had clicked, like the tripping of some ancient combination, and for a moment he had thought that he would say her name – which was perfectly ridiculous, since he had never laid eyes on her before.

For a while, however, he'd been convinced he had – that he knew her from somewhere, from some childhood playground or mountain resort where their families had vacationed together. But that, too, was absurd. They had been at opposite ends of the country. She had been in Florida; he had been in Maine. So where had they met? And when? No. It was delusion.

And yet, even now he could clearly remember the two of them wading in the tremulous shallows of a mountain pond. He knew by heart the water's odor, the sound of the lisping waves, and could see the dancing freckles of light dappling her small brown limbs. He saw the slightly magnified whiteness of her feet in the water, and the nut-brown tan of a back no larger than a large man's palm, which he was following fixedly, following with a terrible, crucial love. This 'memory' was so potent that Higgins smelled the muddy reeds again, and the rich wind of that forgotten summer morning, while above their heads, two glittering dragon-flies, their bodies like scintillating blue needles, clung to each other in the middle of the air, like two iridescent souls embracing eternally in space.

But what was he remembering? For no such scene had ever occurred, and the 'memory' had left him then, as suddenly as it had arrived, the way dragonflies fly, sliding obliquely and fluently away.

Higgins' roommate was in an enthusiastic mood and would not leave Higgins alone, however, to steep in the sweet juices of his dreams. Instead, he stood in the doorway of the bathroom talking to Higgins while Higgins tried to shave.

'So, *mi amigo. ¿Cómo está?*'

'That's what I should be asking you.'

'I am fine; bruised a little, see?' And he hiked up his trousers to reveal two enormous blue hemotomas on his knees. He smiled. 'There is nothing like surviving an attempt on your life to make you feel quite wonderful.'

'I imagine you're right. I hope never to know.'

His roommate grew more serious and confidential. 'You see now, don't you, why we need your help?'

Higgins said nothing. He continued shaving.

'You have thought some more about our . . . conversation?'

'No, I haven't,' Higgins said.

There was a disappointed silence. 'I am surprised.'

'I don't know why. I told you. I don't know anything about this sort of thing . . .'

'Oh, but you *do*!' the young man insisted. 'You can deliver anything; you are quite well known.'

'I am?' Higgins asked, feeling at once both flattered and alarmed.

'In certain circles, I mean.'

Higgins sincerely hoped these certain circles did not include the Office of the United States Attorney General.

Jorge stepped closer and drew something from his pocket. He started to unfold a type-written list. 'If you would only look at this . . .'

'No!' Higgins said. He put down his razor. 'I told you already. You've got the wrong guy. I'm not who you think I am. And even if I was . . . *I don't sell arms.*' He picked up his razor and started shaving again. He nicked his chin. 'God-damnit!' he said as the blood began to spread. '*Now* look what you made me do!'

Higgins was aware he was behaving badly, but he couldn't help it. He didn't want to hear another word. Jorge must have sensed his resolve, for he folded the paper back up and, with a disappointed look, returned to the bedroom.

Higgins went back to shaving, and as he did, he remembered something from earlier that morning. He had risen at dawn to go to the bathroom. Standing before the toilet bowl, half-asleep, his half-lidded gaze had drifted out the window. And there he'd beheld the little odd *mestiza* girl staring up at him from the street below. Higgins was so startled, he had peed on his foot! At which point, the girl had smiled to herself and walked away, disappearing into the misty morning.

It was nothing, of course. And yet, remembering it now, he felt uneasy. Who was she? Was she really crazy? Or was she, too, some sort of spy. And what was she doing staring up at his window?

But no, it wasn't her, Higgins decided now. It was the Doctor's sister! Yes! She was affecting his glands.

That's what it was, his *glands*, he thought, happy at last to have come up with a vaguely scientific-sounding explanation for his aberrant mental state. She had imbalanced them or something. She had thrown off the delicate balance of his endocrine system.

But what was Higgins babbling about? Endocrine system? He was just hot, that's all; his roommate was a deluded, bomb-throwing maniac, and he was in a bad mood – why drag his endocrine system into the miserable picture?

There was an unnerving vibration from the bedroom. It was the shriek of a phonograph needle skidding across the surface of a record, followed by the brittle tinkling of strings, a sobbing glottal tenor, and the unmistakable voice of the *chuaranga*, like an armadillo in pain. It was Lucho Barrios!

Higgins put the razor down and assessed the damage. He had cut himself in four different places. Tiny blood roses blossomed on his cheeks. He blotted the bleeding with toilet paper as the song ended and the next one – 'My Desire' it was called – began. Lucho Barrios sang:

> *My desire will not leave me alone.*
> *The face of a goddess haunts my dreams!*
> *My senses are on fire!*
> *When will I quench my desire*
> *In the cool waters of love?*

After that, Higgins did himself a favor and stopped translating. He wiped his face on the one bald towel, and went back out to the bedroom. His roommate was sitting on his unmade bed looking, Higgins decided, not like death warmed over, but more like death reheated for the third or fourth time. Higgins peeked in the closet. It was open and empty.

'No deliveries this morning, I hope.'

'No. I have made other plans.'

'Good. Cheer up,' Higgins said, belting his pants. 'Don't

look so glum. Hey,' he said. 'Maybe it's your glands. Did
you ever think of that?'

'Glands?'

'Yes. Glands. Maybe the world's problems aren't political
at all. Maybe they're *glandular*.'

'What are you talking about?'

'Forget it,' Higgins said. He was in that kind of mood:
flippant and cavalier as hell. He started unlocking the series of
locks. 'Glands,' he said in farewell. 'That's today's password.'

'Glands?'

Higgins left the garret on the run, slamming the door
behind him. He wanted to get out of there, fast. For it was
suffocating in the stifling garret with Lucho Barrios yodeling,
the *chuaranga* twanging, and his roommate mooning about
with his tragic, hangdog air.

But out on the street, he felt even worse. '*My senses are on
fire . . . My desire will not leave me alone*!' The passionate
torch song kept spinning through his mind, haunting him
with the peculiar force of certain stupid words.

And then, to further inflame his senses, a young Oriental
waitress – lounging before a sign that read *Comidas Chinas y
Criollas* – gave him a hot wink as he passed by, and he felt
the *prana* surge inside him. Higgins imagined embracing the
girl in the restaurant's back room amidst tins of jasmine, dried
mushrooms, and sacks of rice. The moment he stopped to
investigate further, however, the girl blushed, giggled, and
slipped inside. Higgins did not follow. It was nothing to get
excited about. Just a little friendly fire on the part of the
natives.

Passing under a movie marquee, Higgins considered the
pictures that were playing. *La Brujeria con* Raymond Gris.
And *Knife of Death. Con* Arsenio Castellano.

He stopped in his tracks and looked again. But what? He
had misread it, surely. It was *El Cuchillo de Muerte*, all right,
but the Castellano it was *con* was not Arsenio, but Gilberta.
My God, it was the Doctor's sister!

Higgins paused to marvel at this wonder. Then again, perhaps it was some other Gilberta Castellano. But no, an enor-

mous poster, wrought in the colors of sex and hell, advertised the Spanish thriller and showed a woman who distinctly resembled the Doctor's sister screaming in terror as a gigantic bloody knife blade descended from above. But wait! The knife was connected to a meaty hand, which in turn was attached to a monstrous body, for Higgins saw now that in the accepted tradition, several characters and dramatic situations had been drawn together, without regard to comparative size or perspective, so that the knife blade only *appeared* to be descending upon Gilberta – though this, of course, was a part of the poster's charm. Equally charming was Gilberta's torn blouse, revealing a lot of heaving, milky bosom. Higgins smiled. Yes, the poster was clearly what was called an 'artist's interpretation,' since, to the best of Higgins' recollection, the Doctor's sister was not so generously endowed.

At the bottom of the poster, written in ersatz blood, was the legend: '*She fought for her honor. She fought for her life. She fought against the*' – drip, drip, drip – '*Knife of Death!*'

Higgins shook his head in delight at the thing, and feeling very much better for no clear reason, set off once more through the summer morning. Merchants were hosing down the pavement in front of their shops while children on bicycles splashed gaily through the puddles. Rainbows flickered in the windblown spray lending a sense of the fantastic and surreal, as though somewhere Higgins had made a magical wrong turn and stumbled, somehow, into the slums of fairyland.

At last, he reached the studded wooden doors of an *iglesia* – one of the many old and beautiful Spanish chapels with which the *barrio* abounded. Entering it, he left the heat of the day behind and found himself in a space of cool and fragrant darkness, redolent with the scent of frankincense and myrrh. When Higgins' eyes had adjusted to the dark, he walked to a little alcove in the front of the church that housed the statue of the Virgin. This one was especially tawdry and poor. She was little more than a glorified doll, crowned and dressed in a blue satin gown trimmed with scraps of dusty lace.

Nonetheless, Higgins knelt before her and asked for her blessing, without which life is queer and grim.

And yet even when he had finished his prayer, Higgins continued to feel uneasy. What was bothering him? He couldn't say.

It wasn't the fear of assassination. If somebody was going to eliminate Jorge, well, then, let them! He doubted they would also eliminate him. No. There was something else. What was it? And then he felt a sort of subtle inner concussion, like a balloon tapping against the ceiling of his mind.

Of course. He was being blackmailed! Or was about to be.

That was it. Yes. Vazpana had something on him. He knew not only about the deal with Hansei, but about some other less savory transactions as well. And he would use what he knew – if it came to that – in order to get Higgins to do his bidding. Higgins was absolutely certain of this.

Higgins cursed, then caught himself, realizing he was kneeling in front of the Virgin. He had always prided himself on his cleverness and cunning. So how had he ever allowed this to happen? To be caught by the short hairs like this! It was infuriating, absurd!

Through your dishonesty, the Virgin seemed to answer – that little chink in your moral armor through which a host of ills is now entering your life, just as germs might penetrate your bloodstream through an imperceptible fissure in the skin.

His dishonesty, yes. And his defiance! For it was more than greed that had motivated Higgins to spindle the rules. It was rage!

Rage at whom? At life; at God, at the Virgin herself! For he felt that she, by taking his wife, had not played fair with him – and so he would be damned if he would play fair with Life! That's why he had taken the risks that he had, hadn't he? Not for the money, or even the thrill, but to flaunt his rage and his defiance: to give, as it were, the finger to Heaven.

Though Higgins' defiance had rebounded upon him – and it was he, not Heaven, who would pay the bill.

But perhaps he was just over-reacting. Maybe Vazpana

wasn't even an agent. After all, nothing had been said. Then again, nothing had to be.

Higgins closed his eyes and prayed that Everything Would Be All Right, that he would Not Be Blackmailed, Bombed or Shot, that he would be Happy and that his Writing Would Go Well, and that he would find True Love within and without. Finally, he performed some ejaculations, as they are called: O Beauty! O Wonder! O Splendiferous Light! blessed himself, and stood up, his bad knee twinging, but his restlessness relieved.

And that's when he saw the girl again, and his heart stopped, and his blood started dancing. For it was her: the Doctor's sister, the one he had been dreaming of.

Reunion

Chapter 15

Higgins caught up with the Doctor's sister in the dusty alcove between the church proper and the outside door.

'What's a nice girl like you doing in a place like this?' It was a dumb thing to say; nonetheless, he'd said it.

Gilberta looked up at him with some surprise. Then she replied, 'Why not? I'm a Catholic, aren't I?'

'Are you really? I didn't think there were any Catholics left. I thought they'd all gone out with the hula hoop and the uh . . . whooping crane.'

She stared at him with faint amusement, while Higgins drank in her beauteous presence. She was built like a short-stop, long and lean. Save for a certain Latin languor that lived and lingered in her bones, there was nothing particularly 'Spanish' about her. Her skin was fair without being pink, its pallor giving to the mole on her cheek, her black eyebrows, and the soft down above her upper lip a special definition.

'And you? What are *you* doing here?'

'She's my *ishtadevata*,' Higgins said, pointing to a statue of the Virgin visible through the leaded diamonds of the window.

The Doctor's sister turned and stared.

'Your *ishtadevata*'s your chosen deity,' he explained.

She gave him a blank look.

'Your chosen deity's the form of God you worship.' Congratulations! In the first ten seconds of their introduction, Higgins had managed to break into Sanskrit, and steer the conversation toward yogic theology!

'What do you mean, *form* of God?'

'I mean, God doesn't have a form, now does He? Still, He has to assume one to appear to His devotees. To a Christian, He appears as Jesus. To a Moslem, Allah. Hindus see Krishna, Shiva, or Kali.'

'Buddhists see Buddha,' she said either mocking him deadpan or following him perfectly – it was hard to say which. 'And why does He do that?'

Higgins smiled. 'Because wouldn't it be ridiculous if He appeared to the Pope as the Great White Buffalo? Or as the Bleedin' Jasus to some Taoist sage?'

She didn't smile back. Instead, she studied him intently. Then, slowly, but surely, her look lightened. She *liked* him. It was obvious. Higgins felt like breaking into song. What had he ever been nervous about? It reminded him of the morning he had seduced his wife-to-be in St. Botolph's. He had felt exalted like this then. Higgins took a step closer, conscious of every molecule between them.

She turned on her heel and opened the door; the conversation was clearly over. Higgins followed after her, watching her picking her way down the steps, and found he was stirred by an absurd sense of panic and loss. 'Hey,' he yelled. 'Where are you going? Do you know who I am? I'm Philip Higgins. I'm your brother's best friend.' He thought for a moment. 'Maybe you don't know it yet, but *your daughters love me*.' It was an excellent line – full of wild Irish charm.

'My daughters, Mr. Higgins, idolize the dog.'

This was an even better line, and in the caesura that followed, Gilberta turned and looked into his face. And Higgins had the feeling then that she had looked at him this way before. It was a memory so powerful, it was disorienting. On a rain-swollen river, at night, in a boat . . .

Then Higgins blinked, and the river was gone; they were standing once more on the steps of the chapel beside a marble statue of the Blessed Virgin, drizzled with pigeon droppings and the light, spring rain.

Gil lowered her eyes, and disbursed a small smile. 'I know who you are. In fact, I've met you twice before – though I doubt that you remember me.'

'We *met*?'

She nodded slowly. 'The first time was at Harvard – fifteen years ago. You were lying on the floor of my brother's room – drunk – in your underwear.'

Higgins grinned. 'Were you charmed?'

'Shocked is a better word. I was only twelve. I had never seen a man in his underwear before.'

'But you've seen a lot since, I understand.'

She looked at him, but didn't flinch. 'I also saw you the last time you were here – last year? I watched the girls walking you up the block. I was hoping to finally get to meet you, but you went away that night. It was soon after your wife died. I met her, too.'

'My wife?'

'Yes. The day she died. She stopped by to see my brother. We were introduced.'

'That's right.' Higgins said. 'She was in New York that day. I'd forgotten that.'

'I liked her. She was a lovely woman. Very spirited, very gay.'

'Yes,' Higgins said, smiling sadly. 'She was that.'

Gilberta dropped her eyes and started walking again, and Higgins fell in beside her. Mention of his wife had altered his mood, while something had shifted now, and there was a new ease between them – even if they did not speak. Gil kept her eyes on the ground, as though contemplating something, while Higgins, for his part, wondered why he'd made such a nasty remark. And yet the way she had handled it had been impressive. There was something grave about her that he liked – some weight and depth which did not rise to every barb and compliment.

On the corner of the avenue, she hailed a cab. Higgins

opened the door for her, then surprised them both by getting in beside her.

'And where do you think *you*'re going, Higgins?'

'I just thought I'd come along. You know. For the ride.'

'And when we get there, what?'

Higgins smiled. 'I'll just turn around and come back.'

She looked at him, doubtfully, even as she gave the driver an address in the Seventies. So, Higgins thought, they *had* met before. Even in his drunken stupor he must have somehow managed to imprint her image on his brain.

And what a lovely face and form it was! For she was indubitably beautiful with hot Latin eyes that were flecked with gold and a nose as sharp and finely wrought as cutlery, even if a certain pallor – the ghost, perhaps, of a recent illness – flickered beneath her skin.

And Higgins felt such desire for her then, it overwhelmed him, and surprised him, too. For ever since his wife had died, he'd felt little towards women. Oh, he could still admire the way their parts all fit together, but he'd admired it from a distance, the way one admires something clever, and it hadn't moved him – until this morning.

He rested his arm on the back of her seat. It was an innocent move, but it had a future. Gil looked back at it – unamused. He removed his arm and folded his hands in his lap. 'So what were you doing in church today?'

'Me? Praying. I pray a lot. "Lord Jesus, you gotta help me, man. Ave Maria, gimme a break." That's how I pray. Pure complaining.' She smiled. The confession verged on self-parody. 'And you?'

'I meditate,' Higgins said.

'Yeah? I always wondered. How do you do that? What do you think about?'

'That's just it. You don't think about anything. You make your mind completely empty, completely still.'

'Yeah?' She seemed skeptical.

'Look, I hope you don't take this the wrong way.'

'So do I.'

'But are you a lesbian – or what?'

She rolled her eyes. 'Who told you that?' Then she said, 'Mr. Higgins, my brother's a nitwit. I hope you know that. For your sake, as well as his.' She sighed, as if undecided whether or not to go on. 'Look, once upon a time, I told him that. Hokay? Just to get him off my back, you know? About getting married? Well, you should have seen him. He hit the ceiling. I said, "Hey, man, at least I don't get pregnant." '

Higgins laughed. 'And what did he say to that?'

'Nothing. What could he say? His moustache – it waggled a little. Twitched. You know how it gets? Like bugs are gonna come crawling out?'

'And then they disowned you?'

'Who said that?'

'Ambrosio Garcia.'

Gil made a face. 'Look. How can they disown me? I am not a piece of furniture they may buy – or sell. I'm their flesh and blood. They *say* they disown me, but what does it mean? Nothing. It's just something they say to make themselves feel better. I don't even think about it anymore. But let's not talk about that. Tell me more about your . . . meditation. What do you mean you don't see nothing?'

'Well, I don't.'

'So? Why do you do it, fool?'

It was a very good question. For the truth was, Higgins didn't know what he was doing. For six months now, he had been patiently knocking, but the door to his inner sanctum remained locked or jammed. Maybe he was expecting too much from it all, for instead of Bliss, all he had attained from a thousand rounds of *pranayama* was a ferocious appetite, while the yoga he performed made him feel relaxed – peaceful, even – but hardly sublime.

And yet, though his prayers had not been answered, Higgins still called to Her each night and morning, beseeching her to come to him and bring him her love. He had no doubts she would answer him someday soon – he only felt She was long overdue, so that he waited upon her coming the way an anxious host awaits a beloved guest, mysteriously and inexplicably detained.

Then again, he thought now, perhaps She had arrived already in the person of this girl. He looked at Gil with a growing admiration. He recalled a description of the perfect disciple: 'His speech is beneficial. It always brings joy. He is very intelligent and sharp-witted. When he is told something once, he understands it.'

She was like that. She was very sharp. He could see that at once. Even when she spoke to you in that hip, street-smart Latin accent, you could hear the light ironical edge in her voice, as though it was not really she who was speaking, but only the character her destiny compelled her to play.

And suddenly he remembered a country inn with sleds and wagons all round it. And Higgins heard, in the back of his mind, the shivering whinny of overheated horses come to the end of a long and frantic haul. Then the two of them – Gil and he – were inside the tavern before a hot yellow fire. There was the cloying scent of melting tallow, as the innkeeper's wife and children pressed upon them tankards of cider and platters of buns, speaking to them in a language he didn't understand. But what was he remembering?

'Excuse me,' Higgins said. But what did he propose to ask her? Did she remember traveling with him in a foreign country, crossing over a flooded river, and how they had fled in a horse-drawn sleigh through the snowbound back roads of where? Belgium? Flanders? He couldn't have told her. And so he said nothing – he just looked at her strangely.

'Hey, man, you okay?'

'Fine,' Higgins said. But he wasn't really. He was confused as hell, and worst of all the spell was broken. The love he had imagined he had seen in her eyes was gone, and she was looking at him now like a mother of three, a good friend, a concerned United States citizen.

'Maybe you oughta take it easy,' she said. 'You know, after what you've been through.'

'What are you talking about?' Higgins asked. But she didn't answer.

The cab had reached its destination. Gilberta tried to pay

the driver, but Higgins wouldn't let her. 'Where are you going?' he asked.

'That's none of your business, is it?' She opened the door.

'Then when can I see you again?'

'You can't.'

'Don't say that.'

'All right, I won't,' she said, and got out.

The Deviled Head

◆

Chapter 16

When the Doctor awoke, he panicked and felt for the money in his pocket. But blessedly, the wad of bills was still there. Where was he? he wondered, shivering a little as he remembered the dream. A young woman had come for a gynecological examination. He had asked her to strip and to lie down on the examination table. While examining her, he had discovered a lump in her pelvis suggesting an ovarian tumor, and suddenly, as his hand probed, it had plunged elbow-deep into a leathern cavity that was somehow built into the woman's side. This dream cavity was further subdivided into molded cubicles, so that he could feel the hard smooth squares of leather, and he had withdrawn his hand at once, disgusted, frightened, and amazed. Then he had awakened and remembered the money.

'You come when he calls you.' That is what Omar had said. And it was true. The Doctor *was* a coward. He already had the week's payment carefully counted and concealed in his pocket and he was only waiting now for the moment he would deliver it to *El Duende*. A meeting had been arranged for 2 a.m.

'Two a.m.?' the Doctor had cried. 'But I will be sleeping then!'

'You come when he calls you,' Omar had replied, tapping the Doctor's chest with a dead finger so that the Doctor could hear the hollow sound behind the bone. 'When he calls you, *comprende*?' And yes, the Doctor thought he did. Because the Doctor, despite his promises to Higgins and Garcia, was not about to do anything so mad and rash as to stop the payments. Oh no! How could he? And be butchered in cold blood that very next night or the one after that? Or, even worse, have one of the children menaced? Never! For even if the Doctor was not brave, he was, at least, not stupid. Oh, it was easy for Higgins to counsel courage. It wasn't his bones that would be milled and broken, his precious blood that would be spilled and drunk. Still, the Doctor's failure of nerve agitated and depressed him, and he turned on the bed with a secret cry, like a wounded animal.

It took a moment for the Doctor to realize now where he was: the children's room. This explained the sharp pain in his back which, upon inspection, turned out to be caused by a piece of the television. A picture of Jesus stared at him with its soft, reproachful gaze, and he cursed. It was finally getting to him, he swore: the creeping Catholicism that was all around, that was in his *teeth*, for Godsake, like radiation.

The Doctor sighed, turned on the pallet, and wiped his brow. What had happened to him, he asked? He had grown older and the light had died, the way it does, the way they said it would. The world had lost its charm, was all, like an overfucked mistress or a broken toy. And his life which had begun as such a great adventure had turned into an anxious routine, and in this careworn state the Doctor was resigned to pass his days, throwing away his prime like the dice on *la calle*, wasting away in this provincial Godforsaken spot.

For more and more now, the Doctor saw the *barrio* for what it was: a sink of misery in which the first cause of death for males between the ages of fifteen and forty-five was murder. The Doctor had read this dismal statistic only the other day, and it had sent shivers through him. He realized this meant that he would most likely be murdered himself. But no, that could not possibly be right! He must have phrased it improperly. He tried again. Of all the people that died, they were most likely murdered. That way, it still didn't make sense! He had to go pay the money now; he was just being nervous.

The Doctor got up and went out into the foyer. He noted with a minor pang that the sofa in the living-room was empty. He had ordered Higgins, in the interests of safety, to sleep there this evening, and he was irritated now that his order had been ignored. He went out. The street at that hour was like a prison corridor. The rows of shops had an armored mien protected as they were by corrugated steel riot doors or accordian shutters. In fact, these latter guards were found only on those establishments it would have been impossible to rob: poor Spanish fish stores in which there existed all night nothing but moonlight, odors, a gouged table, dripping ice, and on an unwashed knife blade, maybe, like sequins, a few glittering scales.

Below the street was another level of subterranean store-fronts, cellars and passageways, occupied by many 'social clubs,' a few legitimate businesses, and a greater number of crooked ones. Here lived the scum of the earth – men who trafficked in every conceivable vice. This black market the Doctor found particularly obscene, and the low cellar rooms never failed to oppress him.

But by now the Doctor had reached the place where the transaction was to occur: a boarded-up storefront showing no signs of life, until the Doctor knocked and was admitted.

La Club, as it was inelegantly called, was a unique establishment: a private restaurant dedicated to the gluttony of a single man. It was financed by *El Duende*'s drug, numbers, and extortion operations, as well as by annual tax-deductible 'memberships' from the *barrio*'s merchants and business community in sums ranging from $250 for the smaller shops to $1,500 for the larger ones. In fact, this 'membership' bought one nothing more than the right to continue to do business in the *barrio* for another twelve months without serious mental threat or physical injury. It is true that once a year the Goblin gave a fête and then, for one night only, the private nightclub was open to all, transformed into a veritable horn of plenty with tuxedoed waiters, hors d'oeuvres, loose women, and an open bar. But in the morning, the bottles were once again stoppered, the tables cleared, the leftover roasts flung to the pinscher, and the door bolted – so that although you had purchased a nine-hundred-dollar membership in La Club only the night before, you couldn't have drawn a glass of seltzer from its murky depths or made water there now, uninvited, if you'd tried.

It was Omar, *El Duende*'s wounded lieutenant, who showed the Doctor in. 'I am surprised you are up,' the Doctor said. 'The last time I saw you, you were lying on my examining table.'

Omar only grunted – or groaned. The bullet wound had been superficial. On the back of his head, however, he wore like a yarmulke a white piece of gauze where Garcia had brained him. He led the Doctor past the bar, and into the restaurant.

El Duende was seated at the only table that was set. His bulk was so preposterous that an ordinary chair would not support him, and so he sat instead in an upholstered throne specially built to accommodate his immensity, the throne lending him an air of kingship and mystery.

For no one knew where *El Duende* was from. He had simply appeared in the *barrio* one day out of nowhere – a young, obese and unctuous thug with an obsession for food, a head for business, and an eye for beautiful, masochistic women. His reign had begun with the purchase of a funeral home which, under his auspices, had flourished, the Doctor was almost tempted to say. Then he had bought a laundromat and a couple of brownstones, and within the year he owned the block and was the undisputed king of the local rackets, the past *capo* having 'retired,' as they said, meaning he was dead. With each passing year, *El Duende*'s empire had expanded – along with his body. His gluttony was so boundless, he had come to sit perpetually at table, and the Doctor's interviews with him were invariably conducted over these one-sided repasts as *El Duende* ate, or feasted rather, and the Doctor, supplied with a spot of brandy in a crystal snifter, watched the fat gangster slurping down his never-ending meal.

Tonight was to be no different. The Doctor's interview was to be conducted over several dozen oysters and cherry-stone clams glimmering on their half-shells in a bed of cracked ice, the ice in turn resting upon a silver dish, the dish upon a massive table bearing condiments and wine, and the table standing, finally and firmly on the red tiles of the res-taurant floor – as was a large dog: a gray pinscher which, as the Doctor approached, retracted its lips displaying its white teeth and black gums.

'Down, Satan,' *El Duende* said. He raised a shell to his lips and drank off the fresh, salty liquor, then sucked down the living mollusk, bathing it in wine.

The gourmet baptism over, he raised his eyes. 'Ah,' he said, relishing the moment, 'will you join me, Doctor?'

'No, thank you,' the Doctor said. 'It is a strange hour to be eating one's supper!'

'Not if you're hungry. Don't you agree?'

But the Doctor only agreed that the man was an obscenity. Already the Doctor felt light-headed, powerless, and hot. He watched as the gangster absorbed one oyster after another, sucking down the gray iced flesh, then started on the clams with a tireless rapacity.

When he was finished with the shellfish, a rack of lamb arrived, trailing rosemary and garlic. The cooked fat shook and jiggled merrily and the meat bled pink as *El Duende*'s knife worked with neat brief strokes – so that even before it had been re-confirmed that the Doctor would continue his weekly 'schedule of payments,' as the heinous bloodletting was euphemistically called, the roast had been reduced to a rib cage and cartilage, and the fat man was smearing with a linen napkin the soft lamb fat which shone on his lips, while preparing to assault the next object of his bottomless lust: the sweet orange flesh of half a dozen mangoes. The Doctor objected!

'Stop!' he cried. And when *El Duende* looked up: 'Such

habits, *Señor*,' he explained sternly. 'They are an insult to the bowel!'

El Duende paused, and the weight of his sodden, insatiable gaze fell upon the Doctor. Then he tapped a tiny pill – the size and shape of an ant larva – into his fist, and swallowed it with wine. It seemed ridiculous to think that this minute white lozenge might somehow affect his monstrous condition.

'Pass me that, will you?' *El Duende* asked, and the Doctor threw him another immaculate rag which, placed to his lips, came away stained with wine and gravy.

Then the gangster snapped his fingers and two young women appeared from a nearby booth. They were floozies – elaborately coifed professionals, it was obvious – and they quickly slid in beside the fat man in the fawning age-old attitude of such women. *El Duende* put his arm around them and smiled with satisfaction. 'This is Stardust. And this is Jane. Girls,' he said, 'meet the Doctor.'

The Doctor looked away; such women unnerved him. He took a peek. One of them was staring back at him with the flat, knowing insouciance of whores. 'Hi ya, Doc,' she said, cracking gum, even as the other girl screamed, surprised by the fat man's palm upon her cool white thighs.

There was answering laughter from the gangster's attendants who, the Doctor now realized, numbered more than half a dozen persons: Omar, the barman slicing lime, the hovering captain and two uniformed waiters at their stations, the young 'muscle' guarding the door, and the cook – a blue-cheeked non-entity who, momentarily relieved from the tyranny of his boss's stomach, stood in the kitchen doorway smoking a cigarette and looking tired as hell. It was more than your usual animal association; it was a minor kingdom, the Doctor decided, and *El Duende* was the chieftain with all the usual *droits de seigneur*. In fact, no sooner had the Doctor entertained this notion, than *El Duende* grabbed one of the girls by the neck and pushed her head down until she disappeared beneath the table. The Doctor did not know whether he should be insulted or sick. He felt, in fact, both. It was the ultimate indignity, and he realized now that these were the vicious circumstances under which the interview would be conducted – while one harlot reclined upon the monster's breast, and the other performed the despicable service.

El Duende settled himself comfortably and reached for mango. There followed an explosive gush and an aquative slurp as its juices drained down his flapped and folded chins. The Doctor was appalled. The man was diseased! When he finished the mango, he picked up a pear. Would he never stop eating? It was really most disgusting! He just went on and on, swallowing and digesting . . . and shitting, no doubt, the Doctor thought. While the whole time, underneath the table . . .

The Doctor took the lump of money from his pocket and tossed it on the table. It was $1,400. It was more than he could afford.

'There,' he said. 'That is it. That's the end of it, too. I'm not going to pay you anymore. You hear me? I can't.' The protest which had begun so manfully, finished sounding weak and craven.

El Duende laughed and clapped his hands. 'Bravely done. The Doctor is rebelling,' he announced to the house. And everyone turned then and stared into the camera of the Doctor's eyes – the girl, the cook, the barman slicing limes.

'I am not rebelling,' the Doctor said. 'I am just not paying you anymore. I have paid you $47,000 these last two years, and that is quite enough. Too much.' He sounded stronger. The girl beneath the table attempted to come up for air but *El Duende* pushed her head back down with a savage thrust as though he was trying to drown her.

'Doctor,' *El Duende* said, cutting him off. 'Let me tell you a story. Hokay? There was once a man who lost his head. Did you know? Yes. A man who lost his head because it was stolen by a devil who wanted it for his own. Now this devil, he kept the head and lived on it. It was his house. He looked out its eyes and he came and went out its mouth. And sometimes, when the devil was tired, he would sit in the head's mouth like a big black bug. And when he was thirsty, he would sting the head bad, and the head would cry and he would drink its tears.

'Of course, the head did not like this so much.' *El Duende* laughed. 'But what could the head do? I will tell you. It could do nothing. And do you know why, Doctor? Because this head, it was just a head. You see? *It didn't have no cojones!*' *El Duende* barked a laugh. Was it supposed to be a threat – or a joke?

'So in the end,' the gangster concluded, picking up another pear, 'in the end, the devil continued to come and go and live exactly as he pleased. Inside the head. It is a simple story. I think it has happened to you, *cabron*,' he said now with a venomous contempt.

The Doctor was appalled. Deviled heads and headless devils! And yet how appropriate, he thought, that threats of this nature should be couched in the language of psychosis and dream. For it was true: *El Duende* was a devil and he had nested in the Doctor's head and there was nothing the Doctor or anyone else could do about it. That was the story. It was as simple – and as evil – as that.

'You do what we tell you to,' the gangster said, beginning to breathe harder now, 'and I will . . . think about . . . what you said . . .' He closed his eyes as the rapture passed, and the vibration beneath the table ceased.

'However, in the meantime,' he said at last in an unctuous tone, opening his eyes and flourishing a piece of paper in his fist, 'you will keep to the schedule of payments, eh, Doctor? We have an agreement!' and he *thwocked* a pear core out his mouth.

'Agreement?' the Doctor shrieked, outraged and unhinged at last. 'What agreement? Once, in my great stupidity, I borrowed ten thousand dollars from your shylock here,' he said waving a hand in Omar's direction. 'Since then, I have repaid you the original sum plus more than $37,000 interest. This absurd penalty serves me right for ever doing business with the likes of you in the first place. But now I am finished. You hear me? That is all you will get. I assure you.'

The girl came up from beneath the table. She smiled dreamily at *El Duende* and reached for a pear – but he pushed the basket of fruit just out of her reach.

'Doctor, let me introduce you to someone,' he said. 'Mucho! *Venca!*' and a big shambling creature rose from the table at the door and came forward through the restaurant, knocking over a bar stool in his ungainly haste. The Doctor felt sick at the sight of him, for even from afar the Doctor could tell the boy was not right. He was two or three inches taller than the Doctor and had round, sloping shoulders, a wet, loose mouth, blurred eyes, and a short black crew cut strewn with moonshaped scars. The Doctor thought 'boy,' but he would have been hard pressed to give his age, for he had that look of perpetual adolescence common to morons.

'Sorry, Mr. Valpero! Sorry, sorry,' he repeated nervously as he stepped into the light.

'What are you apologizing for?' *El Duende* asked. 'I just called you!'

'Sorry, Mr. Valpero,' he said, looking at the Doctor now and at the girls, then back to *El Duende*. Then he began to laugh – or rather honk – in a most demented manner through his nose.

'This is Mucho, Doctor,' *El Duende* said. 'We call him that because . . . there is so much of him!' It was a joke. And everyone, with the exception of the Doctor, laughed.

'You wanna see my fish?' the boy said in a high, excited voice. 'I got this fish.'

'What are you talking about?' *El Duende* said.

The boy put his hand in his coat pocket and withdrew a small yellow goldfish. He held it out for everyone to admire. The girls went 'ooh,' as if on cue. 'Fish,' the boy said. He looked down at it sadly. 'Before . . . it was moving a lot.'

'Jeez, didn't they give you no water for it, kid?' one of the hookers asked.

'Yeah,' he breathed, admiring the thing.

'Well? What did you do with it? The water, I mean?'

'I drank it,' Mucho said. He looked down at the fish and poked it with a blackened nail. He looked up at the Doctor. 'Before, it was moving a lot.'

'Zip up your fly,' *El Duende* said irritably. 'And straighten your jacket. And put away that fish. Arturo, help him,' he called, and the tuxedoed captain rushed over to Mucho, briskly straightening the boy's jacket.

'Ah,' *El Duende* said with real feeling now as the waiters appeared with a meat pie, two bottles of port, and a virgin round of cheddar cheese.

'May I interest you in some late supper, Doctor?' *El Duende* politely asked.

'You are incredible!'

'I'd like some, Mr. Valpero!' the demented one said.

'Not you,' *El Duende* said unpleasantly. 'You are monstrous enough! Look at this, Doctor.' And with that, *El Duende* lifted the boy's shirt, undoing the work the captain had just finished. Again, the girls oohed melodramatically. For the boy's musculature was abnormal, or at least it was not that of a modern man's. There was a set of vestigial muscles in his stomach – nameless muscles the Doctor had never seen before. 'You may examine him if you wish.'

'No, thank you,' the Doctor said curtly, even while remembering how once in Dorado, in the darkened corner of a mountain hut, he had come upon a boy with an eight-inch tail.

'His mind is equally primitive,' *El Duende* said. 'Mucho, Doctor, comes from the backstreets of Puerto Valle. I am his . . . patron, his . . . godfather, you will say. Mucho will do anything I ask him to. Won't you, Mucho?'

'Yes, Mr. Valpero,' the boy said sniffing, wiping his fingers on the tail of his shirt.

'For instance, if I told you to, oh, go over there and break the Doctor's thumbs, you would do it for me, wouldn't you, Mucho?'

Mucho looked at the Doctor. The idea appeared to stimulate him. He rubbed himself and broke into the most disgusting grin, as though he and the Doctor were about to make love. 'Yes, Mr. Valpero.' The Doctor blanched.

'Thank you, Mucho,' *El Duende* said. 'You may go now.' And with a disappointed look – at the pie, at the Doctor's thumbs – the boy took a great troubled breath and crashed back into the rkness of the club, stumbling over the fallen stool.

'Like I say, Doctor, he will do anything I ask of him. And then some. And don't be fooled by his appearance, either. He's not so stupid as he appears. Why, the poor boy is wanted in Cuba for a series of utterly horrendous sex crimes – beheadings of *putas*.' The girls looked horrified. 'So you see, he doesn't need *my* inspiration, Doctor. Just, as they say, a little push in the right direction . . .' After that the Doctor could not understand what the gangster was saying since his mouth was plugged with cheese and his words were bathed in gravy.

Then the telephone rang and the Doctor was thrown out. It was as fast and as unceremonious as that. *El Duende* made a gesture and the next thing the Doctor knew was he was being escorted by Omar to a back exit that opened upon a series of basement rooms which, he assumed, led eventually to the street. The front door, Omar explained, was not being used any more because of the shootings. And besides, they were taking good care of the Doctor. They wanted him alive and well.

'*Buenas noches*, Doctor,' Omar said. 'We will see you next Saturday night at about this hour, eh?'

'No, you won't,' the Doctor said. 'I told him. I am not paying you any more.'

Omar looked up, surprised. His mouth opened to reveal several gold-filled molars. Then he shrugged as if to say that the Doctor's behavior was most bizarre, but not any of his business, really. If the Doctor wished to dig his own grave, well, yes, that was an option that might be arranged. He could, if he was so inclined, cancel the payments by forfeiting his existence. In which case, if this was what the Doctor wanted – if he was tired of drawing in lungfuls of the marvel-ous spring air – then far be it from Omar to interfere. Still, from a personal viewpoint, and because they were old pals, he thought the Doctor's attitude unwise. He said all this with a shrug and a roll of his eyes.

Then he frowned. 'I tell you, Doctor, I don't like that guy. I don't like that damned *hombre* one little bit.' He grimaced.

'You don't like *what hombre*?' the Doctor said, anxious to capitalize on any divisiveness in the ranks. 'Valpero?'

'No,' Omar said. 'That other one. What's his name? He calls Mucho. That one. That's the *hombre* I do not like. If that one ever got to you, I mean, there's no telling what he might do. Maybe he would break your thumbs is all. Hokay. That's tough enough. But I don't really trust him to stop just there. Do you? Not after what he did to those *putas*.'

'What did he do to them?'

'You don't want to know,' the shylock said. He grinned. 'It would give you nightmares.' He unlocked the door. It gave on to another basement room. 'Good-night, Doctor. My respects to your sister.'

'Your sister be fucked!' the Doctor hissed, but he was shut out by then and the door locked behind him.

The Whore With The Heart Of Stone

♦

Chapter 17

No sooner had Omar gone than footsteps reapproached the doorway and the Doctor slipped behind an upright stand of lumber, flattening himself against the cellar wall. It was stupid of him to have said what he did. *El Duende* had taken umbrage, surely, and dispatched his goon to dislocate the Doctor's thumbs (or, more precisely, to shut them in a dresser drawer, for this is how, the Doctor had read somewhere, that it was done.)

The Doctor held his breath and listened while the latch chuckled and the knob was turned. Then the door opened . . . and a young woman stepped into the basement space. She squinted through the darkness as though she was searching for someone. The Doctor cringed, dislodging a two-by-four, which crashed down like a shot, freezing the woman and stopping the Doctor's heart. When his heart began to beat again, the Doctor stepped out from behind the blind.

'Well, hell's bells!' the girl said. 'You scared me, Doc. What are you hidin' for?' and she began to pick her way across the room towards the physician, her long legs flashing on her teetering high heels. And though the Doctor disapproved of such sexual theatrics, he could not help but admire the legs themselves, for they were long as knives and sharp as blades. These extraordinary extremities terminated at one end in the above-mentioned heels, and at the other in one of these extravagantly constructed *derrières* on which the Doctor could have stood his cup of morning chocolate; or these, at least, were the first things about the woman the Doctor noticed: her legs and her ass – redblooded Cuban coward that he was.

But who said that? The Doctor was not a coward. Hadn't he just told off *El Duende*? *Si*, an old inner familiar snickered, after you paid him, donkey, one thousand four hundred of your dollars! What a man you are! Of course they didn't hurt you. You *paid* them, fool, even as you swore you wouldn't. And the Doctor sighed, because he knew this inner prompter spoke the truth. He had paid the men while crying, 'no, no, no,' even as his hand had guided the shafting – like a certain type of Catholic girl the Doctor had pursued in his youth.

The Doctor looked up at *El Duende*'s whore, at her sleek young lines, long legs and sculpted tail. 'What do you want?' he asked coldly. (And yet, even now, despite his tone, the Doctor was having sex with the girl – mentally, that is; was already nibbling at the tender meat of her neck, and drawing in her perfume where it greeted his system like a rush of speed.)

'Jeez,' she said. 'I'm just being friendly. What the hell's the matter with people around here?'

'You are not Spanish!' the Doctor said.

'Never said I was,' the girl declared in her offhand way. 'What's the matter, sweets? Got something against *gringas*?' And she gave him a smile that said if he did, not to worry – she would soon fix that.

'Of course not,' the Doctor said. 'In fact, my oldest, my very dearest . . .'

'*Friend*? Aw, c'mon, Doc,' the whore said coming closer to him now. 'You can do better than that!' And she gave the Doctor another look that made his blood boil and his tongue freeze.

In fact, the Doctor could hardly look at her now. He found the girl too blatantly sexual, and he was afraid he would explode if aroused. He looked down at the floor as, with a kind of minor amazement, he realized she was coming on to him and he could have her if he wanted.

Of course he could have her. She was a whore!

No, not like that, his heart insisted. He could have her – as a woman.

'What are you *doing* here? Why did you *come*?' he shouted rudely.

She looked surprised, then smiled. At his *passion*, no doubt. What was he getting so hot and bothered about, anyway?

'Huh?' she asked stupidly. She shrugged. 'I dunno. Just liked you, Doc. I saw you coming out here, and so I just followed you is all.'

'I don't mean *here*,' the physician insisted fiercely. 'I mean *here*.' He gestured grandly at the *barrio* around them.

'Huh?' she asked again, wrinkling her brow. 'What's wrong with *here*, Doc?'

'There is nothing wrong . . . with *here*, I mean!' the Doctor said, too stimulated to properly converse. 'It's just that most people . . . girls,' he choked, 'like yourself . . . don't usually . . . try . . .' But he couldn't go on. His throat was constricted with a sickening mixture of hate, tender hopes, and lecherous expectations. He let his gaze fall upon the soft round of her breasts. To be kissing them now would be something indescribably wondrous and fine! He looked up, infuriated. 'How could you?' he whispered. 'Do that . . . to him . . . in front of me?'

'Didn't do nothing,' the girl said sullenly, guiltily, lowering her eyes. Then she raised them defiantly. 'Didn't!'

'My God!' the Doctor fairly shrieked. 'You call that . . .'

'Look. Don't you see, Doc? It was all a big joke. On you, Jack. It's probably impossible, actually. He's too fat!' She laughed. 'I just crawl under the table. I don't even touch him. And then he just pretends . . .'

'Pretends?' The Doctor was thunderstruck.

'If he has one,' the girl declared, 'and I'm not saying he does, mind you, he most probably uses it on boys.'

'What are you saying?'

'That he's kind of a faggot, Doc, if you ask me.' And she

yawned, as though faggots, or the Doctor – it was hard to say who – bored her to tears.

'But . . .' the Doctor sputtered. 'It seemed so . . .'

'Real? Well, it weren't,' the girl said firmly. 'It was all a dumb act. You think I'd actually *do* such a thing?' She appeared outraged at the thought. 'Look,' she said, throwing the Doctor an honest country look. 'I'm not saying I'm no saint or nothing. But I'm not what you think I am neither. Hey, Mister! I belong to the Art Students League! Uh huh! I go to art school! Three days a week!'

The Doctor was not certain what this precarious academic affiliation was supposed to prove, but she held it out to him now as a sign of something – her respectability, he supposed – and the Doctor, for no respectable reason, found himself accepting it as such. She wasn't a whore – just a young *artiste* working her way through college. The ends of the Doctor's mouth strained at this ridiculous fiction.

But on examining her more closely now, he saw clearly she was just a child – she was barely out of her teens. He could read it in her shoulders. It was funny, the Doctor mused, how the truth showed in the body, for in the way she held her beautiful bare polished shoulders he could see the youth of the animal, the matchless female florescence. If he had thought she was older, it was because of her manner, which was seductive and commanding beyond her years, and her body, which was a woman's and a joy to behold. The Doctor should have known; he had examined tens of thousands of bodies in his day, prodding them repeatedly and peering into their sundry orifices. And yet, rarely had be beheld such a beautiful one as hers. She was built like a colt, long legs and wondrous slanting bones, with flesh so fresh it begged to be touched, like wet paint. Her eyes were enormous, green and sad, while the circles beneath them were not unattractive, only unexpected in one so young and, clearly, evidence of a sluggish bowel, lack of sleep, or was it . . . drugs? The Doctor stiffened – then relaxed again as he gazed into her eyes. They were very old. That's why he had thought she was older than she was. She had large old eyes in a sharp, sweet, sensuous face. She was really – it dawned on him all over again – quite beautiful.

'So tell me what are you doing with him?' the Doctor asked, 'if you are not . . . *servicing* him, that is.' He chose the verb with care. 'What and why in the name of hell . . .'

'For the bucks, Doc,' the girl said, cutting his outrage short. 'He pays me hundred and fifty dollars for a few hours' work. Hundred and fifty geetas,' she mused with a quiet greed. 'To humor a fat guy.' She looked at her watch. 'From one to five. Now I think that's just a wonderful gig for a nubile young lady like myself. Don't you? Sure beats slingin' hash or waitin' tables.'

'Tainted money,' the Doctor said. 'Blood money,' he reiterated, realizing with a queer relief that she had no idea who *El Duende* was. Humoring a fat man, indeed!

'What money ain't, Doc?' the girl asked with a philosophical shrug. 'Trouble is, girls like myself can't be all that picky about where our money comes from – not like you big rich handsome doctors. Course, I know some sawbones selling scribs on the side. Lots of others poppin' pills or got a jones. What I'm trying to say, Doc, is no one's perfect. There's a little dirt beneath everybody's nails, only money has a funny way of making you forget it. Look, Mister, homeboy's handin' me a wad of Hamiltons, I don't ask the dude he got a blessing from the Pope. You read the picture, Doc?'

But the Doctor did not, in fact, 'read the picture.' She spoke too fast in a city slang warped by a lilting hill country twang that made the Doctor's translations suspect. It didn't matter. He could tell, at least, that she was coming on to him. And he was pleased she thought him handsome. And amused she thought him rich. He wondered if she'd been paid with his own extorted money. 'It's not like that.'

'Oh, it's not, huh?' she said, showing her displeasure with him by stabbing a cigarette between her too-red lips. 'Look, Doc,' she said, the unlighted cigarette waggling at him like a scolding finger, 'you mind your beeswax and I'll mind mine. That way, we can all be friends. You don't worry about how

I pay the rent, and I don't ask whether you're doing scrapes on the side. What do you say? Deal?'

'I am not like that!' the Doctor said.

'Of course not,' the girl smiled. '*You're* different. And so am I!'

Her logic was admirable. The Doctor looked at her hard. He felt gagged with lust. Should he take her right here, right now, and be done with it? The moment came, the moment went. She seemed disappointed. The Doctor was fossilized. He had taken root. 'Doc,' she said at last. 'Wake up. C'mon. Ain't you even gonna light my ciggie?'

'Forgive me,' the Doctor said, coming to life with a jerk. He fumbled in the pockets of his suit for a match. He leaned forward, cupping the spitting matchflame between his palms. A strand of her honeyblond hair grazed his wrist, stirring him absurdly.

'Thank you, Doctor,' she said, openly seducing him now with her voice, her body, her eyes. She laughed – and made a noise in her throat that was indistinct and yet distinctly exciting. She licked her lips, waited, and sighed. The Doctor was paralyzed. He could not move. For years now he had kept his sexuality at bay, afraid that, once unleashed, it would rise up and destroy him, like a pack of dogs.

And yet . . . to be torn limb from limb by the teeth of his desire seemed to the Doctor now 'a consummation devoutly to be wished.' He wanted to fling himself upon this woman, to lose himself inside of her, the way as a child he had hurled himself into the crashing surf, or later, as a doctor, into his mission with the poor. And he realized now how deeply he had been infected by the miracle of gluttony and lust he had witnessed in the underworld hall.

But there were noises now – small ones, it is true – but noises which, nonetheless, sent the Doctor's heart scudding up against his ribs.

Footsteps were approaching, followed by the familiar timbre of *El Duende*'s voice and, in a panic, the Doctor threw himself against the girl, pushing her behind the stand of lumber, and pressing her, in turn, against the furred and dirty wall.

Then the door flew open with a bang and *El Duende* entered – insinuating himself sideways into the room – and the Doctor, whose hearing was sharpened by fear, thought he could hear the joists in the floor start to scream with the strain. Then Omar appeared, moonfaced, mute, like the satellite of a colossal world, as *El Duende* said to him in Spanish, 'He will pay us. You will see.'

But there was another sound, too; it was like the lisp of dripping blood, but was, the Doctor recognized now, the pinscher's claws upon the concrete floor. And the Doctor's heart, after a momentary sally, sank like a dead weight into his knees. 'It'll smell us,' he whispered in the woman's ear.

'Satan? Don't worry, Doc,' she hissed back. 'That poor old critter's so coked up, he can't smell a thing.'

'What?' It was difficult to believe. Who would ever do such a thing – feeding drugs to dogs? The Doctor peeped out through a chink in the boards. He could see the dog clearly now but, for whatever reason, it did not seem to smell them as he had feared. That was luck. For the dog's needle teeth in the glossy musculature of the Doctor's leg was something he did not even wish to imagine.

'Yes, he will pay us,' *El Duende* repeated. His great bulk seemed to fill the entire chamber, like light, like radiation. It was a disagreeable illusion, and was swiftly followed by two more familiar sensations. The first was a resurgence of abject fear: of the men, of the dog, and of what they would do to his thumbs if they caught him; while the second was lust – for even now, with one foot in the grave, something inside of him was aware of the girl's white breasts pressed and exploding up against his chest like bombs. The Doctor inhaled her hair, shuddering with the peculiar exhilaration of the mixed emotions, lust and dread, so that for one giddy instant he experienced the thrill that comes from having sex in roller coasters, or ravishing the Queen.

But *El Duende* was speaking now. His voice was not unpleasant in pitch, and yet its feeling and effect were like the trickling sweat meandering across the Doctor's brow. The gangster was talking about someone – the Doctor had no doubts who – in a most impersonal way, as though that person was not a person, and existed without subjective reality, without I-ness, like a thing. The mobsters paused in the center of the space, while Omar collected his breath. Then he suggested that since this person was giving them so much trouble, they should leave him alone. This prompted *El Duende* to repeat the assertion: 'He will pay us. You will see.'

'And if he don't?' the shylock asked in English.

El Duende cut a fart. He made no attempt to suppress it, as the Doctor often did. 'If he don't,' *El Duende* said, 'eliminate him.'

'Yes, sir.'

These last words were like a gun going off inside the Doctor that brought down, once and forever, his naive and humanistic cast of mind. 'Eliminate him.' But they must mean . . . something else. They must mean . . . But what else could they mean?'

Though even worse than the murderous order itself was the banal reply. The Doctor could still hear the bland tone in which Omar had responded: 'Yes, sir,' – without surprise, without protest or pause, as though *El Duende* had ordered, say, a pound of coffee, instead of seventy-five kilos of Cuban flesh.

The Doctor had his moustache in the woman's ear.

'Tickles, Doc.'

'Shhh!'

'They're gone, Doc,' she said. 'Hey. You can get off my foot now.'

'What?'

'I asked if you'd mind standing off my foot.'

'Yes,' the Doctor said, and stepped back, his heart pounding, his lust gone. He stared off at the dim brick, the weak bulb, at the blond two by sixes fanned, like a bad hand, against one dark wall. And it seemed to him now that these things should look different than they did, less ordinary, more evil and besmirched, as though blood might boil from the filthy brick, and the mortar shout, 'Foul!' But no such signs of moral distress on his behalf manifested on the walls. The Doctor had noted this heartlessness before: the obliviousness of inanimate things. Though you may be drowning in it, the river doesn't care. No one really cared but the Doctor, and the Doctor was alone. 'Did you hear what they said?' he asked his companion.

'Nah,' the girl said, wiping her nose with a fist. 'You mooshed my hair, Doc.'

'You didn't *hear* them?'

'Don't speak the lingo, sweets. Hey, don't get me wrong,' she hurried to add. 'I *like* the way it sounds.'

'They just said . . .' but the Doctor could not bring himself to tell her what the men had just said. It was too horrible for words. *Eliminate him.* But no, that was not possible. They were extortionists and hoodlums, yes. Not cold-blooded killers. He felt a shiver of disgust – a sad resonance that seemed to vibrate in the pit of his stomach and travel up his gullet, gagging him. And the Doctor beheld a familiar vision then, a vision of himself he had perfected through the years of a sad, long-suffering figure of obscured brilliance and unmanifest destiny who, through some sick whim of Fate's (and no fault of his own, surely!) had been left to languish in this dark dungeon of a slum where, nonetheless, he was engaged, day and night, in heroic healing and ardent self-sacrifice like some urban Schweitzer, or some rural corn god. That his victimization was a myth the Doctor saw clearly now – and this revelation was a ray of hope.

He turned to the young woman. 'You must get out of here.'

'Huh? What's the matter, babyface?'

And something inside the Doctor melted at this silly *Anglo* endearment, even though he knew perfectly well she was the kind of girl who called everyone that – like that brand of waitress who calls everyone 'Doll.' But even knowing this, the Doctor's heart responded, for such is the bewitching power of words.

'It is not safe for you here,' the Doctor explained. 'Take a cab. Get out! Go home,' he said, tendering a twenty which the girl accepted with the speed of light. She made up for her greed, however, by giving the Doctor a kiss on the cheek. It was disappointingly chaste. 'You're a dollface, Doc, you know that?' And she slipped her hand into his.

'Go on,' the Doctor said gruffly, but secretly pleased, as though he was her lover already – or her father.

'Gee, Doc,' she said. 'We hardly even got a chance to chat.'

'Chat? About what?'

'It's . . . *you* know!' She made a face.

'Medical?' the Doctor asked, disappointed. 'Is that why . . . ?' He sighed. 'Come see me Tuesday. I have office hours then.'

'Tuesday? A girl could die by then!'

'I am sorry. I am a busy man.' He handed her his card.

Somewhere in the dark hive of flats that squatted above them, a toilet flushed and water began to gurgle through a pipe near the Doctor's ear.

'Hurry up. Go on.' The Doctor harassed her with his love – it was the way he would have talked to a daughter, had he had one.

'Okay. See ya Tuesday then,' the girl said. She stopped and shook her finger at him. 'Now don't forget!' He heard her heels stutter on the poured concrete, then the door complained on rusted hinges, slammed, and there was perfect silence.

For a moment the Doctor stood there, reveling in the ghost of the woman's presence. Then, blinded by that fierce joy that accompanies the onset of courage – or love – he ran headlong into the darkened cellars – and immediately was lost.

How long the Doctor wandered there, he could not say. The crystal of his watch soon blurred with condensation, and the endless succession of gray cellar rooms defeated time, so that at first it seemed like only minutes had passed since the girl's departure, while moments later, it felt like days.

The Doctor was beginning to feel giddy now, claustrophobic and ill. He looked about him. He was in a dim room with a grilled window. A soft velvet fuzz grew on the walls while things that looked like sticks of fur leaned in the corners.

And it was then he heard music. *Salsa!* Trumpets blew a fanfare like on the Day of Judgment. Then the music ceased as a man's racing Spanish came through a tinny transistor.

The Doctor turned abruptly and pushed open the closest door, yanked back a curtain and staggered, blinking, out into the bright stale air of a little basement shop where two old clerks, counting money at a desk, looked up at him with the rising wonder of faces in a dream. The Doctor nodded to them, casually, and kept right on going, threw open the outside door and lurched into the street. And as the Doctor returned to the world of night and men, he had the lucid delusion he had just been coughed up by the soft throat of the slum or – to put it more crudely – that his thorny personality and horny hide had allowed him to pass unscathed through the bowels of the earth and be shat out, like a turd, on Fifth Avenue. And the Doctor realized then that for all his lost and panicked traveling, he had gone nowhere at all, having exited exactly one door down from the door he had entered with the money – he looked at his watch – less than one and a half hours ago.

The Doctor stopped and searched the night. Its eastern rim was the color of bone though the streets themselves were still full of night shadows and cool violet airs. Above the slum, an Islamic moon hung like a sickle of lightning. The scene recalled to the Doctor's mind the setting for some metaphysical thriller in which an exotic backwater's fetid and picturesque decay is used to replicate the soul's darker quarters.

And yet, despite his ordeal, the Doctor felt reborn. Whether it was his release from the underground maze, his impending doom, or the girl's large, white breasts, his life seemed indescribably sweet to him now, the kissing airs of the breaking day more precious to him than silver pieces. And the Doctor felt himself drawing new life and courage with every breath.

For he was not, after all, some sacrificial victim, some impotent and dismembered god but rather, a cunning, living and resourceful human Cuban physician who would see to it that this evil was remedied at once! And it was then he remembered the gun in his safe.

The gun was not humanism, of course. The gun was something else again. And yet the Doctor was beginning to consider now that something else might be required. For if the Doctor did not protect himself against *El Duende* – if he let *El Duende* sic his goon on him, or on the children – there would be hell to pay. He could guarantee you that.

The Doctor set off – anxious to meet with Higgins now despite the hour – hurrying past a clothesline in an empty lot where a headless, handless, footless figure fashioned out of someone's winter underwear squirmed and darted in the warm dawn wind inches above the ragweed and the mud. This wretched specter seemed to gesture to the Doctor – though whether in blessing or in malediction, who could tell?

Secret Police

◆

Chapter 18

Garcia stood before his bedroom window, gazing down at the dark summer street. He watched the pink pate of Rodolfo Benitez float from a doorway and disappear into the back of a dove-gray limousine. Garcia waved, but *El Presidente* did not appear to see the ex-Captain, and a moment later the limousine drove off. A second car full of Benitez's bodyguards followed. Garcia sighed; he had once applied for this position, but *El Presidente*'s Chief of Security had only laughed at his request, reminding Garcia, when pressed for a reason, of the fate of the Generalissimo – the last man Garcia had been hired to protect.

Garcia lifted the telephone receiver, and though it was past midnight, called his old comrade, Manuel Gomez. Gomez answered on the second ring.

'Garcia here. How are you, Manny?'

'It's two in the morning.'

'You weren't sleeping.'

'How do you know?'

Garcia might have said, because I soldiered with you for forty years and know things about your habits, *chico*, you don't know yourself, but instead he said, 'Because there's a video camera – behind the mirror.'

There was an uncomfortable silence. Then Gomez said in a bitter voice: 'That's not funny, Ambrosio.'

For Gomez lived in fear of his life – ever since someone had put a bomb in his car. The fact that he had not been in it when the bomb went off did not seem to matter. The next morning, he had gone into hiding – erasing himself, becoming a cipher, living in a series of furnished rooms rented under an assumed name. To support himself, he sold information.

'Well,' Garcia said, 'you get my FAX?'

Gomez sighed. 'No one I know who's here from Dorado would want to harm *you*, Ambrosio – unless it's some sort of personal feud. And that I doubt, too. Since I know all the ladies you screwed – and which ones have a jealous husband.'

'You sure?'

'I have researched this thing – extensively. Remember? Somebody tried to blow me away. Don't you think I tried to find out who it was?'

'And did you?'

There was an unpleasant pause. 'No. But I found out a lot of other things.'

'Anyway,' Garcia said, 'the Junior Officers don't have agents here, do they? I would imagine they're too busy fighting the rebels at home.'

'What, are you crazy? This is New York. *Everybody* has an agent here.'

'You mean, they do?'

'Yes.'

'Yes, what?'

'Yes, *sir*!'

'Goddamnit it, Manny. Who?'

Gomez paused. Then he said: 'Apparatus for State Security – External Section.'

'AES!' The name made Garcia sick inside. 'But what would AES want with me?'

'Probably nothing. Then again . . .' Gomez thought. 'Maybe they don't like your alliance with Benitez.'

'*Alliance?* What alliance? Just because we fled in the same fucking boat? Don't you remember? You, too, had to flee for your life.'

'You kneeled on the ground and kissed his ring. You swore allegiance to him.'

'And how the hell do you know that? It was in the middle of the fucking jungle!'

'The trees have ears. You also applied for a job with his security people.'

'And didn't get it,' Garcia said bitterly. 'And anyway, why shouldn't I? I have to eat. I have a sick mother to support.'

'Ambrosio,' Gomez sighed, as though picking up the skeins of an ancient quarrel. 'How many times do I have to tell you? People are not interested in your motives. Whatever your reasons, good or bad, they see you now as allied with Benitez. And President Benitez is a dangerous friend to have.'

Garcia paused for a moment. 'But isn't there anyone here who is on our side?'

'Yes. MIRA.'

'I am right here!'

'I mean MIRA, the Dorado underground.'

'Ah! And they are our friends?'

'Better than that. They are your enemy's enemy.'

'Name?'

'Names. *Dos*. Captain Willie Crespi and Lieutenant Jorge Vazpana.'

'Jorge Vazpana!' Garcia repeated, amazed. The Doctor's boarder was a MIRA agent! Incredible! He tried to make some sense of it all. 'But what are they doing here?'

'Undoubtedly, they are looking for the one from AES.'

'Don't you mean the other way around?' Garcia asked, remembering Jorge's extreme fear.

'Probably they are both looking for each other. Whoever finds the other first . . .' He made a slow wet sound, to signify a throat being cut.

'And who is this one who is here from AES?'

'I couldn't tell you. But there is probably someone working with him – someone helping to direct and coordinate the actions. You might start there.'

'Somebody else?' Garcia's head was swimming.

'Layers,' Gomez said, in explanation. 'Levels.'

'You mean a local contract?'

Gomez was silent.

'Who?'

There was a moment's hesitation. Then Gomez said, 'I don't know.'

Garcia could tell his friend was lying – hadn't he soldiered with him for forty years? – but he could also sense it was fear which froze his tongue. He thought at first of offering him money. Instead he asked, 'Who would?'

Gomez thought for a moment. 'Try *Sangre de Charco*.'

'Pool of Blood?' Garcia asked, using the gruesome nickname from Dorado. 'But I thought he was dead . . . or in hiding somewhere.'

'He's here.'

'Here where?'

'You might ask at The Hen,' Gomez said. He seemed impatient to go.

'Wait,' Garcia pleaded.

'What is it?'

Garcia paused. 'Would AES use *porqueria*? You know. Witchcraft? Little dolls?'

'Dolls?'

'I am serious, Manny.'

But evidently Gomez did not think so, for the line went dead.

Garcia sighed and cradled the receiver. Well, he thought, that must mean no. AES used bombs, bullets, poison. No one used magic anymore – not since Papa Doc and the late Generalissimo. He sighed and ran a hand through his thick, graying hair. Jorge Vazpana was a bonafide agent of MIRA, the Dorado Underground. And he had a comrade here named, what was it now? He looked at his notes. Ah, yes, Captain Willie Crespi.

Unhappily, AES had an agent here, too – someone who was out to get Jorge Vazpana, and maybe to harm Garcia, as well.

Garcia looked at his watch. It was too late to call the Doctor and Vazpana. He would tell them, he decided, first thing in the morning. For the enemy might attack at any moment! And with this understanding there arose inside him a bubble of the purest joy. To be fighting again! To be back in the saddle! If he was a dog, he would have howled.

Summer Solstice

◆

Chapter 19

Though morning was breaking on the *barrio* streets, inside the tenement it was still night. The Doctor, panting softly, climbed the stairs to Higgins' room – then stopped in his tracks. For the door was open; or rather, he saw now, it was ripped from its hinges – making any mention of a password irrelevant.

For a moment, the Doctor stood frozen with fear. The room was dark, an exquisite crescent of moonlight lay on the floor like spilled silver. Cautiously, he stuck his head in the door. He saw the body at once. Thought it might have been sleeping, he knew it was dead. He wasn't sure how he knew this, but he did.

The Doctor felt for the light switch on the wall. Unable to find it, he looked behind him once, then crossed the threshold of the darkened room, easily charting the moonlit chamber.

The body was lying on its back in bed. It was naked, its face covered by a crumpled sheet. Was it Jorge? Or was it Higgins? Even up close the Doctor couldn't tell.

Steeling himself, he drew back the sheet, but what he saw now distressed him even more – for the body was without a head. The severed neck displayed a stub of vertebrae, a sheaf of nerves and bloodless arteries. But whose body was it? Desperately, the Doctor looked around him for the head.

'They took it with them, Arsenio.'

The Doctor shrieked and almost did a double back somer-sault on the spot. He did not mean to scream or to perform the dubious acrobatic.

Higgins was seated on the floor by the window. 'Damnit,' the Doctor hissed, both furious at Higgins and deeply relieved. 'Where did *you* come from?'

'I've been here all along. I thought you saw me.'

'No! What are you doing?' the Doctor said dropping his voice to an angry whisper.

'I was meditating,' Higgins said in a normal voice. 'It's supposed to be good to meditate on a corpse. Except . . . right in the middle of it I . . . got sick.' He laughed in a weird, careening way.

The Doctor had heard such laughter before – in emergency rooms and in the morgue. It was shock. Sometimes it froze the tongue; other times, it loosened it, and the subject became voluble and giddily gay. He made a note to keep an eye on Higgins. Then he turned back to the corpse and sighed. 'He was just a boy; I never thought he'd be worth anybody's killing.'

For though the body was headless, it was young and male; and the Doctor had no doubts any longer about whose it was. Jorge's passport, keys, money, wristwatch, and pistol were on the night table beside it. 'When did you find him?'

'About quarter to three.'

'And why didn't you call me?'

'I did,' Higgins said. 'You weren't around.'

The Doctor frowned. There was little blood in the bed. The boy had not been butchered here. He wondered where the surgery had been performed. You could not cut off a person's head without spilling a whole body full of blood.

'And have you been sitting here all this time?'

'Of course not! I tried to find you. I woke up Rosita. And Gil. We looked in your room. You weren't there. Then I went out to some of the *cantinas*, but you weren't there either.'

'No. I was . . . working late,' the Doctor lied. He turned to Higgins. 'And where were *you* till three in the morning?'

'That . . . I'd rather not say.'

'Oh, really?' the Doctor said. He stopped and looked at his friend. 'Well, under the circumstances, I think you had better.'

Higgins sighed. 'I was out with your sister.'

The Doctor raised his eyebrows.

'If it makes you feel any better, Arsenio, it wasn't a particularly successful evening.'

'Meaning what? You didn't get laid? Surprising. Everyone who goes out with my sister gets laid.'

Higgins frowned, but said nothing.

The Doctor stepped into the bathroom. Here, the odor of blood was overpowering. The tub was coated with it, while the walls and floor were besmeared and spattered. Though the Doctor should have been inured to such sights, he wasn't.

A spent shell cracked underfoot. He retrieved it, noting it was a .22, and tucked it away, continuing his examination. Next, the Doctor reinspected the body. Despite the evidence of shooting, he could see no wound, other than the severed neck – though that, of course, was wound enough. He felt the flesh. It was growing clammy, while on the body's underside there were already signs of postmortem lividity, the purplish striations which appear on a body when the heart stops and the blood pools.

And at this sight, the Doctor felt a sudden filthy joy. Why was that? Because the body's condition meant that the boy had been dead for some time, had died hours before the Doctor's interview with *El Duende*. So the two events were not related, and the horrible gruesome execution had – thankfully – nothing to do with him!

Calmer, almost happy now, the Doctor tried to reconstruct the crime. It was most professional. Someone – or maybe more than one – had blown the door with a small explosive charge at the hinges. They had killed the boy and removed his head. Then they had left, taking the head with them. But what for? To make identification more difficult? And yet there were Jorge's fingerprints and effects – the killer, or

144

killers, had not bothered to remove them. So perhaps they had taken the head for some other reason.

The Doctor remembered Mucho, and recalled the story of the headless whores. But he had been with Mucho about the time the boy was murdered. Which left . . . who? AES? That's what Jorge had been claiming all along.

'Look at this, Arsenio,' Higgins said.

'What is it?' the Doctor asked, having difficulty removing his eyes from the corpse, for, like the body of a naked woman, it was endlessly fascinating.

'Sure you want to touch it?' Higgins teased, dangling it in front of the Doctor's nose.

'Will you stop that!'' the Doctor shouted, battling at the thing. 'What is it?'

This was a bit more difficult to say. It was a length of string to which were attached pigeon feathers, beads, the delicate bones of a bird or a rodent, and a small metal disk with a misshapen rim and a hole drilled in its center. Whatever it was, the Doctor thought, it was hideous and bizarre, like those minor monstrosities the mad concoct and carry with them everywhere like charms.

'Where did you get this?'

'It was next to the body. Isn't it lovely?'

'No. What is it?'

'It seems to be some kind of talisman,' Higgins said. 'Or, more precisely, reverse talisman, it's purpose being to kill you, I suppose.'

'Yes? Well, I don't believe in such nonsense,' the Doctor said, handing the wretched thing back to Higgins and looking around him vaguely for some place to wipe his hand.

'Maybe you don't,' Higgins said. He looked at the corpse. 'But somebody does.'

The Doctor cursed, peeved by this macabre stroke. Mystic disks and pigeon feathers! It didn't make sense. If it was political, then why was there magic? AES wouldn't leave this sort of thing behind. Unless it wasn't political at all. What if it was some sort of ritual killing? Or had the fetish been left only to confuse the issue?

' " . . . Bodies are like garments which the soul takes on and off." '

'What is that?'

'The *Gita*,' Higgins said.

'*Gita*?' the Doctor, asked, distracted. He supposed it to be some section of the Bible – Saint Gita. He did not know. He had not read the Bible in thirty years, and he believed it contained all sorts of things – pillars of fire and animal heads that raved out of clouds! Then the Doctor realized that Higgins was not talking about the Bible at all, but about . . . reincarnation.

'Ah, ha! And I suppose that you will tell me next that this was all his evil *karma*,' the Doctor sneered in order to communicate what he thought of Higgins' train of thought.

But why was he arguing with his poor raving friend? And what did philosophy matter any longer? Right now, all that mattered was finding out who had done this to Jorge. And making certain they didn't do it to him.

For what if this was just the beginning? What if they came for the Doctor next? What if they fractured his knuckles one by one, and then took a knife and sawed off his head?

But no, his imagination was going haywire. He was only scaring himself by thinking this way. His enemies, whoever they were, weren't supermen. They were goons, cretins. It was brains, not brawn, that counted now, and the Doctor had gone to Harvard.

This thought made him feel much better.

But wait a minute. Who the hell was the Doctor kidding? Remembering the bathtub full of blood and *El Duende*'s colossal bulk, the Doctor felt suddenly dispirited and ill. His fears seemed quite insupportable now, their collective mass like the stuff of collapsing stars, one suitcase of which is said to equal the weight of the world.

'Pack your bags and come with me,' the Doctor said.

It was Higgins' turn to look surprised. He glanced at the body. 'But . . . what about . . . him?'

'What about him? There's nothing we can do for him now.

Before?' The Doctor gave a guilty shrug. But that was another story.

'But shouldn't we call the police or something?'

'Why? So that they may cross-examine my nieces and ransack my office? No, thank you. They'll contact us soon enough. Pack your bags. *Pronto*. We're getting out of here.'

'But they'll connect us, Arsenio.

'Perhaps. But so what? We didn't kill him."

'They'll wonder why we ran.'

'Look,' the Doctor said. 'No one even knows we're here. And anyway, do you think they really care? Do you think the police will investigate this matter for more than . . . what? A day? The death of . . . what? A Spanish refugee boy? In a *barrio* garret? Don't be absurd,' the Doctor said, suddenly on the verge of tears. 'Nobody cares! And anyway,' he said very quietly now, 'no one talks around here. It's a rule. If anybody talks, they wind up like him.' He looked at the body. Higgins looked at it, too.

'All right, Arsenio. Let's get out of here then.' Hurriedly, Higgins collected his things. There wasn't much to pack, though as Higgins did, the Doctor saw his hands were shaking.

When Higgins was finished, he dragged his suitcase out into the hall. 'I wonder how long it'll take,' he said, glancing back at the corpse one last time. 'You know. Before they find the poor guy.'

'It's the first day of summer,' the Doctor said. He shut the door as best he could. 'It won't be long.'

Wilderness of Mirrors

Part II

The wilderness of mirrors corrodes gentlemanly constraint, and the discipline of counter-intelligence theory demands rigorous examination of every potential suspect when penetration by a ruthless and hostile intelligence service is suspected.

— John Costello
The Mask of Treachery

Return To The *Barrio*

◆

Chapter 1

At the tender age of twenty-seven, Gilberta Castellano felt kicked to shit. The ruination she was feeling began in her womb, irradiating through the rest of her existence. She dismissed it at first as the effects of the tour. Twenty-two cities in forty-five days, with shows almost nightly and interviews daily, would have sapped the strength of a Brahman bull, much less a hundred-and-seventeen-pound, five-foot-seven-inch mother of three.

But the tour had been over for more than a week; the accident that had ended it was now no more than ancient history. Yet still her blood felt flat and dead, like uncapped, lukewarm Coca Cola.

Gil remembered an old *pensione* on the outskirts of Rome. The large marble building was vacant, awaiting demolition to make way for an American-style supermarket. She recalled the ornate carvings around its windows, the Italian sunset, the dry garden, the empty rooms, the elaborate and antique edifice perfectly beautiful, pink, intact – and doomed. She felt like that.

And again, with a shudder, she remembered the crash . . .

But that was all behind her now. Now she was just tired, shot to the core. Now what she needed was a month of Sundays, a long season of rest and restitution.

But this, it appeared, was the last thing she would be

getting, for immediately upon her return to the *barrio*, she had sensed that there was something wrong. When she went to her brother's bank to repay another installment of the sum she had 'borrowed,' she was curtly informed that his account was closed – even though it was a business account which he had maintained for years. It was always possible, of course, that her brother had, at last, wised up and moved his monies to a 'higher-yielding monetary vehicle,' as she had been urging him to all along – but she doubted it. For her brother did not have a head for money, and he would not have recognized a monetary vehicle had one run him over in Herald Square – and so she could only assume the worst, that he had squandered it all on some stupid gamble, or invested it in another worthless property, like the rat-infested tenement he had recently acquired.

Certainly he had not spent it on his apartment. Maybe it was only in contrast to her European quarters, but her brother's flat seemed to have sunk to dangerously new levels of failure and neglect. Giant dustballs, agitated by the summer breeze, shivered beneath the furniture like frightened pets, and the telephone receiver defied the laws of gravity, adhering, when answered, to your ear and hand. Whole lengths of her daughters' braids were gummed together with melted fudgesicle, or was it beer?

Not that the girls weren't perfectly all right. They were. It was only that, like everything else in the place, they could have used a good, hard scrubbing. Which was the first thing Gilberta did.

On her first day back she cleaned her children; on her second, she cleaned the place from top to bottom, front to rear. Her daughters' bedroom was like an archaeological dig. Chicken bones, credit cards, coffee mugs, Rosita's underwear, pinto beans, and her brother's razor were stashed in little middens underneath their beds. A nondescript plastic knob which Gil foolishly discarded turned out that evening to be a part of the television. She even discovered the source of the odor that was plaguing the downstairs hallway, and, ripping up a floorboard, removed a mummifying rat. Then she went to bed and cried.

Gil didn't know why she was behaving this way. It wasn't like her. She had always been so sure of herself, so controlled and controlling. She had resisted the guilt they had tried to foist on her, the insinuation that she was not a good mother because she would not settle for a waitress job or marry one of the neighborhood boys. Why should she? She hated the *barrio*. She had no intention of remaining poor. She knew exactly what she wanted out of life: *dinero*, luxury, respect, and all the trappings that success, like a queen, brought in its train. For once she had had this. Once her family had owned mansions and *fincas*, orchards, servants, farmland and gold – but that was all before Fidel and his revolution.

And so, at twenty-one, she had fled the *barrio*, renting a place on Riverside Drive. Her people disapproved, accusing her of being a traitor, snob. *La Reina*, they'd called her. The Queen.

And that's how she had felt that first winter by the river, like a queen in exile, cold and lonely. She had worked as a waitress at a West Side restaurant and, on her days off, stalked New York with hungry eyes. The treasures of the earth shone like gold in shop windows. She wanted them all. Surely they imparted to their owner a royal patina, a special sheen. Several times she went quite berserk, buying things she could not afford and had to return, shame-faced, the next day – a sable jacket in which her face had shone like a mink's, a chatelaine of Aegean gold.

It was then she got pregnant – for the first time. Everyone was astonished. Since she wouldn't give you the time of day, everyone had assumed she was too much of a snob to open her legs to a man. But apparently she had, and to the worst type of fellow, too – someone who had laughed about it later with the *chicos* on the corner.

Friends counseled her to get rid of the baby; her family, to put it up for adoption. But though Gil listened patiently to both arguments, she never seriously considered either. The child was hers (as were the two more that followed). They were her flesh and blood, and she no more could have got rid of her children than she could have taken a knife and cut off her fingers.

But she could not get rid of her dreams of glory, either, though everyone told her that her dreams and kids could not live together. Everyone except Rosita, the grandmother of the middle child. She had encouraged Gil to study acting, to become something more than just an unwed mother – and to allow Gil to do this, she cared for the babies for hours at a time.

And so, Gilberta Castellano had tried to make it as an actress, enlisting in that army of lovely young women who make the rounds of the Theater District day after day, out-sized portfolios clamped beneath their arms. Demure from a distance, the illusion dissolves as they approach and you see in their eyes, beneath their carefully applied mascara, the blind ambition of a Tamerlane.

But five and a half years had passed in this manner, and ten thousand telephone and cattle calls later Gil was no closer to becoming a 'someone' than the day she had begun. Not that there hadn't been some minor victories along the way: she'd had screaming parts in two Mexican thrillers, and major roles in a few regional shows. And once, for three perform-ances of *A Midsummer Night's Dream*, she had been the only *Latina* Queen of the Fairies to ever appear in Shakespeare-in-the-Park.

But mostly Gil had supported herself and her kids with voice-overs for industrials, and 'under-fives' for Spanish soaps, the latter meaning you could count your lines – plus the digits in your paycheck – on the fingers of a single hand.

At last, desperate to succeed, she had tried to make it as a singer. It wasn't Shakespeare, but she was on stage, at least, before the public eye, and there was always the off-chance that some agent or producer would discover her. For a while she had sung with a New Wave group downtown, wearing green eye shadow, purple hair, net stockings, and a rose tattoo – the difference between Gil and the others being that she removed her costume at the end of the evening while the rest of the band went home in theirs.

Finally, just as her dreams and bank account were giving out, she was hired as a vocalist by *Johnny Colon y Su Explosion Musical*: a group of professional, red-hot, Cuban *salseras*. Gil happily rinsed the purple from her hair and worked like a dog for the next six months, assuring herself that it would all be worth it if they could only land a European gig. She imagined herself performing on the Continent; she was certain she would feel luminous singing in Rome.

But the worst thing in the world is getting what you want, because on that day your dreams must die, and by the time the band reached Italy, Gil's dreams had been murdered ten times over. All she discovered in the Eternal City was another set of problems, this time in Italian. Worst of all, she missed her kids. And never once, even by mistake had she felt luminous.

Then one rainy morning, just outside of Rome, as they were coming home from a late-night party, the van the band was riding in was clobbered by a milk truck. In the sobering seconds that followed the collision, she was amazed to find she felt no dread, only a gnawing sense of disappointment and chagrin that her life should end in such an undistinguished manner – beneath the wheels of a milk truck in the Italian rain. There were two more collisions as the van richocheted off two retaining walls before slamming head on into a concrete abutment. And as it hit, Gil felt herself go flying through the windshield.

She raised a hand to shield her eyes but, behold, her hand encountered no resistance and she drifted through the pane of glass unscathed – like smoke blowing through a screen door – continuing to ascend into the night until she was hovering just above the wreckage.

It took her the longest moment to understand that she was not in her body.

How could she describe those minutes as a liberated soul? It was different from anything she had imagined. Though her body was gone, her senses were unimpaired and, floating above the lurid scene, unlit by light, unwet by the falling rain, she watched as men with bars and torches burned and pried their way through the twisted wreckage. Once, just by thinking about it, she descended to the road and peered into the van at an unconscious body. It took her a moment to realize it was hers. She looked so different. And it struck her then that, for the first time ever, she was seeing herself as others saw her – not her picture or her mirror-image.

A moment later, she started to float away. She knew that she was leaving then for good and it felt peaceful, fine. She felt like a ship who slips her moorings in the night, finds the tide and begins to drift, heading for the open sea, and the only thing that checked her speed was the memory of her children. And perhaps Gil would have gone for good, had she not seen *them*, hovering in the air above her head, watching her with their burning yellow eyes. They had pointed ears, furred hands, and wizened faces. They looked like . . . gargoyles. She screamed.

The moment she screamed she re-entered her body, like a genie returning to its bottle. When she awoke some hours later she was in a hospital in Rome. And though the doctors kept her there another forty-eight hours, all she had was a sprained wrist and a mild concussion.

The rest of the band, on the other hand, was dead. All that was left of them was their instruments: the black-cased trumpets, the electric bass sunk in purple plush, the robed congas standing in one corner of the empty suite like beautiful children abandoned by their mothers.

After the accident, of course, she was never the same. How could she be? The experience had caused a revolution inside her; the borders of her mind had been permanently redrawn. She felt like someone who, having lived her whole life in a windowless chamber, discovers a door that opens on the sky; or like that girl in a story her Tia once told her, who climbed into the picture above her bed and found herself wandering in a fabulous country.

Stranger still, her ambition was gone. That inner prod or goad or god that had spurred her on so long was dead, and she felt instead as empty inside as a Buddhist nun for whom the world is phantom and unreal.

For it was true! Seven *amigos* – gone! Months of rehearsals and years of dreams – up in smoke. How could one believe in the promise of such a world?

It was all an illusion . . . a trick with string. She knew that now. She had gone behind the scenes and seen how it was done. And yet, instead of feeling privileged, she felt disappointed and chagrined, the way you do when a magic trick has been explained to you, or as she had that first night she had gone backstage as a child and discovered that the radiance in which the brownies were bathing, the fey glow in which Lord Oberon stood, was not a supernatural aura emanating from their bodies – but the effect of pink cellophane clamped over klieg lights.

Man Of The People

◆

Chapter 2

It was two days later, at ten in the morning, that somebody finally reported the corpse. The Doctor knew. He'd been walking past the brownstone on the way to his office when a squad car had arrived with its siren whining, and two big goons with pistols drawn had stumbled out and lunged inside – only to re-emerge a few minutes later with their pistols reholstered, their noses wrinkled, and with faces looking like they had stepped in shit. Then a police video crew had arrived to take moving pictures of the unmoving body, while the sight of the camera had attracted a crowd. The crowd, in turn, had attracted vendors peddling ices, sweat socks, sunglasses, underwear and roasted chunks of meat on spits.

At last, the coroner had arrived in a city limousine, and a few minutes later the Doctor had watched as the boy's remains were removed from the building in a black rubber body bag. The bag reminded the Doctor of those long canvas satchels in which traveling athletic teams carry extra equipment: fungo bats and shoulder pads.

The Doctor had hoped to bid the boy one last goodbye, but by the time he had managed to reach the cadaver, attendants were shutting the morgue wagon's doors – and so the only goodbye the Doctor got was one last whiff and glimpse of the malodorous and undistinguished satchel.

Detectives were starting to question the crowd as the

Doctor slipped away. He passed a fish store where an open-mouthed grouper, nesting on a bed of ice, questioned him with its eyes, the blood shot, hound dog visage of the fish haunting him like the face of his conscience.

For the boy *had* been an agent of MIRA. This much was certain. If Garcia's intelligence had not confirmed it, then the assassination surely had. He had come to the Doctor asking for protection, but the Doctor, in his arrogance, had thought him a fool. After all, what kind of secret agent announces he is a secret agent? But now, inarguably, the boy was dead – and the Doctor wasn't even sure who to contact about it.

The Doctor hurried on through the hot June glare and entered a little park, seeking refuge from the heat and his hordes of Mongol thoughts. He imagined it would be cool and restful in the park, but it wasn't. Vandals had stolen the slats from the benches, and the air was fairly seething with bees. A squadron of yellowjackets was marauding the garbage pails with the mindless, pin-brained and rapacious lust of insects. One of them peeled off from the others now, stationing itself by the Doctor's ear, as though expecting honey to come oozing out. The Doctor swatted at the thing and cursed. He looked around him. On one pocked wall was the English imperative:

Smash the Capitalist Patriarchy!

And below it, in the Doctor's mother tongue, like a cry,

Liberacion!

Liberation! The lovely Spanish sound was like a ringing carillon, a door swinging open in the Doctor's heart. For the Doctor needed liberation now as much or more as any country. A long bloody arm had reached all the way from Dorado, directed, he was certain, by the government there, and murdered someone who had trusted in his protection – and the Doctor wanted to cry out, to tell someone, but knew not to whom or where to turn, certainly not the New York

Police – until fate had brought him once again face to face with *El Presidente* Rodolfo Benitez.

Of course, there were other Doradoan alliances the Doctor might have made – from MIRA to the PRS. But the Doctor, who could no longer bear to sit on the sidelines, needed to talk to a human being, not a set of initials – to a head and a heart, not a political agenda. And what a head and a heart Rodolfo Benitez had!

Thinker, poet, humanist, politician, Rodolfo Benitez Cayetano was the grand old man of South American affairs. He had been Dorado's President for six exhilarating days, fleeing the country – in a boat with Garcia – only when it became apparent he would be assassinated if he remained.

Since then, he had headed both a rebel army and a government-in-exile, consulting frequently with both Washington and Moscow, amid persistent rumors he would soon be called upon to lead his country once again. And while his exiled government might have seated itself in the luxurious suburbs of Mexico City or Madrid, the fact that it should choose to remain standing, as it were, among the poor people of the humble *barrio* was, to the Doctor's way of thinking, just another sign of Benitez's towering greatness.

The Doctor had heard the Great Man speak one summer day, many years ago, during his first and only visit to Dorado, soon after finishing medical school. He had arrived in the capitol at three in the morning after a thirsty, lurching bus ride through a million little tinhorn mountain towns – and when he had risen at eleven the next morning it had been to the fanfare of trumpets, and the oceanic murmur of a gathering throng. Still thirsty from the night before, he had rinsed out his mouth from a bottle of *gaseosa* and then, looking for somewhere to spit, had gone to the window and opened the shutters.

Christ, but it was beautiful! He had never seen such a sight before! The capitol sat in a natural hollow semicircled by the blunt blue peaks of the Siuna Hills. The mountains hugged the city like two blue arms, giving one the sense of being embraced and uplifted by the very terrain. The vent of the

Masaya volcano dispensed harmless puffs of blue smoke into the cloudless sky, while in the *Plaza de Luz* at the mountain's base a crowd was forming: a glittering sea of shirts and hats and banners that surged around the freshly cut lumber of a newly built speaker's platform.

The Doctor dressed quickly and hurried downstairs. Perhaps it was only the effects of the altitude, but he was lightheaded and panting with excitement by the time he reached the ragged edges of the crowd.

A brass band, out of tune, tantalized his soul with its triumphal disharmonies. Indians in bowler hats and ponchos squatted in the dust, roasting guinea pigs over smoking coals. Then a cry went up, and a dizzying roar; a car floated over to the side of the podium and a pink-skinned *hombre* in shirtsleeves emerged, unleashing the people with a wave of his hand. The Doctor stood on tiptoes, straining. It was *el candidato*: Rodolfo Benitez.

He hadn't been running for President then, just some local office, and yet the Doctor would never forget his speech that morning: for his words were not like fire, but food – nourishing and filling as the taste of tacos, black beans and rum. Benitez had spoken for more than two hours, and while his speech had been interrupted a hundred times by the mad *ding-a-ling* of cowbells and numerous little blizzards of confetti, never once had his audience's attention veered. The reason, the Doctor decided later, was simple: instead of talking politics, he had told them about themselves. He had spoken about the life of a miner, about the pride a woman feels on giving birth to a child, and the shame and anger that a person must know when his children are hungry, his wages withheld him, or his humanity denied. He had talked to them about the beauty of their women, the brutality of the soldiers, the courage of the people, the indifference of the priests – so that by the end, his speech was not like a speech at all, but a tour through a hundred tinhorn mountain towns, an oracular rosary, a golden string of sound on which a thousand peasant hearts were strung.

The Doctor would always remember that day. And yet it

was not only Benitez's words that were inscribed inside him; he remembered everything about it: the stainless sky, the dry blue hills, the benign scrawl of the silent volcano.

And so the previous morning when President Benitez, whose physician was away, had returned to the Doctor complaining of another pain, the Doctor had been more than pleased. Benitez's bodyguard, prevented from attending the examination, had waited gracelessly, cracking his knuckles, in the waiting room outside. Finally, toward the end of the exam, the Doctor could restrain himself no longer and had said to the silent, pink-skinned, silver-haired old man: 'You know, *Señor*, I admire you greatly. Of all the many *hombres* who have tried so long to lead . . .'

El Presidente had looked uncomfortable and attempted to cut the Doctor off, but he persisted. And then, without even planning on it, the Doctor had confessed, telling Benitez about Vazpana's murder, and what he knew of AES and MIRA. And when he was done, he felt better than he had in days, as if the pressure on his heart had been relieved.

Benitez listened until the Doctor was finished, then asked quietly, 'And why are you telling me this, *Señor*?'

'Because I trust you. And because I thought that you should know – in case you need to . . . intervene.'

Benitez looked sad. 'If an agent of MIRA is assassinated by the Dorado secret police on the streets of New York City, what can I, the exiled President of Dorado, do?'

But the Doctor was not fooled by Benitez's apparent humility or impotence. 'Nothing, perhaps. Still, I thought that you should know. No one else does; they haven't even found the body yet.'

'Then I am honored by your confidence.'

'Also, your Excellency, I am afraid that Captain Ambrosio Garcia may be next on AES's hit list. He is being threatened as well.'

'Threatened? How?'

'He's receiving . . . little dolls . . .' It sounded stupid now when the Doctor said it.

'*Dolls*?'

162

'Yes, you know. *Porqueria*, pig things.'

Benitez sighed. 'That, I am afraid, is out of my league. Perhaps he should consult a spiritualist.'

'He thinks it is AES who is behind it.'

'AES? Maybe. But if so, they're even kinkier than I remember them. Finished?'

'Yes, of course. As I told you before, it is only a touch of diverticulitis. You may get dressed ... I'm prescribing another antibiotic.'

But as the Great Man dressed, the Doctor found himself saying, 'I hear a lot. You'd be surprised. All kinds of things that might be of interest to you ... and to your people.'

'You are saying ... ?'

'I am saying that while I cannot claim to be much good with a weapon, or a master at military or political campaigns, I think I could, in some small way, be useful to your cause.'

Benitez had looked at the Doctor then, as if the thought had never occurred to him. 'You are offering ...'

'My services,' the Doctor said with a small bow. He hurriedly went on. 'Oh, nothing that would violate my Hippocratic oath, of course, but other things: the names of agents, who is currently loyal to whom. You'd be surprised the kinds of things I hear. For instance, did you know ... ?' And the Doctor had then proceeded to unravel another tiny knot in the great ball of string that was South American politics.

When he was finished, he fell silent, embarrassed. What was he doing? He felt like a high school student trying to land a summer job. But he was even more surprised at how much it meant to him – how much he wanted the Great Man to accept him, to give his life meaning and purpose again.

'You know, Doctor, if I decide to take you on ... my organization is small, I could not afford to ... pay you anything.'

'*Pay* me?' the Doctor nearly shrieked. 'But, *Señor*, it's not money ...' And then the Doctor had gone on at length – a confused and emotional confession – about democracy and humanism and *dinero* and the debt the Doctor, 'nay, the whole human world,' owed Rodolfo Benitez for his masterful leadership of the democratic cause.

When the Doctor was finished, as though put off by his passion, the old man said, 'Well, maybe. We will see. I'll contact you. Don't do anything until then. Thank you.' And then he had left, taking the help of his bodyguard as he made his way down the stairs to the curb. The Doctor followed him, calling out from the stoop: 'I will wait to hear from you, *Señor*. There is much more I can tell you!' But Benitez had only nodded and waved, disappearing into his waiting limousine. '*Man in the Vanguard!*' the Doctor had shouted, as the car pulled away. It was the Great Man's motto.

The Doctor had been on tenterhooks for the rest of the day, uncertain if his help would be accepted. Benitez's *nom de guerre* was *Chino* – the Chinaman – not because of his political sympathies, but because of his opaque and inscrutable air.

But the Doctor's help was not rejected, nor had he long to wait for a reply. In his mailbox that evening was a handwritten note:

Offer accepted. Debriefing tomorrow noon in the confessional at St. Elvira's. Man in the Vanguard!

The Doctor had received this message sixteen hours ago and from that moment on, his life had changed. Suddenly, he was not just another unfortunate Cuban physician shunting between his office, hospital, and home, but a confidential agent *disguised* as an unfortunate Cuban physician, and this slight adjustment in his identity made all the difference. This morning at breakfast, for instance, as he sipped his *café con leche*, a part of him had stood apart and watched himself drink – watched Arsenio Eduardo Castellano, secret eyes and ears of Rodolfo Benitez, fuel himself for the morning's work.

The Doctor's new role also gave him room to dream: though yesterday he had been an unknown no one, today the Doctor felt connected to the very heart and groin of history, to the racing pulse and wet pudendum of the times. He could hardly wait for the midday meeting. And though he had no illusions that the interview would be personally conducted by Benitez, he had no doubts at all that his intelligence – given its import – would soon reach Benitez's ears. After that, it was clearly just a matter of time before Benitez dropped the middle man and began asking the Doctor's opinion on other matters, as well.

Just a matter of time, too, was Benitez's return to the Presidency of Dorado; and after that, who knew on what stage the Doctor would be standing? Perhaps he would be given a portfolio in the President's new cabinet – Minister of Health Services, say. And from *there*, given the kind of job a fellow like the Doctor always did, wasn't it inevitable that his statue would someday be erected in *La Plaza de Luz*? The Doctor envisioned the statue they would build of him. A masterpiece, the eyes were keen, the pose heroic, the nose sensitive and long, its whole effect so inspiring and grand that the Doctor looked around him now, half expecting to see it standing there before him – but all he saw was the filthy park and the yellow bees which were feasting obscenely on the pink cream of a broken cruller.

He looked at his watch. It was time to go.

Leaving the park and crossing the street, he entered the door of St. Elvira's. It was cool and dim in the little church, and the air was sweet with the scent of myrrh. Moisture pilled and beaded on the walls like sweat from pores in the living stone. The Doctor instinctively removed his hat, though he did not bless himself from the stone font of holy water, genuflect before the tabernacle, or bow his head before the gruesome image of the wounded god, but walked directly to the wooden confessional in the rear, drew back a curtain, and slipped inside. He pulled the curtain shut and knelt there in the scented dark until he heard the screen slide open and a man's voice with a cigarette edge declare, 'Man in the Vanguard.'

'Man in the Vanguard,' the Doctor rejoined.

'Go ahead.'

'So,' he said, wondering where to begin, 'the police have found Vazpana's body.'

'When?'

'Oh, about an hour ago.'

'And why was he here?' the voice rasped.

'Why? I don't know exactly. According to my sources, it may have been to purchase arms. For MIRA. Though whether he succeeded in this or not before he died, I cannot tell you.'

'Who killed him?'

'Who? AES, we believe. But I told the President all this yesterday.'

'Tell it again.'

The Doctor wiped his brow. Though it was cool in the confessional, like a penitent, he found himself sweating. 'I understand that AES has an agent here – though as of yet we don't know his name. Do you?'

But there was no response from the faceless presence on the other side of the silken screen – not a word, not a sign. It was, the Doctor thought, like talking to God.

Then the Doctor smelled smoke. A vaporish tendril curled through the screen into the sweet dark box. And though the Doctor's mind no longer believed in the Catholic religion, he was momentarily shocked by this sacrilege – as though his senses still did. Smoking in church! No, it was not immoral, only dangerous. If someone saw smoke coming from the priest's cubby . . .

'Christ, what are you doing?'

'Sorry,' the voice said quickly. 'I forgot where we were.'

'You forget where you were?' the Doctor hissed. 'Well, I'll tell you where you are. You are in church. Pretending to be a priest. My God, what's the matter with you?'

'Have you anything else to report?'

'No!'

'Then tell us this. We understand there is a second MIRA agent here. A high-ranking officer.'

'Yes,' the Doctor said, delighted to be able to furnish the name. 'Captain William Crespi.'

'And where is this Captain Crespi now?'

'I don't know. My informants, however, are investigating the matter.'

'Good. You'll be notified soon of the time of our next meeting. *Man in the Vanguard*,' and the screen slid shut.

The Doctor stood up and snatched back the curtain so fast that it shrieked up on the wooden rod. He stepped into the fragrant dusk and stood there, blinking, his heart racing, still smelling the tobacco fumes. For a moment he considered opening the priest's cubby just to surprise the idiot inside. But such insubordination would have been reported to Benitez. And so the Doctor, good spy and soldier, furtively departed, leaving the church by a side exit with a guilty grin and sliding eyes – the way an upperclass gentleman leaves a lower-class bordello.

The Maiden Makeless

◆

Chapter 3

Early that morning, he had dreamt of her again. In the dream, his wife was alive and they were being chased by some invisible force down a long metal corridor. The power that was pursuing them was like a conscious wind. Higgins pressed himself against his wife to protect her from it and as he did, he felt the spirit's presence brush him with its wings, and could feel it still, searching for them, as it moved away down the long metal hallway.

But when Higgins turned to his wife to tell her it was gone – her head was missing. He recoiled, sickened by the flapping sheaf of nerves and veins protruding from her neck. Though headless, she remained standing, her icy fingers gripping his wrist.

And that was when he saw the young *mestiza* girl levitating in the air before him.

Astonished, he awoke. Though even then, he could feel the grip of his wife's ghostly fingers, and he rubbed his wrist distractedly, as though to rub the dream away.

For a day and a night, Higgins had kept the lid on his terror. In fact, he had managed to be almost blasé about the murder, as if this sort of thing was only to be expected when one vacationed in New York City. But the morning's dream had uncapped his panic, and lying there, he felt at once revolted and appalled. Oh, the horror of it, the butchery!

Only last night, he had found a dried disc of Jorge's blood on the handle of his toothbrush.

But even worse than the feeling of contamination was Higgins' gnawing sense of guilt. It was not guilt over Jorge's death so much – for what could he have done to stop it? Rather, it arose from the *relief* he felt that, with Jorge dead, his secret was safe and he would not be blackmailed. Though Higgins was also acutely aware, that if this were known, it might look as if he had his own excellent reasons for wanting Jorge dead.

Higgins got out of bed. He took a shower, drank some coffee, read the New York *Times*, and then – since no one else was about – went back to his room. He didn't even try to meditate this morning. He was too upset. It was all starting to hit him now; the shock at last was wearing off.

Higgins considered going back to Boston – his weekend in New York was definitely over.

Then again, Higgins told himself, maybe what was bothering him was the Doctor's sister. Maybe it wasn't death – but sex. Yes! Though there certainly hadn't been any of that!

For their 'date' the other night had been a fiasco. 'I can't stay out late. The kids might need me.' On this unpromising note the evening had started. At one, they had gone to a club in the Village where the music was too loud, stayed for an hour, then left, gone home and been in separate beds by three – or would have been if Higgins had not discovered a dead person in his. Real swell time. Had to do it again.

At one point, during the cab ride home, Higgins had asked her why she'd never married.

'Why? Because I didn't want to. That's why.'

'You didn't love the fathers of your children?'

'You could put it that way.'

Higgins wondered why she had slept with them then, but the question seemed rather chauvinistic and naive. Had he loved every woman *he* had slept with? Christ, he couldn't even remember some of their *names*.

More to the point was why she had kept the children?

'We're getting awfully nosey, aren't we?'

'I've been getting a lot of "disinformation" lately. I just thought I'd hear it from the horse's mouth.'

'And *I* am the *horse*?'

It was a bad connection. His timing was off. There was no good-night kiss. As soon as they pulled up at the Doctor's apartment, she nodded and went inside; though later that night, after he had discovered the boy's headless corpse and was lying in shock on the Doctor's couch, she had stuck her head in the living-room doorway and said, 'I thought you will be needing this,' and placed a pillow, sheets, and blanket on a table by the door.

'Come here,' Higgins said in a passionate whisper, but by then she had withdrawn her head and he said it to the darkness.

Needing something to distract him, Higgins opened up a manuscript he'd brought. The words looked like Sanskrit – which, in fact, he saw they were. He read for a while, making notations in the margins, but he couldn't really concentrate. He kept on seeing his dead roommate's head superimposed upon the *devanagari*.

And so now when Gil stuck her nose in the doorway and asked if he was busy, Higgins did not look happy, and with an aggrieved and aggravated gesture, he pushed the troublesome manuscript aside.

'Am I disturbing?'

'Very. But come in anyway,' Higgins said. He closed the folder.

'You were riding,' she said with a Spanish t.

'I was trying,' Higgins said.

'I admire riders,' she said frankly. 'I imagine that it's difficult to ride.'

'It's difficult to ride well,' Higgins agreed.

'May I?' she asked, and took a seat on the couch. She was dressed like a peasant; a modern peasant. It was your Indo-Chinese Boat Person look: cutoffs, t-shirt and cheap rubber flip-flops. Higgins who'd been up for hours had the feeling she had not. Nor, after the other night, could he imagine what she wanted.

'Something is happening to my brother, isn't it, Mr. Higgins?'

'Happening?'

'With his money, I mean.'

Higgins thought for a moment. The Doctor's predicament was well known on the street. There was no real confidence he would be breaking. 'All right,' he said, and he explained to Gil what he knew of the matter. He told her about the payments, the *vigorish*, the threats, and the debt that had grown like a cancerous gland. She listened intently, without interruption, and when he was finished, she paused and considered everything he had told her, then said she still didn't understand why the debt could not eventually be repaid. And Higgins had patiently explained to her then how there are certain people you must never allow to do you favors, people to whom, once you were indebted, you were forever enthralled.

'But who *are* these people?'

Higgins shrugged. '*Pistoleros*.'

'Political?'

'I don't think so.'

'Oh, I am sure of it,' she said. 'For as long as I've known him, my brother has always been involved in some filthy political thing. But you must know.'

'No. He doesn't talk to me about it.'

'That's because he thinks he's a spy. He thinks he is the Simon Bolivar of the *barrio*.' She paused a moment. 'And do you think these people intend to hurt him?'

Higgins didn't care to answer that one. For the truth of the matter was he didn't know.

'And what do you plan to do about it? Or is this whole thing just too dangerous for you?'

'It's dangerous, all right,' Higgins said. He remembered again the headless corpse, and the violence and cruelty sleeping in Omar's bedroom eyes.

'Yes?' she said coldly. 'So then why don't you go back

home where everything is nice and cozy? Or are you like my brother – here to perform some sociological experiment with the unfortunate from which, you believe, you will emerge reborn?' Her irony was not kind.

'The only experiments I intend to perform are on myself, thank you,' Higgins said just as coldly.

She looked away. 'I'm sorry,' she said, 'but this whole thing is quite upsetting. You see, I love my brother. And me and my children . . . we have to live here for a while.'

'Why's that?'

''Cause we can't get back into our apartment. Guy I sublet it to won't get out. Says we signed a contract.' She laughed. 'He's right. We did. Well,' she sighed, relaxing slightly. 'I guess it could be worse.'

'It is,' Higgins said, and he told her then about Vazpana.

She took it well; didn't flinch, at all. He had to admire her self-control. 'And you have no idea who did this . . . murder?'

Higgins held up the queer feathered fetish.

'What's that?'

'Something we found next to the body.'

'But what is it? Where's it from?'

'Nobody seems to know.'

Gil thought for a moment. 'I know someone who might.'

'You do?'

'Yes. She is very secretive. Strange. But *good*. Sometimes when people have questions, they go to her.'

'And?'

'Sometimes she answers them.'

'And sometimes she doesn't?'

'Sometimes she says . . . the Fakir will not let her.'

'The Fakir? And who the hell is that?'

'That, I believe, is her name for God.'

'Oh.'

'Some people say she is a saint.'

'Oh, yeah?' Higgins said. Though he sincerely doubted it, he found himself intrigued. He thought for a moment. 'And if I wanted to meet this person, where would I find her?'

172

Gil shrugged. 'Sometimes you may see her wandering about the *barrio*, but mostly she stays in a house by the river.'

'You've met her then?'

She nodded. 'Once. With my cousin Armando. We went to her to get her blessing when his mother had cancer, but Sara – that is her name – said we did not need it, only to remember this: that God is nice.'

'God is *nice*?'

'That's what she said. *Amable*. Nice. Kind.'

'Oh,' Higgins said, who had never thought that God was that.

'At any rate, the cancer went away. When they looked again, they couldn't find it.'

Higgins was intrigued. 'And where did you say this person lives?'

'Here. I will show you,' Gil said, and she had Higgins stand and face the window. 'Two blocks down there,' – she pointed east – 'everything ends. No one lives beyond there, except some junkies and *putas* . . . and her.'

And indeed, beyond the second intersection, the buildings still standing were untenanted shells, and there began a tract of rust-colored waste so monotonous and drear, it might have been Mars. 'If you follow that street for a quarter of a mile, it will lead you to a house – one of the few that is still standing. Sometimes, you may find her there.'

'Since you know where it is, why don't you show me?'

Gil's mouth developed a listing smile. 'I'm afraid.'

'Afraid of me?'

'Of her.'

'Of *her*? But why?'

'You will see. I tell you, she is . . . very odd. She is not how you think a saint would behave.'

'Ah . . . "like a child or a madman, a ghoul, or an inert thing".'

'What is that?'

'Just a line from a poet I'm fond of.'

'Yes. Like that.'

But Higgins was having difficulty focusing on the

173

conversation. Gil was standing next to him by the window and he knew now that if she moved a millimeter closer they would either come together – or fly apart. Higgins' arms suddenly ached to embrace her, his lips to smudge the soft brown fuzz that ran from her sideburns, dividing her cheek and ear. She was so close, he could smell her now. She smelled of soap and children; it was an odor he loved, simple and good, and impulsively, he curled an arm around her waist and drew her toward him. She looked him in the eye, but did not draw away.

'Your brother told me you were a real airhead, you know that?'

'How kind of him. What else did he say?'

'He said you were gay, and had the brains of a frog.'

'And you believed him?'

'Not any more. I think you're brilliant. Brilliant, and beautiful. And heterosexual.' It was the direct approach. Combined with flattery. This was Higgins' strategy.

The only problem was, it wasn't working this morning. Instead of throwing her hips into his and melting in his arms, she stood rooted and aloof, her heart guarded and unwon, like an animal.

'Do you know what my brother told me about *you*?'

'Let me guess. That I was rich and handsome, a fine poet, a marvelous lover and that I had a superb sense of humor.'

She raised her eyebrows. 'You're modest too.''

Higgins laughed.

'No. He told me to stay away from you, that you had had a nervous breakdown.'

'What!' Higgins cried. 'And you *believed* him?'

'Why not?'

'Damnit,' he said, pulling Gil closer, both anger and desire flirting in his blood. 'I'm not mad and you're not gay. And I didn't have a nervous breakdown! Which means there's nothing in the world to stop us. Is there?'

'Stop us from what?'

'Don't act dumb, Gil.' He looked her in the eye. 'Stop us from becoming lovers.'

She held his gaze for the longest time. 'Yes, there is.'
'What's that?'
'I don't want to,' she said, and slipped from his arms.

The Black Hen

◆

Chapter 4

Years ago, in another country, Garcia and a squad of soldiers had been sent to investigate a report of the plague. Upon reaching the village in question, however, a hard four days' ride through tick- and snake-infested hills, they had found no one alive who could answer their questions – only the grim pantomime of corpses, the drumming wings of waddling vultures, and the terrible eloquence of a hundred human bodies suppurating beneath a jungle sun. An inspection of the dead disproved the rumors: the villagers had not died from any illness, save the mental illness of their fellow men.

Garcia, who had seen a lot of killing, had never seen such a killing as this. A revolutionary slogan, daubed in blood on the mud walls of several huts, proclaimed it the work of *Comandante* Montenegro's People's Forces, a guerrilla army stationed in the hills. But evidence at the scene contradicted this ascription. Empty cartridges unearthed from the mud were stamped *FNM* for *Fabrica National de Municion*, the government factory which sold only to the army, and there was the impression of helicopter skidmarks in a clearing two kilometers from the little town – ammunition and equipment unknown to the guerrillas – while the dog tag of one Leon Blades, a lieutenant in AES, and the filter-tips of a dozen Winstons were found stamped into the grass.

Garcia, of course, had made a full report of the atrocity –

176

including evidence of *AES*'s guilt. But his commanding officer, after studying the matter, had concluded that the massacred Indians were rebels in disguise. 'Disguised as what?' Garcia asked, incensed. 'As pigs and chickens? Women and kids?'

Because Garcia would not let the matter die, a commission was appointed to investigate further. This was not unusual, since in Dorado there were always half a dozen investigations going at any one time. These commissions were like the bruise-colored clouds that piled up in the dry season high over Puerto Valle. The clouds rumbled and glowered and looked menacing from a distance, but except for some thunder and a lot of hot air, nothing ever came from them. This time, as so often happened, the trail of blood and lies had led to the sub-basement of the police station in Puerto Valle and to the office of Colonel Hercules Cordero – at which point, the commissioners had been warned they were infringing on matters of national security, and the investigation was turned over to the secret police who, they were assured, would secretly police themselves.

Now, years later, the 'Garcia Commission' had embarked upon a new investigation, but once again it was running into problems . . .

The Black Hen was not the type of establishment ordinarily frequented by Garcia, but by the poorest of the ghetto's poor. It was, without question, a sink of iniquity, a den of sin, nor was the sin that inhabited it anything exciting or pretty to look at, like some. Mostly, one encountered the demon of inebriation staring out the eyes of its clientele, attended by the trolls of lust, the shades of grief, and the hobgoblins of petty thievery. Its one long room was shuttered against daylight and fulsome with the scent of unclean taps and lines. Crutches stood against a wall, their handles and crosspieces padded with rags. Everything about it was tired, sick and worn. Even the boy behind the bar looked wizened, as did the teenage girl who waited tables, like children abducted by fairies centuries ago.

At the end of the bar, two toothless old persons of indeterminate gender stared in wonder at the distorted shadows flickering across the black and white TV. The show, Garcia noted, was a rerun of *The Munsters* dubbed in Spanish. Here and there, among the ragged clientele, were a few men who were decently dressed. Garcia couldn't imagine why anyone who could afford not to would choose to drink amidst such squalor, unless they wished to chase their rum with the juice of the odious, the wine of the damned.

Garcia ordered a bottle of *Presidente*, and then, on second thought, a glass as well. A particle of hardened foodstuff was stuck to its rim. Garcia, who was not ordinarily a fastidious person, surprised himself by demanding another, annoyed and offended by the dirty vessel, the dark, unclean room and the sweet yeasty fumes of beer. A second glass was clean, if clouded, like a crystal ball. Garcia carried it to a table at the rear where a childish figure was huddled over a bowl of soup. The figure was smoking while it ate, alternating steaming mouthfuls of dinner with silken lungfuls of yellow smoke. The figure had the proportions of a boy, but here the resemblance ended, for its cheeks were clothed with a blue-black beard that was more like fur than human hair. The furred cheeks, slicked hair, and prominent incisors gave the man the look of a rodent – or if not a rat exactly, then perhaps a mink or a ferret. The man's name was Dante Guzman, his nickname, *Sangre de Charco*, 'Pool of Blood.'

'I need some information,' Garcia said, without greeting or affection. Guzman continued sipping his soup. Garcia reached in his pocket and peeled five ones from a small sweaty roll. He folded them once, then pushed the bills beneath the tureen. Guzman kept eating, his movements secretive and quick, like a rat intent on finishing its cheese. Garcia waited, then said, 'But perhaps you are not interested,' and reached for the money. A little paw shot out, trapping it on the table.

Garcia recalled the first time he had met Guzman in the basement corridors of the secret police station. In Garcia's innocence, he had thought that Guzman was a painter, as his face and clothes were speckled red. It was only later, when he learned his occupation, that Garcia had realized the 'paint' on Guzman's flesh and clothing was some poor bastard's spattered blood.

For Guzman had been the Generalissimo's torturer, a master of the *picano*, the *capucho* and the tentacled *pulpo* and a hundred and one other instruments of fright and pain. He had worked in the dungeons of the secret police, gouging eyeballs, screwing limbs and connecting up the electrodes of the *pulpo* and *picano* to various parts of the prisoners' bodies as he roasted them over the *parrilla*, the grill.

'What do you want to know, my *Capitán*?' Guzman said, pronouncing the title with the same leering sneer he always employed, as if to say captains meant nothing to him, or colonels or kings – or archbishops, for that matter. He had had them all in his hands and they had all screamed with terror, whatever their rank, when the rubber *capucho* was strapped to their heads.

'I just told you. Information. I understand you keep track of these things.'

'Have to,' the man fairly snarled with rage. 'Do you know how many pimps and *putas* would like nothing more than to wear my balls around their neck?'

'A lot, I would imagine,' Garcia sighed. 'You were a most unpopular man.'

'Ha!' Guzman said. The dish he was eating was Galician soup. A slimy white knucklebone gleamed in the bowl.

'Yes,' Garcia continued. 'I would imagine you must keep an eye out for those you hurt but did not kill.'

'And their brothers. And their husbands. And their faggoty friends.' Guzman scowled. 'I am a hunted man. And anyway. You yourself brought them to me.'

It was shameful, but true. For while Garcia thoroughly despised Dante Guzman, there had been times he had delivered up prisoners to him. One prisoner, a young lieutenant in the Boars, had begged Garcia to let him use the bathroom, then slit his throat on the jagged edges of a metal sink rather than fall into Guzman's brutal hands.

After that, at the risk of his own life, Garcia had let his

captives go rather than hand them over to Guzman. Once, he had driven to the *Plaza de Paz* and picked up one of the corpses that sprouted there like mushrooms overnight. He had delivered this body to Guzman instead. 'She's dead,' Guzman said. 'Oh, is she?' Garcia asked, hard as nails. 'What a pity, eh? I only meant to help her remember.' He shuddered now to even think of it.

'I came here for information. If you don't have any . . .'

'I have plenty.'

'About AES?' Garcia asked.

'Ah! *AES*, is it?' Guzman smiled a weasel's grin. '*That* information will cost you more *pesos*, my Captain.'

Garcia counted out another four dollars – one of them in change. Both men were so poor, this trifling sum was all Garcia could afford, but more than enough to loosen Guzman's tongue. Perhaps in other circles, political intelligence fetched extraordinary prices, but here in *La Negra Polla* almost anything – or body – could be had for the price of a couple of rounds.

'AES has an operative here. Yes.'

'Name?'

'Schmidt. Lieutenant Colonel Adolfo Schmidt.'

Garcia searched his brain, but the name meant nothing to him.

'I also hear . . .'

'Yes?'

'Two agents of MIRA named Vazpana and Crespi are looking for this Schmidt. Or were. Schmidt, it seems, found one of them first.'

'What are you talking about?'

'Where've you been, man? Didn't you hear? Somebody cut off Vazpana's head.'

Garcia lurched, overturning his glass of beer. 'What? When?'

'You didn't know? They found his body. Sometime this morning. But you didn't need me to learn that, *amigo*. All you had to do was read the papers. Hey, Ambrosio, you don't look so good.'

Garcia watched the river of beer edge toward the end of the table and spill – but it seemed as distant and unrelated to him as a waterfall on some other planet. 'No,' he said faintly. 'I hadn't heard.' He sat back down, remembering the last time he had seen Vazpana. He had been *alive*! He wondered if the Doctor knew.

At last, he turned to Guzman and said, 'Find me this Schmidt. And this one from MIRA . . . this Captain Crespi.' He thought for a moment. 'And their local contacts, if they have them.'

'I will see what I hear.'

'Yes, and I will hear what you see. And, *amigo*,' he said in an ominous tone. 'Don't waste my time.'

Garcia stood up, throwing down a dollar for the girl who waited tables. He started to leave; then, stopped, and looking back at Guzman, picked the dollar bill back up, and gave it to the girl directly.

The Examination

◆

Chapter 5

Helena de Jesus, the Doctor's mistress, was getting on the Doctor's nerves. When she telephoned his office, which she did each day when she awoke around noon, the sound of her voice made the Doctor queasy, besides interrupting his lunch. For Helena's body was a playground for all manner of minor ailments and complaints and she only called to bore him to death with a recitation of her hypochondriacal woes. One week it was a mole on her stomach which she thought was turning color, the next, a yeast infection for which she somehow blamed the Doctor, the week after that it was 'an ache between the eyes,' the following day it was a stiff neck. Would the Doctor please bring over a hot water bottle for the pain?

'You buy them at the drugstore,' the Doctor said. 'You don't get them from your doctor.'

'Oh, Arsenio, *por favor*!'

In fact, the Doctor knew his beloved's medical history far more intimately than a man might wish. He had no desire to accompany her each month on her menstrual cycle, to chart her rashes, or to graph the frequency of her dyspepsia. And yet that was all they spoke about! From the moment the Doctor lifted the receiver, Helena talked about herself with the one-pointed concentration of a mindreader or a fiend. There was no other topic on which she conversed. Though the Doctor led a somewhat interesting life and experienced any number of bizarre and moving occurrences in the course of a day, she never asked about one of them. There were only her anxieties and her all-consuming ills, the restless night she'd passed, the weakness of her stomach, her watery stools. She was not his mistress, she was his patient. He saw this clearly now.

The telephone rang. It was her, of course.

'I am busy,' the Doctor said. 'I cannot talk now.'

'You're always busy,' she said petulantly. 'You neglect me.'

'Oh, for Christsake,' the Doctor said, fed up to here.

'You neglect me and I'm sick. I could die. Then you'd be sorry.'

'No, I wouldn't,' the Doctor said.

'What?'

'I said, no one dies from a stiff neck.'

'Actually, my neck is better today, *caro mio*. It's my stomach, again. Arsenio, are you there?'

The Doctor was there. In fact, the Doctor was there for the next ten minutes as he listened to her familiar harangue, to the humorless, one-sided and self-absorbed litany of ills which she made subtly but perfectly clear the Doctor was somehow responsible for, indirectly through neglect – and before she was through this June noon the Doctor knew he didn't love her anymore and could not for the life of him imagine how or why he ever had.

'I have had a hard day myself,' the Doctor said at last. 'And now I am tired. Never once do you ask me how it is I am. I don't give a fuck about the kink in your neck – is that clear? And now, you will leave me alone.'

The silence was awesome. The Doctor had never spoken to his mistress this way before. Then his unbeloved hung up the phone. She was highly insulted. The Doctor smiled. He drew a deep breath. It was an unexpectedly liberating sensation to finally spit out the truth. It was like the hairball the cat had coughed up last week after months of gagging. For suddenly the Doctor could breathe again. Suddenly – after months? years? how long had it been? – he was free of her sick prattle, her dreary illnesses, her wretched drivel, her stools, her nerves. Why had he not ended their silly intimacy ages ago?

Then the phone began to ring again. It was Helena, of course. Recovered from the initial shock, she was not about to let the Doctor get away with his cruel remarks. The Doctor lifted the receiver, then brought it down again with a sharp crack. An insult to the eardrum! Yes. Let her complain about that one! In Helena's condition, it could prove dangerous, fatal even. Who knows? He cackled happily. The Doctor had never behaved this way before.

But no sooner had he slammed the receiver down than the phone began to ring once more. This time he didn't answer it. He was not obliged. Oh, he could not hide from Helena's wrath forever. He knew that. But he was under no obligation to confront it now.

No obligation. No strings attached, the Doctor said to himself, feeling his newly won freedom throb like blood in his throat. Ah, how good it felt to be free again! And he remembered now the girl he had met the other night at La Club, the 'white girl,' as the Doctor mentally called her (though his flesh was nearly as pale as hers). Clearly, she found him a man after her own heart, a man of magnetism, authority, and charm. Yes. He liked her, he told himself. She was just a girl, of course, but she did not whine. She did not lie around in bed all day sucking mentholated coughdrops and wiping her nose with crumpled tissues. She did not smell of liniment, eucalyptus oil, and middle age. She was not surrounded – in the Doctor's mind at least – by over-the-counter remedies to remove earwax, tobacco stains, and facial hair. Ah, how glad he was to be rid of Helena!

The phone had stopped ringing and the Doctor took this opportunity to eat his lunch. He drew a chicken wing from a grease-stained paper sack and bit into it. But when he looked up again, the white girl was standing in his waiting room doorway. He gasped, sucking down a piece of gristle, and suffered a violent fit of choking until a powerful whack on the Doctor's back popped it back out and he could breathe again. It was an inauspicious start to an unlikely relationship. Still, the Doctor thought, life is neither square nor round.

'Thank you,' the Doctor rasped, wiping tears from his eyes.

'Think nothing of it, Doc,' the girl said in her friendly offhand way. She looked about the examining room. 'Nice setup you got here,' she said, chewing gum.

The Doctor looked up, expecting to see the dingy office transformed – such is the power of words – but alas, it was the same dreary hole he had worked out of for the past fourteen years. And the Doctor realized then – quite clearly – it was funny how the truth will out – that he had jettisoned his mistress a moment ago to clear the way for the coming of this girl.

'Am I interrupting, Doc?'

'On the contrary,' the Doctor said. 'You saved my life.'

'Yeah?' the girl asked in her offhand way, as though she had saved him a parking place instead. Then she frowned at him, studying him hard. 'Hey, Mister. Haven't we met somewheres before?'

'Where?'

'Don't know.' He watched her memory struggle to place him. 'You ever been to the Boom-Boom Room in Philly?'

'The what?'

She shrugged. 'You ain't missing much.' She squinted at him. 'Maybe in some other life, eh, Doc? What's that called? Incarnations? You believe in that stuff?'

But, no, the Doctor did not believe. Such beliefs were merely wishful thinking. And if they weren't, then why did people with the most miserable presents and dismal futures always claim the most glamorous pasts? Everyone, it seemed, had been a Queen of Egypt, a King of Atlantis, or a follower of Christ. The Doctor was acquainted with two young playwrights, both of whom, in their previous incarnations, had been James Joyce. No. Arsenio Castellano was too much of a scientist to be gulled by such magical imaginings invented to glorify lives that were as dull as a day on the unemployment line. 'But you did not come to discuss such matters, I am sure.'

'Yeah, you're right.' She sighed. 'See, Doc, I got this . . . this *thing*,' she said with her hill-country twang. 'It's bothering the hell out of me.'

'What *thing*?' the Doctor said, putting the chicken wing down. 'Where?'

'Uh . . . down there,' she said, with the same maddening prudery of many of his patients.

'Down *where*?' the Doctor insisted. 'Thirty-fourth Street?'

'Doc,' she said, rolling her eyes in exasperation. '*You* know.'

And yes, the Doctor supposed he did. But even more incredibly, at her words, the Doctor's heart took a dive. She hadn't come to him out of interest, out of love, as he had hoped. She had come to him because she was sick, that was all. Nothing personal. Forget it, Doc. Don't get your hopes up.

And then the Doctor had a second, truer thought. That she was not sick at all. That she had come here to spy on him. And at this thought, the Doctor's heart descended into hell.

'Well,' the Doctor coughed into his fist, standing up briskly to cover his chagrin. 'What exactly seems to be the problem?'

'Doc,' she said with real frustration now. 'I don't know. You're the doc! What do you think I came to you for? Ain't you gonna examine me?'

And before he could answer, she had peeled off her blouse, flung it with a practiced flip across the back of a chair, and was sitting there before him in nothing but the filmiest and sheerest of brassières.

The Doctor was not amused. So, he thought, first he would be seduced. Well, two could play this game.

'Yes. But, first,' he said, 'you must answer some questions. You must fill out this . . . *form*,' he said holding up a clipboard.

'*Form*?' she asked, in despair.

'Now, what is your name?'

'Told you the other night,' she said in a surly voice, folding her skinny arms below her enchanting breasts. 'Don't you remember? Janie. Janie Ray.'

'Janie Ray,' the Doctor wrote. A likely alias if he'd ever heard one.

'And where do you live, Janie Ray?'

'Staying with friends.'

'Friends, is it? Ahh.' The Doctor pretended to scribble a note. 'Now – for your medical history.'

'Don't got none, Doc,' the girl said in her atrocious coal country English.

'Of course you do. When were you born?'

'Libra, Doc. Moon in Scorpio, Pisces rising.' And she named a year impossibly late into the nineteen-sixties. 'What about you?'

'I'll ask the questions. Now nod your head please if you have ever had any of the following . . .' and the Doctor ticked off a long list of illnesses – none of which the girl would admit to having had. 'But how is that possible?' the Doctor asked. 'You have never had measles? Never had the chicken pox?'

'Uh unh. Never been sick a day in my life. Told you. Ain't got no medical history.'

'Shots? Innoculations?'

'No, sir. Mom was agin it. Wouldn't allow them dern doctors anywheres near the hayouse. Said it was most unnatural. Said if the good Lord . . .'

'Yes, yes,' the Doctor said, familiar with the argument. 'But what about school? You must have had innoculations to go to school?'

'Didn't go to no school,' the girl said. 'Least not to no public school. You ever hear of the Mennonite Church?'

The Doctor looked doubtful.

'The Amish people?'

The Doctor shook his head.

'The Anabaptists? No? Well, you should of,' the girl said proudly. ''Cause that's where I'm from. My Momma was a righteous Amish lady – practically a saint, till Daddy left us and she shacked up with Mr. Roberts, the moolyon. One day, without uttering a word, Daddy he just up and walked right out of the hayouse.'

'The what?' the Doctor asked, straining his ears.

'The hayouse, Doc. You know. Place where you live?'

'Excuse me,' the Doctor said. 'You mean, *house*. Your accent . . .'

'Doc,' she said sharply. 'If I was you I wouldn't be poking fun of *no*body's accent . . .'

'I assure you, I wasn't making fun . . .'

''Cause it ain't nice,' she said, like the sweet and simple country bumpkin that she was – or was she? He wasn't sure now.

'All right,' the Doctor said firmly. 'Hop up on the table.'

And again, before the Doctor could stop her, she stepped from her jeans and flung them in the same direction as her top, standing there proudly now wearing nothing but her lingerie, pantyhose, bobby pins and her long young bones – clearly the nicest thing that had happened to the Doctor's office in years. Her flesh was so young and fresh, the Doctor had the feeling it would squeak if touched.

'You will lie down on the table,' he barked. 'Head toward the window. Hurry up, I haven't got all day.'

He heard her climb up, or rather heard the squish of her buttocks and the squeak of the paper.

'I am going to wash my hands,' the Doctor said and disappeared into the bathroom with her purse. He emptied its contents into the sink. There were tubes of lipstick, an eyebrow pencil, loose change, keys, cigarettes, tissues, a book of matches from Tito's lounge, 13th and Arch Street, Philadelphia, but nothing incriminating. He opened her wallet. A Pennsylvania driver's license read: Jane Lynn Ray. He flipped through her address book – looking for what? A Spanish surname, a set of political initials? But her friends all had names like Goose, Smoker, Mrs Pennington and Al.

But when the Doctor came out, clutching her purse, her eyes went from gray shock to blue anger in an instant. 'Hey, mister, what the hell you doing?'

'I am trying to figure out who you are.'

'You ain't got no right goin' through my things!'

The Doctor sighed and approached his patient, wearing his most stern and professional air. 'Let's cut the shit, shall we Jane? Now who are you and what are you doing here?'

'Waiting on you to examine me, fool.'

'The hell you are,' the Doctor said. 'Who are you working for? Come on. Tell me. Is it *El Duende*? Is it AES?'

'Who the hell's Ace?'

'*Aparato del Estado Securidad*,' the Doctor hissed. He grabbed her by her silken neck and pressed the carotid cords on either side of her throat, shutting off the supply of blood to her brain. It was a cruel and simple punishment, no more strenuous than pushing a button, and her face went a ghostly gray and her eyes rolled up into her head. The Doctor loosened his grip and asked again, 'Who are you working for?'

'Oww!'

'You're working for *El Duende*, aren't you? He sent you here to set me up. Tell me!'

'Fuck you!' she said, and tried to kick him.

The Doctor pressed again and watched the sweat break out on her brow, and her eyes roll whitely in their sockets, like a dying fish turning belly-up.

'Who are you?'

'You're *hurting* me!'

But the Doctor was doing more than hurting. Shameful to say, he was becoming sexually aroused. He squeezed again and felt a vicious thrill. To control her like that with just a squeeze of his fingers, to watch her struggle in fear and writhe in helpless agony was an unexpected aphrodisiac, so that for one maniacal instant, the Doctor knew the dirty joy that torturers and sex-fiends feel as they strangulate their helpless prey. The Doctor squeezed again, watched her eyes roll sickly in her head, and feasted on her naked back. He could see where the straps of her bra had bitten into her thin, young shoulders, and the Doctor had a ferocious urge to cover her bare trapezius with kisses.

He opened his hand, like a man waking from a passionate dream. What was the matter with him? She was crying now between strangled sobs. He had gotten carried away. She was coughing, gagging and gasping for air. Christ, another minute and he might have killed her.

Shaken, he threw her jeans at her and told her to put them on. He went into the waiting room and waited, amazed by the dirty thrill he had felt, at the way something deviate and ill inside him had responded to her pain. He could hear her whimpering through the door. He was sorry now he had been so cruel. It had all been a near-fatal misunderstanding. He would go back in, apologize, and send her on her way.

But when the Doctor re-entered, even her bobby pins were missing and her soft fair hair spilled down upon her naked back. Two blue bruises were surfacing on either side of her throat. And though the Doctor had seen thousands of naked women in his day, none had ever stirred him more than did this girl this summer afternoon. For her breasts . . . ah, her breasts were more beauteous than bells, while the curve of her rump was more delicious than a pie, and the sweet blond fleece of her groin engendered in the Doctor sensations as ancient as they were pleasurable and new. Unbearably, she was looking at him now with something hurt and wounded in her eyes. And he realized then she was not his enemy. She was not a spy. She was just a girl – a girl who loved him.

'You hurt me, you bastard.'

'You will forgive me. I am sorry. It could not be helped.'

'What the hell's the matter with you? You're supposed to help me – not kill me!'

'I had to make sure . . . who you were.'

'Well?' she said, taunting him now. 'Now that you got your jollies, you gonna examine me or what?' But she did not look at all like a patient waiting to be examined; she looked like a woman waiting to be loved.

The Doctor approached and placed his fingers just above the blond chevron of hair. He pressed. 'Does that hurt?'

'Lower,' she said and took his hand so that his fingers were involved in the soft blond fleece. She was wet, and he realized then with a stomach-churning thrill that they were a pair, that she, too, had been aroused by the torture.

190

She reached up then and kissed his mouth. And the Doctor found himself kissing her back and licking the slick wet silk of her lips lightly salted with sweat and tears. He sunk his face into her breasts, losing his mind in their indescribably rubbery, blubbery loveliness and largesse. And as he did he heard the ripping of his zipper, and a moment later his knees turned to water.

The Doctor was at once ecstatic and amazed – for no one had ever done this to him uninvited. He opened his mouth to ask what she was doing. But by then it was too late. By then, all the joy in all the world had converged upon the Doctor's groin. He contained it for an instant – and then it overflowed.

False Prophets

◆

Chapter 6

Once, in the wilds of Maine, Higgins had seen a chipmunk elude a weasel down a hole. The weasel, in hot pursuit, had come within a tail hair of catching its quarry, and was so upset by the loss of its supper, that it had run around the hole in small, crazed circles, making noises in its throat of extreme aggravation – noises that Higgins did not know that weasels made. Higgins remembered this now because these very same noises were coming from his own. He had had Gil in his hands; his palms had actually been cupping her buttocks, and somehow, *damnit*, she had got away from him.

Higgins told himself to forget about her and to think of other things, but he could not forget her, try as he might. Again and again, he saw the landscape of her flesh, the way an exile cannot forget the features of his beloved country – how the coastline looked in the moonlight, say, or the burning port that frightful night he put to sea. Higgins saw again the subtle groundswell of her young mommy's tummy, the polished ridges of her clavicles, the ivory line of her long, high bones, and the rounded hills of her luscious buttocks curving down and around into that mossy mound and secret cavern into which Higgins' single fervid wish was to enter, engender, surrender and die!

Higgins sighed and to try to take his mind off sex, performed some hatha yoga, including several postures guaranteed to rouse the sleeping *kundalini*. The sleeping *kundalini* remained sleeping, however. When he was finished, he drew the shades, sat down on the couch, pretzeled his legs into the half-lotus, and began to attend to the softly recurring circle of his breath.

It was the first chance he had had to meditate in days and he seized it, praying now that the Doctor would not barge in in the middle of it and thus disrupt his yogic raptures. Though there was little chance of that!

Not that the Doctor or Rosita might *not* barge in, but because Higgins' meditations were skin-deep affairs, and the closest he had ever come to yogic rapture were the two or three times he had fallen asleep. Higgins repeated a *mantra*, combining it with his breath. Nothing happened, however – his mind continued to wander about his head, sniffing at this and that thought like a hungry dog, while the crack of his ass began to itch ferociously.

Part of the problem, Higgins was aware, was that the *mantra* he was using was not a proper *mantra* properly received from a proper guru. He thought of the woman Gil had mentioned, but remained skeptical. For it wasn't that Higgins hadn't looked for such a person before – he had. And maybe it was only his own ego and pride, but he had never found anyone he could accept as his teacher.

He had met the great Protestant theologian T——, for instance, who, during the most exquisite exposition of the divine milieu, had chainsmoked Camels and screamed at his kids. Over dinner, the great man had drunk too much wine, becoming at first merely white-faced, then florescently ill, while Higgins, who had come for the weekend full of marvelous spiritual expectations, had left before the night was through.

Then there was the well-known hatha yogi, Vijayanandaji. Higgins had met him in Chicago at the home of a devotee. Certainly, he was an extraordinary being. Though almost eighty then, he had looked forty, and could do things with his bronzed god's body that Higgins couldn't do at seventeen. Higgins was looking for a spiritual teacher who could give him a vision of his own inner Self. Whereas, the old hatha yogi had talked for hours on end about vitamins, *asanas*, spirulina, *nauli*, diet, and the importance of keeping fit. And though he had found the old gentleman interesting enough, when Higgins had finally left him that evening he had felt no closer to *Nirvana* than if he had been chatting with any other great athlete – Bobby Orr, say, or Willie Mays.

Then there had been Higgins' unfortunate run-in with the Friends of Saint Jerome. Saint Jerome was a fat young fellow from Brooklyn who claimed to be an incarnation of God. Unusual as this might sound, Saint Jerome had no dearth of well-heeled followers, either here or abroad. A friend of a friend had insisted that Higgins hear Jerome speak and Higgins had obliged, only to walk out of the auditorium soon after Saint Jerome's talk had begun. Jerome had said: 'As for myself, this Condition is neither permanent nor fleeting, not transcendent, nor is it ordinary. It is not insights, it is not blisses. Do not think you see me as I am. Meditating me, you see me as you. Meditating you, I see you as your own reflection. And yet nothing you see does stain this Condition, does violate this egoity, does impede the renouncement of that perfect Condition which is, at root, divine. This is why no impediment can arise in the mind of such a one as I incurring that experiential realization . . .'

At which point, Higgins had stood up and walked out – noisily. A man had tried to stop him but Higgins, who was adamant, had pushed him out of the way. Words had been exchanged. Then someone had thrown a headlock on Higgins and Higgins and that someone had hit the floor. There had been cheers from the audience – though, alas, not for Higgins. Finally, Higgins and his assailant had been separated, but not before Higgins had managed to throw a wonderfully unspiritual left to the ear. Then the fight was over. Saint Jerome had looked annoyed, there finally having arisen, it seemed, an impediment to his perfect Condition, and Higgins was shown the door. The friend of a friend followed him out, very much annoyed.

But once out on the Brooklyn street, Higgins had felt

elated, saved! He had gulped down draughts of the cold night air, feeling like a prisoner just released from a stifling hole.

The friend of a friend sighed. 'You didn't like Saint Jerome.'

'You can always tell a fraud,' Higgins said, 'by the way they abuse the language. They don't have an ego, they have "egoity." It's "renouncement" for them, not renunciation. Things just happen to you and me, but to a guy like Saint Jerome . . . why, he "incurs experiential realizations." '

'Everyone else understood what he was saying.'

'Did they? Or isn't it more like the emperor's new clothes? Look,' Higgins said, 'I'm sorry. But I just couldn't *stand* that guy. You don't seem to understand, but this whole business . . .' He fumbled for the words. 'It's . . . it's very *important* to me.'

But important to Higgins or not, he kept on running into all kinds of spiritual lunatics and crazies. Two days after meeting Saint Jerome, he was introduced by the same friend of a friend to a Queens housewife of Hungarian descent named Jo Tekalosian who claimed, among other things, to be an avatar of Kali. Higgins had never heard of an avatar of Kali. 'I thought only Vishnu had avatars,' he whispered to the friend once removed. 'That's what makes her so special,' he was told. To demonstrate her claim, Mrs. Tekalosian went into a trance during which she spoke to Higgins in execrable Sanskrit, cursed like a soldier, and vomited blood. Higgins was not impressed. His Uncle Evan, entranced on gin, had done the same for years.

Finally, there was the tantric yogi Shri Chaitanya Maharaj on whom, for one shining instant, Higgins had almost pinned his hopes. A bonafide Brahmin from Madras, Shri Chaitanya espoused an attractive blend of traditional eastern disciplines and modern western consciousness-expanding techniques, guaranteed to raise the sleeping *kundalini*. This was exactly what Higgins was after. And it wasn't until he had made some pointed inquiries that he discovered that Shri Chaitanya's main technique for stimulating the yogic force was that old East Village standby, the group grope, with the Master himself sometimes coming down from the seat of Vyasa to more closely supervise the 'tantric' revels.

Higgins was disgusted. The last thing he wanted was sex with his guru. When Higgins had asked one of Chaitanya's crimson-clad disciples what any of this had to do with yoga, with *God*, he had been told: 'Look, friend, first you have to *fulfill* your desires in order to transcend them. Hey! You're uptight. You repress. Open up. Just let go. Whatever you feel like doing, man, just *do* it.'

'Whatever I *feel* like doing, I should just *do*?' Higgins asked, amazed.

'Now you're cooking, bro!'

Higgins thought for a moment. 'And what if I feel like punching you in the mouth?'

The man's face sharpened with fear. 'Hey, wait a minute, fella,' he said. 'Don't do *that*!'

Higgins laughed, remembering. But why was he meditating on lefts to the mouth? He was supposed to be concentrating on his breath. A rivulet of perspiration trickled down the washboard of his ribs, doing awful things to the nerves in his side. Higgins tried to ignore it and to make his mind completely blank. And as he did so, out of the blue, the crazy little *mestiza* girl popped into his head. Higgins dismissed her, but she wouldn't go away. She just stood there, hands on hips, laughing at him with a childish insolence.

And it was then there was a subtle shift – almost like a jerk – and Higgins felt himself drawing up from behind his bones and eyes and leaving his body, exiting it suddenly through the crown of his head.

Higgins, who was not trying to perform this wonder, but merely to deepen his meditation, began to scream in fright – though soon he was screaming mouthlessly, it is true. Hollering like that – mouthlessly – Higgins emerged from the top of his skull and ascended balloon-like toward the living-room ceiling, then floated through the sunlit air, heading for an open second-storey window through which, for an instant, it seemed he would slip and drift away into the stainless mid-summer afternoon – but instead, upon reaching the window

196

in question, he stopped, and began to float back the way he had just come – finally calming down long enough now to stop his (mouthless) screaming and gape at the truly bird's eye view which his sudden disincarnation had conferred. It was unreal! Higgins noted the ring of dust on the room's upper moulding and saw himself seated on the couch below, saw himself down to the tiniest detail: to the blond whorl of hairs on the top of his skull. And for a moment Higgins' fear abated and he felt an absolute exhilaration. To just blow out of your skull like that! To just pop like a pip and float like a ghost just below the ceiling screaming in your mouthless no-body – *whoaa*!

Then with a mixed sense of disappointment and relief, he returned. It was an uncanny reunion, this one of circulating spirit and empty corpse. With a shudder he descended and was back in his body, and it was over as though it had never happened, as though he had hallucinated it when he wasn't crazy, dreamed it when he wasn't sleeping.

For a while Higgins sat there in deep stupefaction, his body shaking, his mind completely blown – for Higgins was not used to this sort of thing; he had always had his feet firmly planted on the ground and his head in the *real* world. And though a philosopher might argue that this *real* world which Higgins had thought he was inhabiting was no more 'real' than any other, and that even his business interests, much less his literary labors, were nothing more than a mental construct: a universe of words and numbers and signs as fleeting, and insubstantial as the amber blips on a computer screen – still, in this 'unreal' world which Higgins inhabited, people, indubitably, did not leave their bodies.

Except to science.

The Cause Of Death

◆

Chapter 7

The door burst open, and the Doctor rushed in. He flung his jacket across the arm of the sofa and proceeded to pace nervously back and forth across the room. That Higgins might have just had an OBE – an 'out-of-body experience' – was something the Doctor didn't seem to consider as he paced obstreperously, on long thin legs, only inches from Higgins' folded knees.

Higgins opened his eyes and fixed the Doctor with a baleful glare. The Doctor took this as a sign to begin. 'So. Did you hear? They discovered our friend.'

'What friend?' Higgins asked. He looked about him uncertainly, wondering what world he was in.

'This morning – around noon. I saw them carry him from the building. In a plastic sack.' The Doctor stared into space, as though the sack was permanently tattooed upon his memory.

Higgins looked up. 'Are they sure it's our friend?'

The Doctor made a face to show what he thought of this question. 'If it wasn't, then who is the person who was dead in your room? Just some strange stranger who knew the password, wandered in, chopped off his own head, then got into bed? Hey, are you listening to me? What's the matter with you?'

'I just left my body, Arsenio.'

The Doctor raised his eyebrows. Then he said, 'Oh, really? And where did you leave it? Ha, ha, ha, ha, ha!'

Higgins' meditation was clearly over. Putting on hold his astral travels, and returning now, with some reluctance, to the world of bodies, living and dead, Higgins got up and stood by the window he had nearly floated out a minute ago. At last he turned to the Doctor and said, 'I've been thinking. What if someone tried to kill Jorge and Jorge killed him instead? Then fled.'

'With what? A head? And left behind his gun and passport? No,' the Doctor said somberly. 'You may discard your foolish hopes right now. I spoke with the Medical Examiner. The body is Jorge Vazpana's, all right. It was checked against fingerprints on file in Dorado.'

'That was fast.'

'Yes. Everything's computerized nowadays.' He looked at Higgins mournfully. 'Perfect match . . .'

There was a painful silence as the information sunk in.

'And there is more . . .' the Doctor continued. 'It seems he wasn't killed by having his throat slit, either. He died, it appears . . . from a blood clot in his heart.'

The words played a strange and painful inner chord. 'That's what my wife died of, Arsenio.'

'Why . . . yes. But in his case, it was intentional. That is, they think he may have been injected with something, a drug, that caused the blood to clot and kill him. Of course, we won't know for certain if there's anything to this unless they can isolate the suspected toxin. The lack of blood in the body complicates the procedure, but they think that if the drug is there, they may be able to find traces of it in the body tissues – so they are looking.'

'For what?'

'We don't know exactly. Some sort of hemotoxin, I suppose.'

Which was all well and good. And yet, why was life like this? For it seemed to Higgins now such a cruel and obnoxious joke that his wife should have died from a similar cause. In less than a year, Death had twice claimed the body in the bed beside him – and both times in the same manner, as though the old *maestro* was running out of fresh ideas.

Not that in the case of Higgins' wife, he or anyone else suspected foul play. His wife had been a dancer and such lethal embolisms, he'd been told, were a hazard of the profession. Still, Life – or is it Death? – was strange.

The Doctor picked up the gruesome fetish lying on the couch. 'And have you made any sense of this nonsense yet?'

'No.'

'Of course, you haven't. Nor will you ever. Because witchcraft has nothing to do with this thing. The murder was clearly an AES operation. We believe we've even identified the assassin.' He looked sadly triumphant. 'Lieutenant Colonel Adolfo Schmidt.'

'That's very interesting,' Higgins said. 'But tell me why, if it's a purely political killing, someone took the poor guy's head?'

'Look,' the Doctor said, 'I know what you think. You think this was some sort of *ritual* murder: bloodings, beheadings, *magi negro*.' The Doctor sighed, as though he was speaking to an overimaginative child. 'But our friend was not killed by any kind of magic, I assure you, except that of the knife and the syringe. Or do you think that this thing here . . .' He held the fetish out at arm's length.

Higgins stretched his legs and gazed past the Doctor at the sunlit window. 'I don't know what I believe in anymore.'

'But, surely, not *this*!' He seemed to want Higgins' reassurance.

'All right, I'll tell you what I think. I think words have power. And when you see that thing you tell yourself certain words. Okay, laugh, Arsenio. Go ahead. But we both know men – intelligent, cultured, college-educated men – who were told the words, "You're fired, buddy," or "Baby, I don't love you anymore," and within six months they had drunk themselves silly or wrapped their Mercedes around the trunk of a tree.'

'But it's not the same!' the Doctor protested.

'Sure it is. Except we don't call it *magi negro*.'

But Higgins was saved from further scorn by the appearance of a fresh target at which the Doctor could shoot. Gil had stuck her head in the doorway. 'The children look well.'

'Yes,' the Doctor answered brightly. 'No thanks to you.'

'Gee. It's King Crab. I see *that* hasn't changed.'

'I am not the King Crab,' the Doctor rejoined. 'I am just a bit . . . *under*whelmed, shall we say . . . by the way you've deigned to honor us with your maternal presence after all these weeks on leave.'

'On leave? I was working my tits off,' his sister said. 'Didn't you get the money I sent?'

'Well, yes,' the Doctor said, evidently uncertain what to complain about next. 'And now that you're back, you no doubt intend to . . . pick up where you left off!'

The stupidity of this observation made even Higgins cringe.

'No doubt, Arsenio,' Gil said, lowering her eyes with a mocking smile.

The Doctor opened his mouth to protest, but withdrew instead, muttering unpleasantries, the way a fleeing army scatters mines.

'He doesn't seem to like you much.'

'Oh,' she said, shrugging it off. 'I'm used to it. Don't you know him by now?'

'I just left my body,' Higgins told her.

'Yeah? Well, welcome to the Twilight Zone.' She didn't seem to be overly impressed. Then again, she didn't look at him like he was schizophrenic either, which was refreshing.

'I was thinking . . . maybe I should go see that . . .'

'Hush!' Gil stiffened, straining her ears. 'Did you hear that?'

'What?' For Higgins had heard nothing save the usual patchwork quilt of city sounds.

She stiffened again. 'Yvonne!' she cried, and flew from the room.

Higgins grinned in disbelief. He thought of sea hens in their windswept rookeries who can recognize, it is said, among a million peeping chicks, the voices of their own. But that was different. Wasn't it? That was animals – Mother Nature.

And yet, standing at the window minutes later, Higgins watched Gil returning from the corner, carrying in her arms her wailing daughter.

Schmidt and Crespi

◆

Chapter 8

The first thing Garcia did when he got out of bed that morning was to look between his legs, but the old brown worm was a limp and lifeless thing. Nor did poking it make it grow any longer; instead, obviously irritated by the indecent prodding, it shrunk, retracting its head, so that even its one blind eye disappeared. Garcia sighed. He had drunk a whole bottle of *Malpotane* the night before. He had expected come morning to awake with a veritable *prong* between his loins, but the fabled men's tonic, like everything else he had tried, had had no effect on his purloined nature.

A sense of shame overwhelmed him. These days, he was consumed by shame, though 'consumed' perhaps was not the proper word since shame, though hot, was not like fire but rather like some fishy burning slime. He was an impotent traitor. *Shame*. Whose wife had left him. *Shame*. And he felt shame, too, at Vazpana's murder. If he had only . . . what? Shame said, he should have done *something*. *Shame*.

But it was too late for that now. Now, all he could do was to find the one who had killed Vazpana. And who was probably threatening him as well – for Garcia was convinced the two were related.

The prime suspect was, of course, the AES agent Schmidt. Lieutenant Colonel *Adolfo Schmidt*. It was really not so strange a name. There were many Germans, even ex-Nazis, in Dorado.

Surprisingly, information about the Colonel was not that difficult to come by, as Schmidt had achieved an almost legendary status among Latin operatives. This was due in part, Garcia discovered, to a host of attempts on the Colonel's life, all of which he had survived unscathed, giving him an aura of invincibility. At the same time, Schmidt was credited with a list of terrorist actions so exhaustive that he could not possibly have been involved in them all, from the Cubana Air Lines bombing, to the hijacking of the pleasure boat *Coral Sea*, to the murder of Courvoisier.

Garcia had expected in the course of his mission to meet with half-truths, deceptions, evasions, lies, the slippery, ungraspable trail that a spy and assassin leaves behind, but this mythical Schmidt was even more difficult to trace. Instead of a cloak and dagger, he hid in his aura, his dazzling glow. Facts turned to fable; the line between his life and legend blurred. For example: while it was probably true that Schmidt had been trained as an assassin while still quite young, it was unreasonable to believe he had shot General Lomax at the tender age of nine years old, as the chronologies would lead one to believe.

Again, it may have been true, as Garcia's sources claimed, that Schmidt had murdered his DGI opponent by drowning him in a cask of Amontillado wine, and yet it seemed unlikely, as the story continued, that he had delivered the cask to the Cuban embassy in Rome with the drowned agent floating inside!

Nor was there any evidence to suggest that Schmidt had ever dabbled in magic. It was not his style. The straight-arrow son of an officer in FACH, the Dorado Air Force, Schmidt had joined the right-wing *Libertad Y Patria* when still a boy, and later, in his teens, had been recruited by AES.

But if Schmidt was a legend, then Captain Crespi of MIRA was a myth. If Schmidt was the Devil and the father of every terrorist act, then Crespi, like God, was transcendent, unknown. There were even some who claimed that Crespi did not exist, that he was a notional creation of the democratic forces, while others passionately believed in his existence, even if they had never encountered him themselves. Nor, like God, could any one tell Garcia what Crespi looked like, whether he was tall or short, young or old, black or white, though everyone had a personal opinion. (Some even whispered that Crespi was a woman, though similar rumors were circulated about Him.) No. Crespi's existence, like our good Lord's, had to be taken on faith. That he – or she – was out there somewhere, a beneficent presence behind the scenes, was all he could confirm.

One thing, however, could be said for certain – Crespi was the bitter enemy of Schmidt. If the two were in the same city together, it was only a matter of time before they clashed.

Still, knowing all this did not really help. Having researched their backgrounds, Garcia was still no closer to finding either one. What he needed now was their local contacts. It was the only way he could get to them, the only place where their rarified persons touched the ground. And for this, his best source was Dante Guzman.

There is something irrefutably beautiful about a bar room in the early morning – even The Black Hen. The spears of sunlight lancing the darkened quarters have the look of revelation. The clean zinc countertop, the barman slicing limes, the dripping sinks and sparkling glasses, the heady mix of morning breezes, silence, light and fermentation all conspire to make one wonder why men would want to trade this beauty for the smoke-filled darkness it will soon become.

The door of the bar was open for deliveries. Garcia wandered in. Behind him, something clicked and he wheeled on his heels – but it was only ice cubes melting in the sinks. The place was empty, though he could hear the sounds of someone working in another room, and smell coffee brewing on a hotplate by the bar.

Garcia poured himself a cup, enjoying immensely this petty larceny. Then he moved to the back of the house where he found his comrade sitting at a table in the rear. The table was strewn with baseball cards which the ex-torturer was examining with care. Garcia set his coffee down beside them.

'Watch it, will you? That's a Mickey Mantle, man.'

Garcia tilted his head. 'So it is.'

'You know what that's worth?'

'Worth?'

'Go on, guess.'

'Guess *what*?'

'Six hundred dollars, man.'

'It's a *baseball card*!'

'Look,' Guzman said, pushing a price list across the table at Garcia. Underscored in red was the line: ''54 Bowman Mickey Mantle. . . . $600.'

Garcia felt a spurt of envy. And he had the bitter-sweet impression then that the world was filled with hidden treasures, which he didn't see, or know about, and so always let slip through his fingers. 'This says, "mint condition." That one looks like you wiped it on your ass.'

Guzman conceded, 'Yeah. But if it was a cherry, it would be worth a lot.'

'But it's not a cherry – so it isn't.' Garcia picked up another card. 'Art Ditmar. Didn't he blow the '60 series?'

'Watch it. You're bending it, Ambrosio.'

'Trade?' Garcia said, holding the card just out of Guzman's reach.

'For what?'

Garcia took a lighter from the table and held it beneath the card. He smiled. 'Adolfo Schmidt.'

'Damn you, Ambrosio,' Guzman said, snatching for the Ditmar. But Garcia was too fast.

'What do you want from me?' Guzman growled. 'I don't know where Schmidt is. After wasting Vazpana, he's probably gone to ground. Good luck finding him, *Señor*!'

'If his mission is finished, why doesn't he just go home to Dorado?'

'Maybe his mission isn't finished. Maybe the killing of Vazpana was just the first step. Maybe he still has work to

206

do.' Guzman leered. 'Maybe if you don't find him, he'll find you.'

But Garcia shook his head. 'Why would AES send their best man after me? Any fool could shoot me any evening on the street.'

'Maybe it's not you he's after.'

'Who is it then?'

Guzman ran a hand through his hair, looking longingly at the Ditmar. Garcia brought the flame a fraction closer. Guzman scowled and hurriedly said: 'Schmidt may be interested in President Benitez. What his mission is is still unclear, but there is a general sense, in certain circles, Benitez must be stopped. In that way, they say, they will "decapitate" the movement.

'What does that mean?'

'They've been fighting the rebels for two and a half years. Yet only last month, Benitez's forces overran half of Montazan province. The feeling is now if they can't kill the body, the rebel army, they should cut off its head. Its head is Benitez.'

'And who is this "they"?'

'A lot of people,' Guzman said vaguely. 'However, there is someone here, working with Schmidt, helping to direct the actions.'

'A local contact! Name?'

There was longish pause, but Guzman didn't answer.

Garcia let the flame die out. He sighed and flipped the card onto the table. Guzman picked it up and smoothed it through his fingers. Satisfied it was unmarked, he grinned and said, 'Don't you know, my *Capitán*? It is *El Duende*.'

The Wings Of Love

◆

Chapter 9

The Doctor had spoken the previous evening in the basement hall of the *Iglesia Metodista*. His speech, entitled, *The Phenomenon of Man*, had been sponsored by Latin Workers for an Equal, Just, and Humane Society – one of the *barrio's* less offensive political fronts.

But the Doctor's speech had been a disaster. For the Doctor, in imitation of the Buddha and Benitez, had taken the middle way, the path of reason – and thus offended nearly everyone. In his careful attempt not to stomp on anyone's feelings, he had managed to step on everyone's toes. He had praised Castro as 'a great liberator,' offending the exiles, but had deplored his being 'in bed with the Rooskies,' rankling the left.

Nor could the Doctor prevent himself from ventilating certain anthropological theories which a wiser man would have kept to himself, calling Christmas, for instance, 'a pagan solar fire festival,' while characterizing Jehovah, Lord God of Israel, as 'a minor Arabian volcano daemon, shamelessly promoted and aggressively hyped.'

Had the Doctor stopped here, apologized and sat down, he might have got away with it, but as it was, he had gone on and on with his outlandish pronouncements, claiming, at one point, that dialectical materialism (of which there were more than a few devotees present) was only a late, degraded and

secularized form of the Universal Mother religion – citing as
proof for his heretical thesis the root, *mater*, in its very title,
and the placement of its major feast day on the first of May,
'a day historically sacred to the Goddess from time out of
mind.' Finally the Doctor, who had already dug his grave,
had buried himself and flung some dirt on top by comparing
the May Day parade of missiles and canonry in certain
socialist capitols to the tradition of Maypoles, dolmens,
shivalingams, and 'other models of the erect male organ,' –
an important symbol, the Doctor claimed, 'in fertility cults
of this kind.'

When the Doctor had finished there had been a dumbfounded silence, followed at last by a retarded wave of
strained applause, as though everyone was waiting for everyone else to begin. No, the Doctor's speech had not been well
received. Everyone had reacted so *emotionally* – Catholics,
commies, contras, Jews. No one had seemed to appreciate his
scientific point of view; and following his speech he had
received a spate of abusive letters and life-threatening phone
calls.

But these threats were nothing compared to the silence of *El
Duende*. Since their early morning interview, the Doctor had
been on tenterhooks, certain that at any moment an attack
would come, but not knowing how, when or from what
direction – whether as a bullet, say, through a twilit window,
or as a perfect stranger waiting in his waiting room at noon.
It might appear as a speeding vehicle on the morning street,
as a pinscher unleashed at the stroke of midnight, or as a
knifethrust by moonlight, (or at any time as a dresser drawer
in which the Doctor's knuckles first, and then his neck,
would be shut and cracked – like lobster claws or Rice Cris-
pies.)

The Doctor was prepared, of course. He was armed.
Having picked up the pistol he had not put it down, and he
carried it with him now at all times in an ill-fitting black body
holster. He had never carried a weapon before and it was a

thrill; it made him feel taller, like a slug of rum – even if he wasn't sure how to shoot the damn thing!

But though he waited, nothing happened; while Omar continued to greet him on the street with the same fake smile and tired wave he had been palming off on the Doctor for years.

It was later that night, on his way home from the hospital, that the Doctor came across the goon. Fortunately, Mucho did not come across the Doctor; he was standing in a moon-drenched playground, caressing with his fingertips the powdered cheek of Janie Ray. It was an arresting sight: the boy's great bulk poised protectively above the slight girl, his hand faintly tracing with a sad, almost wistful air her geisha-white cheek, while his lips twittered confused endearments that the Doctor could only barely hear.

Yes, it would have been a touching sight, an artful photograph in black and white whose beauty was enhanced by the cool moonshadows and serpentine curve of the aluminum slide, an image worth a thousand words about human love and human understanding – had it not been that the girl's white face held a look of such stark and unremitting terror.

The Doctor coughed discreetly, hoping to unfreeze the scene, but nothing shifted, save the girl's frightened eyes which fastened on the Doctor's own with a terrible and secret plea as if to say, *save me, save me*, like the look in the eyes of a mute person, drowning. The Doctor coughed again, harder this time, and the goon turned his pumpkin head and scowled. Seizing the chance, Janie lunged for the pavement, losing a shoe in the sand of the playground but hobbling hurriedly on, nonetheless, until she had reached the Doctor's side. She grabbed his hand. 'C'mon,' she said, as they hurried off.

'What was *that* all about?' the Doctor asked.

'You *know* that guy?'

'Well, yes. We met. The other night. Remember?'

The girl shuddered. 'He's not right.'

'What did he want?' the Doctor asked, remembering with

a jealous pang the tender way he had stroked her hair. The Doctor noticed she was limping. 'Your shoe.'

But the girl only shivered and kept right on walking. 'You don't know what he was saying to me, Doc.'

'No? Let me think. He wants to marry you.' The Doctor laughed.

'Uh unh.'

'What was it then?'

'He was telling me how he was going to cut off my head.'

'What?' the Doctor said and stopped, appalled. 'He *said* that?'

'What do you think I was so scared about? What do you think I grabbed you for? He goes, "And then I'm gonna take my knife, see, and I'm gonna . . ." '

'Knife?' the Doctor said, his very worst phobias coming true. 'He has a knife?'

'What did I just tell you, Doc? Sheeit, yeah. For one hot minute, I thought I was done for.'

Just then they heard footsteps and Jane's face paled. 'Hell's bells!' she said, and pulled the Doctor into one of the hundred darkened doorways that lined the street where they waited, in a forced embrace, while the goon lumbered by. He didn't walk so much as blunder, dragging the rest of him after his out-thrust head. Most horribly, he was making noises in his throat as he passed. It was not English or Spanish, not words or speech, but an animal guttural emanating from some lunatic region inside of him which, entering into the Doctor's consciousness, opened holes inside his head.

'Freak,' Jane hissed when he'd passed. The Doctor shuddered. And yet, something else stirred inside him, as well – some deep, sweet, regal feeling. For the Doctor had not seen the girl since that day in his office when they had so passionately examined each other. Her pang assuaged, there had been no further consultations. And though the Doctor had mastered this manfully, deeming it the wisest course, he realized now that he had missed her, too, – and more than he had thought.

She turned to him now the danger was past, and offered

him the sweetest smile. 'Doc,' she said, and picked a thread off the shoulder of his coat. It was the simplest of gestures, it was probably unconscious, and yet it affected the Doctor in the strangest way. It summoned up a secret world he had rarely known – the lovingkindness of a girl, the sweet attentions of a woman, like spring in the arctic or rain in the desert.

For the Doctor had been so long out of love, he had nearly ceased to believe in its existence. He did his work, he kept a mistress, but his life had always been too serious and problematic to allow himself to fall in love, especially with such a lovely, silly child.

And yet now Fate, in the form of a goon, had thrust them once again into each other's arms, and the Doctor felt a happy fire melt his arctic heart.

The Doctor bent and kissed her lips. She kissed him back, and a marvelous feeling, like awakening wings, fluttered in the space between his heart and throat, leaving him breathless and more than a little thrilled.

And looking at her now, the Doctor was moved by a vision of connubial felicity and marital bliss. What if he married this child? What if he took a wife? Why shouldn't he? Because the girl was exactly half his age? Nonsense. That was part of the charm of it all. He would take a young wife. And she would be a great comfort to him in his declining years. Yes. He liked the sound of that. It had what he supposed to be a Biblical ring. And this young wife would pick lint and cat hairs off the Doctor's shoulders and feed him wonderfully delicious meals, and then, after dinner, after she had washed and put away the dishes, his young wife would fuck the Doctor slowly in their twilit room – in a great generous second helping of love and feast of feeling as the evening sweetened and the shadows deepened into night. Ah, yes, this is how it would be! And this all would come to pass so that the Doctor might be exalted and glorified above the other dervishes. The Doctor's eyes shone with the splendor of this hope and with the luster of his Moorish blood.

'My office,' he said, 'is right down the street. Would you care to come up? I think I could dig up a bottle of brandy.'

She smiled at him. ''Kay.' She was like that, easy. Then she frowned. 'But first I got to find my shoe,' and they started back the way they had come.

The Doctor did not feel so nervous this evening. Perhaps it was the gun he was wearing or the look of love in his companion's eyes. Whatever the reason, he felt strong and confident about everything. Janie must have sensed this change in him, as well, for she glanced up at him now with a girlish smile and gave his hand a series of secret squeezes that sent fire through his senses, promising as it did the bliss of embraces yet to come.

But when they returned to the playground, they could not find her shoe. They could see her footprints in the loose gravel and they could find the spot where she and the goon had stood – but the shoe was gone.

'Freak,' she said again and shuddered. 'He took it, Doc. I know he did.'

The Doctor laughed. 'Your Prince Charming,' he said, 'has got your slipper.'

'It's not funny, Doc. Them kicks set me back half a yard.'

The Doctor looked confused; the reference seemed to be to football. 'Come again?'

'I said, them shoes cost me fifty dollars.'

The Doctor laughed. 'I will buy you another pair. All right?'

'Jees, you will?' she said, brightening at once, and rubbing herself against his chest, like a hungry kitten. 'You're a prince. You know that, Doc? I mean, I'm really starting to like you a lot.'

The Doctor searched her face, wishing desperately to believe her, but afraid. He wanted to take her in his arms, to lose himself in the intoxication of her flesh, but something stopped him, held him back, so that he felt like a dervish who cannot quite make the leap of faith, and so stands apart, on the edge of the whirling dance, sober and unpossessed.

'Hey,' she said reading the sorrow in his eyes. 'What's the matter, babe?'

And reaching up she kissed him then, and with her tongue removed his unbelief; and something in the Doctor's belly whirled, unfurling lovely, shivery wings.

The Secret Queen

◆

Chapter 10

That same evening, after supper, Higgins set off in search of the holy woman Gil had mentioned, and soon found himself wandering on the outskirts of the *barrio* in that little no man's land where the woman was supposed to live. He was impressed by the area's extreme devastation. The landscape was a sunburnt waste of bricks heaped into shapes that reminded the heart of its ruination, a planet of powdering mortar and dust and standing pools of rainwater, while the windows of the empty tenements he passed – a surreal blue and gilded with the evening sun – shone now in the failing light with that peculiar sadness innate in all reflections.

Eventually, the road he was following ended, blocked by a mountain of bulldozed debris. Higgins stopped and looked about him. Behind, there was nothing but the vast expanse of razed and naked lots blazing with the last rays of the summer's day. The declining sun burned the few remaining planes of brick that stood erect amidst the rubble; while above the earth in the purple heavens, jets had left a luminous and blurring scrawl. And looking around him once again, at the desolate fields and gathering darkness, Higgins realized he was lost.

Leaving the road, he clambered up a hill of rubble, picking his way among the splintered studs and shattered masonry. From the top of the mound, he saw the house several hundred yards away. He wondered now how he could have missed it; it was the only building still standing in the brick field, a lone brownstone whose companion habitations had been sheared away on either side.

Taking his bearings, he descended the mound, attempting to ignore the personal effects with which it was littered: a twisted bed frame, a set of false teeth, a woman's shoe – giving one the distressing impression that the building had been razed while its occupants were sleeping.

Higgins, again, set off across the difficult terrain, avoiding pits and skirting hills and puddles. At one point, he flushed an emaciated animal, though whether it was a cat, a rat, or a starving dog it was impossible to say. The longer Higgins walked, the more peculiar it seemed that the woman should live in such a remote location, but he restrained his annoyance, telling himself it was all an adventure. He planned to ask her about the murderous fetish, though Higgins knew in his heart it was not that which had drawn him here, that he was going to her – whoever she was – for what the Carmelites had failed to give him: spiritual guidance and religious instruction.

For the truth of the matter is that Higgins was scared, and it wasn't just the murder, either. He felt as though some opening was taking place inside him, the blossoming of some inner dimension he wasn't sure he wanted any part of, the widening chink in a wall between two worlds, and through this fissure strange dreams and memories and out-of-body experiences were drifting – so that one part of him wanted to seal the chink and run, just as another part of him was watching, rapt, in fascination.

At last, he reached the rundown house. He hesitated on the porch, looking in the windows through cupped hands. The first floor was deserted, showing no signs of human habitation. He tried the door, and when it opened, stepped inside and went up the twilit stairwell, keeping an eye out for monsters, muggers, maniacs and rats, but nothing attacked him, not even mosquitoes. The rooms on the second and third floors were empty as well, and it wasn't until he reached the fourth and final storey that Higgins came upon a door. He knocked timidly at first, and when no one answered, hammered louder, not liking the prospect of finding himself alone in the empty house after dark, a quarter of a mile from nowhere on this ragged edge of the world. The stairwell was lit with the radiance of the sunset, and with that part of the day which had still not drained from the sky. The house appeared to have no electric power, and Higgins wondered how he'd get down in the dark. He'd borrow a candle, of course. What was he so frightened of?

He knocked a third time and, when no one answered, tried the knob. The door opened on the hallway of a modest flat. To his right was a kitchen with some dried beans soaking in a bowl. A narrow bedroom just beyond it was furnished simply with a metal cot, a painted, wooden dresser, and one of those grisly religious calendars in which Jesus is holding his own sacred heart.

There was a third and final room at the end of the hallway. Though carpeted with several threadbare kilims, it was empty of furniture, and illumined only wanly by the last pink traces of the day. Higgins was convinced he had found the right place, and he sat down to wait. But though he waited for several minutes, no one appeared. He glanced around him. The room was growing darker by the minute and he was trying to decide if he should get up and leave or look for a candle, when his peripheral vision spied the hooded hulk, the black humped shape stationed like his death in the shadows behind him, and he screamed, leaping to his feet.

'My, you're a jumpy one,' a high-pitched, girlish voice declared, as though it was Higgins who was crazy, Higgins who was weird, when everyone could see it was she who was queer as a hooty owl, sitting there like a phantom in the dark, living in a place like this. Higgins could not see her face in the dusk – he could not tell her age or even her race – only the flickering jewels of her eyes beneath the blanket's steep peak. 'Are you always so nervous?' the voice inquired. 'What a shame. A young man like you.'

'I've been through a lot recently,' Higgins said.

'I'm sure you have. Screaming like that. You're peculiar all right,' she pronounced, as though it was decided.

Higgins fell silent. He had only just met this person and already she was insulting him. 'Please,' Higgins said. 'I'm sorry if I disturbed you. If you'd like, I'll go.'

The figure laughed. 'First you come. Now it's go. Well, which is it?'

Higgins opened his mouth to speak, then closed it again, like a goldfish in some summer pond.

'Staying then? All right. So what do you want?'

Higgins thought for a moment. 'Some answers, I guess.'

'To what sort of questions?'

He remembered the title of a book he'd once read, '*Questions Relating to the Liberation of Beings.*'

The figure sighed, as though she had been afraid of that. 'Why me? Hey, I have an idea. Why don't you go see a priest?'

'You can't be serious,' Higgins said. 'You know what priests are like these days?'

She didn't reply.

'When they talk about the Inner City, they mean Roxbury . . . or Newark!'

The creature smiled; he saw her teeth glint in the dimness. 'And what makes you think there is some other?'

Higgins was not prepared for this line of questioning. He had expected unwavering support. 'Well, isn't there?' he croaked. 'I mean, isn't there a spiritual realm or something that we can, like . . . enter into or something? Goddamnit! Excuse me, *Señora*, but what are you saying?' he asked, with a note of real panic in his voice. Because if there wasn't a spiritual realm or something that he could, like, enter into or something – if there was no God – if Life was a meaningless chemical experiment hazarded by Time in Space, then the whole complexion of Higgins' universe changed: his life became pointless, his devotion a joke, his suffering belittling and unredeemed.

'Ah,' the voice said, not unkindly. 'How worried you look when you think you will not find what you are after. Well,' she said, settling herself comfortably, 'go ahead then. Ask your questions.'

But Higgins didn't know now what questions to ask. He felt oddly sleepy, drugged, as if he was coming down with something. His scalp had begun to prickle and burn, and he had the sensation of heat in his neck and head. He remembered the dream of the English doctor and the strange memory on the steps of the church, and finally, out of desperation said, 'What about . . . rebirth? I mean, is there really such a thing as reincarnation?'

The creature frowned. 'I don't read past lives, if that's what you've come for. Most people can't figure out who they are in *this* one.'

'But they have them?'

'Have what?'

'Past lives?'

There was a disbelieving silence. 'Where were you educated?' the voice asked with a genuine note of pity and concern. 'Didn't anyone explain these things to you?'

'No,' Higgins sighed, thinking of all the useless crap he'd learned in school. They had taught him everything, all right – chemistry, Spanish, history and math – everything except the basic ground rules of existence.

'But of course there is rebirth,' the voice declared.

'Still, some people would say it was just wishful thinking,' Higgins objected, meaning by 'some people' almost everyone he knew: his family, his friends, the Doctor, the teachers who had taught him.

'Wishful thinking?' the voice cried, aghast. 'To be born over and over and over again? No! It is *they* who are guilty of wishful thinking, I fear.' She laughed, like a child. 'To believe that after just *one* life – without ever getting it right – you will be united – forever – with *God*! That, my friend, is wishful thinking!'

'I see,' Higgins said, never having looked at it quite that way before.

'Hey, what makes you think it gets any better after you

die? You think you die and all your problems just . . . go away?'

Higgins shrugged, for the assumption did seem now rather optimistic and naive. Of course, it didn't get magically better when you died – he should have known. And yet . . . 'What about heaven? Don't you go to heaven when you die?'

She shrugged. 'You do if you deserve to. But even in heaven your freedom and happiness are imperfect and, in the end, you must return to earth to try again. No. You don't improve your personality by doing anything so undistinguished as dying.'

Higgins contemplated this answer a moment. By now the room had grown completely dark. He could scarcely see his hand before him, when the figure suddenly leaned forward, lighting a candle at her feet. And as the bloom of light revealed her features, Higgins screamed all over again, leaping to his feet. For it was her, the little mad *mestiza* girl, the one who had been haunting him!

'Who *are* you?'

'Don't you know? I'm Sara Devi.'

'But I thought that you were deaf. And dumb!'

'Only when I'm around the Doctor,' she said, grinning like an imp.

Higgins could see her clearly now, her little body camped beneath the blanket's tent. How old she was exactly he couldn't say – somewhere between eleven and thirteen. Her flesh was dusky, with Indian tints, her braid blue, her eyes a crystal gray where the Spanish blood had surfaced in her face. She was really quite lovely: a Caribbean blend.

But her age and her cuteness didn't keep Higgins from being angry with her. He felt tricked and ripped off. Then he realized he wasn't angry so much as disappointed. He had sincerely hoped to find a master, and instead he had come upon . . . a twelve-year-old girl!

'Where's your guru?'

'My guru?' She brightened. 'I'm afraid she's not here.'

'That's obvious,' Higgins said. 'I meant, when will she be coming back?'

The child shrugged.

'Tonight?'

'She might.' The girl shrugged again. 'And then again she might not.'

Again, he felt a strange exhaustion, and giving in to it, he sat back down. He looked around him at the room which was at once both beautiful and bare. 'And is she really as great as they say?'

'Oh, yes,' the child hastened to reassure him. 'She is a great being, a great saint.'

'Really?' Higgins was unconvinced. Despite the beauty of the candlelit chamber, the child's shawl was patched and threadbare, the house in state of disrepair. 'Well, if she's so great, why isn't she rich?'

The child's laugh was like a silver bell. Then she said, 'Oh, *deva*, though she may appear to be poor to you, inside she doesn't feel that way at all. Inside she feels . . . like a secret queen!'

Higgins studied her. 'What are you saying?'

The girl contemplated her answer for a moment. Then she said, 'Imagine how you would feel if you had just been awarded some fabulous prize, or if the girl of your dreams confessed to you her love. Imagine that sudden thrill of pride – that throb of joy – so that, for one moment at least, you felt perfectly fulfilled inside, whole and brimming.' She searched his face. 'That's how she feels *all the time*.' She laughed. 'For no apparent reason.' She laughed again and looked around her. 'No one has awarded her any prize. There is no boy she specially loves, and yet . . . she feels . . . as if her heart would burst with joy, and her soul was filled to overflowing!'

And at her words, a thrill ran through Higgins' body and the hair of his neck stood on end, for Higgins had never heard of such a thing. He had only heard boring discussions about *maya*, and windy lectures on salvation and the void. He stared at the child for the longest time, uncertain whether to believe her or not.

'And it's permanent? I mean, she doesn't feel this way only when she's meditating or something?'

'Oh, no. Even when she's eating or bathing or taking a nap, that happiness, that ecstasy is there.'

'So she never feels sorrow then? Or anger? Or grief?'

The child considered the question, then frowned. 'It's not like that. You see, in this state, nothing is lost. You continue to experience all your emotions. It's just that . . . even in sadness, you taste great bliss. While pain seems . . . disconnected to you. It's there, yes, but . . . on the margin of your being, like,' her eyes drifted to the evening window, 'we experience the color blue.' She paused for a moment, then her face grew livid. 'And when she gets angry, Heaven help you!' Her eyes blazed and her voice trembled, 'She's like Zeus, like Thor, like Rudra himself!'

Higgins looked at her in awe. Clearly, the child was crazy. And yet, at that instant, she seemed to be experiencing the very state she was describing. Imagine the face of a woman united with her lover after many years. Envision the breaking light of her smile, the wells of love that are her eyes. For this was how she was looking at him now, and how she regarded the simplest things: the shadows from the candle, the evening light, a fly on the window – as though wherever her gaze wandered and fell, there her Beloved stood waiting for her with open arms.

Then Higgins asked her the only question that had ever really mattered to him. 'And do you think that I could feel this way, too?'

She nodded. 'When the universal Power is awakened inside you. You smile. But you will see.'

Higgins *had* smiled – though it was not because he disbelieved her, but because he felt so happy to hear what she was saying. The power of the universe unleashed inside him! It went beyond his most Napoleonic dreams! And yet it seemed to be a phrase he had read somewhere before. And then he remembered where – on the back of GI Joe and Casper the Friendly Ghost comic books he had read as a kid. 'A split second in eternity. The Rosicrucians.' And he saw again a picture of a man spread-eagled on a rock, an arc of white light shooting from his third eye, and a stopped clock, and it seemed suddenly all too crazy and absurd. Didn't it? He knew better than this. Didn't he? Re-birth. Third eye? Eternity. And if this was all true, then why had there been no discussion of it at Harvard?

No, the Doctor had been right all along. The child was mad. The only thing was that, unlike every other lunatic he had ever met, she did not seem ill. Was that possible? To be mentally mad, but not mentally ill? Higgins had never thought it was, before today. And then there was the question of his own mental health, for what was he doing sitting at her feet, and why did he find himself believing what she told him with the perfect faith of a child in its mother?

Tired of all his questions, Higgins leaned back and closed his eyes. How long he sat there, he couldn't say. It seemed like only minutes passed, but when he opened his eyes again, the moon was in a new position in the sky.

Higgins got to his feet. His knees were stiff. Otherwise he felt quite excellent, really – quiet inside, light-hearted, *good*. He promised the child he would return again – when her guru was present. In the meantime, however, he asked the girl if there wasn't something he could do to deepen his meditations?

'Dance,' she said. 'As much as you can.'

'Dance?' Higgins asked. 'With who? With you?'

'Just dance,' the girl said, raising her arms like a bat and flapping them with a peculiar beauty, as though she might ascend from the chair. 'By yourself. Alone. In your room. And twirl.' She flung her head into motion; it moved apart from her body as though on a greased bearing in her neck, and her braid whooshed and whooshed, singing by Higgins' nose. 'Twirling is very good to do,' she assured him in an untaxed voice empty of effort or motion, her head gliding, falling and rising like a top, her braid singing like a *bola*, and her arms and fingers waving with the dreamlike grace of underwater vegetation.

'As you dance,' she said, stopping now as abruptly as she

had begun, her hands spiraling to rest in her lap, 'leap, twirl, until you begin to feel, within yourself, the center of your gravity, that place that is not moving. And when you find it, put your mind on that spot. That is all. You may go now.'

'Go?' Higgins whispered, in a state of shock. For the child was mad. It was obvious now. She wanted him to dance. In his room. He imagined what the Doctor would say about that, especially when Higgins explained to him that he was dancing to unleash the power of the universe. Higgins would begin his residence at Bellevue within the hour.

Thanking the little girl, Higgins borrowed a candle, by whose flickering light he easily made his way down the stairs.

Outside, the night was drenched in moonlight; the waste-land glittered with broken glass. He looked at his watch. It was 12:37. Higgins could not believe the time! He must have been meditating for several hours!

He put his hand in his pocket, only to discover the eerie fetish. He had forgotten it completely. And standing there in the moonlit morning, he realized now that in all the time he had been with Sara Devi, he had not thought of his dead roommate or wife.

The Fisher King

◆

Chapter 11

'Arsenio, my darling. There's a man at the door who is wanting our blood!'

Before this cry had died upon the summer noon, the Doctor took defensive action: dropping his shoulder, he rolled away from the dinner table and sprawled flat out on the kitchen linoleum, even as his other hand drew the gun from its holster, cocked the hammer, and aimed it at the door. The move was so swift, athletic, and inspired, it was a thrill to behold – even if now, sighting down the barrel of the pistol, the Doctor beheld no sign of a threat, only his mother-in-law and a Red Cross volunteer standing open-mouthed in the doorway.

The Red Cross worker paled and pawed the air. 'Er, uh, only if you want to give us some, Doc,' and he dived behind the stairwell.

Rosita, on the other hand, seemed positively enchanted by the Doctor's performance. Perhaps it recalled her criminal youth in the nightclubs and brothels of pre-revolutionary Cuba. 'Oh, Arsenio, you *macho muchacho*, you!'

'Stay away from me, woman,' the Doctor barked, menacing with the pistol. Then remembering who, what, and where he was, he got to his feet and reholstered the weapon.

The Doctor, of course, should have felt like a fool. But he didn't. He felt like an *hombre, macho* and grand. His heart

225

was pounding and every cell in his system was flooded with a radiant energy that, for the first time in ages, had nothing to do with dexedrine spansules, loose women or cheap rum. The Doctor glimpsed the Red Cross worker's timid face and, throwing back his head, laughed a real belly laugh this time – not those humorless horsesnorts he had been palming off as laughter for years.

For the Doctor – how does one say it? – had regained his *corazon*, and this sudden access to his inner power was almost more than he could bear.

One would have thought it more than his neighbors could bear as well, but, strangely enough, this was not the case. For instead of the Doctor being stripped of the pistol, promptly arrested, and clapped into jail, he was now glorified by all and sundry for his great bravery and nerves of steel, until soon a little *fiesta* developed, with Rosita telling the story over and over and the Red Cross worker showing how he had dived for cover again and again, while a stream of unemployed adults and truant children traipsed through the kitchen watching their hero finish his chili, while peeking and peering in worshipful wonder at the lethal machinery strapped to his ribs.

By the end of the meal the Doctor was feeling cocky as hell. He smoked a cigar and put his feet up on the furniture. At the hospital that afternoon he ordered about the younger doctors, the nurses, security guards, and anyone else he thought he could. The Doctor even made a suggestive remark to a pretty young technician who worked in the lab, something he had done only rarely before, though afterward, the Doctor's cheeks had burned more brilliantly than hers.

By six o'clock, the Doctor was so full of himself it was becoming dangerous – and boring. Stopping off at The Seventh Heaven, he lectured the *cantina*'s clientele on the nature and message of atheist humanism; then, somewhere in the middle of his second tequila, the Doctor received a visit from Garcia, who recounted to him the latest intelligence purchased from Guzman. The Doctor listened, and when Garcia was through, the Doctor thanked him, bought him a drink, swallowed his own, quit the bar, and with an air of great self-importance headed directly to Benitez's office: a four-storey brownstone with an armed guard lounging on the stoop. The building looked less like a political headquarters than the house of a gentleman, though on entering the iron doors, instead of a butler, the Doctor was received by a second armed guard seated at a desk who asked the Doctor to state his business – whereupon the Doctor declared he was Sr. Benitez's personal physician, and that he required an audience with his Excellency at once.

The guard looked doubtful. But some lever in the Doctor's voice, patrician and commanding, moved the man to lift the receiver at his elbow. He asked the Doctor his name, repeated it into the mouthpiece, then hung up the instrument and told the Doctor to wait. The Doctor took a seat and looked about him. A bittersweet genius pervaded the hall, like the perfume of a woman with whom one has quarreled and parted long ago.

It was money. He could smell it, taste it in the air, see it in the gleam of the brass doorknobs and in the roseate glow of the teakwood paneling. He could hear its laughter, girlish and seductive, in the tetrehedrons of the crystal chandelier that the ceiling fans and evening breezes tinkled overhead. The Doctor smiled and sighed, like a man remembering an old affair. It had been pleasant and exciting, yes, but not for him.

Then the telephone rang, and a moment later the Doctor was escorted to a private elevator and lifted up above the great bright slum. When the elevator doors reopened, he was greeted by a third guard, also visibly armed, who said to him in Spanish, 'He is very busy, but he says that he can see you briefly,' and, leading the Doctor down a carpeted hallway, he opened the doors to a magnificent room.

It was the Presidential Office of the President of Dorado – in exile, of course. Flags stood in stanchions on either side of a bay window; a seal of the Republic was woven into the rug. The seal showed a plumed serpent-bird rising, phoenix-like, from some fiery, adobe ruins, with the words: *Man in the Vanguard*, inscribed below. Just beyond, a massive desk of varnished mahogany finished with silver stood on carved, clawed legs while behind it was the pink, cleanshaven visage of Benitez himself, looking dwarf, bland and frankly anti-climatic when compared to the furniture and the fabulous beast.

The Doctor was always surprised by *El Presidente*'s appearance. He looked like a greengrocer in his Sunday best.

'My greetings, your Excellency,' the Doctor said with a florid bow.

Benitez said nothing, tapping his pencil. The Doctor had hoped to be welcomed with a good deal more excitement and respect, but Benitez was clearly anxious to get the interview over. The Doctor was offered neither rum, nor cigars. He was not even asked to sit down.

'What is it?' Benitez asked abruptly. 'Doctor, I am occupied, as you can see,' and he motioned impatiently to a couple of persons who were also present. A male secretary sat motionless, his fountain pen uncapped and poised over a note pad, while a second man about the Doctor's age, whom the Doctor thought he had maybe seen before but wasn't certain where, used the opportunity to belch lavishly and unbuckle his belt a couple of notches so as better to expand his flourishing tummy. The Doctor decided he was a German businessman. He didn't know why. Perhaps it was his strudel-padded paunch, the European glasses, or the wispy, foreign-looking goatee that sprouted without conviction from his chin. Whoever he was, he seemed to be harmless enough. He nodded at the Doctor in a frank, pleasant way, clearly the friendliest of the three men.

'Yes?' Benitez impatiently asked, building a steeple with his fingers on his desk blotter.

The secretary fidgeted. Everyone was clearly 'on hold' until the Doctor finished his business and withdrew.

'I thought, *Señor*,' the Doctor began, 'that given the nature of our communication, it might be wiser if the two of us spoke—'

'Alone?' Benitez finished the sentence. 'There's no need. Guido is my confidential secretary and the Commander,

228

well . . .' Benitez shrugged. '. . . Commander Rabon is quite all right.'

The Doctor jerked. So that's who the fat 'businessman' was: Benito Rabon, one of Benitez's rebel chieftains. The Doctor had not recognized him bearded, in a suit and tie. The guerrilla nodded vaguely at the Doctor in acknowledgment, and the Doctor nodded back, feeling that sudden ecstasy that an ordinary man knows in the company of the great. He turned to Benitez. *El Presidente*'s pink, weary face was crisply counterpointed by his spanking white collar.

'Your Excellency,' the Doctor began. 'Your life is in danger. You have been targeted for assassination by AES, the Dorado secret police.'

'Have I?' Benitez asked. He was hardly being helpful. Even now, his voice patrolled the borderland between civility and irritation.

'I am almost certain of it, your Excellency.'

Benitez looked at the Doctor, then at Guido. The private secretary was rather preciously dressed in a brown linen jacket, mauve cotton sweater, and pink silk tie. He looked like an English schoolboy, not a South American revolutionary. Commander Rabon raised a cheek and expressed wind. It was meant to be a covert, guerrilla operation – and he flushed, then grinned at the unexpected sound.

'And how do you know this, Doctor?' Guido asked with a strained overpoliteness.

'My informants tell me. Think about it. Why else would Schmidt be here?'

'Schmidt?'

'Lieutenant Colonel Adolfo Schmidt. Of AES.'

Benitez and Guido exchanged significant looks, as if the name was not unknown to them. 'And why would AES want to eliminate me? I am just—'

'Please, your Excellency. That is not true. You are a great man, a great symbol. By eliminating you, they would . . . decapitate the resistance.'

Benitez thought for a moment. 'I see. Who else knows this?'

'No one. Not even your man in the confessional.'

'What are you talking about, Doctor?' Benitez said, his voice making an incursion now across the borderline of irritation into genuine pique. 'Do you know what he's talking about?' he asked the foppish Guido.

'I have no idea, your Excellency.'

'Come, come,' the Doctor said, annoyed himself. 'I am speaking of the man who debriefed me just the other day.'

'What *man?*' Guido asked.

'Why, the man you sent me to in the confessional of Saint Elvira's.'

No one said anything. Benitez and his secretary exchanged looks so unreadable, they might have been in a foreign tongue. The Doctor appealed to Benitez with his hands, his eyes. 'That day in my office, *Señor*, I offered you my services, you said—'

'That I would think about it, yes,' Benitez harumphed. 'And I did. And I decided, Doctor, for purely political reasons, I'm afraid, not to take you up on it.' He smiled sadly. 'Generous as your offer was.'

'Yes,' the Doctor said, nodding avidly, 'you decided not . . .' He stopped. His mouth was a hole. 'Excuse me, *Señor*. But what did you say?'

Benitez sighed, and shook his head.

Guido sat up stiffly and capped his pen. 'His Excellency means that we didn't ask you to do anything.'

Benitez looked away as though the subject was embarrassing. And it seemed to the Doctor then that the terrible petal of some sickening flower were blossoming in his bowels.

'Then . . . if *you* didn't hire me?' he asked, thinking aloud. He looked around the room. 'Who have I been giving information to?'

'I am sure I don't know,' Benitez said, clearly annoyed. 'It is not us, that is all I can tell you.'

Commander Rabon looked philosophical, as though such stupidity was an important part of being human. 'Intelligence,' he offered now with a knowing smile, by way of consolation, 'is a very tricky business, *Señor*.'

The Doctor felt his face and neck prickling with heat. But as he reached into the pocket of his suit for a handkerchief, the Commander launched himself from his chair like a shot. In an instant, he was on the Doctor's back, one steel hand digging into the Doctor's shoulder.

'Aaagh,' the Doctor cried, more in fright than anything else and, bending over, threw the man off – though as Rabon dismounted he held aloft, for all to see, the Doctor's gun.

Benitez's eyes bugged at the sight.

'I spotted it when he came in, your Excellency,' the Commander said, hardly winded by his effort. He seemed pleased with himself for having snatched it the way he did – and pleased with the Doctor for having given him the opportunity.

'How did you get in here with that damned thing?'

'Your Excellency . . .' the Doctor began.

But Benitez, deaf with rage, jumped to his feet and screamed for the guard. The man came running and stood at attention while Benitez gave him such a vicious dressing down that the Doctor soon felt embarrassed for them all.

The essence of Benitez's tirade was this: the man had shit for brains; his prostitute of a mother also had shit for brains, as did the man's homosexual ancestors going back for countless generations. The guard's lineage thus established, Benitez wished to know how many times he had *commanded* this person (whose countless deviate relations had shit for brains) never, under any circumstances, to allow a visitor in his office who had not been thoroughly frisked and disarmed? Then, having asked this question, he demonstrated its rhetorical nature by slamming the door in the shitbrain's face so violently that a little flurry of plaster was aroused from the ceiling. Benitez walked over to the window and meditated angrily on the evening slum, while Commander Rabon, who seemed quite unperturbed by the great man's seizure, inspected the pistol, asking the Doctor in a conversational tone, 'Why do you carry such a stupid little thing?'

'What's so stupid about it?'

'Twenty-two caliber? You could shoot a big man three times with these things and not slow him down.'

'Oh, yes? Well, I happen to like a small-bore weapon,' the Doctor said. The words just came out of him. He wasn't even sure what 'small-bore' meant; it was something he must have read somewhere.

'And why is that, Doctor?' The guerrilla looked perplexed.

'Why? Because it leaves a smaller hole.'

Commander Rabon looked at the Doctor as though he were mad, but amusedly so. 'And why such aesthetic considerations? I think you are confusing medicine and murder. Perhaps with surgery, *Señor*, the smaller the hole the better, but when you are shooting someone, Doctor, you try to make the biggest and bloodiest hole you can.' He frowned again. 'No, I don't like these guns.'

Benitez said something that got lost in the drapes.

'What was that, your Excellency?' Guido asked.

Benitez turned. He was composed. 'I said, it worked all right on Robert Kennedy.'

'Ah, that stupid little *bedouin*. He got lucky,' Rabon said. He laid the gun on the corner of Benitez's desk, like an offering. Benitez looked at it with scorn, as though it might have been a turd that the Doctor had been caught carrying around in his pocket. He picked it up, examining it with distaste. 'You could at least clean it, Doctor.' He set it down. 'I mistrust a man who carries a dirty weapon.' He glared at the Doctor. 'I hope you keep your medical instruments cleaner than this.'

The Doctor didn't know how to respond. It had never occurred to him that the gun was dirty, much less that it needed cleaning, and so he remained silent.

'What are you carrying a weapon for, anyway?' Benitez asked in a cranky tone. He softened a little. 'I know you were not going to use it on me.'

'Because, your Excellency, I need protection. Threats have been made upon my life as well.'

'Really? I don't know why,' Benitez said, sinking down in his chair. 'I read a transcript of the speech you gave the other night. I must say, I couldn't make hide nor hair of the thing. Whose side are you on, anyway? Something about fertility cults, wasn't it? And, ah yes, there was something else, what was it? Guido?'

' "Penis envy," your Excellency.' Guido smiled.

'What? Yes. *Penis* envy!'

The Doctor blushed. 'I was quoting Freud, your Excellency. It's not a point essential to my argument . . .'

'Penis envy! That's what it was. Look, Doctor, let me tell you something. Central America has thousands of problems, but *penis envy* . . . it is not one of them.'

Everyone laughed, including the Doctor, and though the laughter was definitely at the Doctor's expense, he was grateful that at least it was laughter and not recriminations or the third degree. And now, as if to further smooth over any hard feelings (and as an expression of his trust in the Doctor) Benitez gestured to the pistol on the desk, and bid the Doctor reclaim it.

'Wait a minute,' Commander Rabon said sharply, snatching it up. He broke open the chamber, made some minor adjustment, and snapped it shut. 'You have only three bullets in the cylinder, my friend. Now . . . if you need to use it . . .' He smiled.

'Thank you,' the Doctor said, grateful not so much for the services rendered as for all the guerrilla was not saying: to wit, that the Doctor knew absolutely nothing about guns.

The Doctor tucked the gun into its holster and, prior to leaving, started to bow.

'There's just one more thing, Doctor.' And there was something hard and hidden in Benitez's voice, like the gun beneath the Doctor's jacket. 'This man in the confessional . . .' He looked the Doctor in the eye. 'What did you tell him about us?'

'About *us?*' the Doctor repeated.

'Yes.'

'Why, nothing, your Excellency,' the Doctor said. 'What would I say to *them* . . . about *us?* After all, I thought I was talking . . . to *you.*' He laughed nervously, hoping they would understand, as though the whole problem was nothing more than a few mixed-up pronouns.

Only the guerrilla smiled. Guido and Benitez remained unamused.

'Are you certain of that?' the secretary queried.

'Well, yes.'

'Think, Doctor,' Benitez said.

The Doctor thought. 'I am certain, your Excellency. Absolutely.'

Benitez closed his eyes. 'Your notes on my examinations. Where are they?'

'They are in my office, of course.'

'Bring them to me, Doctor. Leave them at the desk downstairs. Thank you,' he said, and, turning away, dismissed him like a servant.

The Doctor did not know whether to feel insulted or relieved. He nodded and bowed to Benitez. He nodded and bowed to the Commander and Guido as well, but his presence had already been forgotten; the guerrilla was listening to the gases trapped inside him, while the secretary had already uncapped his pen and resumed writing.

How the Doctor got out of there that night, he couldn't say. He might have passed through the walls like a ghost or floated out the third-storey window and descended to the street like a hot air balloon. All he knew was that sometime later he was outside again, walking through the summer twilight in a very different state than when he had entered. He felt bereft. Gone were his visions of political glory, or of that land made of music where Mozart lived, and instead he wished only for a room somewhere he could go and lie face down in the dark and think of nothing whatsoever for a long, long time – but instead he kept on seeing a re-run in his head of the morning he had offered himself to Benitez.

What a fool he'd been, screaming his allegiance like that! No wonder Benitez had ducked into his limousine. It was obvious what had happened next. Someone had overheard the Doctor's offer, and taken him up on it, and the Doctor, instead of checking with Benitez, had gone right along with the ridiculous arrangement *because he wanted to believe in it so much* – and he could almost hear Benitez's voice scolding him now, saying: 'If I had something to ask you, why would I send you to the confessional of St. Elvira's? Why wouldn't I just call you up on the phone? No, you've been reading too many spy novels, Doctor . . .' And the Doctor wondered now how many other key paragraphs in the book of his life he had similarly misread.

He shivered a little and hurried on. Except for Jane, he had no one now. He was alone in the world. Not only was he not working for Benitez, but he was the agent and pawn of an enemy he could not name. And though the Doctor tried repeatedly to attach a face to the voice in the confessional, the only image that came to mind was hopelessly confused with a painting he had seen at an exhibition some months before . . .

Helena had insisted they attend an opening at the Guggenheim, and the Doctor, who had gone expecting to spend a pleasant hour viewing still-lifes and nudes while sipping champagne, had been disturbed to discover that a number of the paintings were of tortured people, men and women bound and gagged with screaming mouths and amputated limbs, rendered in a style that was far more frightening and express-ive than if it had been realistic. The Doctor, at once riveted and repelled, had inquired as to what kind of paintings they were, and was informed by Helena, rather snidely as he recalled, that it was the largest collection of German expressionism ever brought to the United States. And yet the painting that he remembered now had showed no blood or broken bodies, so why had it been the most sinister of all? A large canvas, it showed a Viking king of mythic dimensions seated on a stone cube on a northern promontory overlook-ing the sea. The sea was gray and cold; the figure bulky, remote, and crowned with either Viking horns or a diadem, the Doctor couldn't quite recall. What he *could* remember, and could not forget, was that, like no other portrait he had ever seen, the figure had its back to him, as though he, the viewer, did not matter in the least.

But more disturbing was what the figure held in hands which were little more than blurred and curving yellow claws. For he held in them, like some evil fisher, the drawstrings of a tremendous net.

Map Of The Heart

◆

Chapter 12

'Kid's stuff,' Sara Devi said, flinging the fetish out the fourth-storey window.

'That's evidence in a murder case,' Higgins told her.

'So why do you bring it here? What do you think I am? A detective?'

It was evening and Higgins was once again sitting with the girl in the candlelit flat on the edge of the world. It was already full night. The sky was a livid purple, with a crescent moon tilted above the slum. The child was in a fiery mood – and despite her gender, age, and size, Higgins found himself oddly intimidated by her. She grumped. 'I thought you wanted to learn meditation.'

'I do,' Higgins said.

'So why are you asking me questions about murder?'

'I don't know,' Higgins said. It was a point well taken.

'If you want to learn meditation, you need a master.'

'Exactly,' Higgins said. 'That's why I've come. Where is she?'

'Actually,' Sara said smiling beautifully, like a girl in love, 'she is nearby.' She glanced at Higgins quickly. 'Are you beginning to understand?'

'I think so,' Higgins lied.

'And if this one was to bless you, why your heart would

leap upward, and your soul would open, like those Chinese shells that flower underwater, transforming you from within.'

'Into what?'

She seemed surprised. 'Why, into a being just like her. Ecstatic. Mad with love. I know. You see, she touched me. Here,' she said pressing her breast and closing her eyes.

'Okay,' Higgins said at last. 'So, where is she?'

The girl opened her eyes, and smoothed the thighs of her skirt with slim brown hands. 'That's for me to know and for you to find out.'

'What?' Higgins said. 'You won't *tell* me?' How cruel! That she would string him along so far, only to deny him!

The child hunched forward. 'Look, this stuff is not for you. You're obviously not ready for it. Why don't you go home and just forget about it. Marry someone nice. Raise a big family.'

'What are you talking about?' Higgins cried, upset at this unexpected turn of events and by the child's low opinion of his spiritual condition. 'What's the matter with me?'

'You have no faith. Even now, you only half believe what I'm saying.'

It was true, Higgins thought. But then again, what could she expect? What she was telling him was unbelievable. Imagine! An ecstatic soul so great and bright that merely by her thought or touch you would rise up awakened!

'Anyway, I already have a teacher,' Higgins said.

'Who?'

'His name is Bhartrihari.'

She rolled her eyes.

'What's the matter now?' Higgins asked annoyed.

'The poor man's dead.'

'So what?' Higgins said. 'Don't you believe his spirit is immortal?'

She looked at him with pity. 'And do you really think that if you pray to Bhartrihari he will teach you meditation?'

'Why not?'

She smiled. 'And if you pray to Mozart, will he teach you the piano?'

238

Higgins scowled.

The girl leaned closer. 'If you wanted a wife . . . would you marry a dead woman?'

And something tore and spilled in Higgins then, something cold and ugly, a bag of pain.

'All right,' Higgins said, at his wit's end. 'So tell me where the guru is.'

'Can't,' the girl said. 'I told you. You must find her for yourself!'

Higgins jumped to his feet and began to pace. His cheeks smarted with the pain of her refusal. He looked at her with sudden hate. She was going to keep the secret to herself and taunt him with it. He knew that now. He tried to think what he could do. He thought of hiding in the dark outside the house and following the child to see if she might lead him to her. Then, when she did, he would burst in the door and fling himself before her feet and receive the great blessing. But damnit to hell, why wouldn't she just tell him where she was?

'It was peaceful in here before you came. If you're going to pace,' Sara said, 'I wish you'd go outside and do it.'

'Oh, you do, do you?' Higgins said suddenly incensed at her beyond words.

'Ha!' She laughed. 'You have had your feathers ruffled.'

'I have not,' Higgins cried.

'Of course you have. Now you're pouting. What a baby!' And she dismissed him then, just like that, with an airy wave of her little hand, as if he was some bothersome insect that had flown in the door.

'You'll be sorry for this,' Higgins said, losing it at last.

'No, I won't,' the girl replied.

Higgins stormed from the room and fled down the hallway, slamming the door behind him. But no sooner had he done so than he found himself floundering in the blackness of the darkened stairwell. And suddenly Higgins began to cry; Higgins, whose pain was dry; Higgins, who had rarely cried even as a child, hating to give anyone the satisfaction of his tears; Higgins broke down and began to weep as if his head was melting. And as he wept he asked himself what he was crying over. Over every rejection he had ever suffered at the hands of a woman – his mother's years ago, Gil's the other day, and someone else's tomorrow, of which Sara Devi's cruel refusal was only the most recent manifestation. And yet contained in all of them was that final and most uneqivocal rejection of them all: *her* death!

How it still haunted him! With what ancient power! How it still clung to him! With what sturdy ropes! He'd thought that he was over it and yet with a single lancing word, Sara had re-opened the wound, exposing the abscess, the festering sore.

Hardly realizing what he was doing now, Higgins started back up the stairs, feeling with a hand ahead in the dark while praying from the bottom of his heart that he would not encounter that dreadful monstrous hairy something he had been afraid of meeting all his life. He was relieved when he reached the top of the stairwell and found the door ajar and the landing lit by the crescent moon. He ran down the hallway only to find the girl unmoved and seated in exactly the same spot where he had left her. The sight of her made him cry all the louder, like a wailing child at the sight of its mother, and he fell at her feet and cried for the longest time into her slippers and the hem of her gown. He felt as if there was a river inside him and this river was rising and flooding his heart, washing away the dead wood and bones and useless emotions that were buried there, even as another part of him watched in amazement this torrent of emotion, feeling and tears. And from the depths of this flood there arose again that question which three hundred sleepless nights had not resolved.

'My wife and I . . . I loved her so much. She loved me, too, and we were very happy together for almost a year . . .' He gasped for breath. 'And then one night, one goddamn night, for no good reason, she just . . . *died! Why?*'

Sara stirred then, and looked at the window, as if the answer was scrawled in the dust of the sill. She closed her eyes. 'It was her destiny,' she said.

Even before he understood her words, he knew that they were true, for their sound passed inside of him, sovereign and unopposed like the truth. The effect was astonishing. Something removed its beak from his heart. His tears stopped and his jaw dropped open. And yet it was the last thing in the world Higgins had been expecting her to say, for in all his mind's mad and melancholic meandering, that the reason might be something as simple and as innocent as 'her destiny' had never once occurred to his addled brain or tortured heart.

It was her destiny, her fate! It had been written in the heavens long ago, planned and ordered by the powers-that-be. It was *supposed* to happen. They were to be together for a certain span of days and when that span was done, their bond would be dissolved – but not their love. Oh, no, never their love!

He gave a cry. Birds of guilt flew away. Ropes that had bound him snapped and broke. He felt like Atlas relieved of the world. And some vicious thing inside of Higgins that had been eating him slowly every second of every hour of every day and night since the night she had died fled his heart then forever and for good.

Kidnapped

◆

Chapter 13

At 3 a.m. the phone rang, waking her. It stopped. Then it began to ring again.

Leaving her daughters' bedroom, Gil went out into the darkened hallway to answer it, just in time to hear its ringing cease as her brother's groggy voice answered the extension in his bedroom. For no good reason, she lifted the receiver. And that was when her breathing stopped, and her blood clotted, and a sickening *frisson* ran all the way up her spine to her scalp, as though she were some great crested reptile whose scales were erecting in the dark – for a man's voice in gravelly Spanglish was saying, with all the emotion with which one announces the time, 'You like the children, Doctor? *Si*? So. You do not pay us, we take the children. *Los niñas*. Hokay? And then every week, we mail you back a piece of them.' *Click*.

The sound of the disconnection was no louder than a kiss, but to a mother's heart it might have been the world exploding. Instantly, she was wide awake. Her brother's bedroom door swung open and he stumbled out into the hall. He stopped when he saw her. She replaced the receiver.

Neither of them spoke, but something passed between them then as they looked into each other's eyes. Her brother seemed at once frightened and ashamed, and then he mumbled something and sidled by her with a moan, disappearing into the darkened toilet from out of which there quickly came a tinkle and a splash, and then the sound of nightpent water roaring in the bowl. At last, it ceased and he reappeared in the hallway, fussing with his shorts. And this time when he reached her side he said, softly and sincerely, 'I am sorry.' That was all. Then he sucked in his breath, and stumbled on, disappearing again into the darkness of his bedroom. And Gil had felt some inner vessel founder inside her – for she knew then that her brother could not save her children, would not, could not even save his own self.

After that, she wasn't certain what happened. Only isolated scenes stayed with her later: the taxi ride through the just-lightening streets, the littlest one crying inconsolably, as the two older girls suffered wooden-faced as totems on the dawn journey with their crazy mom. She remembered the stanchions of the George Washington Bridge and the cliffs of New Jersey, and the motel on Route 4 she checked them all into under an assumed name and which ten minutes later she checked them all back out of when the name she had registered under disagreed with the signature on her Traveler's Checks, and she could produce no identification to confirm either one.

Then – somehow – they were all back in New York ensconced in a small hotel in the East Thirties. By 10 a.m., the children were bathed, fed, in bed again and dozing happily as they watched Roadrunner cartoons on the color TV. Twice, she almost called the cops – but what would she have told them? *Someone is threatening to murder my children.* Who, ma'am? *I don't know.*

Instead, she called Rosita who an hour later arrived as summoned and, after listening to her story, promised upon the Teeth of Jesus that she would shoot the next *hombre* to set foot in the door.

She had a gun, too, a derringer, so little, silver and trim it might have been a piece of costume jewelry, but with which, she told Gilberta, she had once shot at a man who was bothering her sister. 'Actually, he was a handsome fellow and I was sorry to have to do it.'

'Christ, Ma, how can you think of that at a time like this? You're obsessed.'

'This is true,' Rosita said speculatively, as though she had just been given a deep insight into her own nature. She shrugged and sighed. 'But what can I do?'

'Raise your consciousness,' Gil said. 'About six inches.'

'That is where my stomach is. And then, you see, I just get hungry.'

Gil sighed. 'Shoot the next fucker who walks through the door. Will you do that for me?'

'Don't worry. I will aim for his *cojones*.'

'No,' Gil said seriously. 'Aim for the heart.'

Gilberta Castellano kissed her children and went back out, ignoring the pointed stares and glad eyes of the male idlers milling about the lobby. She purchased a pack of cigarettes, even though she hadn't smoked in years. It was her one outward concession to panic. She needed something to do with her fingers. She was tired of shredding tissues and picking at her nails.

She went through the hotel's revolving doors and got into a taxi. But when she gave the Doctor's address in the *barrio*, the cabbie, a washed-out old *Anglo* said, 'Hell, lady. I ain't goin' anywheres near that hole.'

Gilberta thought she might cry, but instead she got out and into another cab driven by a young Hispanic man deranged on drugs or his own male hormones who was banging out the rhythms of a disco tune on the bongos of his dash. Gil gave him the address of her brother's office. 'Gotcha, babe,' the young man cried, and floored the car so violently she wrenched something in her neck. Whiplash. It was a wild bucking ride. She tried to sit back, relax and smoke a cigarette, but that was not possible. In the bumping cab, she could not get the cigarette lit and all she managed was to scorch the paper and raise a blister on the inside of her thumb. She cursed beneath her breath and put the stupid things – the matches and the cigarettes – back in her purse.

Someone was threatening to murder her children.

She got out in front of her brother's office, paid the driver, and climbed the three steep flights of stairs. It was a great place for a doctor, she thought; a great place for sick people in wheelchairs with heart attacks to have to get to. At the top of the stairs she let out a sigh – the steel door was shut, and a laminated plastic sign hanging crookedly from the hooked steel handle read:

The Doctor Is Out
He Will Return At:

below which a clock's broken hands pointed their stubs to no time at all.

For a moment, again, she thought she might cry. She'd been up half the night and one part of her felt very tired and shaky. And yet standing there, gripping the banister at the top of the stairs, another part of her felt supernaturally lucid and calm, like a statue of some Egyptian goddess, five times life-size, carved out of hard green stone.

She shook herself, went back down the stairs at a coltlike clip and out into the summer street. The minute she hit it, the comments began, the leering suggestions and the kissing, clicking noises which the mustachioed lips of her admirers felt compelled to bestow upon her sumptuous womanhood. She had lived with this harassment so long she hardly even heard it any longer. It was just background noise, like the hum of the traffic.

Reaching her brother's brownstone, Gil bounded up the steps, got out her key and let herself in. Before entering, however, she looked about carefully: the world was real, it had hard edges on it. She felt almost grateful for the vicious phone call. She had been in a fog; and it gave her a reason to live once again.

Upstairs, she checked all the rooms, but there was nobody home. A sport coat of Higgins' was flung across the sofa. Instinctively, she started to hang it up, then stopped and thought angrily, I'm not his maid. *Or* his wife. So, what am I doing? But she hung it up anyway. She hated messes.

Someone was threatening to murder her children.

She wished that Higgins was here to talk to. Maybe it was only the soft nap of the jacket's wool twill, but suddenly he seemed to her a powerful ally, an intelligent and sympathetic man. There was something a little stiff about him, to be sure, something slightly formal. Sometimes when he saw her, he would smile mildly and, placing his hand upon his heart, bow slightly from the waist, and antique gesture, like a count in some old novel. Still, she had to talk to *someone*, to come up with a plan, to find out who had made the threat against them. But there was nobody home.

She went back downstairs and stood on the sidewalk, scanning the street for Higgins or her brother. She lit a cigarette and inhaled with a guilty pleasure. A disapproving voice mumbled something inside her. What was it saying? Oh, yes. *Nice girls don't smoke cigarettes on the street.* God, where had that come from? Well, the hell with it. She had stopped being nice at nineteen – when she'd seduced the Italian movie director, Ermenegildo Ferre.

A Cadillac drifted up to the curb. An unctuous voice invited her in. God, she was sick and tired of being hassled by men. 'Fuck off,' she said.

Then she felt the gun. It was touching her belly. It looked extremely real, realer than anything she had ever seen. She looked in the car. It was full of wild-looking men and her brother, stonefaced, sandwiched in between them.

Gil did not feel frightened, only cold and monumental, like something heroic carved out of hard green stone. Girl, this is not a dream, she told herself.

'C'mon, sweetheart. In!'

El Duende

◆

Chapter 14

'You owe us, Doctor.'

'I owe you nothing. I told you. No more money. Nor do we like being kidnapped off the street by your thugs.'

'It's not your money we want, *amigo*. It's intelligence. And that you *will* supply us with,' *El Duende* said. 'If you know what's good for you.' He smiled at Gil. 'And for those kids.'

Gil didn't blink or speak. She only stared at *El Duende* as though she was recording his words on the disc of her memory and fixing his image on some film in her head. Then she said: 'So it's you who threatened them last night.'

Omar laughed. 'We just didn't want you to sleep too soundly.'

'And it's you who set up that charade in the confessional, isn't it?' the Doctor asked.

But Omar only frowned. 'What confessional?'

Then he presented the Doctor with their latest offer. He made it seem so reasonable. The Doctor's debt would be forgiven him in return for a small favor.

'What kind of small favor?' the Doctor sneered.

'Find out for us what Benitez is up to.'

The Doctor guffawed. 'You must be crazy. Rodolfo Benitez? You think President Benitez discusses his war plans with *me*? You think he tells *me* what he does or does not intend to do?'

'We know he does, Doctor,' Omar said. 'You are his physician. He came to your office twice last week. And just last
night, you conferred with Benitez and Commander Rabon.'
He looked at his notes. 'For almost one hour.'

'And how do you know that?' the Doctor asked, surprised.

'We know everything about you, Doctor. Every step
you've ever made. Omar, show the Doctor his file.'

Omar lifted a file from the table and set it on the Doctor's
lap. It was not the few pages of handwritten notes the Doctor
had expected, but a thick black notebook. And every word in
the astonishing document was about him: Arsenio Eduardo
Castellano.

'Go ahead,' *El Duende* said. 'Read a little, Doctor. It's
amusing.'

The Doctor, opening the notebook at random, read a profile of his father, 'a neo-liberal physician' – then skipped a
few pages and studied a photocopy of a confidential report
made about him by his English teacher, Master Jeffrey Parks,
to the Headmaster of the Miami prep school the Doctor had
attended twenty-five years ago.

'Where did you get this?' the Doctor asked, amazed.

'Read on, Doctor,' *El Duende* said. 'It will soon become
clear.'

But as the Doctor read on, nothing became clearer, only
more and more amazing. The file might have been the journal
kept by the omniscient Saint Peter, for every page was crammed with facts and fancies about the Doctor and his life.
There were even interviews with people he had only slightly
known years ago. The first woman he had ever slept with,
Evangeline Guare (whose image was permanently enshrined
in the Doctor's heart and toward whom he still felt a certain
stupid, stubborn love) claimed not to remember who the
Doctor was.

'I told the other man,' the Doctor read, 'I slept with about
a hundred and fifty guys that summer. So how you expect
me now to remember this one *hombre*?'

The Doctor, his heart mangled, skipped a few pages and
read some more: 'Believed to have experimented with halluci-

nogens from '66 to '69 when drug use abruptly ceased, according to Informant G. Reason for sudden cessation unknown.'

Ah ha! So they did not know everything, whoever they were. They could only see outlines, they could not see inside his head. They did not know about the rush that had kept on rushing, the high that would not die, and then the thousands of ravenous blue *langostas* that had exploded from the ivy-covered walls of the campus, nipping at the Doctor's toes.

The Doctor shuddered and continued reading: 'A typical bleeding heart liberal, the subject showed little talent for managing his resources and was frequently in debt. From '80 to '83, credit rating poor.'

The Doctor looked up. 'Who the hell wrote this?'

'Our friends. Your enemies, Doctor.'

'But why would anyone keep a file like this' – he thumbed through the pages, riffling years; he saw his grades at medical school, his trip to Dorado, and the license plate number of a car he no longer owned – 'on *me*?'

'They keep one on everyone important,' Omar said. 'Though not everyone, of course, ends up with a dossier as fat as yours. Obviously, you interest them.'

'I do? But why?' the Doctor asked. experiencing alongside a sick, sinking feeling a rising sense of self-esteem.

'Come off it, Doctor. Don't be so modest. You are well respected. You give speeches, don't you?'

'Well, yes, but . . .' The Doctor laughed. 'I never thought anyone listened to what I said.'

'Ah, there, you see? You are wrong. You will find summaries of all your speeches here. Plus the names of those persons who were in attendance.'

'Really?' He was amazed. And though he was aware that the reason for their interest was to use and manipulate him for their own evil ends, their attention was flattering, nonetheless, and somehow made the Doctor feel like he was someone who was wanted, someone who was *loved*.

'It's funny, but I never noticed anybody following me around.'

'Ah,' Omar said, 'and think what else you may not have seen.' And the Doctor saw Mucho then, standing behind him by the curve of the bar. He was staring at Gilberta while eating ice cream with a tiny wooden spoon. He turned and smiled at the Doctor, sweet cream bubbling between his teeth. Then he went back to staring at Gil in his frankly perverted way.

The Doctor put the notebook down. 'I won't do it.'

'Oh, yes you will, Doctor.'

'What my brother's trying to say, *Señors* . . .'

'I don't need a translator, damnit!' the Doctor shouted, aware he should not be talking to his sister this way in the presence of their enemies. 'And you, you big tub of lard! You still can't get it through your head, can you, that I am not your dog anymore. I told you once—'

He did not see the blow. It came from behind. And now, looking up from the floor where he found himself lying, it was with some surprise the Doctor realized it was the goon who had hit him. He had not thought the boy could have covered those fifteen paces so swiftly. He was looking down at him, still eating ice cream. 'You shouldn't talk that way to Señor Valpero.' He licked the inside crack of the little ice cream cup with his wet red tongue. Then he licked both sides of the wooden spoon. He frowned. 'Señor Valpero doesn't like it.'

The Doctor glanced at his sister. She was sitting up, calmly smoking. She did not appear to be at all concerned that her brother had been so grossly and feloniously assaulted. And for one small, heartrending second, the Doctor felt completely abandoned and betrayed.

'Get up,' *El Duende* said, as though it was the Doctor's fault he was lying on the ground, as though he'd done a pratfall.

But as the Doctor tried to rise, the goon came over and stepped on his fingers, for no good reason – because his shoes were just itching to step on something, with the vicious reflex that makes you squash a bug.

'Mucho! No!' *El Duende* barked.

Mucho stalked off, his feelings clearly wounded, though as he left, he threw up the licked utensil and the empty Styrofoam container with a spoiled cry. The little wooden shovel paddled through the air with a lovely whirring motion, skidding as it touched the shiny tiles by the Doctor's fingers.

And it was then the Doctor remembered the gun. How could he have forgotten it? He did not have to take this shit. He was armed, after all. And standing up, he drew the pistol and pointed it at Omar's head.

The shylock seemed surprised – but only for a moment. Then he reached up and turned the Doctor's wrist so that the barrel of the gun was pointing back at the Doctor, and the joint of the Doctor's hand was painfully bent against the bone. The move was calm, deliberate and certain; the Doctor had had all the time in the world to fire – but didn't. Why? Because he was not about to blow Omar's skull to smithereens at six o'clock on a Monday evening.

And the Doctor realized then that he'd been watching too much television. On television, when a character drew a pistol, everybody froze. Never in any of the shows he'd seen had someone reached up and twisted the pistol so it was pointing at the assailant's head.

The shylock released the Doctor's wrist. He seemed to have no fear of the gun. Why should he? The gun was harmless if the Doctor did not intend to use it – which he didn't For what could the Doctor do, shoot them all in cold blood then sit down and wait to be arrested for murder? The Doctor put the gun away and rubbed the subcutaneous bracelet of blood left by the shylock's grip, but he only succeeded in making it redder.

'Doctor,' *El Duende* said, 'let me tell you a story. Once there was a fairy who lived in a pumpkin, eating moonbeams, dressed in starlight. Then one day, the man who owned the pumpkin got mad at the fairy and took her out. He squeezed her till the blood broke through her eyes. Then he pulled off her head and wings.' *El Duende* ripped a chicken wing from the carcass on the table and cartwheeled it past the Doctor's nose. The pinscher caught it in its teeth with a hollow *clock*.

'And fed them to his dog.' He paused, his chin and fingers glistening with grease.

'What's that supposed to mean?'

Omar answered: 'It means that if you do exactly what we tell you to, your debt will be forgiven and your nieces will remain unharmed. You don't, and we'll kill the children. Then we'll kill you. And as for your sister . . .' He licked his lips. 'She's too good-looking to kill. We'll give her to Mucho . . . as a pet.' And they all laughed.

The Doctor got to his feet, enraged. 'Devils!' he said. 'You're devils, not men.'

'Take them away,' *El Duende* said, losing interest in the sadistic proceedings. 'The Doctor is bleeding. Find him a cab.'

The Doctor waited for his sister to cry, but as the cab drove home, she neither spoke nor wept. She stared out the window, frozen, unmoving, like a creature made of ice. If she had cried, the Doctor might have cried along with her, comforted them both and felt better, but as it was her silence was a great recrimination. They had not even bothered to take away his gun; it was the final humiliation.

The Doctor sighed and spoke at last to fill the anxious vacuum. 'That idiot. Did you see him? Shoveling ice cream into his face!'

Gil said nothing. Then she said: 'Your cheek is swelling!'

'Of course it's swelling,' the Doctor said, 'what did you expect it to do? Sing *Juantanamero*?'

'I only meant . . . here, let me, Arsenio.'

'Get away,' the Doctor said peevishly, swatting at her hand. 'You'll only make it worse.'

But despite his protests, Gil began to dab at his cheek, even as she told him something which the Doctor did not hear. For the Doctor was remembering another summer evening, now already more than a quarter of a century old. The Caribbean was near, the stars were eyes, the moon was yellow, they were afraid of her getting pregnant. He had entered her quickly, then withdrew and in a sweet erotic panic she had milked him with her hand. And afterward, she was not ashamed or disgusted as he had feared, but showed it to him, the steaming handful of his sticky, pearly seed, and laughed and touched it with her tongue and smeared it on the sand, and gave to him her breasts to suck and stroked his head and said that he was very good, very *macho*, very strong. And the Doctor who lay down a boy stood up a man.

Evangeline!

A Bed In Hell

Part III

Whither shall I go from thy spirit?
Or whither shall I flee from thy presence?
If I ascend up into heaven, thou art there:
If I make my bed in hell, behold,
Thou art there.

– Psalm 139

Renunciation

◆

Chapter 1

Higgins woke up, elated, before dawn. He rose on an elbow and raised a shade: purple vapors and violet airs still lingered in the streets. The shops were dark, their iron gates securely shut against the vandalic night and the only sound was of an engine throbbing, catching and sobbing, starting and failing again and again, until it caught with a sputter, sang for an instant, then swiftly died. The morning was then very quiet and dim – except in the east, where Higgins saw a sight that made his hair stand on end and his innards quiver, for there, just below the curve of the world, something inconceivably brilliant was rising.

Higgins lay back down in bed, remembering now the previous evening. After he had finished crying, Sara Devi had wiped his eyes with the hem of her shawl, given him a sip of freezing tea, and sent him packing. He had wanted to sleep there, at her feet, but she would not permit it. The truth of the matter was that Higgins had been afraid to cross the moonlit waste alone at that hour – though as it turned out, he had made it back without incident. Even a bunch of drunken thugs, hanging out on the Doctor's stoop, had broken ranks to let him through. Clearly he was under somebody's aegis, though whether it was the young *yogini*'s or *El Duende*'s, he couldn't say.

Higgins tried to fall back to sleep, but he was too excited.

He didn't know why. He felt as though a light was rising in his body, something he couldn't see as yet, something just below the curved horizon of his mind.

Yes! Something great was about to happen. He could sense it, feel it coming, like birds presage the changing weather, or spirits the approach of day.

Restless, Higgins got out of bed and went to the kitchen. He found Gil sitting there in the dawn gloom. She was dressed and smoking, staring out over a cup of untouched coffee in which the *leche* had separated into ghostly swirls. The room had an uncanny stillness, an emptiness he couldn't quite define. Then he could.

'Where are the kids?'

'On a plane.'

'A plane?'

'To Puerto Rico.'

'What for?'

She didn't answer.

Higgins went over and stood above her. 'Hey, are you okay?'

'Uh huh.'

'No, you're not. What's the matter?'

'Nothing.'

'You've been crying.' He took her hands. They were freezing. 'You miss them?'

She nodded.

'So why didn't you go with them?'

She didn't answer. She stubbed out her cigarette and looked away. Higgins drew her to her feet and took her in his arms. He only meant to comfort her, but in that instant his brotherly affection blurred into passion and instead, he bent and kissed her lips.

It didn't count. She wasn't there. He might have been kissing an inflatable rubber dolly. Her body was present, but her soul was not. Her soul was cruising at 30,000 feet, and on a plane to Puerto Rico.

There are few things more humiliating than kissing a woman

who does not kiss you back. It's worse than kissing a woman who resists you, since such a woman may eventually be won, whereas kissing a woman who just stands there with her mouth open and her eyes on the ceiling, thinking of Puerto Rico, is worse than kissing even a corpse because in the latter case the corpse can't kiss, while in the former one, the woman can and won't.

This, or something close to it, was the tape that was running through Higgins' mind, in an endless loop, driving him mad. He tried to meditate, then to do some writing, but his concentration was ruined, and his unhappiness only deepened as the morning progressed. Gil's non-kiss burned on his lips, while his soul felt like it was spiraling down into some tar-black pit of failure and pain.

Face it: he was defeated. Beat. Life, he told himself, is like some pretty tease who excites and entices and leads you on, but in the end, will never sleep with you. He thought of Gil, but it wasn't even her he wanted; it was *her*; no, Her! It had always been Her.

But though he had loved and courted Her for ages, still he had received nothing, attained nothing, no measure whatso-ever of certitude or peace. Why? What in the world had he left undone?

Higgins thought of his mentor, Bhartrihari, who had given up a kingdom, and of the rich man in the Gospels who Jesus had commanded to sell all he owned. And it struck Higgins then, with the force of a hammer, that he would never attain anything until he gave up everything he had.

This idea pained and depressed him. And yet bitter as it was, he could think of nothing else to do. Some austere spirit of renunciation was urging him to give up all his loves and possessions so that he might, at long last, know God fully. For how could he ever hope to embrace Her when his hands were full of *things*?

Yes, that was it. He must renounce everything. He must renounce the world! He gazed out at the trees and the summer sunlight. But how did one renounce the world?

Well, first of all, he would renounce women. He would

give up sex. And why the hell not? He had been very unlucky with women, with love. Sex was a millstone around his neck, his penis more a torment than a pleasure for all the little thrills it had enjoyed.

Higgins took out his address book with the names and addresses of all the women he knew and threw it on the floor as a symbolic gesture. In the book were the names of his family and friends as well. Well, he would renounce them, too.

Then he went to the closet, pulled out his favorite jacket, and threw it on the floor. It was a beautiful garment, splendidly tailored in silk and wool with natural shoulders and bone buttons. It was the most beautiful and expensive piece of clothing that he owned. Ah, but it, too, would have to go!

Then he remembered the property in Maine: the two hundred acres of deer-fraught forest, of lakeshore and blackberry bushes and beautiful blue lichen-stained stone walls. He thought of the pond that kissed the forest, and the restless tongues of water that lapped and licked the northern woods as secret inlets and trouted streams. He remembered the firs in the morning with a cottony mist clinging to their needles. Damn it! He would get rid of every watery inch and piney acre of it – though he loved it more than any place on earth. He would give it away and never see it again, he swore!

But the more that Higgins attempted to renounce, the more he realized what he owned, big and small: there were his cars and his condominium, there were belts, shoes and scraps of paper (ticket stubs to Symphony Hall from his first real date with *her*), underwear, t-shirts, ties and tie clasps, thousands of books and hundreds of tapes and records, furniture, paintings, and kitchen utensils: skillets, teakettles, cups and knives. The list was endless, like stars in the night sky. And like stars in the night what you saw with your eye was only a part of an infinite whole – for behind this whole visible fortune was another invisible one of stocks and bonds and certificates of deposit, of treasury notes and IRAs.

Well, damnit to hell, he would renounce it all! He threw his checkbook on the growing midden as a symbol of his good intentions. He would renounce his wealth – every *shekel* of it – even if it took him years to do so.

Now, what else must be renounce?

Looking around him, he saw the pages of his manuscript and his heart took a fall. O, but he had loved books and writing so, ever since his boyhood! *Charlotte's Web! The Count of Monte Cristo*! He remembered the first day he had ever heard of a literary symbol. He was probably eleven. An older cousin, Gary Harmon, had showed him a passage from *The Red Badge of Courage* in which the setting sun was likened to a bloody wafer and had announced it was a 'Christ symbol.' And Higgins remembered how the short hairs on the nape of his neck had stood on end and how a shock had gone through his prepubescent body at the sudden marvelous inner dawning that such a thing could be: that a sun could also be . . . a Son – that a word could stand for two entirely different entities at once, that there existed such mysterious and exalted things as signs, levels, symbols!

Now Higgins regarded the pages of his manuscript with pain. For he knew he must renounce his writing. What else could he do? He loved it too much. He took a sheet from the couch and spread it on the carpet. He piled his jacket, his address and checkbooks in the middle of it, then tossed his manuscript on top, and after it a dozen felt-tipped pens. He would renounce women, he would renounce writing, he would renounce the world. He would give up all those things that gave him pleasure and then, that One he had loved and longed for, courted for so many lifetimes, ages, would have pity on him and reveal Herself at last.

Higgins thought of all the money he would have to give away – it was staggering. He thought of Gil and all the women he would never love, all the novels he would never write, all the friends he would never see again. Then he sat down on the edge of the couch and wept. He didn't know why. Why, when he had done God's bidding, should he still feel so miserable, bereft, and empty?

'Why? Because you're an idiot. That's why.'

Higgins looked up, expecting to see Gil, but it was Sara

Devi who stood in the doorway, beaming at him with great delight. Higgins, who had never seen her in daylight before was amazed by her appearance. Her eyes were a crystal gray, her braided hair an Indian blue, while her dusky flesh held such a glorious luster that for one crazy instant Higgins thought he might see himself reflected in her face.

Stepping in, she looked about her. Clearly, she was not impressed. The room was a mess – a mound of papers, pens, and clothing heaped upon the rug.

Higgins explained how he was renouncing the world. But instead of the praise he had expected to win, the child only laughed in amusement and said, 'And where do you intend to live, if not in this world?'

This was a question that Higgins couldn't answer.

Then she leaned forward and said in a whisper: 'O *deva*, just as everywhere on the sun is fire, so every part of this world is God. When that's the case, what can you renounce?'

Higgins stared at her for the longest moment, trying to decipher what it was she was saying. 'You mean . . .' he said at last, 'I don't have to give up . . . all these *things*?'

She looked at him kindly. 'If you give up your clothes, you'll only be naked. If you give up your wealth, you'll only be poor. Do you really think Truth can be bought so cheap? Renunciation is an inner state. Give up your anxiety, your pain and greed. If being poor and idle made a man holy, then every derelict would be a saint!'

And listening now to Sara Devi's wisdom, Higgins felt a fist of joy arise inside him that smashed his ignorance, and broke his pain. What a fool he'd been! What a simple, literal-minded fool! It wasn't the *world* he had to renounce – but his attachment to it and his wrong understanding.

With a happy cry, Higgins retrieved his book and jacket. And as he did so, there arose within him a great rejoicing – as though he had offered his life to the Virgin and she'd been so pleased by his act of devotion, she had given it back to him, multiplied a hundredfold.

Then Higgins turned to Sara Devi. He looked at her anew,

wondering to himself who she was to see the world in such an extraordinary manner.

And as he did, the scales fell from Higgins' eyes. It was more dramatic than the day he had first put on glasses and the green blur outside the optometrist's shop had resolved into a thousand saw-toothed leaves. Only now the change was in his inner vision.

For though she was perched on the radiator cover wrapped in her patched and threadbare shawl, Higgins' inner eye was finally opened and he saw her now for who she was. No wonder she had been appearing in his meditations! No wonder she had been haunting his thoughts and dreams! She was his guru! There was no other.

No sooner did Higgins have this revelation, than Sara laughed and began to sing. Chanting softly, she arose and approached him, placing her hands upon his forehead, and pressing her fingers deep into his eyes. Higgins was too surprised for it to hurt! Then she touched her knee to his spine – and held that pose for several seconds. Finally, she made a sound of satisfaction, stroked his head the way you would an infant's and, very quietly, quit the room. In this way, Shrimati Saraswati Devi, secret queen, who the world regarded as a beggar and a fool, gave to Higgins her divine initiation.

Initiation

◆

Chapter 2

Higgins had imagined that if he ever had a 'spiritual experience' it would be very 'spiritual' and very subtle – but what followed Sara Devi's touch was about as subtle as being hit by a brick.

First, he felt a voluptuous physical chill ripple through his body, breaking as an ecstatic wave on the shores of his soul. This was followed by a tapping sensation in the space between his eyebrows, like the switching on of a nerve; and then, suddenly, something like a spring made out of light exploded at the base of Higgins' spine, shooting up his back-bone, and light supernatural burst from his eyes!

Higgins gave a shout and fell back on the couch, blinded, mad, his eyes streaming gold. Nothing in his life had prepared him for this experience, for it was different from anything he had ever known. He tried to sit up but found now that his body had a will of its own, guided as it was by the miraculous power that had erupted inside him. He could feel an actual current of energy streaming up his backbone and lapping softly at the base of his skull like a jet of warm water. Lightning-like thrills and chills were zipping through his body. And then there was the light – he seemed to see every-thing through sheer gold curtains that waved and evanesced at the corners of his vision.

Higgins laughed in astonishment, only half believing that such a thing could be. And yet even as he doubted it, an ecstasy like he had never known ballooned inside him. It was like falling in love without an object – and so he kept on falling, falling.

Suddenly, Higgins leaped to his feet and began to dance about the living room, hissing like a serpent. His body was moving of its own accord, following the circulating currents of *prana* that were flowing inside him. Then he stopped and began to whirl like a dervish, instantly becoming drunk on the perfect circularity of his movements, his motion emulating the Spirit inside him, that same spinning Power that pin-wheels galaxies, spirals seashells, sperm and stars. Higgins didn't understand what he was doing, or why, only that it felt wonderful to do so; his back cracked and the muscles of his neck and torso stretched and flexed. Inspired by the awakened Power, he seemed to be dancing with joy, or performing some sort of spiritual gymnastics. And then, in an inspired instant, he realized it wasn't gymnastics at all. It was yoga!

No sooner did Higgins have this revelation than his legs locked and he sat down in the full lotus. Higgins was amazed, for he had never been able to sit in this posture properly before. It was as though his body had been commandeered by a Goddess. What was more, this divine afflatus had taken control of his autonomous nerves, for She ruled his breath and moved his limbs according to Her will.

Then, just as suddenly, the movements ceased; Higgins breathing hushed, his mind became still, and he fell into a state of deep meditation.

How long it lasted Higgins couldn't say. He was in bliss. Morning turned to afternoon, afternoon to early evening. At one point, he opened his eyes and gazed out the window, expecting to see the same raggle-taggle slum with its rhinestone lights and threadbare beauty, but the cityscape was transformed. The buildings were bathed in a shimmering radiance. The tarnish on his vision had been removed and he could see the divine monogram imprinted on everything. Everything declared the glory of God – even the stones were scriptures!

Eventually, his meditation ended, and getting up he left the flat. He would never forget how he felt that night as he staggered out into a summer evening of old rose and lacquered

Spanish gold. He was drunk on inner drafts, dazed by the brightness of an inner sun. The feeling was stronger than being on drugs. His mind was swimming, while deep, sweet chills kept coursing through his body as though a hundred hidden springs had surfaced at his breastbone, or his heart, which had been dry and dead, had split and spat forth the first shoot of some fantastic new life and no one, anywhere, was more amazed by it than Higgins.

After a while – not because he was tired, but because it was late and he should have been exhausted, which he wasn't – he returned to the house and lay down on the couch. And still Higgins' ecstasy continued! He lay in the dark of the Doctor's living room, feeling the serpentine energy moving inside him, undulating like a sea filling his throat and then rolling out his mouth past his teeth and lips in the form of *OM*. *OM* was the name the energy chanted. *OM* was the name it called itself out of Higgins' mouth. Higgins had nothing to do with the voices. Some inner chorus had pulsed into being and the pulses of its being were the waves of bliss and light that lapped his heart, exiting his mouth in the form of *OM* – what more could he say?

All sorts of images arose before him. He saw quite clearly an Arab port. It was somewhere in the African Mediterranean with blond mud huts, flies, and a crude bazaar; next, he saw somewhere that was not of this world: a serene blue valley full of twists of blue smoke and unearthly blue and silver deer.

Finally, around midnight Higgins got up and went to the kitchen where he drank a glass of tap water, just to see if he could still function, for in between the onslaughts of ecstasy that assailed him he wondered if he had not gone mad. For a moment or two he felt perfectly normal, the fiery Presence having abated in the dark. But then, once again, there was a throbbing sensation at the base of his spine and a white inner flame flashed from his head to his heart in a supernatural arc, and the next thing he knew the glass had fallen, and he was whirling in the darkened kitchen, his steps light as helium, twirling and whirling in the pork-scented darkness, dancing with a secret and unspeakable glee.

The Double Agent

$\blacklozenge$

Chapter 3

'They want me to spy on you, *Señor Presidente*. They want me to worm my way into your organization and report everything I hear back to them.'

'And who is this *they*?'

'*El Duende*. Who is working, we believe, with Schmidt of AES.'

'And what makes them think you'll do this for them? Are they offering you money, Doctor?'

'No, your Excellency.'

'What is it then? Do they think you're one of them?'

'They're threatening to kill my nieces.'

'I see,' Benitez said. 'How very persuasive of them.'

It was early evening and the Doctor was alone with *El Presidente* in the third-floor office of his lavish home. The room, with its books and flags and dozens of mementoes, its pre-Columbian artifacts and framed photographs of Benitez shaking hands with assorted politicians, looked more like the office of a college president than the lair of an exiled lord. To the west, through windows that ran from floor to ceiling, the Doctor had a marvelous view of the East River bathed in the gray gold light of the evening sun which alternately glared and dimmed as it blundered through some puffy clouds. The view was marred only by the sight of a garbage scow, which for the past five minutes had been chugging about the harbor.

'Cigar, Doctor?'

'Yes, thanks.'

Benitez plucked from the humidor behind him a *Romeo y Julieta Churchill*, clipped one end with a silver cutter, ran its length beneath his nose, and passed it to the Doctor. Then he lifted an antique lighter and uncapped its flame, urging the Doctor to take his time and to draw slowly on the glorious Havana – until its tip was glowing brightly and the room had filled with its sweet gray fumes.

The ceremony over, Benitez leaned over an intercom and pressed a button. 'Guido, get me the file on *El Duende*, and on Lieutenant Colonel Adolfo Schmidt.'

'Yes, your Excellency,' the box responded.

Benitez lounged back in his chair and waited. The Doctor, who had been afraid of a tongue-lashing, was glad to see *El Presidente* in such a benign and sympathetic mood. Benitez sat, patiently, silently absorbed, while the Doctor tried to imitate his manner and failed. He could not get comfortable in the overstuffed chair. When he leaned back, he had the sense of sinking, ass-first, into a soft morass, while when he sat up, his legs were a problem and he couldn't decide what to do with his knees. And so, he concentrated on the Havana and on the spirals of smoke rotating in the evening light like distant galaxies.

Then the double doors flew open and Guido waltzed in. Benitez, who was staring at the wake on the river where the garbage scow had passed, stuck out his hand and took the proffered file without removing his gaze from the water. '*Gracias*,' he murmured – at once a thanks and a dismissal.

Guido glanced at the Doctor ensconced in the chair, smoking the cigar. 'Your Excellency . . .' he began in a petulant voice, but Benitez silenced him with a raised palm, and the secretary, forced to swallow air, gave the Doctor another withering glare and exited the chamber. Then the door was closed, and the two men were alone again in the silver dusk suffused by the twin illuminations: the great one that played upon the river, and the little one at the end of the Doctor's cigar. Benitez snapped on a desk lamp and began to read the files.

When he was finished, he passed them to the Doctor. Schmidt's file consisted of a short biography, half a dozen scissored newspaper articles, autopsy reports, and a blown-up telephoto snapshot of Schmidt that was so blurred and unrecognizable, it might have been Nessie or the Abominable Snowman.

Each of the articles reported the killing of a Doradoan exile. Schmidt's *modus operandi* was remarkable, it seemed. His choice of weapon was not the long-range rifle and telescopic sight. Almost all of his hits had been performed up close, *mano a mano*, in your face, as it were.

The Doctor examined several autopsy photos of Schmidt's victims – including one of Courvoisier. In almost every one, there were powder burns where the muzzle had been pressed against the flesh. This was all the more remarkable as many of his victims were prominent individuals who knew their lives were on the line. And yet, in every case, Schmidt had managed to get them alone, and close enough to press a gun to their flesh as though, whoever Schmidt was – or was pretending to be – his targets had trusted him. In every case, too, he had managed to slip away – leaving no more trace than a bad memory in the mind of a frightened maid and a brief description so general as to be useless: Latin, 5'11" to 6'1", 175 pounds, brown hair, brown eyes. And the Doctor understood now why Benitez was so concerned about security. Schmidt's description fitted a million *hombres*, including himself.

Most disturbing, however, was the list of exiles whom Schmidt was alleged to have killed. It read like a veritable 'Who's Who' of Dorado. If Schmidt had done the same to a dozen great works of art, the world, the Doctor thought, would have screamed bloody murder. Imagine one man destroying Michelangelo's David, blowtorching the Mona Lisa, and bombing the Parthenon? And yet Schmidt had destroyed something far greater. He'd sought out and offed Dorado's best and brightest – the flower of a generation.

He'd gone up to Courvoisier and shot him in the head. He'd put an icepick through the heart of *La Bafana* – and oh, the Doctor knew, from listening to her records, what a beautiful and generous heart it was. And once again the Doctor felt a deep and visceral revulsion for this destroyer of human souls.

However, while Schmidt was certainly a brilliant assassin, he was not, the Doctor read, believed to be the brains behind the string of executions, though who that was was still unknown.

Next, the Doctor turned to *El Duende*, but *El Duende*'s file, with the exception of a few handwritten notes, was empty.

'Hmmm,' Benitez said, leaning back in his chair. 'I bet they've done business together before. Come in. Make a deal. Yes. But why *now*?' The Doctor was having trouble following the conversation, which was not surprising since Benitez was not really speaking to the Doctor – merely thinking aloud. Benitez paused. 'Unless they got wind of . . . the negotiations.'

But at the word 'negotiations,' a ratchet clicked in the Doctor's brain, and the face of the man he had seen downstairs earlier that evening reappeared before him.

For Benitez had been busy when the Doctor had arrived, and so the Doctor had cooled his heels for more than an hour on the hard wooden bench in the ground floor lobby. This time the Doctor had been thoroughly frisked. The guards had done everything but look up his rectum. At last the elevator doors had opened and a tall, *Anglo* gentleman had glided out and crossed the floor. The man's face was familiar. The tanned, patrician features, the strict lips, the pale, ironic eyes, the hair that was a blend of silver and gold. Why it was . . . it was . . . But the Doctor could not attach a name or title to the face, try as he would. And it was only now, at the word 'negotiations,' that his memory was jogged. He could still not remember the visitor's name or official position, but that did not matter, for he knew where he had seen that face before, even if it had aged in recent days, lining lightly and well like expensive glove leather, and graying at the brow. It was a face he had been seeing since the early seventies at news conferences on Vietnam, and Congressional hearings on Cambodia and Chile, the face of a man who for years had been, if not the chief architect of US foreign policy, then certainly one of its main carpenters and masons.

'You're negotiating with the State Department,' the Doctor said.

Benitez turned and looked at the Doctor like he might have to kill him for reaching such an accurate conclusion. He seemed to weigh this option for a fraction of a second, then decide, once and for all, against it. And it was at that moment, the Doctor realized later, he became one of them.

'Not negotiating, Doctor, only negotiating about negotiating. We are talking about talking, meeting about meeting. You see, at the moment, we cannot yet agree on an agenda, or where or when these proposed negotiations will take place.'

And the Doctor remembered another war, not so long ago, where, while fire rained and children burned, the peacemakers argued about the shape of the table.

'But what does it all mean?' the Doctor asked, lowering his voice to a conspiratorial whisper. 'Your Excellency, can it mean that soon you will be back in power?'

Benitez shrugged. 'Who knows? Perhaps I am a fool, but I have always thought that someday it would come to pass. And not because I am one of those people who believes that liberation is inevitable, and that justice is sure to one day triumph. No. The only thing I regard as inevitable is death.'

'And taxes,' the Doctor added.

'Hardly. Look at the generals and ruling families of Dorado. They've paid no taxes for twenty-two years.' Benitez smiled sadly. 'No, if I am returned to power it will be, I think, for deeper reasons.' He paused and gestured to the design in the rug. 'Do you know what that is, Doctor?'

'The seal of the Republic.'

'Very good. And who is *that*?' he asked, pointing to the fabulous figure coiled at the center of the seal.

'It's Quetzalcoatl, isn't it?'

'Tell him, Guido,' Benitez said to his secretary who had

once again entered the office and was eavesdropping at the door.

'That's his Aztec name. It's Cukulcan, actually, the Mayan version of the same divinity. A snake-bird. Fabulous. Plumed. He gave the Indians fire by rubbing his sandals together. In that way, he is a sort of a Central American Prometheus. And yet there are other things about him that are strangely familiar. His symbol was the cross and he was born of a virgin. He died, and on the fourth day, his heart was resurrected as the morning star. No wonder the Spanish *padres* thought their own beliefs were being mocked by the devil.'

'But why is he on the seal?'

'Because,' said Benitez, 'he represents the spirit of the people of Dorado. Unquenchable. And though he left our golden land, the legends say he will return someday from out of the east to usher in a period of righteousness and truth. The poor Indians thought the Spanish were him.' He looked at the Doctor over his reading glasses. 'Obviously they were wrong. For in fact, the truth is, Doctor, I am Cukulcan. I am Quetzalcoatl.' Benitez frowned. 'Oh, don't look like that, Doctor. I have not gone mad. I do not believe I am some plumed divinity. Do I look plumed, Guido?' the great man said, tapping his bald pate. He smiled mildly at his joke. 'And yet, you see, I *do* represent the legitimate spirit of righteousness and peace for the people of Dorado. Perhaps you forget, Doctor, that despite the bandits in power, *I* am Dorado's duly elected President, and I fully intend to serve the term that the people of my country elected me to. And so, that is why, along with our motto: *Homo Primus* – Human Beings First, or "Man in the Vanguard," as my more left-leaning brethren choose to translate it – Cukulcan appears on our seal.'

'In Montazan province during the elections,' Guido volunteered, 'we always had his Excellency fly in from the east. Often we would schedule it for early morning so that his plane would appear literally to come out of the sun.

'You don't understand, Doctor, I can see. But the Indians

did, I can tell you that. These old beliefs persist. Many of them are Christian in only the most nominal sense. They believe that the crucifixion was some sort of . . . human sacrifice, and the Eucharist, the cannibal meal that followed.'

'Guido,' Benitez said. 'Don't bore the Doctor with your comparative anthropology.'

'And the volcano . . .' the Doctor said, vaguely remembering something. 'Don't they have some myth about that?'

'Yes,' Benitez said. 'They say their ancestors, rather than embrace the Christian faith, threw themselves into it – several thousand at once. Then, when the Spanish *padres* tried to purify the mountain, the volcano erupted, drowning in lava the Spanish mission and army garrison stationed on her side. The Indians say that on the day the feathered serpent returns, the spirits of their martyred warriors will arise from the volcano and drive the foreign invaders from their land.'

'Recently, Doctor,' Guido concluded, 'the government has taken to disposing of its political enemies by dropping them into the volcano alive – from helicopters overhead. Their bodies, of course, cannot be recovered. The army congratulates itself on having discovered a unique solution to a modern political problem, but, in fact, the volcano has been devouring virgins and captured enemies for centuries.'

'And so you believe,' the Doctor said, drawing thoughtfully on his cigar and summing up the great man's thesis, 'that because of reasons of historical inevitability, because of a certain predisposition on the part of the collective psyche of your people going back for thousands of years, it is inevitable you will be returned to power in Dorado.'

'Not at all, Doctor,' Benitez interrupted flatly, like a magician suddenly tiring of his tricks. 'I will return to Dorado because the bandits in power will soon ruin the economy, and when that happens the guerrillas will attack the capitol and all hell will break loose. Rather than have hell loose in such a sensitive and strategic spot, the Administration will decide that my government in exile – repugnant as it is to them – is the lesser evil, and certainly a better regime than the guerrillas would establish if they shot it out amongst themselves.'

'In other words,' the Doctor said, 'if they can't have a capitalist paradise there, they'd rather see your socialist limbo. Better that, at any rate, than a communist hell.'

Benitez smiled. 'I told you he was clever, Guido. Yes. And so that is why I have never doubted that these overtures I mentioned to you would be made, and that negotiations would come about, and that someday I will return to Dorado.'

'In triumph,' the Doctor hastened to add.

Benitez seemed pleased by the Doctor's optimism, though Guido did not. 'Your Excellency . . .' he protested.

'It's all right, Guido,' Benitez said. 'The Doctor is now . . . one of us.' He turned his sad, brown, red-rimmed eyes upon the Doctor. 'It's what you wanted, isn't it, Doctor?'

'What? Oh, yes,' the Doctor said. 'I am one of you – and honored to be so, I might add.' For even as he said these words, the Doctor felt a delicious sensation spreading across the surface of his skin, a feeling of belonging to something greater than himself, so that the Doctor looked at Benitez now with something approaching adoration, and even gazed at the difficult Guido with a feeling akin to brotherly love. He was one of them! He was a man of the people. If he had been translated to heaven and made into a deity he could not have been more pleased.

'And so, being one of us, you will follow my orders to the letter. Do you agree?'

'Whatever you tell me to do, your Excellency.'

'Swear it on the Virgin.'

'I swear it, your Excellency, on the soul of Man.'

'Good. I will remember that. And Doctor?'

'Your Excellency?'

'If you betray us,' Benitez said, smiling sadly, 'don't worry, we won't kill your nieces.'

'What? But, of course, you wouldn't.' The Doctor gave a nervous laugh.

'No,' Benitez said even more sadly. He looked at the Doctor. 'We'll kill *you*.'

The Fire Of Yoga
◆
Chapter 4

'You *wanted* yoga. I *gave* you yoga. Now you ask me what it is!'

Higgins, who was standing in Sara's doorway, watching the darkness blossom with light, had evoked this response by merely wondering – albeit aloud – what she had done to him, and if what she had done to him had some kind of name.

'*Yoga*! Yes! That's what it's called.'

Higgins looked out at the moonlit waste. The air was suffused with a soft blue fire that danced and burned at the edges of his vision. This light was so real and bright that Higgins had thought the *barrio* was burning, until he had realized the fire was inside him and it was he, not the city, that was rapt in flames.

But now that he knew what Sara Devi had given him, Higgins couldn't help wondering – again out loud – why she had waited so long to give it.

'Why? Don't you see? Because it wasn't up to me, but *you*. It's not the guru who selects the disciple, but the disciple who accepts the guru. As long as you didn't recognize me . . .' She shrugged. 'What could I do?'

'But you tricked me. You said the guru wasn't here!'

'I said *my* guru wasn't here. and she isn't. But *your* guru was seated before you!' She grinned. 'The truth is, *deva*, you tricked yourself. Though your heart had found her, your

mind insisted it could not be so. How could your guru be a
skinny little brown-skinned girl? I thought when I told you
that she was nearby, you would get it, but . . .' she laughed,
'you didn't.'

It was true; Higgins had not recognized her due to his
prejudices and preconceptions. For he had always imagined
that when he found his guru he would be a fine old man with
a long white beard, who would be gentle and kind and say
things to Higgins like, 'Thou art my beloved son in whom I
am well pleased,' whereas instead he had got this magical
child, this mischievous teenage fairy queen. And regarding
her now, Higgins had the feeling he had seriously misjudged
her. He felt like a man who marries a goddess only to discover, as he goes to embrace her, a form of fire, a face of
flame.

Higgins sat down at Sara's feet. He told her about the firey
power, the ecstasy, the sound of *OM*. Sara listened gravely
then nodded and said: 'When the Feathered Serpent awakes
there is no doubt. The whole body begins to quake and tremble. The mind glides into meditative states and *mantras* and
holy sounds hum in the breath – *OM* and names of God you
did not know you knew. Don't be afraid. It's natural for you
to see visions at this time and whatever you see is auspicious
and true. For you, it is fire. For me, it was flood. One evening, after supper, I watched the whole world drown before
my eyes.' She looked at him and grinned. 'Not even *I* survived.'

This remark was so preposterous that Higgins couldn't
help but laugh. Sara Devi laughed as well.

And as she did so, once again, Higgins found himself falling
into meditation and as he fell, flames seemed to shoot up all
around him, with a noise like burning acetylene. And Higgins
beheld now, seated within them, an old woman on a funeral
pyre. Though bathed in flames, she was undisturbed. Then
she raised a burning finger and, looking into Higgins' eyes,
beckoned him to join her there.

Higgins gave a start and the vision ended. He looked about
him, but there was no old woman, no pyre, no flames. He

stared again at Sara Devi, wondering again what it was that she had done.

For he had come to her seeking spiritual counsel, fully expecting that this would be a civilized affair – like the sherry suppers he had enjoyed at Harvard – but instead it was like being flung to the wolves, or hurling oneself into a chasm of fire. Behold, the crucible! Whatever in him was human would be consumed, whatever was not gold or god would be burned and eaten. And Higgins felt a moral terror as he understood at last the meaning of the fiery visions. A holocaust was about to happen – and he would be its victim.

'Now go,' Sara said. 'It's getting late.'

'Go?' Higgins protested. 'But you even haven't told me what I'm supposed to *do*.'

'There's nothing to do,' the child said, blithely. She was fluffing a pillow in preparation for sleep. 'Before tonight, you pursued yoga.' She lay down quietly and closed her eyes. 'Now yoga will pursue you.'

Who Is *El Duende*?

◆

Chapter 5

The Garcia Commission had been investigating non-stop, but progress was slow. Though Garcia had followed up more than a half a dozen leads, the legendary and elusive Lieutenant Colonel Schmidt was still no more than a wraith and a mystery. And so Garcia had decided to focus instead on someone else.

Now Garcia re-entered the Black Hen. He had no desire for small talk this evening. He peeled off two fives from a dwindling grease-smeared bundle and pushed them across the table. '*El Duende*,' he said.

Guzman's eyes gleamed – like the fires of hell. 'What would you like to know, my Captain?'

'Everything. Who is he? Where is he from? Or don't you know?'

Guzman smiled. 'Of course, I know. Didn't I use to report to him personally when he was an aide to Colonel Hercules Cordero?'

Hercules Cordero, Garcia recalled, had been a colonel in AES even before the four-storey fall of the Generalissimo. In fact, there were some who said he had engineered it.

'I don't know, did you?' Garcia rejoined, relying now more on Guzman's ego to extract the information than on the curled and wrinkled dollars he had pushed across the wood.

'What? You think I was just some breaker of skulls? *Ptah!*'

he spit invisibly in the dark. 'Well, *hombre*, I'll tell you who I was. Every morning I would report to *El Duende* the results of the night's interrogations. One copy of my report went direct to Cordero, the other straight to the Generalissimo.'

'Are you telling me *El Duende* once worked for AES?'

'Probably still does.'

'But why didn't you tell me this before?'

'You didn't ask me, Captain.'

You mean, Garcia thought angrily, you were waiting for more money. 'But when the Generalissimo was overthrown, *El Duende* must have been arrested. No?'

Guzman sniffed. 'Arrested – and exiled. But it was all a sham. Cordero protected him. He was given a new identity, Salvador Valpero, and relocated here where he continues to do what he has always done so well – neutralize our enemies. Don't look so shocked, Ambrosio. They did the same with you.'

The torturer drew a glassine bag from his pocket and did a line of cocaine. He took it in the Spanish manner, like snuff, tapping a pinch of it on the fleshy web between his thumb and index finger. He raised it to his nose and vacuumed expertly twice, filling both nostrils. Two round tears of synthetic bliss rolled down his face and ran off the blood gutters in his cheeks toward his ears. Guzman snorted with satisfaction and tucked the bag away. The drug, Garcia thought, explained his talkative mood.

'Of course, it's not surprising you don't recognize him. He's always been secretive, and in the last few years, he's put on nearly three hundred pounds. His appetites are gargantuan. And it's not just food. He goes through women . . .'

But Garcia wasn't interested in *El Duende*'s women. 'What about magic?'

'Who told you that?' He was suddenly close-mouthed, his insolence gone. 'There are rumors. If you want to know more, you should go see Mathilde.'

'Mathilde? The witch? Ah ha!'

At last, Garcia was getting somewhere. Not only was *El Duende* working for AES, but he was evidently involved with witchcraft as well. Even more remarkably, he had stumbled upon *El Duende*'s superior. 'So,' he said slowly, running it down, 'both *El Duende* and Adolfo Schmidt report to Colonel Hercules Cordero.'

'It's a good possibility.'

Garcia considered the intelligence he'd purchased, while Guzman again withdrew the little silvery packet and put its contents up his nose. In a more innocent era, Garcia remembered, such bags had been used for collecting stamps and coins.

Plan Of Battle

◆

Chapter 6

In the satellite photo at which the Commander was waving, Dorado's capitol looked like a backward L. Its horizontal bar was the dusty road that entered Puerto Valle from the west and threaded between Lake Hurakan to the south and the town to the north, until it met the Masaya Volcano and the iron spine of the Siuna Hills. Unable to proceed further east because of the hills, the road made a sharp left-hand turn and ran north for forty miles, becoming with every one of them less a road and more an idea in the mind of God. At last it entered the Indian village of Ayres where it seriously dwindled, getting itself confused with the memory of a town square and, barely alive, came crawling out the other end of the town as nothing but the vaguest hope of a road: a faint goat track scratched in the jungle.

The well-to-do of Puerto Valle lived, Commander Rabon explained, in the acute angle of the L, surrounded by slums on every side, while a series of forts lay along the northern approaches. This meant there were three possible avenues of attack: one, from the west along the horizontal bar; two, from the south, across the lake; or three, from the north, from the direction of Ayres. Attack from the east was ruled out as the mountains were impassable. Questions?

'If we're interested in negotiations, why are we looking for a military solution?'

'Contingency plans,' Benitez answered. 'Purely contingency, Doctor.' He turned to Rabon. 'Are there forts along the western approaches?'

'No, sir. Only barracks.'

'And why is that?' Benitez asked, steepling his fingers and wondering aloud. 'Build forts, I mean, along one flank of the city and not the other? What general thought of that?'

'General Avarice. And Major Greed, your Excellency.' The Commander smiled. He tapped the map. 'If you'll recall, the Generalissimo's family owned property in the northern sector. Every time they built a fort, the army had to reimburse the Carreras for the land. Since the Carreras didn't own land on the western approaches, the Generalissimo wasn't interested in building forts on it. It had nothing to do with the defense of the nation – only with his own personal gain.'

Benitez sighed and said in wonder: 'These tyrants accrue such enormous power, then use it for such piddling ends! The Generalissimo – he could have done anything. He could have built a *dome* over the entire country. He could have turned the course of rivers; he could have made Puerto Valle into a paradise on earth. And what did he use it for? What all of them use it for. For nothing! To line their pockets. And to have their way with the nigger maids.'

'There are *barracks*, however,' Rabon continued, pointing to a series of gray rectangles just north of the western approach. 'These garrison nearly eight thousand soldiers. With such a concentration of personnel on the main road, I suppose they must feel very well protected.'

'And *are*, damnit,' Benitez said, sitting up and pounding the desk once, hard. 'Eight thousand soldiers? How the hell do we get past eight thousand soldiers? Christ, a thousand men could defend that road if they had to.' He squinted at the map and summed up the military options with increasing ill humor.

'There are two approaches to the capitol – forget the lake, Commander, we're not going to go across the lake. The first is from the north. But this approach is defended, you say, by a line of forts spaced roughly every thousand yards, and by as many as two thousand soldiers. We can't go around them because of the mountains and swamps, which means we'd have to fight a major battle every few miles. Absurd. The second approach is from the west, but that road is defended by General Cuzo and his eight thousand regulars. The only way we could possibly get past them is to fight our way. And while our men would be exhausted and our supply lines stretching back for two hundred miles, they would be sitting on top of theirs. In other words, we'd be attacking their headquarters.' He looked at the commander. 'Stupid!'

'Yes, but your Excellency,' Rabon hastened to add, 'if we *did* get through, it would be wonderful.'

'Damnit,' said Benitez, becoming visibly wroth. 'Nobody said it wouldn't be wonderful. All I'm saying is that, as of yet, no one has shown me a way such an attack might conceivably succeed. And until someone does, I am not going to sit here and waste my time and your breath.' He rose to his feet. 'We are pressing ahead with the negotiations.'

Everybody stood up, including Rabon.

'Good-day, gentlemen.'

The meeting was over. The men filtered out. For now, at least, there would be no offensive. Still, the Doctor was impressed with the briefing. Benitez had shown a perfect willingness to war, given the right circumstances and plan of attack. He mentioned this to Guido, who stopped and bristled.

'*El Presidente hates* war. Though he is entitled to wear one, you have never seen him in a uniform, have you? Nor does he wear a loaded pistol on his hip. He abhors the "man on horseback" image so dear to the hearts of our *compadres*. He loathes the "cult of violence," as he calls it in his speeches, the *macho* madness with which our hemisphere is obsessed.'

'I only meant . . .'

'The other day in Mexico City – this is a true story, Doctor – his Excellency went on a picnic with a senator's family. As he got into the car, he noticed the senator tuck a pistol in his belt. His Excellency asked him if he was expecting trouble up ahead – you know, guerrillas, assassins. The senator laughed. Oh no, he said. He *always* carried a pistol, just in case some wise guy got funny with his daughter, or while he was driving, some son of a bitch tried to cut him off!'

Just then, the American diplomat loped around the corner, escorted by an aide and two uniformed guards. He raised his silver eyebrows at Guido and the Doctor, then disappeared within the Presidential suite.

The two men watched the double doors click shut, then turned and faced each other.

'His Excellency is a man of peace,' Guido insisted – like a bastard defending his mother's honor.

Scum Of The Earth

◆

Chapter 7

The letter was like an envelope of sunlight that brightened her eyes and warmed her heart the instant it was opened – for there in the photograph were her three children playing on a sunny stoop in Puerto Rico, and Rosita behind them, like a big brown hen, wiping her hands on a checkered apron. Behind Rosita, Gil could see one pastel wall of the house in Arecibo cut by the saw-toothed shadow of a palm frond, like a blade stamped out of sheet metal. She looked for a letter or a note, but there wasn't one – only the photograph. It was candid – neither Rosita nor the children were looking at the camera. Again, Gil searched the envelope for some sort of explanation, then she turned it over and saw her name misspelled on the front.

Gil gave a cry of such dismay, it surprised her – as though it had been made by some animal inside her. And it was then her blood turned to ice and her joy to smoke, and the saw-toothed shadow of the tree in the photograph seemed to tremble, leap, and stab at her heart.

Gil went inside and tried to call Arecibo, but for twenty-five minutes she could not get through and while she waited, she chanted a weird and meaningless prayer, 'O Mother help us don't let anyone nothing answer damn you why don't you answer operator what's the matter what do you mean the lines are Mother help her bastards if you hurt them murder

I'll . . ' until finally she heard the distant telephone ringing, someone lifted the receiver and said, 'Hullo, Hullo?'

'S'me, Ma!'

'Gilberta!'

Then offhand, though her voice was shaking, 'Kids okay?'

'What? Can't hear you!'

'Said, Kids okay?'

Then her littlest cried, 'Mama, Mama,' and she heard the two others squealing in the background and she knew they were sitting happily at breakfast wrapped in the warm bright tropical sunshine, and it was only she who was sunk in darkness and fear.

After talking to the children, she said to Rosita, 'You didn't send a picture? Did you, Ma?'

'Picture?'

'Of you and the kids?'

'What am I? A *turista*? You think I got time to be taking you pictures?'

Gil thought for a moment. 'Come back home, Ma.'

'Home? Wha? We just got here . . .'

'I know,' Gil said, 'but I can't live without them.'

Garcia did not look well this morning. He was seated on a broken-slatted bench, squinting at the sun, holding his stomach with his palm in a queer, sick sort of way. Gil sat down beside him and took his hand. His old face softened when he saw her. They had always liked each other – they were *simpatico*. Though he was aged, he breathed a splendid masculinity which she respected, like a old lion with chewed ears drowsing in the sun.

She showed him the photograph.

'Ah. Your babies.'

'Yes,' she said, 'aren't they beautiful?' When he was finished admiring them, she took back the picture and put it away. 'I wanted to ask you. This *El Duende* . . .'

Garcia shivered though the sun was hot. '. . . *es muy peligroso*.'

'Dangerous, yes; but he would not hurt children, would he?'

'He would hurt God and rape His Mother if he could.'

'Yes. But *children*?'

'Children, women, old men, boys. I have seen his work. He kills,' Garcia said, 'without conscience or pity, like a pistol.'

'And how do you know this?'

Garcia sighed and wrinkled up his nose, as though she'd exhumed a rotten memory. 'Because . . . I used to work for him, Gilberta.'

'Arresting children? Ambrosio! How could you . . . ?'

Garcia gave her a feeble smile.

'My God!' Gil cried in revulsion and looked at Garcia through new eyes. 'Monsters!' she said.

Garcia sighed. 'Not monsters,' he said sadly. 'Men.'

'And how could you . . . Ambrosio! . . . be a part of such things?'

'What would you have had me do, Gilberta? Resign from the human race?'

'Not race. From the army . . . government . . .'

'The other side did the same. There's a guerrilla chieftain named Ruben Montenegro. He hangs kids from trees. All in the name of brotherhood and liberation!'

'Oh, the Spanish!' Gil said with hate.

'It was the US who built the police station in the first place. And who trained the police in their "methods of interrogation." '

'*Yanguis*!'

Garcia shrugged. 'The Russians are worse. In Afghanistan, they dropped these bombs. They looked like children's toys . . .'

'Shut up,' she cried, sickened, and put her hands to her ears. She began to weep. She didn't want to know these things. She didn't want to hear them. She didn't even believe that they were true. How could they be? No; she had met *El Duende*. He was gross and disgusting, yes, but not insane. She remembered a Haitian maniac who had decapitated a little boy with a machete for no apparent reason. She had seen the man on television after his arrest – he was raving, delusional, wild. Such a man, maybe. Commanded by the voodoo spirits! But please do not tell me there were people who looked like you or me who leaned into intercoms and commanded, 'Break the baby's fingers, Miguel. Break them slowly. Break them one by one. What's the mother doing? Does she feel like talking yet? All right. Keep it up. Break the wrists. Report to me this evening. I have to run home and say "hi" to the wife.' No; she did not believe it. 'Who told you this. About *El Duende*?'

'Someone who used to work with us both. My old *compadre*. Dante Guzman.'

Gil made up her mind at once. 'I will go and talk to this *Señor* Guzman.'

Though it was ten-thirty-seven on a Saturday morning, the Black Hen was already home to a dozen or so patrons – and a hundred or so flies. Things glowed on the walls: trophies, beer signs, small-shaded lanterns like votive candles, giving the room the feel of a chapel – if you didn't feel too closely. Gil closed her eyes, wondering how many evil cells like this there were in the world, and saw in a twinkling a million filthy hovels, some of rock, some of mud or wood, where men and women numbed themselves in an escalating blur and paralyzing dream of gin – or its local equivalent – amid the smoke and flies.

Gil's entrance caused a ripple of excitement. The boy tending bar looked up from the glasses he was smearing with a dirty towel, while several patrons swiveled completely around on their bar stools to better view her progress through the room.

The room ran back and down several steps into a darker, windowless area. Guzman was right where Garcia had said he would be: asleep at a table in the rear, his head buried in his arms.

She stood before him for a moment, but he didn't wake. 'Excuse me,' she said and prodded his arm. Guzman opened one eye.

Her beauty had an effect on people – though Gil could never be certain precisely what that effect might be. Some men became more chivalrous in her presence, others obsequious, nervous or dumb; women became either icy or fawning; while there were those who it drove to rapine and riot. The torturer, Guzman, appeared to be of the first order. He stiffened at the sight of her, sitting up quickly and making a halfhearted attempt to look presentable by combing his fingers through his hair. He rubbed the stubble on his chin as if to say, I am aware I look like an evil weasel dragged from some unused corner of Hell, but looks, *Señorita*, can be deceiving. I am very charming. He smiled, exposing several blackened stumps and a large incisor inlaid with gold. Gil sat down as Guzman motioned for the waitress.

'Not for me.'

But Guzman insisted, clapping imperiously until the plain-faced girl appeared at their table. The child was only a few years older than Gil's eldest daughter. Her hands were cracked and red from wiping tables. She would not look Gil in the eye.

'Dewars!' Guzman said, and made a circular motion with his finger.

Gil did not want scotch. Not here, not with this man, not at ten-forty-one on a Saturday morning. The thought made her faintly queasy and ill. 'Ambrosio sent me. He said you might be able to help me with a problem.'

'Anything for you, my lady,' Guzman said, as though he was her champion.

The child reappeared at their side, holding a pen and a piece of paper. It took Gil a moment to realize the girl wanted her autograph. She took the pen and asked the girl her name.

'Illuminada. I saw you, lady, in *El Cuchillo de Muerte*.'

Gil scratched her name, and the child went away. Gil fumbled for a cigarette in her purse and found a light awaiting her even before she found the pack. Guzman was a gentlemen, all right. And yet, she couldn't help but wonder how many times he had pressed lighted matches to lips that held no tobacco. And Gil had the intuition then that this thing called 'civilization' was the thinnest of veneers, a mask to hide the fangs of a beast. It was all lip service and window dressing.

'Ambrosio says you know *El Duende*.'

'Everyone knows him.'

'He tells me that you worked for him.' Nor could she resist adding: 'If that's what you call torturing children.'

Guzman made a face. 'Communists, *Señorita*.'

'Communist children?'

'The mother was. The father and brother, as well. Why not the child?'

'Torturing children is a dirty job. But someone's got to do it. Is that what you're saying?'

But Guzman could not be shamed. He smiled pleasantly. 'What do you want?'

'Since you worked for *El Duende*, I thought you might tell me how he could be stopped.'

'Tell you? Or stop him for you?'

Gil looked at him. 'I am not in need of a hired gun. If it came to that, I would do it myself.'

Something dangerous and authentic in her voice made him pause and change his manner.

He leaned back. 'And why do you want him stopped? Or are you a patriot also? Like your brother.'

'Patriot? You could say that. Except for me, you see, my children are my country.'

'Ah ha,' Guzman said. And he thought for a moment. Then he said: 'What if I gave you evidence, *Señorita*?'

'Evidence of what?'

'Crimes.'

'By him? Or you?' Then she relented. 'What good would that do?'

'You could go to the police with it. You could have the man arrested, jailed – deported, even.'

Gil considered this. It was the first semi-sensible suggestion anyone had yet made. Why hadn't Higgins thought of it? Or her brother?

'Evidence of crimes committed where?' she asked carefully.

'In Dorado. And in this city as well. Crimes that would put him away for the rest of his life.'

'And the police, they would believe this?' she asked unsurely.

291

'If you had evidence, they would have to believe it, wouldn't they?'

'What kind of evidence?'

'I will show you.'

Gil thought for a moment. 'If *El Duende* knows I am doing this, he will kill me.'

'And if he knows I gave it to you, he will kill me, too.' Guzman smiled at the symmetry of their predicaments. 'But how will he know? I will tell no one, nor will you – or we both die. After you see the evidence I have, you will need only to give this information anonymously to the police.'

Gil thought for a moment. 'Of course, you will want some money for this.'

Guzman smiled.

'How much?'

The torturer rolled his eyes in thought. 'Let us say . . . five hundred dollars?'

'I will, of course, want to see this evidence first.'

'But of course, *Señorita*,' Guzman said. He rose from the table. 'Please, come with me.'

Perhaps it was the drink she'd had, but as Gilberta rose to follow Guzman she felt an unexpected sense of gratitude and hope. Why shouldn't she? Despite his viciousness, his avarice, and his sins, he was going to help save her children.

At the rear of the bar, a spiral stairwell descended to the basement. Guzman went first; Gil followed. At the bottom of the metal spiral, there were a half a dozen battered kegs with copper lines running up through the ceiling. Beside them was an unused kitchen filled with pieces of mysterious machinery. She felt a small exhilaration. Again, she had managed to slip behind the scenes.

Halfway down the basement corridor, Guzman unlocked a battered metal door. He flicked on a light, revealing the lair of a demon. A pallet with twisted blankets took up half the floor. The other half was littered with dirty clothes, empty bottles, and stained containers of Chinese food. Guzman smiled and waved her in. Every sense and instinct in her body told her not to cross the threshold. But then she remembered she wasn't doing this for her own enjoyment. She badly needed the evidence he had, and so, for her children's sake, she entered. Guzman brushed some clothes off an orange crate and motioned her to sit. Some sort of black beetles which she did not want to see were swarming over a paper plate in the corner. She could hear the faint sickening click of their shells.

She turned and caught Guzman watching her intently – but when their eyes met, he looked away and began rummaging through a cardboard carton. 'Yes,' he said, 'it is all here.' She wondered what kind of evidence he had. Documents, pictures, tape recordings, a confession . . . what?

A small glass vial on an orange crate by his mattress caught her eye. It looked like perfume. Idly, she picked it up.

'Careful, lady.'

'What is it? Drugs?'

Guzman sneered at her naivete.

'Potassium cyanide.'

'You mean . . . *poison*?' Gil asked, putting the bottle back down. Her hand wiped itself against her leg. 'What on earth for?'

Guzman shrugged. 'There are times when a man is better off dead. Believe me. Just one taste of that stuff and you're out of here forever. You never know when it might come in handy.'

'But you shouldn't leave it out like that. I mean, what if some children . . .'

Guzman looked at her like she was crazy. 'Children? I have no children.'

Perhaps it was the word and the memory of why she had come, but Gil felt suddenly weak and exhausted. She closed her eyes and, for a half a moment, rubbed them with her fingers. Mistake! For no sooner had she dropped her guard than she felt the weight of the man's desire (or perhaps it was only the heat of his peppered breath) fall across her like a shadow. And so when his hand reached around her throat and tried to cup her mouth, she reacted swiftly, biting down so long and hard into one of the black, foul-tasting fingers, that she actually felt the knuckle crack. For a moment, despite what must have been excruciating pain, Guzman held on, lifting her up, even as his other hand groped her belly. Then she drove an elbow with the force of a piston back into his stomach and felt the dirty wind of his out-rushing breath. She turned, batted away the crate with her hand, took a step and drove her instep into his groin like a person trying to punt a football a hundred yards down field.

Guzman dropped as if cleavered at the knees. He kneeled before her, helpless, drooling, making mouths like a goldfish, two clear tears filling the deep runnels of his cheeks.

'The evidence. Where is it?' And then, like a shiv in the ribs, she understood.

There was no evidence. It had all been a ruse. 'Come here, little girl. I'll give you some candy.' It was the oldest of tricks. She had warned her daughters against it, then fallen for it herself.

In a rage, she overturned the cardboard carton. It was filled with hundreds of baseball cards mixed with pictures of women in bondage. She saw the chains, the clamps and gags.

Gil recoiled, scalded by the sight, as though someone had splashed hot coffee in her face. It was less the attempted assault that upset her than the deceit. Evidence. Christ!

She clamored up the metal stairwell and headed for the door.

A drunken young *hombre* opened it for her, waving her through it with a solemn and exaggerated show of respect.

Blue Light

◆

Chapter 8

Higgins was not unaware of what was going on around him; he could read the distress on the face of Gilberta and overhear the arguments between her and her brother, or rather, overhear the Doctor yelling at her in the evenings while Gilberta answered him in firm, low tones. He felt the stress at meal times, the vacuum of the children's absence, and the moment of frozen tension that ensued whenever the phone or doorbell rang. It wasn't that Higgins was oblivious to these things, only that they left him curiously undisturbed. He did not feel worried, threatened or afraid. He felt ecstatic.

For what was going on inside of Higgins was so amazing that it overshadowed anything that was happening in the outer world. It was like falling in love in the middle of a war – even the twisted, smoke-blackened ruins look beautiful. Or like a person who is dying – what does he care anymore about the gossip on the street? For inside of Higgins, a revolution was occurring.

And as these inner worlds were opened, his experience of the outer world was transformed as well. Life regained its savor and its sweet delight. Some days he felt so glad-hearted and full of glee, that whatever happened made him happy. If it shone, hooray! If it rained, all the better! And when the telephone rang, instead of cringing and worrying anxiously who it could be, he answered it with a jubilant and humorous anticipation – while the fact that it was no one important, not even for him, only the undertaker calling to speak to the Doctor, did not diminish his delight in the least.

Sometimes, disbelieving, Higgins looked inside himself for the sorrow which had tormented him so long, but it just wasn't there. It had vanished. And, in its stead was an exquisite stillness, a sense of rest and ease, an authentic and natural happiness. He felt he had found some secret spring, a blissful pool of peace and rest, peace and rest, which, by turning within and drinking from, his tiredness was relieved and his fears erased.

Of course, Higgins' association with Sara Devi did not go unnoticed in the fishbowl of the *barrio*. The Doctor gave him all kinds of flak. 'You've been bewitched. You've been hypnotized. Why do you associate with that crazy person?'

But nothing the Doctor or anyone said to Higgins could keep him from her. He felt so happy in her company. Nor was it only Higgins who benefited from the blessing he'd received.

Sometimes in the evenings, after an argument with her brother, Gil would burst into Higgins' room, white-faced and distraught. She would pace for a while without speaking, sinking down at last before the burning candle, until her breathing evened, and she was once again quiet, dignified, and still. Sometimes, too, drawn by the irresistible, blissful silence, the Doctor would come, lean in the living-room doorway and yawn. And at those moments, his face would go as blank as paper, as though the yawn had erased his mind of everything it had ever known: the way a cash register is cleared of a long list of totalled charges and sums – the night's receipts – *brinngg*! – and the tumblers whir back to zero.

Then Higgins, too, would close his eyes, and the three of them would abide that way in perfect silence for the longest time, so that four floors above the teeming marketplace, in the middle of the troubled city, they experienced the quietude and peace of a cave.

Why it was that Gil and the Doctor were also so affected, Higgins didn't understand – until one night he had a dream.

In the dream, his room was filled with a shimmering blue radiance. The light was strongest and brightest near the little makeshift altar, but it was everywhere else in the apartment as well. It spilled out the living-room doorway, sparkling in the kitchen and shining brightly in the air of the hall. It blew through the bedrooms like blue snow, drifting beneath the furniture, catching in the Doctor's moustache while he slept, making the children's pillows glow, and bestowing protectively on everything it touched its peace and benediction.

Promotion

◆

Chapter 9

'You idiot! He's furious. That was top secret! Now it looks like you've gone and queered the whole thing. At any rate, he wants to see you, Pronto!'

The Doctor, who was sleeping when Guido called, dressed swiftly and ran to Benitez. Upon entering the brownstone he was patted down, then ushered into a downstairs room. The secretary, who was drinking coffee, showed him the story in *The New York Times*, page 3, column 4.

U.S. DENIES SECRET TALKS

NEW YORK, July 23 – Administration officials today denied they were meeting secretly with the exiled former President of Dorado, Rodolfo Benitez Cayetano.

But a spokesman for the rebel faction, Dr. Arsenio Castellana, maintained that secret preliminary talks between Benitez and State Department Under-Secretary George Cole were underway.

Comparing the secret contacts between Cole and Dorado rebel leaders to the arduous process of the Paris Peace Treaty, Castellana said, 'They're talking about talking. They're negotiating about negotiating. You might say, they're still arguing about the shape of the table!'

'They spelled my name wrong.'

'You idiot!' Guido said. 'You *told* them.'

'Yes,' the Doctor said. 'I did.'

For as the Doctor had left the brownstone the previous evening, he'd been surprised by two men with a video camera. Even more surprising, when the Doctor had tried to walk past them, they had turned the camera on him. On of them had probed him with a microphone, asking, 'Can you tell us how they're going, Doctor?'

'What?'

'The negotiations.'

'No negotiations,' the Doctor had said. And that's when he had made his now famous pronouncement.

Guido and the Doctor went upstairs. The Doctor felt like a man on the way to his execution. He only hoped it would be swift. His political career had lasted all of forty-eight hours. Rabon joined them in the corridor. He smiled at the Doctor and shook his head – in wonder at human frailty, perhaps. A guard appeared and whisked them into the Presidential office. Benitez was talking on the telephone. 'Yes, Ambassador. Perfectly acceptable. I'm glad we agree on *something*.' He listened and laughed. 'And you, too. And your family . . .' The Doctor was waiting – for the firing squad and the *coup de grâce*. But when Benitez hung up, he did not appear angry, only thoughtful and bemused. He had a smile on his lips which, like a visitor from another planet, didn't seem to quite belong. Then he laughed and got to his feet.

'It's what the Administration needed all along. A swift kick in the butt! Gentlemen, Under-secretary Cole has agreed to meet with us in Mexico City. Miguel Fry, Dorado's Mexican Consul and Jimmy Sanchez, their Ambassador to Costa Rica, will attend as well. Meetings will begin next week with details of the agenda to be worked out then.' There was a dumbfounded silence, then the Commander whistled as Guido broke into sharp applause.

Benitez said, 'Even more strangely, Montenegro has agreed to the negotiations. That's the only thing that worries me. Such a move is not like him. He must have something up his sleeve.' And the visiting smile went away and the ironic frown that had lived for sixty years on Benitez's lips returned. He looked at the Doctor. 'Well, Doctor. How did you do it?'

The Doctor was not so sure what he had done; he only knew that he was being praised for what he had thought, a moment ago, he would be hung. 'It was nothing, your Excellency. Some . . . selective leakage, that's all. Occasionally . . . it has its effect.' He was being modest; he should have been.

'Remind them of their failures, eh, Doctor? And if that doesn't work, embarrass the hell out of them!'

'Well . . . yes,' the Doctor smiled.

'There was a risk,' Benitez said with iron in his gaze. 'A risk for all of us.' The iron turned to steel, and for a moment the Doctor thought he might be in for it yet. 'But . . . you won! *We* won!' he cried, and with a hard slap on the Doctor's back, Benitez joyfully embraced the Doctor, then Guido and Rabon, as the room dissolved into excited talk and laughter.

For several minutes, a party ensued. A bottle was called for, and Havana cigars. The doors to the Presidential suite were flung open, the news was let out and several secretaries and aides were let in. There were toasts. To negotiations! After years of steadfast refusal, the Junior Officers had finally given in!

Then Benitez put the cork back in the bottle, took the unfinished drinks from the lips of the secretaries, chased out the aides and closed the door. The party was over. They had business to attend to.

For now that they were entering into negotiations, they had to come up with something to call themselves in press releases and communiques. The papers referred to them as the 'rebels' or 'guerrillas.' But how, Benitez asked, could *they* be the rebels when they were the legitimately elected government of Dorado? The present government was the rebels, and the rebels were the legitimate government. It was all upside down. The solution? A new name. Suggestions?

Rabon offered 'government-in-exile,' but Guido said it sounded too out-of-it and dull. He proposed, in turn, 'insurgents,' or 'insurgent forces,' but Rabon claimed the word 'insurgents' made you think of the feeling in the pit of your stomach right before you had to puke. He suggested 'freedom fighters.' But 'freedom fighters,' the Doctor objected, made you think of teenage Hungarians throwing rocks at tanks. 'Well then, Doctor, what do you suggest?' There was a thoughtful pause.

'What about "the Resistance"?'

There was another pause as this word went inside everybody and set off a series of semantic explosions.

'I like that, Doctor,' Benitez pronounced at last. 'It sounds . . . strong.'

'Yes,' said the Commander. 'It reminds one of the Partisans. You know. Who fought against the Nazis.'

'It sounds legitimate,' Guido concurred, 'as though we were invaded or attacked – which, of course, we were.'

'The Resistance,' Benitez said. 'Yes, all right. That's very good.'

But if they were the Resistance, then who were the forces they were resisting? Certainly not 'the Government' – a name Benitez deplored.

'How about "the Junior Officers"?' Guido volunteered.

Benitez squirmed. 'It summons up the maternal instinct, I'm afraid. The poor *Junior* Officers. It makes you want to cuddle them, no?'

'The Oligarchy?'

'Too intellectual.'

'The *Momios*?'

'Too obscure.'

'How about "the *Junta*," my President?' the Doctor said.

There was another longish pause, while the word bounced around inside them. Benitez looked at Guido and Rabon for their reaction.

Rabon shrugged. 'Pretty good.'

Guido frowned. ' "The *Momios*" seems . . .'

'I like it, Doctor,' Benitez said. 'The Hoonta. Yes. Those long o's are scary. You don't feel much like cuddling a hoonta, do you?' He looked at the Doctor. 'Two for two. You seem to have a real facility . . . for this sort of thing.'

The Doctor glowed with the praise. You could not see it, but his whole body was awash with a delicious radiation. 'Thank you, your Excellency,' he said modestly.

'Perhaps . . . we've underestimated you. Your remark to the reporters. That was quite good, too.' He looked at the Doctor. 'I used to think you were a stupid fool. Now I am beginning to wonder. Perhaps I misjudged you. Either that or you have changed. And change . . . that is something few men ever do. What do you think?' Benitez asked the Commander.

The Commander, who was lounging on the sofa in the most languid and unmilitary of poses, slowly jack-knifed his body and leaned forward with his palms on his knees. 'If you want my opinion, I think the Doctor would make one hell of a political spokesman.'

'Yes. That's exactly what I was thinking. And you, Guido?' Benitez asked, sighting down his nose over the steeple of his fingers.

'The Doctor has certainly been useful to us,' Guido conceded, without sincerity or joy. 'But your Excellency, as for such a position . . .'

'Good. Then it's unanimous,' Benitez said. 'I am appointing the Doctor our new press secretary – or shall we call you our new "political spokesman"?'

'But your Excellency,' Guido cried.

'Calm down, my friend. I know what I promised you, but you can't do everything. You have plenty of other important chores. And, you know, Guido, I depend on you dearly . . .'

'But, my President . . . it is I who—'

'Stop whining! This is exactly why I am naming the Doctor. I won't have you whining in front of reporters. Where are you going?'

For the personal secretary, in a spasm of humiliation, had thrown down his steno pad and run from the room.

Benitez sighed. 'Let him go. He'll be back. Guido is an excellent secretary – smart, discreet, super-loyal, but he's too emotional, and his, uh, image is not all that it could be. We need someone er . . . uh . . . stronger, more forceful,' Benitez said, choosing his words with care the way a man in a mine-field chooses his footfalls. 'That's why I think you'll be perfect for the job, Doctor. Moustache. Harvard. Yes. From now on, you will be our political spokesman.'

'But there's so much to learn!' the Doctor protested.

Benitez asked. 'What is there to learn? There are five rebel factions operating in Dorado including MIRA and our own United Front. There is also . . .' Benitez ticked them off. 'This last, the so-called People's Forces – is a real problem. It is headed by an absolute fanatic named Ruben Montenegro. Now Montenegro, Doctor, is not right in the head. One of his tactics is to hang his enemies' children from lamp posts. Being a bachelor I can't speak from experience, but I under-stand from those who know that it can really take the wind out of your sails to wake up one morning and find your kid swinging from the tree outside.'

'We have tried to talk to him repeatedly, Doctor, but have gotten nowhere,' Rabon declared. 'He has entered into only the flimsiest of alliances. After victory, he will promise nothing. We think it's clear he intends to try to take control of the nation himself. Anything else?'

'Well, yes. What, for instance, is the social program of . . . the Resistance? What are we fighting for, and what do we want?'

'Look, Doctor,' Benitez said. 'If I return to Dorado, I have no intention of making a big revolution. It's not my goal to grow a beard, and stand everyone on their heads. My visions are more prosaic than that: a little more *taco* in the people's mouths, some rural health care for the Indians, pure drinking water and more electricity, land reform and agricultural development, universal literacy and, for the people in the capitol, some decent housing rather than those cardboard boxes that half the country lives in now. No, all we want is a negotiated settlement. We have never asked for anything more.'

'A negotiated settlement? Then why do we have a guerrilla army?'

'That is just a bargaining chip, Doctor. To exert some

pressure. . . . And remember, if anyone asks you, we're in favor of a *mixed* economy. With a *strong private* sector. You got that!'

'We are? But I thought we were . . . socialists or something.'

Everyone looked horrified. 'What? Never! And anyway, even if we were, why would we tell them? It's like calling yourself an Indian while riding herd with a bunch of cowboys. No. Better tell them you're a cowboy like them. Of course, it may be true your skin is red, and your cows are really buffalo, but still, as long as you *say* you're one. . . . Remember, Doctor. Names are important. And here. I have something else for you.'

'Is it . . . for the press?' the Doctor said taking a typewritten sheet.

'For *El Duende*. You will memorize this information and pass it on to him tonight.'

'San Miguel?' the Doctor read aloud. 'But this gives the time and place of our attack!'

'This is *dis*information, Doctor.'

'I see. And what if he finds out?'

'He won't, will he? And if it does nothing more than keep them from developing alternate sources of intelligence, you'll have done your job well. And by then . . .' But Benitez had not finished the sentence.

The Doctor sighed. He was already feeling the burden of his new position. 'I only hope I can live up to your and the Commander's expectations.' The Doctor looked to the guerrilla, but Rabon was snoring.

'Don't worry. Of course you will. And Doctor? Who's your tailor?'

'Tailor? I don't have one.'

'Obviously,' Benitez smiled. He handed him a card. 'Go see mine.'

Heart In A Box

◆

Chapter 10

One evening, leaving Sara Devi's, Higgins came across a figure standing in the downstairs hall. He was an older gentleman, smoking in the shadows, and he was waiting patiently, as though he'd been waiting there all his life. 'Mr. Higgins? Captain William Crespi. MIRA.'

In the darkened hallway, with the moonlight at the stranger's back, Higgins could not readily make out his features. He was nothing but a strong and stocky silhouette.

The man stepped closer and quietly said, 'First, I want to thank you for the support you gave our dead *companero*. And also for your support in the future. You see, the day he died, Jorge told me of the assistance you will be rendering.'

'What assistance?' Higgins said, feeling his blood turn to ice.

In answer, the man withdrew from his pocket what appeared to be the same goddamn sheet of paper that Jorge had once waved at him. Higgins stared at it dumbly, as though it was a hallucination. He couldn't believe it. He felt tricked, gulled. It was as though the dead had risen from the tomb.

'Look,' Higgins said. He searched the empty house and night, at a loss for words. 'I don't know what Vazpana told you, and I don't really care. I'm sorry he's dead. . . . I really am. But that doesn't *change* anything. Do you understand me? I'm not going to help you – or anyone else – purchase arms.'

'Not arms. *Parts*! Here,' Crespi said, and thrust the list again at Higgins. 'Just look it over for us, *please*.' And stepping forward, he pressed it into Higgins' hand. Higgins smelled smoke and nicotine and felt a kind of grizzled energy. Why Higgins didn't simply drop it then and there, he never knew. But before he could object, the agent raised a staying hand. 'Just think about it. That's all I ask. Just think about it. Okay?'

'I don't need to think about it,' Higgins said. 'I already know what I think. I think you're trying to recruit me for a foreign intelligence agency.' And Higgins wondered then, if he went along with the whole mad scheme, if he'd have a codename and a handler.

The man must have smiled then for Higgins had the impression of strong yellow teeth. His tone changed completely. 'Recruit you! How absurd! Why, this is . . . strictly business. I'm approaching you as one businessman to another, as someone who sells goods to the highest bidder in the best Yankee tradition. What you would be doing is no more subversive than Goodyear, say . . . selling tires to . . . England.'

'Yeah,' Higgins said. 'Except that this isn't tires. And the sale of spare military parts to some foreign intelligence agency just might be construed, by some finicky and over-zealous DA, as a violation of US law.' His voice was dripping with sarcasm.

'*You* could get away with it, however.' The man smiled. 'You always have. In the past, I mean.'

So there it was again. The threat. His secret had not died with Jorge, as he had hoped. What a fool he'd been to think it had. And everything seemed to tremble then, framed in that perfect and eternal *suchness* which Buddhist sages love to praise – though perhaps it was only the light of his candle.

'Think about it. This is all we ask. Think about it. And I will call you in the morning. For, *amigo*, remember, we don't have much time.' And giving Higgins a crisp salute, Crespi turned and slipped into the outer darkness.

Higgins watched him disappear. Well, he thought, let him go – right to the US Attorney General. For even if Higgins had to go to jail, he was not about to get involved in *this*. Oh, no. Then they would *really* have something on him. Then they would own him. Better to bite the bullet now, than to eat one later.

For Higgins had done some stupid things in his day. But, God, thus far, in His infinite Mercy, had shielded him from their consequences. And Higgins wasn't about to try God's infinite Patience by doing something so infinitely stupid again.

Blood On Your Hands

◆

Chapter 11

While Higgins pursued inner peace, the Doctor prepared for war, dedicating all his energies to *El Presidente*. He had taken a leave of absence from the hospital while Julio Cruz, the young doctor on call when the Doctor was away, had absorbed the bulk of the Doctor's practice and appeared to be in no hurry to give it back.

It was just as well. For the Doctor's time had finally come. Like a new star ascendent in the heavens or like a comet blazing round the sun after years on the frigid rim of the universe, or like the avatar of some powerful new god, the Doctor's light was being seen, his power felt, his name and praises sung. *Jay! Jay!* Hallelujah!

The Doctor, unfortunately, had little time to bask in his brightening aura. The week following his promotion and first press conference, he hardly slept, cranking out instead a mountain of paper – like the hero of some impossible fable who must write a book as high as heaven overnight in order to wed a giant's daughter. You would have thought they were fighting with ink, not guns; waging a battle of words, not bullets. Documents on every conceivable topic under the sun flowed from the Doctor's pen, underwent Benitez's scribbled revisions, and were poured into word processors, emerging at twenty-two characters per second as political tracts and social positions which they must now defend.

Once, a single missing comma had almost derailed the negotiations. The unfortunate omission of something the size of a rice grain had subverted the intended meaning of a phrase, appearing to call into question a certain ally's testicular resolve. Only bushels of assuaging words and baskets of praises could convince their friends the slur was unintended, but by then the infinitesimal missing crescent had done more damage than a bomb.

The Doctor was appalled. To think a misplaced punctuation mark could have such a devasting effect! Was history an equation that one false value or erroneous sign could hopelessly subvert? Or were they riding upon a victorious flood that nothing in heaven or earth could stem or turn? For this is how the Doctor and his comrades often felt: as though they were merely instruments of fate, as though they were doing the will of heaven.

But even heaven's will is not accomplished without human effort, and it fell to Benitez & Co. to do the actual legwork. Each small piece of the campaign broke up into a multitude of parts. The Doctor handled copy mostly, but he was well aware that all around him a gigantic war machine was grinding into motion; and though it was invisible, from time to time he could feel the jarring thunder of its machinations.

Given his exhausting, stressful schedule, the Doctor's time alone with Jane was more important and precious to him than ever. On nights when she was not with *El Duende*, they had taken to meeting secretly late in the evening, then retiring afterward to the Doctor's office where they made love on his waiting room couch which was almost but not quite big enough for the two of them, so that the Doctor invariably ended up toward dawn on the floor, with a void in his groin, and the sharp flanges of a hangover cutting into his skull.

This particular summer evening Janie watched as the Doctor undid his tie and unstrapped his holster. Then he removed his shirt and pants as well.

'Hey, Doc,' she said. 'You don't kid around.'

The Doctor, in his socks, summer undershirt and boxer shorts, poured himself a pony of brandy and joined her on the couch. 'Health, love and money,' he proposed. 'And the time to enjoy them!' He took a sip and drank her in, astonished once again by the living, shivering consciousness that brimmed her eyes. It was *this* he loved, this quicksilver spirit, this shining nymph that inhabited her body and moved her long and beautiful bones.

'Marry me,' the Doctor said. The words just flew out. He had not planned them. He himself looked quite amazed, then he threw himself upon her in a flux of passion, nibbling at the sweet white meat of her throat.

'Hey, hold yer darn horses, son. We don't have to get married just to do *that*!'

'I am serious,' the Doctor said, feasting on her flesh.

'What? I can't hear ya, Doc. Quit it, will you?' she said, forcibly removing his prying hand. 'Hey, will you behave yourself?'

'Marry me,' the Doctor said again.

She looked in his eyes for the longest time to see if he was serious or crazy – then seemed to realize he was both. 'Well, jeez, Doc. I hardly know you. I mean, I gotta think about it.'

The Doctor was somewhat taken aback. It had never occurred to him that a simple country girl like Jane might hesitate to wed a grand and important personage like himself. Still, upon reflection, she was probably right to be so cautious, and the Doctor praised her for it, urging her to make inquiries into his 'background,' as he called it, hinting broadly he was descended from kings.

She herself was common, of course. There was no getting around that. And though the Doctor might once have wished for a wife closer to his social station, after the inbred bloodline of Helena de Jesus, he found Janie's origins bright and refreshing, like the sparkling notes of a country banjo after a concerto for oboe, viol and bassoon.

But by seven o'clock the following morning, after another orgy of love-making and an enormous breakfast at the luncheonette downstairs – a breakfast which the girl devoured with a farm hand's appetite – the Doctor began to have second thoughts about his proposal of marriage and Jane's suitability as a mate. If he wasn't careful, he realized, she would eat him out of house and home, and it was with great difficulty he got her to stop eating and to come back upstairs.

Now, in the sober light of day, he looked at her again. She was chewing gum and reading a movie magazine on the couch, wearing only her bra and panties, which, in fact, was a sensible choice of attire given the heat. Her feet, planted on one arm of the couch, were wiggling in a profoundly frivolous way, and something inside the Doctor told him then that he was deluding himself – that she wasn't the type who would cook for him a big fancy meal when he came home, but rather the type who would expect *him*, after a hard day's work, to take her out for lobster and cocktails at some overpriced clam bar in the Village. Yes! But no, the Doctor would change her if that were so. Like some Spanish *Pygmalion*, he would take and shape her, molding her into the ideal companion and his life would become like a Moorish heaven – a garden of Allah where he was titillated and comforted by sloe-eyed *houris*.

'Assholes!' his celestial companion said, winging the movie magazine at the table. 'I'm thirsty, Doc,' she whined in an unpleasant and infantile way. 'Be a dollface, will ya, and crack me a frosty?'

The dollfaced Doctor disapproved. He did not think it seemly that his fiancée should begin on the *cerveza* at eight in the morning. It was not dignified. It was not what he had had in mind. Nor did it seem right that a forty-one-year-old doctor should be waiting upon an unemployed twenty-year-old girl. Who was the *houri*, after all? Finally, it seemed peculiar that, though they were lovers, she still called him Doc.

'I don't have any beer,' the Doctor said. 'What do you think this is, a *cantina*?'

'C'mon, Doc,' she whimpered. 'Pretty please?' And she gave him a wink that promised all sorts of shameful and salacious joys if he complied.

'All right, but put some clothes on, will you?' he asked throwing her her frock. 'My God. This is a doctor's office.'

But five minutes later, when the Doctor had still not left – he was standing just inside the doorway wrestling with his holster – he heard the words, 'Hey, c'mon, Doc. Toot sweet!'

'I am coming *toute suite*,' the Doctor growled, annoyed by her tone and the French expression. He came out of the door way wearing the ill-fitting holster. She looked at him and shook her head.

'Doc, sometimes I think you're not too bright.'

'*I* am not too bright!'

'Doc, sometimes I think you're a nice guy *but* . . . you read my meaning?' and lifting her hair from her eyes with a jet of breath from her outthrust jaw, she expertly readjusted the holster so that it fit him now, the gun snug and tight beneath his left armpit.

'Where did you learn that?'

'Doc, put on your hat and buy us some brew?'

The Doctor started down the stairs, muttering to himself. He did not like taking orders, especially from a girl. Even in bed she bossed him around, shouting out directions and commands with a Protestant practicality that appalled the Doctor, and which no good Latin Catholic girl in her right mind had ever dreamed of doing.

But out on the street the Doctor found his stock had soared. His association with Benitez and with the lovely blonde *mujer* had captured the rabble's imagination, and the Doctor's resurrection this morning was greeted by a cacophony of hoots and whistles, trills and leers from the men and boys in front of *El Encanto*, so that the Doctor moved in an effluvium of sound, hailed as a hero by the people, celebrated for his phallus, like a local corn deity. Even the old man who sold the Doctor *cerveza* paused before bagging it to wink and make an obscene and ancient gesture with his hands while whistling appreciatively through the interstices of his teeth.

Thus it was love, not war, that was on the Doctor's mind as, passing the newsstand, his gaze fell upon the morning paper.

REBELS AMBUSHED IN DORADO

The Doctor stopped in his tracks, snatched the paper up and practically inhaled the copy. How many killed?

'*Fourteen*,' the paper said, '. . . when *government forces*

312

repelled a rebel attack on the San Miguel police station, twenty miles south of Coban.' San Miguel. But why did the Doctor know that name? Because that was part of the intelligence he had given *El Duende* less than a week ago and now, incredibly, already it had been used to slaughter soldiers – fourteen of *their* soldiers, or of Benitez's really, or of Commander Rabon's, or of whoever in hell was in charge of them, finally.

The Doctor was horrified. Up until now, it had all been unreal – words and paper – and somehow he had forgotten that real people were on the other end of those papery words. Fourteen men dead, and God knows how many more wounded! He read on further. The government admitted to six casualties; three dead. Seventeen dead in all. They were probably lying. There were probably more. But what did it matter – seventeen or fifty or seventy-five? After one, the numbers soon became meaningless. He wondered how many patients he had saved in his day? And it seemed to him now, in the course of the morning, he had just undone the good works of a lifetime.

And yet, the Doctor told himself, he really was not to blame. These deaths were not his, but Benitez's responsibility, after all. The Doctor had been no more than a conduit. Yes. He liked the word. *Con-dweet*. Surely the Doctor was no more to blame than a telephone is guilty of carrying murderous instructions. When the Doctor looked at the thing from this perspective, he felt better. All he'd been doing was following orders. Soldiers had to follow orders in order to fight a war.

For somehow (don't ask how) the Doctor had managed to get involved in a hot little war without even setting foot outside of the *barrio*. It had been fun and quite exciting for a while. But now, with the first blood, the play had gone out of playing soldier. And though no more than a minute had elapsed since he had read about the ambushed squadron, the Doctor felt many lifetimes older.

Forgetting about Jane, he headed straight for Benitez's headquarters. The Doctor relinquished his weapon at the door, passing easily though the first two sets of guards, then got into a shouting match with the sergeant at the elevator. It was the same guard who had failed to search the Doctor on his first visit there and, while the Doctor cursed, the man frisked him with an humiliating familiarity. Eventually, Guido appeared, attracted by the noise. 'It's all right, Sergeant. The Doctor is expected,' and he pushed the Doctor through the elevator's folding gate.

'Have you seen this?' the Doctor asked, flourishing the paper.

'Yes,' Guido said. He closed the gate and pushed the button. On the third floor landing, the gate was reopened and the Doctor again was frisked. Then he was led by a guard down the carpeted hall to Benitez's quarters.

Benitez's office was looking less and less like a college president's and more and more like a military camp. Maps spilled out of a map room behind his desk. A telex machine had been installed in one corner, and in another room, telephones were ringing.

'Your Excellency,' the Doctor said. 'I came immediately. As soon as I heard.'

'Heard? About what?' Benitez said vaguely.

'The ambushed squadron.'

Benitez frowned. 'That was *days* ago, Doctor. Where do you get your intelligence from? The newspapers?'

'But, my President, fourteen dead! And all because of the information . . . I, that is, *we* gave to *El Duende*.'

'It's unfortunate,' Benitez admitted, furrowing his brow. 'But then again . . .' He shrugged and the lines left his face and his demeanor lightened, as though this briefest regret was a passionate Act of Contrition and his soul, in that instant, had been cleansed of sin.

'But your Excellency,' the Doctor persisted, wringing his hands. 'Such a tragedy. I fear things are not going well for us at all!'

'What tragedy?' Benitez snapped. 'Everything is working perfectly . . . according to plan. Because of the information you gave, the government flew eight hundred troops into

Montazan province. We threw four hundred men against them, gave them hell, killed twenty-seven and lost nine. Not fourteen either, as they're claiming.'

'But even *nine*, the Doctor said.

'Look,' Benitez said patiently, laying a fist on the Doctor's shoulder. 'We can't fight a war without killing people.'

'Yes,' the Doctor asked, 'but our own men?'

'Don't you see, Doctor? They had to die. To make the Junta believe our intelligence is accurate.'

'What?' the Doctor said, appalled. 'You mean, we . . . you did it on purpose?'

Benitez opened his mouth to explain, then stopped. He looked down at his hands, then back up at the Doctor. Evidently he found the subject distressing, for he tried to change it. 'Do you play chess, Doctor?'

'Yes, but . . .'

Benitez used the Doctor to help himself up from his chair. A pocket chessboard sat on a corner of his desk. 'Are you familiar with the Giocco Piano? A fine opening. How does it go?'

'I really can't remember, your Excellency. I haven't . . .'

'Pawn to King four, isn't it? Then pawn to King four. Then Knight to King's Bishop three. Hurry, Doctor, you have three seconds to make your move. There you go. And I respond with . . . Now you. Now me. Quick. Quick.' At which point, the Doctor saw an opportunity, and seized Benitez's undefended knight.

'You gave it to me,' the Doctor said, surprised.

Benitez smiled. 'I didn't *give* you anything, *Señor*. I *sacrificed* it to achieve position. For, if you are such a fool as to take it – which you are – then,' Benitez quickly moved their pieces, 'three moves later, my move is check. There. You have but one move open to you. That's right. And now . . . mate.' Benitez smiled. He looked at the Doctor. 'So, you understand?'

'Understand?'

'About those soldiers.' He placed a hand on the Doctor's shoulder. 'It hurts to lose a single one of them. I, too, am pained they died, but their lives, I assure you, were *sacrificed*; they were not thrown away.' His smile returned. 'The problem with you, Doctor, is you want to liberate a country but you don't want to get any blood on your hands. Is that how you perform an operation? A doctor, a surgeon like yourself should know better. You can't remove a tumor without spilling some blood, hey? Or do you think that God will blame you for it and you will suffer some sort of—'

'God? No.'

'. . . retribution? Because I'll tell you, Doctor, God is not like that. God is not some fairy with a weak stomach who blanches at the sight of blood. No, Doctor, God is a *man*! C'mon now,' he said, placing an arm around the Doctor's shoulder. 'Look, why don't you take a few days off? You're . . . upset. I'll see you again on Monday morning. There you go. And, Doctor?'

'Yes?'

'Please secure my medical file.'

Downstairs at the desk, the Doctor picked up his pistol and the bag of *cerveza* he had bought at the store. It was certainly true that he needed a rest. But first, there were some reporters' phone calls to return, and then he had to meet with Guido, and by the time he was finished and had called his office, it was already past noon and Jane was gone.

Hungry, the Doctor left the brownstone and headed off for *El Encanto*. His mouth watered in anticipation of the pickled eggs and chilies served *gratis* by the bar.

But as he passed beneath his office window, he thought he saw something glide across the pane. He stopped and stared, shading his gaze against the noonday sun – but now he saw nothing, save the flaking lettering of his name.

The Doctor wondered if it could be Jane, but if it was, then why hadn't she answered the phone when he'd called? He looked once again, but still he saw nothing. He gazed longingly at *El Encanto* not four doors away; then, cursing his over-conscientious conscience, entered the building and mounted the stairs. For the Doctor was driven by inner voices which asked him the most infuriating questions at the least opportune times, questions like, 'Did you turn off the flame beneath the coffee in the kitchen?' as he arrived at the airport to go on vacation. And now these same taunting inner familiars were insisting, 'What was that you saw in the window?'

Damn them, he thought. It was probably nothing.

Then he saw his office door was open. 'Jane?' he called. 'Jane!' But there was no answer.

The Doctor's first impulse was to rush inside, but he mastered it manfully. His second impulse was to call the police, but the phone, alas, was in the darkened office. Then the voices inside him began screaming like crazy, 'Jane could be in there, hurt and dying!'

The Doctor slipped through the doorway. He peered through the gloom at the familiar shadows, the table stacked with magazines. Then he saw a canvas bag he had never seen before lying on the sofa. There was no doubt about it; someone was in here!

He drew his gun, locking the office door behind him. He scanned the room, then went to the door of the examining room and listened. Carefully, he turned the knob and let the door swing open. With the utmost caution, he snaked in his head.

His office had been sacked. The drawers of his files were open and listing. For a moment, he wondered if Jane could have done this – but that was absurd. Why trash the place? She could have taken whatever she wanted, without his ever knowing it. No, it was his enemies who had done this to him: *El Duende*, Omar, Schmidt, Cordero, and the faceless voice in St. Elvira's.

With a battle cry, the Doctor entered. If the intruder had shown his face at that instant, the Doctor would have surely dispatched him on the spot. The room, however, was empty. Unless the intruder was hiding in the bathroom!

The Doctor flattened himself against the wall and screamed, 'Come out of there with your hands up. I warn you. I am armed. Throw down your weapon and you will

317

not be injured.' For this time, the Doctor was prepared to fire.

But there was no response to the Doctor's summons and when at last he kicked open the door – his gun drawn, his eyes blazing – he found the bathroom, too, was empty.

Immediately, he went to the ransacked cabinets and searched them for Benitez's file. Gone! He gave a cry of pure dismay.

Then he remembered he had filed it under Z. How brilliant of him! Yes. Here it was! For it would not have been an easy matter explaining to his Excellency that his medical records had been stolen. Nor, thank God, was Janie here. He tucked away the pistol, greatly relieved.

And so now when the Doctor stepped back into the darkened waiting room and encountered a figure, he was amazed. He was so astonished, he dropped the file. 'Who *are* you?' he asked.

But in answer, the figure sprang at the Doctor.

The voices cried, 'Fire!'

The Doctor obeyed.

Lupe Maria

◆

Chapter 12

'Hello, my friend. How are you today?'

'That isn't what you called to ask me.'

'No,' Crespi said. He paused a moment. 'You've looked over our list?'

'I looked at it, yes.' It was indeed a list of military parts, from armored radiators to nuts and washers to infrared night-scopes.

'And?'

'And as I told you last night. Count me out.'

'Why is that?'

Some of it, Higgins had concluded, could be bought legitimately over the counter with a lot of money and a little *savoir faire*. Much of it, though, was highly restricted. To have bought it, legally at least, would have been difficult for anyone – impossible for Higgins. Not that Higgins was even faintly considering the idea. 'I'll tell you why. And this is the last time we're going to have this conversation, okay? I'm getting tired of it. What you're asking me to do is to cut my throat, from two different directions.

'For example, say I approach a dealer on MIRA's behalf. Since the whole thing's completely illegal, the dealer can always conclude the deal, then go straight to both the US Attorney General and the Director of AES. The US Government would have me arrested; AES would have me killed. The old double whammy. And for what, for what?'

'For freedom!' Crespi said with a sudden flux of passion. 'For our comrades in arms.'

'What comrades in arms? Who are these parts for anyway?'

'Haven't you guessed – they are for the rebels in Dorado. And by helping them,' he added quickly, 'you will, of course, be helping yourself.'

'Oh, really? Explain that to me, please. How shipping parts to the rebels in Dorado does something wonderful for me.'

'It is very simple. *El Duende* is an agent of the Junta. You help to crush them, and he will fall, too.'

'C'mon,' Higgins said. 'I'm going to start a *war* in Central America because my friend has a problem with some shylock here in New York?'

'It is more than just a problem with a shylock, friend. I was thinking of Gilberta. And the children.'

'What about them?' Higgins asked, feeling a chill steal over the conversation.

'You don't know? Gil was abducted the other night. And her children threatened.'

'And how do you know that?' Higgins asked suspiciously.

The agent sighed. 'The whole *barrio* saw it. But you – you prefer to close your eyes and look the other way. Or were you *meditating*,' the agent said with a faint sneer. 'However, if you were, then you must regard yourself as a man of . . . principle. Well, here I am offering you the opportunity to do *real* good, to help liberate the people of Dorado while destroying those who are out to hurt the ones you love. And you . . . you shun it.' He sighed with exasperation. 'And on top of it all, there is your commission. *Dios mio*, anyone else would be overjoyed.'

There was another pause, on Higgins' part now. 'What commission?'

'Your commission. You didn't think we were asking you to do this for nothing? We know you are not running a charity. We are prepared to pay the standard ten per cent for your services. I did not bring it up sooner because, frankly, I thought it was understood.'

First, it was the stick, now it was the carrot. And yet, though he knew what they were doing to him, surprisingly, Higgins found himself pursuing the conversation. 'And do you have any idea how much this little shopping list of yours would cost?'

'You tell me.'

'I would say, conservatively, seven million dollars.'

'That is high. A man of your abilities could bring it in for under five. So your piece of it would be around half a mil. US. Cash, of course.'

For one suicidal moment, Higgins luxuriated in the thought of all that tax-free money. 'Just tell me something. Will you? Why me? Why don't you go through the Doctor or Benitez?'

'No!' the voice fairly shouted. 'You must tell them nothing. No one must know.'

'Why not?' Higgins said.

'Why not? Don't you understand?' Crespie's voice was incredulous. 'Somebody tipped off AES about Vazpana. How else did they manage to go right to his door?'

Maybe it was sheer incompetence, Higgins wanted to say. He didn't though, in deference to the dead. 'And do you really think the Doctor did it?'

'We don't know *who* did it. That is the problem. It could have been someone in Benitez's camp.'

'Maybe *I* did it.'

There was an awkward pause. Then the voice said, 'You're a foolish man to joke that way. If I thought it was you, I'd have killed you last night.'

Higgins reddened, concluding this was probably true.

'We chose you precisely because we think you can be trusted. And because of your past record. We were impressed with your . . . finesse and discretion.'

Higgins almost wanted to believe what he was saying, and yet how could he? The intelligence he had been waiting for had finally come through.

321

'According to his birth certificate, Jorge Vazpana was thirty-two years old. He had light brown hair and blue eyes. None of which squares with my dead roommate.'

'Oh, is that what's bothering you?' The agent laughed. 'I will admit, Jorge Vazpana was a very different man from his records – by the time we got through with them. Or do you think all the secretaries in the Hall of the People are loyal to the Junta? What does it take to change a few words on a birth certificate? I will tell you. Nothing more than a girl named Lupe Maria.'

And when Higgins heard the name, he knew intuitively what Crespi said was true. In every office there is such a girl. She is plain and docile, though she, too, has her dreams of love. A sweet look here, a kind word there, a romantic dinner, tickets to a Lucho Barrios concert and soon you have her heart in your hand. You explain to her intimately, your lips brushing her ear: 'Lupe, sweet one, I need a favor from you. . . . Just a little thing.'

And Higgins realized then that all the so-called 'facts and figures' on which this world runs go through the hands of girls like Lupe Maria – and are subject to her whim.

The Sickbed Of Castellano

◆

Chapter 13

For the next two days the Doctor refused to leave his bedroom. He was distraught. For it had not been the Doctor's enemies at all. It had only been that wretched Solano boy – the seamstress's son – stealing drugs again. Whenever the Doctor threatened to remember this, he would swallow another pill, so that he rose and fell, like some blubbering seabeast, in the ocean of his own drugged consciousness and dreams, surfacing just long enough to take in the dreary unreality of the curtained chamber, recall the boy's bloody face (and the image of the ambushed squadron), then rolling over in the sweaty bed, plunging downward once again, embracing oblivion and rippling dreams.

The telephone rang incessantly, but the Doctor did not answer it, nor when Rosita did, would he acknowledge the hundred voices that called for him, crying for him half the night. Many of the calls were from worried patients – patients worried about themselves, not the Doctor – while others were from perfect strangers who wanted to congratulate or condemn the Doctor for firing the shot. The fact that the congratulatory phone calls greatly outnumbered the others was just a further irony that the Doctor, by staying in his bedroom, hoped to ignore.

For there were many people who were actually heartened that the Doctor had shot a child in the head. The *Post* gloated:

323

'Doc Plugs Drug Thug'; the New York Better Business Bureau sent the Doctor tickets to the Met and coupons good for two complimentary dinners at Tavern on the Green. The National Rifle Association was using the occasion to issue a major policy statement on the place of hand guns in a free society. Just to think of it made the Doctor ill, and he burrowed down more deeply, pulling the covers over his head.

> *'Whence comes such faintness of heart*
> *and lowness of spirit?*
> *It ill becomes a nobleman,*
> *brings dishonor,*
> *and will never win you heaven.*
> *Do not play the eunuch, O son of Pritha!*
> *Shake off this base faintheartedness,*
> *and arise,*
> *O scorcher of your foes!'*

Higgins, who had invaded the sickroom to deliver this harangue, raised a shade and snatched the bedclothes from the Doctor's fingers.

'What time is it?' the Doctor asked.

'Five o'clock. Sunday evening.'

'Really? And what was that you just said to me?'

'The *Bhagavad Gita*.'

Now the Doctor, who was still rather drugged and befuddled, could not for the life of him remember this evening who or what the *Bhagavad Gita* was. After some thought, he decided it was a *person*, or more accurately, the *title* of a person, whom the Doctor envisioned as a middle-aged gentleman with a shaved head topped by a hair tuft, a small skullcap, and the jeweled robes of an oriental chieftain. The *Bhagavad Gita* was standing in the Doctor's mind, his arms crossed at his chest, a powerful look in his eyes, as if to say he had everything under control. This august personage had replaced the fish-eyed figment that had once been the face of the Doctor's conscience.

'Did you hear what happened?' the Doctor asked Higgins.

'Hear? It's all over town. Read this!' Higgins said, and tossed him the paper.

The paper had got the story wrong – which was not surprising since the Doctor had lied a little bit about what had happened to protect Benitez, and the police had lied a little more to protect the Doctor, and the paper had lied a little further to sell more papers – until all the littles had added up to a lot and the printed version was nothing at all like what had occurred. According to the newspaper's account, the Doctor had surprised an armed intruder stealing drugs from his office and, in the ensuing struggle, the intruder's gun had accidentally discharged – whereas, if the truth were known, the Doctor had, out of cowardice and fear, shot an unarmed child at three paces.

The Doctor wandered out of the bedroom and went to the bathroom. His urine had the stale stink of the sickroom. He wished he could go back to bed, but the *Bhagavad Gita*, looking very much like Yul Brynner, was standing in the doorway, his arms folded, barring the way.

The Doctor wandered down the hall into the living room. He noticed with distaste the small altar that had been erected in one corner, while a book with a long unpronounceable Sanskrit title that hurt his mind to read lay beside it on the couch. It was some sort of eastern scripture, without pictures, he was sure. He picked it up. Higgins was addicted to books of this nature – heathen bibles full of lies – and boring! Oh, my God! The Doctor had once cracked a couple of them sideways and the odor that issued forth was not a pleasant one to smell. For the Doctor could conceive of no more inane and boring pastime than brooding over *Sat* and *Tat*. Give him a fast mama any night doing a slo-o-o-w mambo!

And yet the Doctor would have liked to believe. One small corner of the Doctor's heart wanted to, and waited for a sign, but the signs, when they came, were never encouraging. And yet now, without warning, a tiny prayer escaped the Doctor's heart, like a refugee fleeing a totalitarian country. It was a prayer that was hardly a prayer at all, but more a superstitious wish, a plea: 'God, if You exist (which I sincerely doubt) tell me what I need to know.' And the Doctor closed his eyes and opened the book at random and stabbed his finger and read where his finger stuck – a message from chance – a letter from the universe:

> *O gazelle-eyed One,*
> *The Guru protects you,*
> *If you are cursed by sages,*
> *Snake demons, or even gods . . .*

and with an outraged snarl, the Doctor snapped the book shut, furious that he had been swindled once again by a weak mind and a trusting heart.

So this is how it was! *Snake demons*, for Christsakes! The world was going to hell, *real* people were dying from *real* bullets and Higgins was reading and *thinking* about . . . snake demons. It was in bad taste, to say the least. It was an offense against . . . modernity, yes. But it wasn't really Higgins with whom the Doctor was disappointed; it was himself. Even in his weakened condition, how could he have ever fallen for such crap? And anyway, why would a god damn you, or a sage? Gods were supposed to *bless* you, weren't they? The accursed philosophy was contradictory even on its own terms.

Using his outrage as fuel, the Doctor went back into the bathroom, took a shower, and managed to shave and dress. Rosita tried to feed him dinner, but the Doctor refused, as his stomach was still unsettled from the drugs. Outside, the evening sunlight dazzled. After the sickroom, he felt weak, almost two-dimensional, like something made of paste and cardboard.

But when he arrived at the hospital and saw the comatose boy, the Doctor's own weakness vanished. A square of blood-soaked gauze covered the boy's right eye and temple. Machines and bottles stood around him. The Doctor studied the boy's charts, but they told him little that he couldn't see. The boy was on the edge – and slipping. It would be a wonder if he even made it through the night. He sighed. Oh, well . . .

Just then, there was a high-pitched shriek from the corridor outside. The Doctor started, then ran out just in time to see Higgins and the *mestiza* girl – what was her damned name? – coming right at him, as a nurse reeled after her crying, 'She's the one. She's the one.' A security guard, aroused by the nurse's cries, grabbed the young *mestiza*'s arm. Higgins interposed himself between the girl and the officer, indignantly removing the man's arresting hand.

'Stop it,' the Doctor ordered. 'You idiot! These are my guests.'

The guard froze and looked at the Doctor, one hand still gripping Higgins' shirt. Meanwhile, the nurse, a Jamaican with frizzled gray hair, floated up behind them. She seemed quite hysterical, with grief or joy.

'What's going on?' the Doctor demanded.

'She saved his life . . .'

'See,' the Doctor said to the guard. 'Nothing wrong. Now you may go.' And when the man did not move fast enough for the Doctor's liking: 'Dis*missed*!' and the guard fled.

'Now then,' the Doctor said, trying to smooth things over. 'What's going on here?'

'She raised him from the dead,' the nurse sobbed.

'What are you talking about?'

'Brought him back to life. Praise God!'

'Brought *who* back to life?'

'*Señor* Gonzalez. Room 293. Doctor, he be dead. No heartbeat. Nothing. I be just about to call you, Doctor, when she' – the nurse pointed at the girl with awe – 'touched his face.'

The Doctor stared at the girl as he imbibed this information, but she would not even meet his eyes. Then he turned and walked down the corridor, stepping into Gonzalez's room. The old man was sleeping peacefully. There was no indication he had almost died. The Doctor looked from the trembling nurse to the *mestiza* girl. She was very still, a little half-smile playing on her lips.

'Well,' the Doctor asked, turning to the girl with a nervous laugh, 'did you bring the old fellow . . . back to life?'

The child smiled but made no sound.

'She touched his eyes . . . and he opened them and spoke. . . . I saw him. Oh, she be a perfect wonder. Bless me, bless me,' the nurse wept.

'Well? You heard her.' He smiled benignly. 'Did you wake him from the dead?'

In a soft, matter-of-fact voice the child spoke. 'I woke him, yes. He was sleeping.'

'Not sleeping,' the nurse said fiercely. 'No heartbeat, Doctor. No breath.'

'Your faith is great. But . . . you are mistaken,' the child said kindly. Then she turned from the nurse to the Doctor. 'This is the second time you've helped me, Uncle. I owe you one.' She looked at him and grinned. ' "One hand washes the other." '

The Doctor said nothing for the longest time. He stared at the girl, at the nurse, at Higgins and at Gonzalez. Then he said, thoughtfully, 'Will you come with me?' And the Doctor led the girl out into the corridor and down the hall to the bedside of the unconscious boy. They stood there, studying him for several moments.

'Well?' the Doctor asked at last. 'Will he live?'

The child smiled. '*You* are the doctor.'

'He won't. Will he?'

The girl took the boy's hand and said something to Higgins beneath her breath.

'What was that?'

'She says, "His *prana* is weak." '

'I see,' the Doctor said. He was quiet for a while then he said, 'You promised me a favor. I claim it now. If it's true you have the power, you must . . . save this boy.'

The girl smiled, then shook her head. 'I told you, Uncle. I have no such power.'

'Oh, no?' the Doctor said. 'You don't heal the sick?'

'*You* do, Doctor.'

'You don't raise the dead?'

The girl rolled her eyes at the foolishness of his suggestion. The Doctor didn't know what to say. He felt rather silly.

What a stupid idea it had been. Raise the dead! He sighed and reached to close the curtain.

'But . . .' the child said, 'sometimes . . . if I ask the Fakir . . . he will do it for me.'

'Ah ha! So you *can*!' the Doctor cried, coming to life. 'And who is this Fakir?'

'That is her name for God,' Higgins said.

'All right. You must ask him then!'

The child nodded and closed her eyes. Then she opened them and said, 'The Fakir says, it would be unwise.'

'What?' the Doctor said, dismayed. 'And why is that? He saved an old man just now. Why won't he save a young boy?'

'This one,' the *mestiza* said, gesturing at the bed, 'is a troubled soul. The Fakir says, it is God's will he leave us now.'

God's will! The Doctor almost choked with rage. He felt like a gentleman who, against all better judgment, deigns to make a pass at a scullery maid, only to find himself rejected as unworthy. 'He is a boy,' the Doctor said. 'A young boy with a bullet in his head. You . . . you religious people! You . . . make me sick. The world goes to hell, innocent children starve and die before your very eyes and you can only say, it is God's will! What the hell is wrong with you people?'

The girl shrugged, unmoved. 'You should ask for something else.'

'No,' the Doctor said, remembering some mythic conversation between a man and a fairy. 'I ask for that.'

The girl shook her head. 'It is ill advised. Sometimes, things look different than they are. You should reconsider, Doctor.'

'Well, I won't! Tell him, I demand it,' the Doctor said, furious with himself for carrying on a conversation with a spirit – a spirit that did not exist. 'Tell him, he – you – promised me a favor. Now I hold you – him – to your promise. Tell him to let this poor boy live.'

The girl shrugged and again grew still. She closed her eyes, 'The Fakir says, you don't need his intercession. If you wish it, you yourself have the power.'

'What? To save this boy?'

'That's what he says. And the Fakir, he is never wrong. Good-bye, Uncle!' She turned to go.

'But what does that *mean*?' the Doctor called, taken aback. 'You mean, that's it? No laying on of hands? No lighted candles? No special incantations?'

But Higgins and the girl had already turned their backs and were halfway down the hallway.

'Watch out for the snake demons,' the Doctor yelled. 'There are several in the nurses' lounge! Ha, ha, ha, ha!'

But the Doctor was not really laughing. He was disgusted with himself. What was wrong with him? To be begging favours of the spirits. A humanist like himself!

He sat down at the boy's bedside and took his hand. And as he did, the girl's strange words disintered a long-buried memory. He remembered the first time he had fired a rifle. Aiming in the air, he had pulled the trigger – and brought a lovely sea-green parrot parachuting down from out of the trees. His cousin, whose gun it was, had laughed in surprise, and told the Doctor to wring the parrot's neck.

And it was then, while standing over the wounded creature whose breast and wing were stained with gore, that something inside the Doctor had stirred, sending forth a tender shoot which, unfolding cotyledons of mercy and concern, had grown in due time into the wondrous tree of the Doctor's doctorhood.

For instead of wringing the parrot's neck, the Doctor had flung the rifle down and, cooing in the bird's feathered ear, had brought it inside the seaside *finca* and attempted to undo the damage he had done by deftly and expertly extracting the pellet. Then he had dressed the wound and set the wing – things no one had ever taught him how to do – keeping his patient in a bamboo cage until it was well.

And when the day finally came for the parrot's release, no one was more excited than the Doctor-to-be. Thirty years later, he could still remember that green Cuban evening: how his father had made a little ceremony of the occasion, gathering the family in the shadows of the avocados, and how the parrot had looked puzzled at first, then, testing its wings, had remembered their power and leapt into the twilit sky.

His aunt had wondered aloud if the parrot would ever come back someday, to thank the Doctor, as it were, but the Doctor, at eleven, had had no such illusions. It would not return, any more than a fish thrown back into the ocean returns to the fisher's hand. And anyway, he didn't care. For it wasn't the parrot that had made him so happy. What had made him so happy that green Cuban evening (and that he would marvel at forever after) was not the bird at all – but his own miraculous power to heal.

That night had been a turning point. And the Doctor felt a surge of gratitude to the girl for unlocking the door to this sweet, sweet memory. He disengaged himself from the boy's limp hand. Oh, well. He had given it the old college try.

He stood up and stretched. His body ached from the days of bedrest. He put on his jacket and was starting to go, when on an impulse, the Doctor bent and kissed the child upon the brow.

For a moment, he waited, half expecting something to occur. But unlike those tales of fairy enchantments, the boy neither stirred nor opened his eyes.

Nectar

◆

Chapter 14

The ex-witch, Mathilde, was nearly eighty – a skeleton in a wheelchair. Garcia had tracked her down in the hope that she could throw some light on his enchantment, and on *El Duende*. She lived in a public housing project defaced with spray-paint and composed of four identical brown towers, each facing in a different direction, like monsters loitering on the horizon. Across the grounds, clotheslines looped in the late hot sun, wet wash dripping into the smoking dust.

Gil had insisted on accompanying Garcia. Garcia led them through the maze of apartments to the concrete balcony of the flat in which the woman lived. New slums, Gil thought. When the old ones succumb to age and fire, the city builds new ones – complete with concrete balconies.

Garcia introduced the two women, and the elder asked Gil what she did. 'Me? I'm a mother,' Gil said, surprised by her answer. A week ago she would have said 'actress' or 'singer.' 'And you?'

The woman smiled. 'Me, I was a witch. And not a very good one at that!'

'Witch?'

'Yes. Does that surprise you? It was I who fashioned dolls out of human feces, and then, with the use of certain syllables and drugs—'

'Feces?' Gil asked, wrinkling her nose. 'But . . . why?'

'For powers. And pleasures. And to appease certain spirits who would then grant us boons. For, as I told the Captain here, it *can* be done . . . this *magi negro*.' She looked at them both. 'But first you must eat balls of shit and other dead things and perform certain unusual and disgusting practices. Sexual congress with the dead is highly efficacious in these matters.' She looked at Gil and laughed. 'I am *trying* to be delicate.'

'And where was this?' Gilberta asked.

'In Dorado, on the southern plateau, where the old ways are still practiced.'

And Gil had a vision then of an iron-gray plain on which the chaparral gesticulated in the wind, where skeletal balls of tumbleweed rolled forever through heat-choked days and there the stars burned like an obscene declaration.

'You did all those thing, *Señora*?'

'Ah, the young,' the woman said. 'They think that sin is new and only they are bad.'

It was full night. The sky was a livid purple. The moon had debuted above the surrounding ruins, crescent and old, like the golden horns of a black bull. In the distance, a small fire was bleeding smoke into the evening.

'In Dorado,' Garcia asked, 'did you know a man named *El Duende*?'

The woman was silent. 'Why do you ask?'

'Because,' Gil said, 'he is threatening to murder my children.'

The woman stared at Gil for the longest time, though she showed no emotion.

Then she looked away and said: 'I met him once. Yes. He was a young lieutenant then.'

'What was his name?'

'His name? It was Lieutenant Leon Blades.'

'Leon Blades?' Garcia repeated. Where had he heard that name before? And then like something glimmering in the overgrown grass of his memory, Garcia saw the name's punch-pressed letters glint again on a tin dog tag crushed underfoot in an Indian village.

This recognition must have registered in his eyes for the sorceress asked: 'You knew him there?'

'Not personally. No.'

'He and several of his fellow officers came to my hut in Chaltopec.'

'What for?' Gil asked.

The woman smiled. 'They wanted . . . nectar.'

'Nectar?'

'Yes.' She laughed and looked at Gil. 'Of course, I told them I knew of no such thing. I explained to them how I could sicken a cow or make a moustache sprout on the face of a girl, but *nectar* . . . ?' She shook her head, 'I didn't even know what it was.'

'And what did they say to that?'

The woman paused and looked off at the river. 'I will never forget. They said . . . it was the sweetest thing in this or any world – sweeter than women, sweeter than money or music or youth. They said, the man who tasted it became . . . forever satisfied.'

The woman frowned and smoothed her skirt. 'A man I knew learned of their desire and foolishly promised to produce it, through alchemy. He sold *El Duende* a powerful drug, but it was not nectar, and when *El Duende* discovered this, he had the man killed. I knew the man well. That is all I know of *El Duende*. That one meeting. And the fact that he had Don Carlos murdered.'

'When was this?'

'Seven years ago. On the outskirts of Puerto Valle. Nectar.' She smiled, drifting back into the past. 'The Generalissimo was behind it, I assumed, but *El Duende*, he really did seem to believe in its existence.'

'And what do you think, grandmother?' Gil asked.

The old witch contemplated the question for a moment. She looked out at the river and adjusted her shawl. 'In eighty years, I have seen a lot – more than most – high and low, bad and good. But . . . *nectar*?' She shook her head. 'I do not think that such a thing exists.'

Gil and Garcia left the building and stepped back out into the twilit evening. Gil spoke at length, but Garcia was not listening. He was seeing inside himself the sunwashed walls of an Indian village daubed with the blood of children, and the nauseating tendrils of the sickening memory, entwined with the vines of his own complicity, made him feel ill.

What had he done? He felt like the butt of some cosmic joke. For years in Dorado he had searched for Lieutenant Leon Blades, perpetrator of the atrocity in the Siuna hills, when all the while, he realized now, he himself had been working for the man, delivering up to him nightly innocents to be broken and killed.

'Ambrosio, how could you?' Gil's ringing accusation still echoed in his ears. For in Gil's voice and eyes that other morning, he had seen reflected for the very first time the enormity of his crime.

And yet it had not seemed criminal at the time. It had all been rather dull and boring. It was as though a cloud had settled over his eyes. And now the cloud had lifted and everything looked changed.

He sighed. At eighteen, you make a vow. You know with every atom of your being, every cell of your heart it is the right one to make: you will fight for this cause! You will marry this woman. How is it then that many years later one is so full of bitter regrets?

Traidor. Yes. He understood now why the word on the wall had entered him with such force. For, walking through the summer night with Gil, Garcia saw at last who it was he had betrayed. It was not any country, any party or friend.

It was Garcia.

Out Of This World

◆

Chapter 15

With the threat of blackmail now upon him, some of Higgins'
bliss departed. Nor was this the only strain that summer; the
heat was bad, while the living conditions were not ideal, or at
least, not what Higgins was used to. The children had
returned, but since Gil would not permit them out on the
street, they played inside, from six in the morning to nine at
night, making more noise than the childless Higgins had ever
imagined three small bodies could produce. It was difficult
to write or meditate undistracted, as there was no place in
the spacious apartment he could not hear Rosita's voice, not
even in the bathroom with the door closed and a pillow
pressed against his ears – while the Doctor seemed less a
living presence than a ghost. He floated in and out at all hours
of the day and night, untalkative and exhausted.

Along with the children came Garcia, newly installed as
their bodyguard. This move had coincided with the death of
his mother only days before. The dignified old soldier sat in
the kitchen, mourning, drinking endless cups of Spanish
coffee which stained the fringes of his white moustache,
cracking his knuckles, and listening to Gil. It was clear they
had a special understanding; he was her champion. She fussed
over him in a manner Higgins envied, and poured out her
heart to him in a way she refused to do with him. When the
doorbell rang, it was Garcia who answered it.

And yet, Higgins was aware of how helpless they were. It was all well and good for Garcia to answer the door, but what if he opened it to a man with an automatic rifle? Who wanted Gil. Or the kids. What would he do then?

Now and then, in search of some solution, Higgins caught himself thinking of the parts deal with MIRA and of the half million dollars that dangled at its end. He couldn't help it. He did not consider it seriously, however. He thought of the money the way one will think of another man's wife . . . knowing she is untouchable, unattainable – though most desirable, all the same.

Half a million dollars! Gee, he could live quite nicely on that. He imagined traveling to the east somewhere or to a clean Greek island in the middle of the blue Aegean. Higgins saw himself seated in the sunlight at a rough plank table eating grilled calamari, olives and bread.

But, there he went again, dreaming of escape to some sunny Greek isle or Himalayan cave when Gil had been kidnapped; the Doctor, blackmailed; the kids, threatened; and everything else was sliding straight to hell. Yeah, that was it. He'd fly off to Corfu and eat seafood leaving the Castellanos to fend for themselves. And when he returned, he'd be arrested at Customs. Jesus, what was the matter with him?

Still, despite his growing worries, Higgins continued his meditations. He lengthened them to an hour and a half each morning and to half an hour before he went to sleep. He was always attempting to go deeper, deeper.

And then one morning in meditation, Higgins went deeper than ever before and something most amazing happened – he traveled to another world.

Higgins, of course, did not visit this world in his physical body. His body was seated on the Doctor's couch, sunk in meditation. It was that other part of Higgins, that part of him that once was called 'the soul,' which somehow quit its earthly tenement and wandered through the astral streets. Nor was Higgins *trying* to visit this celestial region. He was only trying to meditate, focusing on his breath, and by merging with which one slips the bonds of space and time.

337

The next thing Higgins knew, he was standing in a field outside a great walled city. The light was good, and though there was no sun, the sky glowed like mother-of-pearl. The city was astonishing. It was very neat, brilliant and serene, with rain-rinsed roofs and dripping drainpipes, as though it had showered only moments before, while off in the distance, in a copse of blue trees, Higgins could see a herd of sleek silver deer.

Then he saw *her*. *Her*! She was seated on a broken wall, caring for a dark-skinned child. It was the first time he had set eyes on her in nearly a year – and Higgins was amazed at the specific personal beauty of her actual face, as opposed to the idealized blur that had been his recollection of her. She looked different, younger than when she'd died, as though, unlike him, she was growing backwards in time.

Then she lifted her gaze and saw him, too, and for one radiant heart-stopping instant, they looked into each other's eyes. 'Philip!' she cried, and rose to her feet. And she looked at him then with such surprised delight – her look making him love himself in a way he had forgotten how to, and to love her, too, all over again.

Suddenly her expression clouded.

'I'm not dead,' Higgins hurriedly assured her, afraid that she might think he was. And he made an expressive gesture with his hands which somehow explained it all. She laughed and clapped her hands together. Then she approached and he took her in his arms and drew her to him and kissed her lips.

And it was not like in those ancient fables where the spirits of the dead cannot be touched and the living hero, attempting to embrace them, embraces only heartache and empty air. They kissed! They touched, with bodies that were made of light, not flesh, though the bliss of their embrace and kiss was no less sweet because of it.

Drawing back, he looked into her eyes – those dear, gray eyes he had missed so much. 'Why did you leave me?' he asked her now.

She seemed surprised. 'Don't you know? I was bitten by a

serpent.' And she turned her left elbow, showing him its mark.

Then the child began to cry. She bent to comfort him, and in that instant, the world dissolved. A moment later, Higgins opened his eyes and found that he was back on earth – the room filling up with gray dawn light.

For the longest time Higgins sat there, holding the last image of her in his mind. It had *not* been a dream – he had seen her so clearly! He had gone somewhere where she had been – another country where the light was good and there were children. He didn't know how or why he had traveled there, or why it had so abruptly ended. He only knew he had. And though they had parted once again, their love was still intact and true; he had even kissed her, and for one exquisite mystic instant held her in his arms.

Higgins marveled; he laughed out loud. She must have been *amazed* to see him there. And he was certain now that even as he sat there remembering her face, she was sitting on a wall in heaven remembering his.

Then he recalled her remark about the snake, and saw again the tiny fang mark just below the curve of her arm, and suddenly, his certainty faded. *Bitten by a snake?* It wasn't possible. She had not died from snakebite in their Boston condominium!

And if *that* wasn't true – then perhaps the whole vision was a mirage, some sort of wish-fulfilling fantasy, some sick and potent dream. And if the vision was a lie, then perhaps the inner path that he was following also was untrue – the refuge of a hurt and tired mind. And when he thought like that, Higgins felt his spirits wither.

But that evening when he described the city he had visited to Sara Devi, she said at once: 'The world you saw is Pitru-loka – the region of departed souls. Everyone there is healthy and young, and people are much happier there than here. Did your wife want a child?'

'Yes! But we couldn't have one.'

'So, in heaven she's been given one to care for.'

But though Higgins was overjoyed to have the truth of

what he'd seen confirmed, he couldn't help but be bewildered by her remark. 'She told me that she'd been bitten by a serpent. Why would she say a thing like that?'

Sara Devi thought for a moment. Then she asked, 'Was your wife a liar?'

'*Liar*?'

'Yes. Did she like to tell lies?'

'*Lies*! Of course not!'

'Well, then,' she said, with the sweet logic of a child. 'Then it must be true.'

Higgins considered that. 'Bring her back to me,' he asked.

'What?' Sara Devi asked, sitting up, her eyes growing wide. Apparently even her supernal bliss was not immune to the madness of his request.

'Bring her back to life. I know you can.'

But Sara only shook her head. 'I told you before. It was her destiny. And even God Himself, try as He might, cannot undo your destiny, *Señor*.'

Over The Volcano

◆

Chapter 16

The idea of new elections infuriated Benitez. There had *been* elections, he informed the Doctor, not three short years ago and he, Benitez, had been duly elected President in them by a plurality of the populace and in conformance with all recognized standards of civil and international law. But he had not been President for more than a week before the wolves had descended and the Junta, who had never expected him to win in the first place, had driven him from his country, his palace and home. And now, certain persons, certain *American* persons whose memory was as short as his was long, were insinuating, nay, actually verbally insisting that he, Rodolfo Benitez Cayetano, run for the office of President *again* and against the very men who had sabotaged his presidency, murdered his people, and driven him into exile in the first place!

'But how can I run for President when I *am* the President?' Benitez had shouted. 'How can I run for an office I already hold?'

'Ah, your Excellency,' the silverhaired American person had urged, 'you must put away your pride. For the good of your country.'

But Benitez's stubbornness had nothing to do with pride, he said, but with the rule of law. He had been elected President for a seven-year term, had served six days of that term,

341

and fully intended to return to Dorado to finish serving the six years, eleven months, and twenty-five days left of it.

'Ah, your Excellency,' the silverhaired person had said, extracting a cigarette from a platinum case. 'And is there anything that might induce you to relinquish this claim?'

'Yes. There is one thing,' Benitez had confessed.

The silverhaired personage had lifted his eye with a look of hope or expectation.

'A bullet through my head!'

Benitez was recounting all this to the Doctor now not out of rage or pride, he said, but so the Doctor might better grasp the political situation.

No, the negotiations were not going well at all. And though they would continue for now, it was time to think seriously of a military solution.

Of course, there was another reason why Benitez was so dead-set against elections, the Doctor thought. If elections had been held today – after his close victory and his long exile – it was somewhat doubtful whether Benitez would have won.

Now Benitez got up from his desk and unfolded before him a large paper rectangle colored with the blue lakes, green fields, tan swamps and brown mountains of Dorado.

'Please, Doctor. On the floor here, where you can see the map. Look,' Benitez said, pointing to the dark brown hills. 'We have a force of twenty-four hundred here. Though we are only eighty miles east of the capitol as the crow flies, we can't attack from that direction. If we wanted to attack, we would have to march two hundred miles around the mountains and the lake and come in from the west, the direction in which they're expecting us to come. So . . . Commander Rabon wants to know if . . . there is some way we could go *over* the mountains, and come in the capitol's backdoor.'

'Go *over* them?' the Doctor asked. 'But that is impossible.'

'Yes; or so I am told. I'm not a native of these parts – I'm from the south; but they tell me there are only tracks in places and these are only navigable a small portion of the year.'

'Why is that?'

'The weather. It's very bad, Doctor. And then there is the *chinchincacacia* . . .'

'*Chinchi* . . . ?'

'A grass that stings a man like a scorpion and makes his whole body swell. The Indians are immune to it, but to a white man, it is like fire.'

'Still, why couldn't an army simply proceed due west until it reached the capitol?' the Doctor asked.

'Because of the terrain, Doctor. The terrain, they say, is like a bad dream. Steep ravines intersect the mountains. Tracks end in sheer drops. Paths that appear to be headed in one direction turn slowly, over the course of many miles, backwards upon themselves. In winter, there are avalanches; in the spring and summer, floods and mud slides. Everywhere there are thorn bushes, wild boars, ticks, scorpions, poisonous plants and serpents. It's devil's country. Most of it has never been mapped. You couldn't get a jeep through there, much less an army.'

'What *does* get through there? Anything?'

Benitez shrugged. 'Birds. Birds fly over the mountain, I suppose.'

'Helicopters, your Excellency! Airplanes!'

'We don't have any,' Benitez said with a touch of pique. He looked at the Doctor. 'The question is, could a hundred or so men on foot carrying automatic weapons go over these mountains and attack the capitol from the east, from here?'

The Doctor looked at the map. 'That's what Lawrence did at Medina.'

'Lawrence?'

'Of Arabia.'

Benitez approved. 'Oh, so you're a student of his campaigns?'

'No, your Excellency.' The Doctor laughed. 'I saw the movie.'

Benitez frowned – then laughed himself. 'Well, what about it?' he pressed, making the map paper crackle with his jabbing finger. 'Can we do it? Could it be done?'

'I don't know,' the Doctor said. 'I've never heard of it being done before. But then again, I was only up there once fifteen years ago.'

'Nothing's changed up there in fifteen years, I assure you, Doctor. Nothing's changed up there in fifteen *hundred* years.'

'Then there is the weather. Right now,' Benitez sighed, 'it's the rainy season and very muddy, and by November the mountains are covered with snow. Then comes spring and it's muddy all over again. There is only one season one can get around.'

'And when is that, your Excellency?'

'There's a six-week window when the weather is fair, beginning in mid-September. But it's best to be out by the Day of the Dead.'

'It's best to be out of the whole damn country on that day!' the Doctor said, remembering the Day of the Dead in Dorado when bread is baked in the shape of bones, and friends send you poems referring to your funeral. 'If I may make a suggestion, *Señor Presidente*.'

'Of course. What is it?'

'There is someone we should talk to about this.'

'Who is that?'

'An old friend of mine who knows these mountains well. He fought in them for years.'

'Really? Who was he fighting?'

'You, your Excellency.'

'Oh?' Benitez looked up. 'You must be referring to Captain Garcia. Why, I spoke to him only yesterday. And you know what that maniac wanted to do? He wanted permission to assassinate *El Duende*. Claims he put a hex on him or something, the evil eye.'

'You gave it?'

'Gave it? I forbade him even to *think* of it. *El Duende* is our contact with the Junta. It would be a total disaster to lose him now.'

Benitez paused for a moment, then said of Gracia, 'Thank God, he was enough of a soldier to come to me first. The chain of command, Doctor, is so vitally important. Some hothead decides to save his country by assassinating the Archduke. And boom, you have World War One.' He sighed. 'At any rate, perhaps he could be useful – if we ever decide to go into these mountains. Ask the Captain to come in tomorrow morning. When the Commander is present.'

'As you wish.'

The telephone purred. Benitez absently lifted the receiver, listened without speaking, then hung up.

'The boy you shot in your office, Doctor . . .'

'Yes?'

The President smiled. '. . . has opened his eyes.'

Snakebite

◆

Chapter 17

'They've isolated the toxin,' the Doctor announced. 'Our friend was poisoned. In fact, it's made them reopen several old cases – of exiles who died of what they thought were "natural causes." '

Higgins, who had just returned from Sara Devi's, looked up at the Doctor from the book he was reading. The mention of poison made his mind return to the morning's meditation. Higgins set down the book and said, 'The day my wife died, she visited you.'

'Yes. She'd had a performance the night before at Lincoln Center. The next morning, on her way to the airport, she dropped in to see us.'

'And while she was here . . . was she bitten by a snake?'

The Doctor tilted his head at Higgins. 'Are you out of your gourd?'

'What exactly happened that day? Can you tell me, Arsenio?'

'Tell you? Of course, I can tell you. *Nothing* happened. I took her to lunch.'

'Just walk me through it once again, will you, please?'

The Doctor sighed, clearly irritated by Higgins' mysterious line of interrogation. 'She must have arrived around, oh, I'd say, eleven-thirty. Gil and she had coffee, talked, and played with the kiddoes, I understand. Around one, I myself arrived home and found her here. We went to lunch – at *La Princessa*, one of those tacky little *chinas y criollas* places. I would have taken her some place *nice*,' the Doctor guiltily avowed – 'but she *insisted*. She wanted *real* Spanish food – the kind, you know, *the people* ate.'

'Yeah.' Higgins smiled, remembering with love his morning's visitation. 'She's like that.'

'Then when we were finished eating, I put her in a cab to the airport.'

'And that was it? Nothing else happened?'

'Nothing!' The Doctor frowned. 'Except . . . for one stupid thing. As we were leaving the restaurant, some idiot jabbed her with his umbrella.'

'Jabbed her? Was she hurt?'

'Hurt? No. She laughed it off. He just stuck her with the point. In fact, I thought he was trying to jab at *me*, but at the very last moment . . . she didn't see him . . . she . . . kind of turned, like this, into him' – the Doctor demonstrated – 'and he stuck her instead.'

'Who was he?'

'No one I've ever seen before – or since. Then again, it's not unusual in this crazy place. Do you know how many times I've been assaulted for no apparent reason?'

'Let me ask you something, Arsenio. And think very carefully before you answer. When this person stuck her with the point of his umbrella, where did the umbrella strike?'

'Where? Why, here,' the Doctor said, pointing to his left forearm just below the elbow.

'Jesus,' Higgins said softly, turning away.

'What's the matter?'

'Did you examine the wound?'

'No wound. Just a pinprick.'

'And this poison,' Higgins said, 'which the police discovered in Vazpana's body, could it take up to twelve or fifteen hours to work?'

The Doctor looked at Higgins in disbelief. 'You don't believe . . .'

'Answer my question.'

347

'A small amount. . . . It is conceivable it could cause an embolus to form over a period of . . . several hours, days. Then, if it detached itself from the wall of the vessel. . . .'

Higgins closed his eyes. Of such stuff are mortals made: to be unearthed by a pinhead of clotted blood dropped like a monkey wrench into the delicate machinery of the heart. Suddenly, he understood everything. Lights went on all over the universe. 'This toxin is made from snake venom, isn't it?'

The Doctor froze. 'How did you know that? Yes. It's made from the venom of a serpent found in Dorado.'

So there it was for all to see, everything as plain as day. The only question left was why? *Why?*

Higgins must have spoken these anguished words aloud, for the Doctor, after several moments, said in a dead and wooden voice, 'I think I can tell you. Two days before her death, I made a speech condeming AES and the Junta.' He looked at Higgins. 'Oh, my God. They weren't trying to kill *her*, Philip. But *me!*'

Both men turned their backs on each other, to be alone with their horror and pain. Neither spoke for the longest time as they wrestled with the ugly revelation.

'I don't think we could ever prove it,' the Doctor said, at last. 'An amount that tiny. I doubt, after all this time, an autopsy would find it.'

'I don't need an autopsy,' Higgins said. 'I know what happened.'

Higgins didn't sleep that night. He sat by the window, his room lit by the trembling taper on the altar. He had thought he would not feel the pain so much, but he was mistaken.

His wife had been murdered! At the thought of it, a black glory filled his soul. And the irony was, it hadn't even been on purpose – it had all been a fuck-up, a fatal mistake.

Bunglers! Fools! They had the most diabolical technology and fiendish weapons and still they couldn't even manage to stick the right person! It was incredible – like some twisted, slapstick version of 'I Spy.'

Who had done it? AES, for sure. The rare Doradoan poison

was as good as a confession (even if the technology was Russian.) But *who* of AES? Schmidt? Higgins wondered. According to the Doctor, it fit his hands-on, in-your-face m.o. But even if it had been Schmidt, then he was just the button man. Someone higher up must have ordered the attempt on the Doctor's life in which an innocent woman – Higgins' wife – had died.

For several hours that night, before they retired, Higgins and the Doctor had tried to determine who that someone was and, after much soul-searching and several phonecalls to both Garcia and Benitez, they had come up with the name of Hercules Cordero. Cordero was the reputed head of AES's 'extraterritorial capabilities,' that is, the elimination of exiles, foreign enemies and spies. Above him there was only AES's Director, and the members of the four-man Junta itself.

And this is where things got rather sticky. For even if Higgins could pin the blame on Hercules Cordero, what did he propose to do about it? Assassinate a senior-ranking intelligence officer? It was a pipe dream. He was a yogi, a poet, a businessman and scholar – not a spy or a soldier. Higgins could not have killed anyone in cold blood. He did not have it in him. Not even for his wife's assassin.

Of course, he could always go to the police, but that, he bet, would be a wasted effort. He saw himself seated in the 110th Street station house attempting to inspire two bored and overworked detectives with a stories of poisoned umbrellas and other tales of derring-do. Then there was the FBI – but they didn't inspire much confidence either; he had no desire to have the *federales* probing his past, as they surely would. And anyway, as the Doctor had reminded him, the FBI had still not caught the killers of Courvoisier, Dorado's Ambassador to Washington, blown away by AES more than two years ago.

Still, Higgins had to do *something*. He could not just live with his wife's murder, and let it go unpunished and ignored. Nor was it only Higgins' wife: if he didn't do something to stop the assassins, the Doctor, Gilberta, or the kids would be next. And Higgins himself would live the rest of his life afraid of every rainy day and of every stranger with a rolled-up umbrella.

No. The longer he thought about it, and the later, and then earlier, the hour grew, the more attractive appeared the parts deal with MIRA. At least it was something tangible he could do. And yet, supplying washers, lynchpins, and radiators to a guerrilla army was not exactly striking a heroic blow for freedom or exacting a thrilling revenge. Still, it was the best thing he could think to do right now. As with a stubborn knot in a piece of string, Higgins would begin by pushing here, pulling there, and seeing what loosened and opened before him. You never knew. For just as Vazpana's effort had brought Schmidt to town, so maybe now, Higgins' involvement with MIRA would lure Cordero. Higgins didn't know. He didn't have to. He was proceeding purely on intuition. Shake the tree, and see what happens. See what comes down. And in his mind he saw himself, like Samson of old, shaking the pillars of the temple, and the whole corrupt edifice crashing down upon the heads of *El Duende*, the Junta and Cordero while Higgins himself died beneath the rubble.

But why should he die? No. He did not have to die. Not if he was smart and careful.

The Doctor was a different man these days. There was something about him, a new calm and stature, that not been there six weeks ago. Dressing in the bathroom that morning, putting on his tie and suit, he had the air of a statesman, a leader of men – and while this role may not have fitted as well as the suit (which shimmered and fell like flowing water) it was a role he was growing into.

'What could we do that would get him, Arsenio? Get him where he really lives.'

'Win this damn war in Dorado.'

'And what are the chances of that happening?'

'Not good. Our troops are brave . . . our equipment atrocious.'

'And so spare parts would make a big difference?'

The Doctor paused. 'Look, let me be honest. Parts alone

aren't going to win a thing. And yet, who knows? One tiny washer in the right piece of equipment can mean the difference between a failed and a successful attack, and on that attack can rest the battle, and on that battle. . . .'

'So why don't you go out and get some then?' Higgins interrupted.

'Because, *these*, my friend, are *special* parts,' the Doctor said in a patronising voice, as though Higgins was retarded. 'It's not that easy. You don't get them from the hardware store down the street. Plus, there is an arms embargo against Dorado.'

The Doctor shot his cuffs and turned to adjust his tie. 'We do have offers, from various governments, but *El Presidente* is extremely fastidious about whose help he will accept. He doesn't want to be beholden to anyone upon his return to office.'

If he's too fastidious, Higgins thought, there won't be any office to return to. Instead, he said, 'Why don't you let me see what I can do?'

'You?' The Doctor stopped and laughed. 'Buying arms is not like buying and selling a tanker full of oil, my friend. Or whatever it is you do for a living.' He smiled. 'And anyway,' he said, growing more serious, 'it is extremely dangerous. The Junta would like the same parts and equipment, and AES will go after anyone who attempts to supply it to their enemies. If you need proof, look at Vazpana.'

'But if Jorge *had* succeeded, would Benitez have accepted it from him?'

'Why not? MIRA is our ally. Unfortunately, MIRA is dead – without a head. Unless you count this Captain Crespi – who no one seems to know.' The Doctor paused and looked at Higgins, 'About *her* . . . your wife. I feel . . . I am . . . somehow . . . guilty . . .'

Higgins cut him off. 'The hell you are! But thank you anyway, Arsenio.'

So there it was. It wasn't much, perhaps, but it was a beginning, and it was all he could think of doing just now. That it was dangerous was a given. Nor was he even sure that he could pull it off. That he could end up dead or in jail was a distinct possibility. And yet, Higgins wasn't thinking of himself just now.

No, if he did it, it would do it for *her*. He would do it for Gil, for the kids, for Dorado, and for his friend, the Doctor; the Doctor who once, years ago when Higgins was in dire straits, had opened a silver box filled with twenties and told him, 'You take whatever you need from here. You take as much as you want whenever you want it, and you spend it on whatever you need to, clothes, whatever. And you do not keep track of it, or ask me for it or tell me what you took, or pay me back forever, you are my friend.'

The telephone rang. Higgins answered it in the hall. It was Crespi's morning call: part threat, part sales pitch, part patriotic exhortation. Higgins interrupted him. 'Update the list you gave me. I'll get you what you need.'

There was a shocked silence. Then Crespi said, 'You seem to have had a change of heart. What's come over you, *amigo*?'

Higgins was in no mood for explanations. 'Let's just say . . . I saw the light.'

'The *light*?'

'Yeah,' Higgins said, remembering the radiance of that heavenly city. 'The *Light*.'

Operation Rorschach

◆

Chapter 18

'At 0300 hours on November first, a hundred shock troops come down the volcano and infiltrate Puerto Valle. They seize the police and radio stations, and surround the Presidential Palace, taking up positions on the edge of the town. At 0400, a team of sappers blows the bridge on the northern road and seizes the bridgehead, cutting off this route for retreat or reinforcements. That is the signal for the assault to begin, and for my men in the capitol to open fire on Cuzo's forces from the rear. At the same time, *Comandante* Cereno's troops attack from *their* positions on the western front. General Cuzo's army is trapped in the middle – his soldiers cut to ribbons by the enfilading fire.' Rabon paused a moment. 'Well, what do you think?'

'It's fiendish, *Comandante*,' the Doctor said.

'It is risky,' Benitez said. 'But admirably bold. Of course, all of it is predicated on the fact that there's a way across the mountains. And you heard what Captain Garcia said. The mountains are impassable.'

'Ah, but there *is* a way, your Excellency,' Rabon insisted. 'The Indians know it, even if we don't.'

'Then why don't they tell us it?' Benitez asked.

'Why should they? And have half a dozen warring armies traipsing through their villages?'

'Well, even if there is a way, and they do agree to show us

it, the question remains: what would they do if an army of soldiers came marching through?'

'Do?' the Doctor inquired. 'Surely, your Excellency, you're not worried that a modern army could be hurt by . . . by . . . what? . . . *sticks*?'

'It's not sticks – or stones – that concern me Doctor. But rather – how does that rhyme go? – names, yes, names that can hurt us.

'The success of this operation will depend entirely on secrecy and surprise. And it is hard to keep the movement of a hundred soldiers secret for very long. Especially when these troops are moving on foot through unsecured territory for a period of several days.' Benitez pointed to the map. 'The question remaining: can a hundred men cross the mountains, here, and come down into the capitol, there, without the Junta finding out?' He answered his own question. 'I doubt it. All we would need is one disenchanted Indian to consider it his patriotic duty to bring this intelligence to the attention of the police, and in so doing collect a fat reward and—'

'And what . . . ?'

'And we would be trapped in the mountains with the Day of the Dead and winter coming. Then what would we do? Gentlemen, I will tell you. Sit down and write poems about each other's funeral.'

A silence fell as the three men meditated on the problems the proposed plan presented.

Rabon smiled. 'But let's look on the bright side, shall we? Think what would happen if we succeeded? Let's say we *haven't* been spotted or betrayed by the Indians. Our men descend the volcano under cover of darkness, make their way west through the streets of the capitol and take up positions behind General Cuzo's defensive line. Since never in their wildest dreams will they be expecting a force to attack from the east, all their artillery and fortifications will be facing in the other direction. Then, at dawn, we open fire.'

'With what?' Benitez asked. 'A hundred men?'

'Of course not, your Excellency. We'll have a hundred men attacking from the rear, but, as I said, I fully intend to have

Commander Cereno and the rest of our army, twenty-five hundred able-bodied fighters, attacking from the west, the direction from which they're expecting us to come. The only thing is, now the enemy will be caught in our cross-fire. Instead of having Cereno before them and the capitol at their backs, there will be enemy commandos between them and Puerto Valle.'

'You are right, Commander,' Benitez admitted. 'It is the only way that twenty-six hundred soldiers can possibly defeat twelve thousand defenders.'

'Twenty-six hundred?' the Doctor protested. 'But I thought our strength was *ten thousand*!'

'All together, yes,' Benitez said. 'Explain it to the Doctor, Commander.'

'For other battles an alliance is fine, but for an assault on the capitol, we would only use our own forces and those of MIRA. If Montenegro or even the PND got into the Presidential Palace before us, it would take dynamite to get them out. And none of us have fought so long and so hard and risked so much for *that*.'

There was a pause while the men contemplated briefly this unhappy possibility.

The Doctor looked at the map and said, 'But won't there be the same problem of secrecy and surprise with Cereno's force as well? I mean, how do twenty-five hundred men march two hundred miles without the Junta getting wind of it?'

'They don't,' Rabon answered. 'We *want* them to get wind of it. We want them to know we are attacking from the west. We want them to draw troops from their northern forts and beef up their western garrison. We want them to wait and wait for our frontal assault until their nerves are screwed to the breaking point . . . and then . . .'

'We'll attack!' the Doctor said.

'No, Doctor. We'll retreat.'

'We'll what? You just said . . .'

'At 1700 hours, our western front, under *Comandante* Cereno, will begin a general retreat back into the hills without a shot fired. At the same time, you will tell *El Duende* the attack has been called off.'

'But . . . why?'

Rabon shrugged. 'We have reassessed their strength. We are *maricons*. We were bluffing and they called our bluff. It doesn't matter. You will think of something. This intelligence will be relayed to Dorado. It will confirm the situation on the field. It will be the night before the Day of the Dead, after all. None of their soldiers will want to fight anyway. At the news of our retreat, there will be great rejoicing.'

'Everyone will get drunk,' Benitez said with sober staring eyes, as though he was reading the future.

'Meanwhile, part of Cereno's retreating force will halt with the fall of night and secretly return to their original positions under cover of darkness. At 0400, the attack will commence as our men come down the volcano.'

Benitez shook his head and said very softly, 'It just might work.'

'It will, my President,' the Commander said in a boyish voice. He winked at the Doctor. 'Have no fear.'

'All right. It has my tentative approval – provided, of course, there's a way through those hills. We'll need a name for this operation. Doctor?'

'Uh . . . Operation Rorschach.'

'Rorschach?'

'Yes. You know, like the inkblots?'

Benitez laughed. 'Perhaps I am old and slow. But I'm not sure I follow you there. What's this got to do with our plan of attack?'

'Everything,' the Doctor said. 'As in a Rorschach, one only sees what one already knows. Since it's inconceivable that we attack from over the mountains, our attack will be invisible. It's not the outer night that will shield us from their sentries' eyes, but the night inside their minds. And since they can only see and hear what they already know, they will interpret all intelligence to fit this pattern.'

'I see,' Benitez said. He thought a moment. 'I hope you're

right.' He struck his palm with his fist and said, 'If only we knew there was a way across those mountains.'

'There is, my President. I would stake my life on it. At any moment I hope to hear. . . .' Then Rabon stopped and his face froze, as if he'd just remembered something. 'The moon.'

'Moon? What about the moon?' Benitez asked.

'We need a moon. The question is . . . do we have one?'

'And why is that so necessary, Commander?' Benitez probed.

'Because, my President, have you ever tried to climb down a three-thousand-foot-high mountain in the dark? We'd break our necks.'

'I see,' Benitez said, furrowing his brow. He hit the inter-com. 'Guido, an almanac. Right away.'

'And let us pray that we have a moon, because if we don't have a moon, or if it's new, or it rises too late or sets too early . . .' Rabon shrugged like a peasant and began to pray, 'O Mother in heaven. Give us a moon.'

'Couldn't we use flashlights or something?' the Doctor asked.

'No. O mother of Marx. O mother of Engels. O mother of sex with beautiful women. We beg you . . . we beseech you. . . . Give us a moon!'

'I hate this,' Benitez nervously griped. 'To think one's whole carefully planned political career comes down to this!'

'To what, your Excellency?' the Doctor asked.

'To fate. To Fortuna. To the *phases of the moon*!'

'Mother of cows. Mother of peasants. Mother of Elvira Martinez who I swear I will marry and make an honest woman if only, if only . . .'

The chant was infectious. '*Give us a moon!*'

'Where is Guido. Damn!' Benitez fretted. 'Oh, here he is. Did you get it? Well?'

'I don't know how to read these things. . . .'

'No one asked you to.'

'Give it here,' the guerrilla said.

'Thank you, Guido,' Benitez said. 'That will be all.'

Rabon took the almanac, broke it open and started to read.

One finger moved vertically down the page, while another moved horizontally until the two fingers touched. 'Shit!' he cried. 'It's dark that week!'

There was a collective groan.

'Of all the . . . ! Wait a minute,' the Commander said. He smiled and turned the page. 'I'm sorry, gentlemen. I was looking at September.'

'Goddamn it,' Benitez said, convulsing in his seat. 'Will you read it right?'

Rabon was mumbling: 'Subtract for daylight savings . . . then . . . for Puerto Valle time . . . Un hunh. Uh hunh. Gentlemen.' He shut the book and looked up. 'We have a moon!'

'Thank God!'

'Yes. A lovely three-quarter moon rising at exactly 1:26 a.m. on the morning of November first. By three, it will have cleared the hills. Perfect. It will give us just enough light to see by but not enough for them to see us – unless, of course, they're looking. Now if only we'd hear from our scouts in Dorado.'

Benitez picked up the phone and spoke into it sharply. He listened, then replaced the receiver and reported to Rabon, 'A telex arrived from Dorado this morning. They say, they didn't think it was urgent.'

Now a red-faced aide hurriedly entered the suite bearing the forgotten message. Rabon snatched it from his fingers, read it quickly and broke into a grin. 'Just as I'd hoped. Commander Cereno has found two Indian boys who can show us a way through the mountains. They have agreed to guide us – for a price.'

'How much?'

The Commander frowned. 'Can our war chest afford it? Ten dollars apiece!'

The room exploded with relief and laughter. Benitez sat smiling, staring out the window, his fingers laced into a tent. When the excitement had subsided, he nodded and said, 'All right, then. We have a moon. We have a way across the mountains. We have a plan of attack. We even have a name for

358

our little operation. Let us only pray the gods are with us. Gentlemen,' he said, raising his cup, 'I give you Operation Rorschach.'

Master Of Maya

◆

Chapter 19

Crespi was a hard, short, stocky warrior, getting on in years. His face was stressed and deeply lined, as though he had survived countless battles. His hair suggested sculpted metal; it was iron-gray and combed severely back to cover the bald spot in the back, the marks of the comb's teeth still visible in it. His moustache was a small gray brush, the tips of its bristles stained orange with smoke. He had a soft, intolerant mouth. His suit was quite beautiful, Italian, expensive, the wool a soft gray worsted – and yet its effect was only to highlight the lined harshness of his face.

They were seated almost opposite each other in an Italian restaurant at separate, but adjacent tables. Higgins, per Crespi's instructions, had taken two subways, a cab, and a bus to get here – all to end up within walking distance of the Doctor's office.

The agent turned to take the menu from the waiter and as he did so, Higgins noted the deeply scored and crosshatched flesh just above the smooth band of his collar, and was reminded of the term 'leatherneck.'

Crespi put the menu down and signaled for Higgins to retrieve it. Inside was a piece of paper – an undated list of spare parts and assorted munitions.

'You want hand-held Stinger missiles?'

Crespi winced. 'You will please refer to everything as . . . *peanuts.*'

Higgins was embarrassed. 'C'mon. This is silly. No one can overhear us. Or do you think the sugar bowl is bugged? Aren't we both too old for games?'

'This is not a game. It is a craft, like any other. And if you wish to be successful at it, you must respect its rules.'

But Higgins did not believe that it was craft that made them act like this – covering their tracks, so shamelessly dissembling. It was instinct. The child lies hidden in a pile of autumn leaves spying on the mailman – why? Who taught him? No one. It is in his bones.

It was difficult for Higgins to think, or breathe, for that matter, wreathed as they were in clouds of cigarette smoke.

'You think you could put that out for moment?'

The agent squished the butt on a lovely porcelain butter plate, disfiguring a china rose. Two jets of smoke plumed dragonlike from his nostrils. 'So, can you help us?'

Higgins slipped the list into his pocket. 'Why not? However, I want you to understand something. This is not an ordinary deal.'

'Which means?'

'Which means, I get the money up front. The people who sell these sort of . . . *peanuts* . . . aren't going to wait for payment later. You give me the money, I swap it for the product, I ship it to you.'

Crespi frowned. 'If it's as simple as that, then perhaps we should buy them ourselves and save half a million dollars in commissions.'

Higgins flipped the list across the table. 'Be my guest.'

Crespi's eyes searched Higgins' own looking for something: weakness or greed; then turned away at last, defeated.

'And how do you get it to us?'

'There are lots of ways. Don't worry.'

'I *do* worry.'

'Okay, if we buy them on the blackmarket – which we'll probably have to do – then we load a plane in secret and fly it to an airfield in rebel-held Dorado. We don't file a flight plan or anything like that. We just . . .' Higgins fell silent as the waiter brought their coffee, '. . . *do* it – like smuggling dope. I would prefer not to go this route if we don't have to, but we may have no choice.'

'You said there were a lot of ways.'

'Another, which I'd prefer, is to buy the product legally, in Europe, say, and load it on to some old tub. The papers I file will show that the end user is a country other than Dorado. In mid-Atlantic, we off-load the cargo to another vessel. We scuttle the first, and claim the *peanuts*' – he made an ironic face – 'went down with the ship. Meanwhile, the second ship brings them in.'

'Scuttle? You mean *sink* it?'

'Why not? It's insured, and the captain gets $25,000 for his trouble. You get the parts, the owner gets a new ship, the captain gets rich, and the crew gets drunk and laid in every port from here to Hong Kong. Everybody's happy.'

'Everyone except the insurance company.'

'Insurance companies are never happy.'

Crespi said nothing, and yet he seemed to regard Higgins with a growing appreciation. 'You would need cash?'

Higgins shook his head. 'You can electronically transfer the funds to an account we have in Europe. However, as I said, after that you'll have to trust me. There is no way I can get these goods without the money in hand.'

'And how fast can you deliver them to us?'

'I don't know. I'll have to see. It's not like going down to the *bodega* and buying a bunch of plantains, is it?' He snapped a breadstick and popped a section in his mouth.

Crespi stared at him for a moment longer, appraising once again Higgins' apparent confidence and aplomb. Then he gave Higgins a number, made him memorize it, and told him that in the future they would communicate by phone.

Higgins left. It was raining. He would liked to have stayed in the warm *groceria* drinking *cappuchino*, but Crespi was adamant that he and Higgins not be seen together for any longer than was strictly necessary.

But out on the street, with his audience gone, much of

Higgins' confidence faded. He was in for it now, he thought to himself, as he wended his way back to the Doctor's. Parts were one thing; munitions another. Hand-held Stinger missiles? He tried to imagine what sort of sharks and slime worms he would have to deal with in order to get them. And then there was always the US Attorney General who frowned on private citizens, like Higgins, selling arms to guerrilla armies. And if that was not enough, there was Schmidt and Cordero. God forbid they got wind of the deal. And then, of course, there was *El Duende*.

Higgins stopped in this tracks, suddenly bewildered, his confidence leaking away like air. His eyes opened wide, as though he beheld before him, arrayed upon the field of battle, his enemies with all their mighty armies. The vision was overwhelming. Even his concern for the children and his outrage over his wife's death could not support him in the face of what he saw. And for a moment, at least, he wanted to throw away the list and run, back to Boston, back to the comfort of his condo and his old, sad, safe life. But even as he thought this, something stirred the air, and he knew it was *her* spirit's reproach.

And anyway, he told himself, watching a stranger unfurl his umbrella, it should be easy enough to stay inspired – especially if the weather held.

Tank

◆

Chapter 20

As far as the Doctor could gather, the Junta's arsenal looked terrifying on paper, but in real life was considerably less so. Though they had bought seventeen F–80C Shooting Star jet fighters, only three were believed to be operational due to a dearth of trained technicians and parts. Not that they couldn't be *made* operational. In some cases, Benitez said, it was nothing more than a few screws and split washers that kept the million-dollar death machines grounded, their six 50-caliber machine guns silent, and their bomb bays closed.

But the F–80 didn't have a bomb bay. The ordinance was stored on two external hardpoints beneath the wing.

Really? But was the Commander certain? Or perhaps he was thinking of the F–84.

No, he was not! Why, hadn't he been bombed by F–80s? In Juticalpa?

It was in this vein, in fits and starts, that the review of enemy firepower proceeded. While Rabon and Benitez digressed, diagnosed, and argued, the Doctor, bored by the discussion, stared out the window, dreaming of a war plane grounded by the smallest flaw. It was, he thought, not unlike the human conditions in which a man of extraordinary pre-science and power, at the height of his career, in the pink of health, could have his happiness sabotaged by a single defect in his existence: a live-in mother-in-law, say, or a jealous mistress, a toothache, or even a dripping tap.

Then his mind returned to Jane. He thought of sinking his face between her breasts, and coming up gasping like a man whose head is held too long under water. And the Doctor felt his stomach flutter as he remembered the taste of smoke and spearmint on her tongue.

But the men were discussing gunships now, and the Doctor, who believed a gunship to be some sort of boat, rejoined the discussion by remarking on the inadequacy of Dorado's navy – only to be informed, after a quizzical pause, that a Cobra gunship was a type of *aircraft*, a helicopter to be exact.

'Oh, a *helicopter*,' the Doctor said, disparingly. 'What can *they* do?'

Rabon and Benitez exchanged looks. 'You have never seen one press an attack, have you, Doctor? Well, *Señor*, I hope you never do. For I would rather see the Angel of Death coming at me than one of those. With the Angel of Death at least you stand a fighting chance, but with a Huey Cobra . . .'

Rabon looked at Benitez for permission to continue. 'You see, they come right over the treeline at you, and start unleashing rockets while still more than two miles off. You see only a puff and a flash of fire in the distance, then – *blang, blang, blang* – the rockets strike. Each rocket is armed with a white phosphorus warhead equal to a 107-mm mortar round, and they can fire fifty-one of these at you in less than six seconds.This means the rockets come in almost altogether, and what they don't blast to Kingdom Come they set on fire. The phosphorus cannot be quenched. It burns on contact with air – or flesh – and even inside you it continues to burn so that you you may see your *compadres* – or yourself if you're unlucky, Doctor – with puffs of white smoke coming from your wounds. At this point, you still don't know what hit you.

'Then you hear a kind of stuttering cough. These are the grenade launchers throwing 40-mm grenades at your position at a rate of four hundred and fifty per minute. The grenades skid when they hit the ground – impossible to handle – they pop and flash, each bursting into hundreds of deadly shards. A moment later, two mini-guns erupt, rattling in bursts. The name mini-gun does them a disservice, since each gun has six barrels and can fire anywhere from two thousand to six thousand rounds per minute, achieving almost instantly what munitions manufacturers like to call "lethal density," which is just a fancy way of saying that the air around you is now completely filled with flying lead. At this point the helicopter, as you call it, Doctor, is still more than a half a mile away. Shall I continue? Yes.

'All right. If somehow you are still alive, which I sincerely doubt, at last you will see it approaching through the phosphorus plumes. Imagine, if you will, an insect and a war machine mated. This is what it looks like: a deadly metal dragonfly. When the gunship reaches its target, it hovers and begins to swing in the air, darting back and forth again and again, like a striking cobra. This is how it got its name. Meanwhile, the two mini-guns hose down the area at one hundred and fifty rounds per second. Per *second*! The noise is, frankly, indescribable. The Vietnamese who faced these things called them "the muttering death." ' The Commander smiled. 'So you see, Doctor, these helicopters . . . they can do a lot.'

The Doctor felt hot and stupid. 'Do they have many of them in Dorado?'

'That's what we were just discussing. Nor would you have to ask that question if you'd been following our discussion, instead of mooning out the window, dreaming of your *mujer*.'

'I'm sorry, your Excellency,' the Doctor said. He had underestimated Benitez once again. 'And how did you know I was thinking of her?'

'How?' Benitez asked. He barked a laugh. 'You were playing with your zipper!'

There was loud, happy laughter – the harsh, aggressive sounds of minds under pressure venting their stress. Rabon clapped the Doctor on the back, while Benitez smiled in his thin-lipped sardonic way, as though he had said something devilishly clever.

'It's all right, Doctor,' the Commander rejoined. 'If she was my woman, I tell you this, I'd be playing with more than just my zipper!'

This remark was not so witty and so was not greeted with the same degree of enthusiastic laughter. Still, everyone guffawed. Then, just as suddenly, they grew serious again as the conversation, like a Cobra gunship, swung back again from sex to death.

'Now, as you were saying, Commander,' Benitez said, 'they have several of these Cobras. And what else?'

The Commander listed the planes in Dorado's air force. In addition to the Huey Cobras and the F–80s, they had recently purchased four Cessna Dragonflies. These last posed a major problem, as an all-out rebel infantry offensive could be decimated by them before it even got underway.

'Which means we have to get to the planes,' Benitez said, 'before they become airborne.'

But Rabon shook his head. 'There's no way we can do that short of an all-out attack. The airport is heavily defended. The Dragonflies are their pride and joy and it would be a colossal embarrassment if someone blew them up while they were sitting on the runway. So getting to the planes is out, I'm afraid. They're expecting us to try that.' He paused. 'We can, however, do something even better.'

'What could be better?' Benitez said.

The Commander looked up with a mischievous grin. 'We can get to their pilots.' He sat back, expounding: 'They're a rowdy, randy, thirsty bunch. We know some girls who are friendly with them. We can arrange for these girls to drive by the barracks and drop off some champagne on the night in question. It's the Night of the Dead, after all, and after our ignoble retreat they will want to have a little celebration.'

'What will *that* do?' Benitez asked sourly. He sounded impatient, annoyed.

'The champagne, my President? Nothing much. But the twelve ccs of chloral hydrate injected by syringe through the cork of each bottle will, the Doctor tells me, unglue their gastrointestinal tracts at both ends and ground the entire air force for the next twenty-four hours.' The Commander grinned.

Benitez studied the Doctor and Rabon with a widening smile and a deepening appreciation. 'I am glad you two are working for me,' he said at last. 'I would hate to count you among my enemies.'

The two men laughed loudly and beamed at each other. The compliment was like an unexpected kiss and the Doctor basked in the joy of his leader's approbation. There was for that moment a marvelous sense of power in the room, a current of bliss, a wind of joy, as though the air had been stirred by the pinions of some winged victory.

And so now, having disposed of Dorado's air force, Rabon went on to a discussion of the Government's artillery and armor – and the rebels lack of it.

'We have one tank and one half-track. We have two M–113 armored personnel carriers which we captured from the Junta last May.'

'Continue, Commander,' Benitez urged.

'That's it, my President.'

'That's *it*?'

Yes, Rabon said, but not to worry. They would use sleight of hand to make themselves look more formidable. This would be accomplished, according to Rabon, by marching Cereno's men out of the jungle and past the village of Macondo, where there would be government informants waiting to report their strength. As soon as the one tank and two personnel carriers passed the provincial capitol, they would turn around and circle back through the jungle where their serial numbers would be re-painted, and their crews replaced. Then several hours later, two more M–113s would stream through the village; then toward evening another tank. They would do this maneuver half a dozen times. That they were the same three pieces, Rabon believed, would not be apparent, giving the enemy an erroneous and exaggerated estimate of their strength. To defend against such an armored assault, Rabon said, Cuzo would have to commit all his forces to protect the western flank of Puerto Valle. While such a shield might be nearly impenetrable, the hand that held it would be bare, exposed to the shock troops coming over the volcano.

This second front, of course, was where the operation would live or die and would be spearheaded by Commander Rabon himself. But the success of this whole military venture, Rabon reminded them, rested upon the strictest secrecy and surprise. If Cuzo's men got wind of the operation, they would no doubt wait for Rabon to start down the mountain, then turn their floodlights on them and open fire. Rabon's men would be picked off its face without hope of retreat or resistance, as once, he said, he had watched the flickering tongue of a crested iguana pluck from a wall its luncheon of fat, black flies.

Were there any questions or objections? The Commander was lathered in sweat.

The Doctor asked: 'But won't the Indians in the mountains report the movement of our troops?'

'We have thought of that and have taken measures – you will see.'

'And don't forget one last division here,' Benitez said, pointing to a part of the map far removed from the scene of the battle.

'There?' the Doctor asked. 'But the Junta has no soldiers there, my President.'

'They are not meant for the Junta, but for Montenegro. We will ambush Montenegro, destroy his army, and rid ourselves of this pestilence once and for all.' There was a dumbfounded pause at this major crevice in what had been until then a solid front.

But there was no time now for doubts or questions. It was Rabon's birthday. A cake with thirty-one candles was brought in and everyone sang *Happy Birthday* to the Commander. Rabon made a wish and blew out the candles, but one winked back on – an inauspicious sign, the Doctor couldn't help but think.

But there was no time for evil omens, either. Rabon had a plane to catch. He was leaving for Dorado that very afternoon. Everyone ate a piece of cake, followed by a round of fond farewells and warm embraces, and then the Commander ran down the stairs and jumped into a sports car parked at the curb.

'Can I drop you off somewhere?' he asked the Doctor and they took off like a bat from hell, followed frantically by a black sedan full of bodyguards. The wind laved their faces like a warm bath.

'Do you really think we're going to win?'

The Commander shrugged. 'Confucius say: "When the thunderclap comes, it is too late to cover your ears." An attack may lack ingenuity and even power, but if it can be delivered with complete surprise . . .' He shrugged. 'Who the hell knows?'

The Doctor sighed. He felt suddenly wasted. It had been a long day, a long meeting, a long hot summer and fall. He looked at the Commander who was beaming broadly, the wind in his beard as he tooled the sports car through the city traffic. 'How is it you are always in such a happy mood?'

'Why shouldn't I be?' Rabon laughed. 'Ah, I used to be like you, Doctor. Petulant. Always dissatisfied. But six months in a prison camp cured me of that. I swore that if I ever got out of that hellhole alive, I would make it my business to be happy. Those Russian novelists are right. Suffering is good for you. It does wonders for your perspective.'

The Commander swerved and stopped the car. They had reached the Doctor's house. 'At your service, *Señor*,' he said and offered the Doctor his hand.

The Doctor shook it warmly and got out. He had the feeling he just had made a very good friend, a true *companero*, someone he could listen to and talk to and drink with for hours, someone he could count on for the rest of his life, someone he could make the godfather of his children. 'We will continue this conversation. I assure you, Commander.'

'Four p.m., November first. *Los Dos Hermanos*. Don't be late.'

'. . . *Dos Hermanos*?'

'On Acacia Street. In Puerto Valle. I'll be the one with the pistol on his hip drinking rum at the bar. The good-looking girl I'll be with is my fiancée, Elvira Martinez. Remember, *companero*. Four o'clock sharp!' and he turned the sports car into the rush hour traffic.

Lovers

◆

Chapter 21

At four in the morning, a slim, silken-limbed body invaded his bed. 'Hold me.'

'Huh? What's the matter?'

'I'm afraid.'

'Afraid of what?'

For the longest time Gil didn't answer. She just lay there against him, her face buried in his chest. She seemed to be smelling him, drawing strength and comfort from his skin.

Then at last she began to weep. It might have been exhaustion, fear, or relief. The sobs made her whole body shudder. Higgins held her, firm but gently, until her sorrow found a track, flowing more easily now in a steady rivulet of sound and tears. She was full of so much pent-up feeling that she cried for quite a while, reaching a peak then slowly ebbing in pitch, like a falling siren or a cistern slowly emptying itself of water. And holding her like that, close to his heart, Higgins could feel streaming inside her that same subterranean river of emotion which runs in everyone, which flows through the entire world.

At last, she was spent. There was nothing left to spill. A few final drops splashed out of her as sighs and whimpers, and then she was mute and remote as the moon.

Higgins lay with his arms around her, one hand on the small of her back, the other on a blade of her shoulder. He didn't feel tired, he didn't feel excited, he didn't feel anything but empty and still. He listened to the traffic and watched the lights of the passing cars wrap themselves around the bedroom walls.

Then, from inside her, another engine pulsed into motion and she began to press herself against his body – push, then stop, rock, then stop, and start again. The couch springs began a rhythmic creaking as, slowly, her exertions increased. At last, she grew frantic and moved her mouth to cover his. Her breath was scalding: hot and erotic.

Higgins slipped from beneath her. He heard her body slap the sheet. She turned and looked up at him, insulted, stunned.

'What was that for?'

'Nothing. It's just that for the last two months you've been barely civil. You act like I bore you. Then one night, you're scared and lonely – and I'm the nearest warm male body. Maybe I should be overjoyed, but for some reason, I'm not.'

Gil sighed and rolled over on her back. 'You've changed, you know that?'

'Oh, yeah? Since when?'

'Since about a month ago. One morning, you didn't want me anymore. Oh, you still looked at me like you . . . liked what you saw – but there wasn't anything behind it. You were like . . . on some other plane.'

'So?'

'And so, damnit, don't you see? That confused me. Was it me who'd changed or you?'

Higgins sighed. Was the human heart really so predictable? Was the human mind really so perverse? He remembered as a five-year-old complaining to his Uncle Evan that a little girl he liked didn't want to play with him. Evan told him to ignore her, not to talk to her for a couple of days, and within twenty-four hours she had invited him to her house to make mud pies. Ah, his first conquest! Victory in love!

'And then yesterday, you changed again. You decided something, didn't you? I saw it on your face when you returned from your luncheon.'

'Christ,' Higgins said honestly appalled. 'Is it really so obvious?'

'No,' she said, 'only to me. Because . . . I know you.'

'Of course, you know me.'

'No,' she said. 'I mean . . . from before.'

'Before where?'

'I don't know. But sometimes at night, when I look at your face, I almost think . . . I'm going to say your name.'

Higgins laughed. 'What is it?'

She shook her head. 'I keep on seeing this awful port. It's hot and dirty and full of flies.'

And at her words a chill went up Higgins' spine.

'You remember it, too, don't you?' she said, squeezing his arm.

'Bits, pieces. That port. And . . . a country inn.'

'Yes! With sleds . . . and horses! And once, you were bending over Nina, tying her laces, and I thought, "of course, he's a doctor." It didn't make sense. A doctor doesn't tie shoe laces.'

And as she said that, Higgins saw again the waters of a summer pool. He saw the reeds and weeds and rubbery lilies and the brown arms of a little girl, above whose head the overarching branches freckled blond and gold the brown shallows through which they were wading, Indian-style. He saw again the child's tan back, her sweet trapezius flexing as she swung her braceleted arms at the shoulder. And Higgins knew it was not a fantasy, but a memory. A memory, yes. But of what and when? Of where and who?

Higgins lay back down in the dark. She put her arms around him, and he stroked her hair. She drew him to her, and kissed him then. '*Te ha amado*,' she whispered in his ear. It was not 'I love you,' but 'I've *loved* you.' And at that moment, Higgins felt a delicious thrill as his love for her uncoiled inside him.

He drew her to him. 'I've loved you, too.'

For Higgins wasn't falling in love with her. Nor was their love for each other growing. It wasn't like that. It was like some sleeping creature, fully formed, which once again had opened up its eyes.

At first, there was some awkwardness between them. But only for a moment. Then they were lost in exploring each other's form. Higgins felt her strong thin arms, the delicate fluting of her ribs, her high small breasts with nipples that were as tiny, fine and brown as raisins. He cupped and parted with his fingertips the silken slickness that cleft her like a hidden stream. And as they met and merged and parted, lip to lip, heart to belly, Higgins knew they had done just this, precisely this, a million times before.

They dozed. When he opened his eyes again, the light was already gray and grainy. He kissed her throat. 'Hot tamale.'

She shied from the kiss and compliment like a skittish colt. 'Please,' she said, 'you'll ruin my reputation.'

'And what is that?'

'I'm supposed to be the ice queen, don't you remember? At least, those are the parts I always get. That way when I'm murdered in the end, everyone can say, she had it coming.'

Higgins laughed; his stomach growled.

'Hey,' she said, 'you want some breakfast? There's some leftover chicken in the fridge. Or I could toast a bagel.'

'Toast a bagel.'

'My, you're easy. It took Howie hours to make up his mind. And then when he did and I made it for him, he never liked it anyway.'

'It must have been wonderful,' Higgins said, 'having breakfast with Howie.'

Gil laughed and then he laughed, too. They looked at each other in the lightening dark and the love that flowed between them then was as thick and rich and sweet as honey.

'Hey,' Higgins said. 'What are you doing?'

Kaboom!

◆

Chapter 22

'How do you feel?'

But the boy wouldn't answer. He turned on his side and stared out the hospital window. A nurse fussed with his bed clothes.

'Look, I brought you something,' the Doctor said, taking a small brass telescope from his pocket.

The boy made a noise that sounded like 'asshole.'

The Doctor sighed and sat down on his bed.

'What have you got against us anyway? I know I shot you, but you were robbing my office. Apart from that, what have I ever done to you?'

'You killed his father,' the nurse told him.

'I killed *who*?'

'In Dorado. His father was kidnapped by your people and murdered.'

'What people?'

'The People's Forces.'

So, it had been Montenegro! And what could the Doctor answer to that? Could he say: yes, it is true; Montenegro and the People's Forces are our allies, but we are not responsible for any atrocities they commit. Of course not. So he changed the subject. 'I am glad to see you are looking so much better.'

The child's recovery had hardly been 'miraculous;' rather, it had been cruel, painful, and slow. The boy had simply refused to die, crawling back from the brink of non-existence inch by inch, until now he could sit up and eat solid food. Still, he would not speak to the Doctor – or even make eye contact. The Doctor talked for a while, but it was a one-sided conversation, and finally he gave up and went away.

'Open the suitcase.'

'What for?'

'Just open it, Doctor,' *El Duende* insisted.

At first, the Doctor didn't know what to make of the mess inside. There were several cake tins wrapped with wire bolted to the inner surface. They were filled with a dense tan substance that might have been blocks of hardened brown sugar. The spaces between the tin and blocks were crammed with a white, gum-like putty. More wires, tape, and a small electric device completed the ensemble. 'It's a bomb,' the Doctor said.

'Brilliant. Any questions, just ask Omar.'

'My God,' the Doctor said and shut the cover. Then he started – as though the tiny shock might make the thing explode.

'Don't worry,' Omar reassured him. 'It is not armed. You will do that yourself, Doctor, prior to detonation.'

'Prior to . . . ? What are you talking about?'

'You will bring this suitcase to this afternoon's conference. At a suitable moment, you will excuse yourself, leave the room, and take out this channel selector. Select channel three. Then depress this button.'

'This is stupid,' the Doctor said. 'Do you really think there is any way I could get this thing into the mansion? My God, the security . . .'

'We've thought of that, Doctor. When you enter, someone will be leaving. This person will be carrying an attaché case identical to your own. You will meet at the front desk and both of you will set your bags on the floor. Then you will reach down, lift the other case, open it and show it to Security. Once it is inspected, you will close it and set it back down at your feet. Then both of you will pick up your

original cases. You will enter. The other person will depart.
It's as simple as that.'

'And who is this other person?'

'You'll find that out soon enough.'

'I won't do it.'

'You *will* do it. You will call Benitez now. And then you
will call us, and tell us what time the meeting is scheduled.'

'To arm it,' Omar added flatly, 'you just flip this little
switch.'

The Doctor left La Club, the bomb in hand, and called
Benitez from the first payphone he came to. His fingertips
felt blunt and numb with fear and he had difficulty inserting
the quarter. While the phone was ringing, he discovered a
ferocious desire to pee.

'President's Residence,' a voice announced.

'Give me *El Presidente*,' the Doctor said, and was almost
immediately disconnected. He moaned. He couldn't believe
it. He rummaged in his pockets but, of course, he had no
more quarters. He cursed and, picking up the suitcase with
care, crossed the street to *El Encanto* where he cashed a dollar
and drained his kidneys in the loo – and then, inspired, swallowed a quick *ron* for his nerves. The jukebox, he noted, was
grinding out a *Latino* version of Ghostriders in the Sky.

The Doctor re-dialed the number from the payphone in
the bar and said, 'If you cut me off again, you son of a bitch,
I'll have you taken out and shot. This is Doctor Castellano.
Give me *El Presidente. Pronto!*'

This time, there was a troubled pause and a series of elec-
tronic clicks. Benitez phone did not ring, it purred.

'Yes?' Benitez asked.

The Doctor, in a rattling, high-pitched whisper, recounted
the plot.

When he was through, Benitez paused thoughtfully, then
said, 'So you are to blow me up. Well then, we mustn't disap-
point them, Doctor. Bring the device, and put it in my study.
Then come downstairs to my basement office.' The Doctor
knew enough by now not to ask questions. He phoned La
Club and informed Omar of the meeting. Then he hurried to

the brownstone, lugging the lethal suitcase. Though the bomb was not armed, he found himself walking with extreme care and circumspection.

But when the Doctor entered the brownstone, Guido was waiting at the desk. In his hand was a briefcase identical to the Doctor's. Seeing the Doctor, the secretary looked shocked, and the color drained from his cheeks. Then, without a word, he turned and ran off into the depths of the mansion.

'Give me the President,' the Doctor said to the guard. But instead of replying, the man stiffened to attention. Benitez was standing at the Doctor's shoulder. He was half a head shorter than the Doctor.

'You saw him?' the Doctor asked.

The President looked grim. He set the Doctor's attaché case on the marble entrance table, clicked it open, and examined its deadly innards closely. 'Schmidt,' he said, as if reading a signature. He close the cover. 'Where is the trigger?'

The Doctor drew the channel selector from his jacket pocket. 'Channel three.'

Pocketing the remote control, Benitez handed the briefcase back to the Doctor. 'Place it beneath my desk upstairs. Arm it, Doctor. Then call *El Diario*, and tell them there will be a big explosion. When you are done, meet me in my downstairs office.' He turned to go. 'Oh, and Doctor. The device is serviceable enough, but somewhat crude. There is a miniscule chance – say, one in ten thousand – that some residual current is left in the circuit. If that is the case, when you arm it . . .' He shrugged, fatalistically. 'I want you to understand.'

The Doctor understood too well and, sickened by this understanding, went up the stairs. By the time he reached Benitez's study he was bathed in sweat. He set the device on the desk and went to the window. He gazed at the stanchions of the bridge in the distance but, in fact, he hardly saw them. He was wondering what death by explosion was like. He probably wouldn't even hear the bang. He would flip the switch and Nothing would happen; Nothing, that is, with a capital N. No Doctor, no office, no bridge, Nothing . . .

He calmed himself and turned back to the device. He opened it, identified the arming lever, and took another deep breath. A prayer attempted to escape his heart, but the Doctor shot it dead before it was airborne. He would die like a man. He closed his eyes and flipped the switch.

Benitez was standing with Guido in his basement office. A wrought-iron door opened on a small overgrown garden sodden with the rain of late October. Stacks of files and boxes of papers sat on the office floor, as though hurriedly removed from somewhere else.

'Guido has uncovered a traitor in our midst.'

'Who is it?' the Doctor asked.

'Guido says that it is you, Doctor.'

'Me?'

'Yes. He says that you have been plotting against us with *El Duende*.'

'And how does he know that?'

'That's a good question. Maybe because Guido has been plotting with *El Duende*, too. Haven't you, Guido?'

'Your Excellency!'

'The Doctor says you have.'

Guido looked outraged. 'And who are you going to believe – him or me?'

'I am going to believe the truth,' Benitez said. 'Whoever speaks it.'

'The truth?' Guido asked. 'I will tell you the truth. For five and a half years . . . I have been your faithful servant. For five and a half years, I have given my life to you. I have felt for you, *Señor*, the kind of loyalty that most men only feel for their country.

'And now . . . this one,' he said, turning on the Doctor with bitter gall, 'comes along and within a month, you have promoted him above me, excluded me from your meetings, and taken his word over mine. It isn't fair.'

'Maybe not,' Benitez said. 'And yet for that you would betray us?'

'I *didn't* betray you,' Guido said, though his voice was

weaker now. 'I only pretended to in order to find out who
the real traitor was. And I did. It's Castellano. As soon as I
found out, I came straight to you, your Excellency.'

But Benitez only shook his head. 'But why pretend,
Guido? When they asked you to, why didn't you just tell
them to go fuck themselves? And why didn't you tell me
what you were up to?' He paused a moment, growing colder.
'What did you do for them?'

'Nothing! I swear. Just little things. To keep them happy.'

'Little things? Like helping them blow me to Kingdom
Come?'

'Blow you to . . . ?' He looked at the Doctor, then down
at his case. '. . . Oh, my God.' And he buried his face in his
hands.

'Why, Guido,' Benitez asked. 'Why?' His voice was ashes.

Guido bit his lips and looked away. 'They had pictures.'

'Pictures of what?'

'I'd rather not say, your Excellency.'

'Sailors, Guido?'

The secretary looked startled. 'They showed them to you?'

'They didn't have to. I have some myself.' And manipulat-
ing a key chain, Benitez opened a locked file and withdrew a
glassine envelope stuffed with negatives. Curious, the Doctor
craned his neck. He whistled.

Guido hid his face in his hands. 'They said that they would
send them to you – and to my mother.'

The Doctor imagined Guido's old mother receiving the
photos. He saw her opening the envelope and studying them
in the Caribbean sun, orange trees in the distance. And then
what? Would she keel over backwards? Of course not. It
would be a nasty shock, but one she would get over, surely.
Anyone her age must have suffered many more rude surprises
in her day. She would burn them and say, perhaps, a tearful
prayer to the Madonna. And that would be that – if they had
even bothered to send them. No. All things considered, it
was not a compelling reason to blow your beloved President
to smithereens.

'Guido, Guido,' Benitez said shaking his head. 'Did you

really think, after all these years, you could hide from us your . . . true feelings?'

'Your Excellency. I was most discreet.'

Benitez sniffed. 'Evidently not discreet enough.'

Guido's face was that of a man entertaining a wondrous realization. 'And so you knew . . . all along . . . and didn't care?'

'I knew,' Benitez said, 'from the very first day you walked in my office and planted your faggy butt on the table.'

At that the secretary gave a startled laugh, then cried for several minutes. There was pain in the sound, but also joy and much relief that the long charade was finally ended.

'Why should I care about your sex life, Guido? You did good work. You were loyal and true. I once knew a General who had a thing for chickens. Don't ask me why. This is what he liked. *Los Pollos*! Mad! Hell of a general though. Great tactician! Won twenty-nine battles in forty-eight days. One of the bravest men I ever knew. It's all right, Guido.' Benitez got up and came around the desk. 'There, there. Dry your eyes. There's no need to cry. I have forgiven you.'

'I didn't betray you. I didn't, your Excellency!'

'Of course, you didn't,' Benitez said. 'It was all some sort of . . . misunderstanding.'

Guido stood up and the two men embraced. Benitez said, 'I love you, friend. You are like a son to me. I want you to know that. Always.'

'I do, your Excellency.'

'Good,' he said curtly, as though growing embarrassed by his display of affection. 'Then it's finished, forgotten. Here,' Benitez said, handing Guido the negatives. 'If they bother you again, you can give them these – from me.' He patted his breast and jacket pockets. 'Damn, where are my glasses, Guido?'

'Perhaps upstairs, my . . .'

'Eh? Oh, damn.'

'If you'd like, I would be glad to get them for you.'

'Don't trouble yourself . . .'

'No trouble, my President.'

'Oh, all right. Would you, Guido?'

If the secretary had had a tail, it would have wagged. He threw the Doctor a look of victory.

'When you get up there,' Benitez said, 'call me on the intercom, will you? Perhaps by then I will have remembered where I put them.'

The Doctor watched as the secretary, without a backward glance, left the room – in far better spirits than he had any right to be.

When he left, Benitez activated the intercom himself and said, 'Roberto, Guido is coming up to look for my reading glasses. Let him through, will you? And as soon as you have, check again to make certain that all third and second floor personnel have been removed. Then report here yourself.' That done, he sank down on the edge of the desk. He seemed older and wearier than the Doctor had ever seen him. Benitez looked out at the wet gray alleyway. The Doctor could hear manic strains of *salsa* coming through the garden from some nearby apartment. A wet red leaf was pasted on the glass of the rain-streaked doors.

'He's dangerous,' the Doctor said. 'What are we going to do with him?'

Benitez stared out the window for the longest time. Then he sighed and said: 'In Leon province, years ago, one of our recruits gave away our position to the daughter of an enemy officer. The girl told her father, who set up and ambush, and two of our very best men were killed. We discovered the informer, and sentenced him to death. A young lieutenant was assigned to carry out the execution. He had never even shot an enemy in battle, much less one of his own men in cold blood.' Benitez sighed, as though the story was a burden.

'So the lieutenant marched the boy off into the forest. It was a cold gray rainy evening – like tonight. The boy became hysterical. He begged the lieutenant to have pity on him, to let him live. He claimed it was all . . . a tragedy. You know. He'd been drunk, in love. He had only wanted to impress his sweetheart. When the officer raised the pistol, the boy urinated on himself. The young officer had never seen a person do this before. He could not shoot. He lowered the pistol.

'He told the boy to run, to run for his life. Perhaps, he thought, it would be easier to shoot him in the back, but he couldn't do that either. When the boy had run a little ways, the lieutenant fired a single shot for the benefit of the men in camp – but it was wide by a mile and only made the boy run faster. That was the last the lieutenant saw of the boy – his backside running madly through the forest.'

The Doctor coughed, moved by the confession. He remembered a speech his sister had rehearsed morning, noon, and night till he, too, knew it by heart. ' "The quality of mercy is not strained . . ." '

Benitez raised a staying hand.

'At daybreak, our camp was overrun. That damn boy had gone straight to his girlfriend's father and given away our position. In the battle that followed, fourteen of our men were captured or killed – everyone, in fact, but the young lieutenant.' Benitez stared unseeing at the rainy garden as though the massacre was etched upon the lenses of his glasses.

Then, methodically, he began to rend his garments. He tore the sleeve off his jacket, ripped the pocket of his shirt, and, dipping his fingers into the tray of cigar ash on the table, smeared it on his face. The Doctor wondered if he had not gone mad, or if this wasn't some strange and primitive ritual imported from Dorado.

Just then the intercom rang.

'Yes, Guido?' Benitez said.

'I'm at your desk, your Excellency, but I don't see your glasses.'

'No, I've found them,' Benitez said sadly, drawing them from his breast pocket and slipping them on the bridge of his nose. He picked up the channel selector and, sighting down it in a nearsighted manner, flipped the switch to Channel 3.

'Your Excellency?' the secretary asked. 'What's going on here? Your office is nearly empty.'

'We're cleaning house, Guido,' Benitez said, and pressed the trigger.

The Hands Of Time

◆

Chapter 23

Now that they were lovers, Gil was sweet as pie. She couldn't do enough for him. She might have been the ice queen in the movies and the bitch goddess to the world at large, with a *kris* in one hand and a noose in the other, but to Higgins she revealed her beneficent aspect, and her many hands held breakfasts and made beds, kind words and warm embraces, and nights of the sweetest love. Their love affair seemed to have lifted her spirits and for the first time since Higgins met her, she began wearing make-up and a skirt. With a dab of lipstick and a little eyeliner she looked sensational, and it occurred to Higgins then he was consorting with a movie queen, albeit a minor one.

In the meantime, Higgins worked on securing parts for MIRA. It wasn't easy. He began by trying to buy them legally from established suppliers, but given both the time frame and the items requested, he soon turned to several arms dealers and black marketeers, none of whom, to put it mildly, were nice or honest men. Doing business with such people was sometimes likened to getting into bed with them, but to Higgins it felt more like getting into a canoe. Any sudden moves by either party were taboo.

Nor was there anything particularly glamorous about it. It was dangerous, unnerving work, requiring days of traveling, endless phonecalls, innumerable details, and hours of hard-nosed bargaining.

And yet, despite the oppressive circumstances, Higgins found a strange elation bubbling up inside him, taking him by surprise. He didn't understand it. He should have been terrified. Here he was risking his life and liberty, consorting with people who might turn on him at any time – and yet he felt so protected, *free* – as if everything he touched would turn out just right, and whatever he forgot would be looked after by fortune.

Of course, Higgins was also very careful. The paperwork and financial transactions were funneled through a series of dummy corporations, each of which further blurred and distanced his involvement in the affair. Not that Higgins could not have been traced with great diligence and effort. He could have. But then again, who was going to do it? What police force or government agency, already grievously over-budget, could afford the thousand and one man-hours that would have been required to follow the paper-trail back to Higgins? Even AES had better ways to spend its money.

Still, Higgins took every precaution. He avoided phoning certain clients through his Boston office, calling, instead from the bank of phonebooths on the street. When traveling, he employed the techniques which Crespi had taught him: changing cabs several times in the course of his journey to make sure he wasn't being followed, and, when he arrived at his destination, registering under an assumed name. He paid cash. He did not use credit cards, inconvenient as it was. He had seen too many people who thought they were traceless leave behind a trail of paper thousands of miles long. Later on, the authorities would reconstruct your every meal, the site of every gas pump and telephone booth you'd stopped at, along with the names and numbers of everyone you'd called – and there was no use protesting they had confused you with someone else, for, at every stop, you had signed your name.

Even stranger, as the days progressed, the whole mad effort began to come together. The thousand and one things that can and do go wrong with deals did not – with this one. Connections occurred like clockwork, while coincidences abetted him again and again. A supplier from Eastern Europe, whom neither Higgins nor his agents had managed to locate in Belgrade, Gdansk, Cracow, or Prague, walked through the door of a New York restaurant while Higgins was eating dinner one evening and took a seat at a corner table. Obviously, for now at least, the gods were on his side.

Of course, if he was a little paranoid that was only to be expected, and if he read too much into little things, well, that was to be expected, too. Once an old classmate tried to phone him at the Doctor's, ostensibly to solicit funds for their school. Higgins felt sickened when he read the message, convinced, as he was, it could not be from his prep school since no one other than his secretary knew where he was. It was not until Higgins returned the phonecall that the mystery was resolved. At a think-tank on Madison Ave. he reached his old classmate Bradford Buck III, who, under Higgins' persistent grilling, reluctantly admitted that, unable to reach Higgins at home or at work, he'd had one of his 'whiz kids,' as he called them, get a read-out on all calls made to Higgins' office. Since the Doctor's number had appeared almost every morning . . .

Higgins was so relieved by this confession that he had pledged his school a large donation.

'Oh, that's splendid,' Buck said. 'Splendid! Hey, since you're in town these days, let's get together, Phil. Number's in the book.'

And Higgins had hung up then, secure in the knowledge that if he was ever held hostage by MIRA or AES, his prep school would find him.

Then, one night, while buying in Miami, as he closed his eyes and slipped into sleep, Higgins saw a forest. It was green and old and spangled with the sun. The trees were big around as pillars and in the distance was a mill built of rounded stones and the sound of flowing water. And at the sight of it, the thunder of a paddlewheel filled his senses, and he was seized with a vivid joy.

It was a saw mill, not a mill for grain, and he smelled once more the sweet, clean scent of the freshly cut lumber and saw it stacked and whitening in a sunlit clearing, so that suddenly he was *there*. O, how he loved his mill, the towering woods ringing with birdsongs, his pretty wife and little daughter!

And then what happened? His wife had left him. His wife whom he had loved so much and whom he had thought was so happy living in the mill had run away one summer morning on a coal-black roan, her sunburnt arms tightly clamped about her lover's waist.

He awoke, with a shock. What wife was this?

And yet closing his eyes again he could see once more the mill pond's waters, the rounded stones, the angle of the light slanting through the tall old wood, and he knew it was an ancient memory. When was it? It felt like the twelfth or thirteenth century. And yet, despite its great antiquity, it seemed no different than any other memory – that of his Uncle Evan, say, sudsing the windows of his '53 Coupe de Ville.

The next day Higgins got started early in order to purchase a dozen reconditioned nightscopes – AN/PVS–4 Starlight Night Vision Systems.

But that morning while shaving in the bathroom, he remembered another piece of that life. It came back to him like a man recovering from amnesia. For his daughter, he remembered now, had drowned in the millpond. How could he ever have forgotten that?

Higgins saw again in the steamy mirror the little soaking body laid out upon the fern-sweet bank, and himself standing over it, stupid and disbelieving with grief. He saw again the sopping ringlets of his daughter's hair, the drowned and empty face, the outstretched form, more limp and lifeless than he had ever known a thing could be.

And reliving it, Higgins burst into tears, crying for a daughter whom he had loved and lost lifetimes ago in an old French wood. The sorrow flowed inside of him like blood. And yet how was it possible that his grief was still so fresh and real after all these many hundred years?

Higgins tried to blot out what followed, but the memories

unfolded inexorably now. He saw smoke. What was he doing? Burning down the mill? Yes. And disappearing into the forest, an enemy of Fortune, a hurt and bitter man. There, he'd fallen in with brigands: men who rode horses, and preyed upon travelers who wandered the byways unprotected or alone.

Now, instead of the innocent embraces of his little daughter and the discipline of the mill, there were drunken bouts and endless arguments about booty, cruel raids, and vicious couplings with captured women. And there were fights – deadly, muddy brawls of flashing fists and swinging elbows, kicking feet and slashing knives – from out of which one autumn morning – completely unexpectedly – an axe had flown and split his skull.

Standing in the hotel bathroom, Higgins watched himself collapse and die – a big, unkempt sand-haired man with a savage headwound and red, chapped hands. Even before he was a corpse, his companions had stolen his boots and money, abandoned him, and broken camp, leaving him with not so much as a crust of bread or a sip of water. So had Higgins died, once upon a time, on a gray November morning, with the promise of snow in the medieval air and a crusting of frost on the rutted mud byways.

Later that day, peering through a reconditioned nightscope, observing men in a far-off corner of a darkened warehouse magnified and bathed in fluorescent green light, it occurred to Higgins that something similar had come to him. Somehow he had acquired an inner instrument that allowed him to pierce the night of time and see close up what could not be seen. For these visions, he believed, were not meaningless; they were showing him something, something about the work he was doing, though what it was exactly he still couldn't say.

In this way, over the course of several weeks, Higgins' far-off past was revealed to him – in bits and fragments, like shards of ancient pottery. Mostly, he saw moments of *extremis* – his death and the deaths of those he loved – though sometimes, he saw some curious detail, a scene from his life as an English doctor, a strange black ceremonial hat he had worn as a Japanese monk. Other times, in the middle of a conversation, he was overpowered by the memory of certain places: the old French wood and sylvan pool, that rancid, fly-infested port, the British slums at winter dusk.

Nor was it only he, Higgins realized now, who had gone from life to life. Those he loved had accompanied him as well.

And when he realized this, Higgins tears had dried and his grief departed. How could they not? For he saw, oh, so clearly now, that the child who had drowned in the medieval millpond – in the sun-dappled waters of the mountain pond – had been born since then many times over, now as his wife, now as his daughter – now as the beautiful Cuban actress, Gilberta Castellano.

Then one morning, in meditation, Higgins found himself wandering through blood-spattered rooms. Everyone was beheaded, dead. His wives were dead, his children, his cousins. An old retainer lay dismembered on the stairs. There was evidence of resistance – but it had soon been over. The palace had been overpowered swiftly, with no quarter given or mercy shown. The dogs were dead, as were the horses in the stable.

The prince of some minor northern fiefdom, he had returned from the hunt to find his kingdom gone.

And it was only then it dawned on Higgins that his enemies, like his friends and lovers, had followed him from life to life as well. The same vicious beings who had slaughtered his family centuries ago in some northern castle had been reborn again in different wombs, pursuing him through time and space, even beyond the final sanctuary of death and the refuge of the grave. It was they who had chased his sled through Belgium, who had drowned his daughter in the forests of France, and murdered his wife on the streets of New York. Sometimes they had triumphed, sometimes he had won. Yet even if he triumphed now, what did it matter? The dead would only rise again.

Hunter's Moon

◆

Chapter 24

The picture in *El Diario* was worth a hundred thousand words. It showed Benitez and the Doctor on the steps of the brownstone. Smoke was billowing from the upper stories. *El Presidente*'s brow was blackened with soot, his clothes dramatically torn and frayed. 'INVINCIBLE!' the caption yelled, going on to say:

A powerful blast ripped through the headquarters of the Dorado United Front shortly after 5 p.m. yesterday afternoon. The explosion left one person dead and caused extensive damage to the upper floor of the landmark building. This dramatic photograph snapped only minutes afterward by *El Diario* staff photographer, Richard Diaz shows Dr. Rodolfo Benitez Cayetano, exiled President of Dorado, being helped from the building by Arsenio Castellano, a spokesman for the rebel movement. Today's incident is only the latest in a series of miraculous near-misses for the ex-President, who survived an assassin's bullet in 197—, as well as a dramatic escape from the capitol when thrust from power in 198—.

The story went on to explain how the Doctor and Benitez had left the room moments before the bomb went off. The dead man was identified as Guido Ricardo Herrera Sanchez,

Benitez's personal aide. The paper said it had been fore-warned of the blast by a caller. The Doctor was also quoted as saying, 'this vicious outrage – the explosion of a powerful device in a crowded city – shows the true terrorist nature of Dorado's enemies.'

But Benitez had other things on his mind. Tomorrow was the Day of the Dead. In seven or eight hours the attack would begin as Rabon and his men came down the mountain. 'Never mind that,' he said, pushing the paper aside. 'Look at these,' and he slapped at a set of blown-up photos.

'What are they?' the Doctor asked.

'You tell *me*!'

The Doctor picked the photographs up and found himself staring down from a tremendous height into the smoking, tree-lined vent of a volcano, beside which gleamed an ink-black lake. At the top of the picture, he could make out a dusty ribbon of highway, beaded with vehicles. The estates of the rich were clearly visible in the midst of large walled compounds, and to the south he could discern the formless sprawling slums running down to the water – a town of rain-soaked cardboard, mud, and corrugated tin, interlaced by a hundred malarial sinks and alleyways.

'Puerto Valle,' the Doctor said, pushing back the photos.

'Yes. Taken from a glider yesterday morning. The question is: what the hell are these?' And Benitez underlined with a clipped pink nail two pale rectangles at the foot of the volcano. One of them was hollow, the other solid, and there were faint bulldozed tracks leading between them.

'I don't know. What are they?'

'Damnit! That's what I'm trying to find out!'

They sat for a while in anxious silence. When the phone rang, Benitez jumped on it. He listened for a moment, then hung up. 'Pre-fab Army barracks,' he told the Doctor. He paused a moment. 'God*damn*it!'

Benitez got up and went to the window. He stood there motionless, clearly upset. Then he asked: 'Who would ever think of building barracks there? And why? What for? The

farthest point from any front? It makes no sense. Unless . . .
Unless they *know* . . .'

And at the thought, Benitez looked defeated, dazed, like
an old general blinded by the smoke of cannons, trying to
fight a battle he could no longer see.

'Or unless, your Excellency,' the Doctor said, 'some
important person owns the land on which they're built.'

Nothing in Benitez's face changed, but a hand floated out
and depressed a button. Immediately, a uniformed aide
trooped in – a handsomish young man with a too-short military haircut, a chestnut moustache, and a look of such fierce
loyalty in his eyes it verged on the cusp of religious adoration.

Benitez introduced the man to the Doctor as Lieutenant
Victor Calderon, his new secretary. Then he said, 'Find out
for us, Lieutenant, who sold the land to the army, when it
was sold, and who is building barracks on it.'

'Yes, sir.' The lieutenant saluted, and withdrew.

For a long time, neither man spoke. The Doctor sat in the
chair by the desk, studying the photographs, while Benitez
continued to stand at the window, staring off at the river.
The Doctor recalled that day years ago he had climbed the
volcano and looked down into its living core. The sight was
unearthly: on the crater's inner walls grew stands of pines
older than the century, while flocks of red-eyed parrots
wheeled through its smoking depths like souls of the damned.

The phone rang. Benitez lifted the receiver. He listened for
a minute, saying, '*Si. Si. Si. Si.*' When he was done, he turned
to the Doctor and said: 'The land for the barracks was for-
merly owned by Isabella Cuzo, mother of Javier, Supreme
Commander of Dorado's Armed Forces. The deed is dated
January fifteenth. Bidding for the barracks began on April
twelfth and on May third was awarded to El Jaguar Construc-
tion Company, own by Axel Sugarman and Antonio Cuzo,
the General's brother-in-law and elder brother.'

'All in the family,' the Doctor said.

'Yes. But more important, Doctor, note the dates. The project was begun well before we devised our Operation Rorschach – so . . .' he breathed a small sigh of relief which quickly

grew into a larger groan of apprehension. 'And yet, it still presents us with a major problem. One of the barracks is clearly occupied already.' He slammed his fist. 'Damnit, Doctor! Do you see? This is what comes from fighting a stupid opponent. He does things that are so inept and witless, he makes you look stupid, too! A week ago, when Commander Rabon went up into the mountains, there was nothing there. Tonight, when he and his men descend, they will come down on top of two hundred soldiers!'

He looked at the photographs and thought for a moment. 'Unless for some reason, the barracks were empty.' Suddenly Benitez's agitation ceased. He sat down behind his desk, growing calm and still.

'Doctor, you must deliver for us one last message. I don't have to tell you how important it is. You must return to *El Duende* and tell him you were deceived. Tell him General Cereno's retreat is a feint and that the rebel attack is on. Tell him that at 0100 hours, Cereno will attack from the west, hitting them with everything he's got. Tell him . . . the US will be lending us air support!'

'The US Air Force!'

'Yes. They'll call Washington, of course, and Washington will deny it. But they're such paranoid bastards that will only make them believe it all the more!'

'And what if they don't?'

El Presidente turned to the Doctor now, fixing him with his powerful and soulful brown gaze. 'You must *make* them believe it. We must empty those barracks before four in the morning. We must draw those soldiers away from the foot of the mountains or all our plans will be undone.

'Are you carrying a pistol, Doctor?' Then without waiting for an answer, he said: 'The sergeant will issue you ordnance. If *El Duende* gives you trouble – do not hesitate to use it. Then put the message through to Dorado yourself.'

The Doctor, who just a moment before had felt so good, felt suddenly awful. 'You can't be serious, your Excellency. You don't mean you want me to *shoot El Duende*?'

Benitez shrugged. 'If it comes to that. So be it. I can tell you right now, there would be few who would mourn. Or do you think you are the only one who is under his spell? No. There are many *hombres* and not a few *mujeres* whose blood he drinks, whose guts he eats, like a tapeworm in the belly. You kill that monster and you will be releasing them as well. Yes! You will be liberating a whole realm of enchanted knights and ladies!'

'But I am a doctor. It would be against my oath.'

'It seems to me you swore another oath as well.' Then Benitez's sternness dissolved. 'Look, Doctor. I'm not telling you to do anything except to deliver that message and take whatever steps are required to see that it gets through. And anyway, you are not alone. You are supported from within.'

'By Captain Crespi?'

Benitez seemed surprised. 'You know the Captain?'

'By reputation only.'

Benitez quickly changed the subject. He looked at his watch. 'Now we have some time to kill. The girls are not quite ready yet.'

The Doctor was confused. 'Girls?'

'From The Pickled Prince. C'mon. Get with it, Doctor. It's a brothel. In Puerto Valle. The girls from there will be meeting the pilots at ten for supper. Now girls like that are always a little late, and anyway, we have to give them time to have their champagne toast.' Benitez looked at the clock on his desk. 'It's nine forty now. The Commander and his men will be down by four. That means General Cuzo must receive the message by midnight. So, you will deliver it to *El Duende* no later than quarter to one, our time.'

The telephone rang. Benitez answered it, listened, then cupping his hand over the receiver, said, 'Now, Doctor, why don't you go and get some supper? Oh, and Doctor,' he said, smiling brightly, as the Doctor turned to go, 'relax.'

Deva

◆

Chapter 25

Sitting on the porch of the solitary brownstone in the warm summer twilight, Higgins told Sara about the latest of his visions – the cold castle walls splashed with blood, after which the memories ended.

'Don't you want to know what happened before that?'

'Not really,' Higgins said.

'It might be important.'

'You told me yourself, I shouldn't get caught up in that stuff. And anyway,' said Higgins, who had just returned from three days' of hard bargaining, 'I'm feeling rather tired.'

'Well, then, you had better wake up!' And picking up a water glass, she flung its contents in his face.

The water never touched his face. Before it did, the porch dissolved, floor and ceiling fell away. What had he been thinking of? A water glass? How absurd! For he was fleeing now with fear, flying over jeweled rooftops on the outskirts of some tremendous city. The memory of someone named 'Philip Higgins' flickered for an instant, then disappeared, like the flame of a lamp extinguished by the wind. He took a turn on invisible wings and felt the throb of mystic power in his belly. For his name was Rudradrishti, and he was a *deva*, a god.

Rudradrishti soared, impelled by thought. He was fleeing, yes, but where could he go? The King had ordered his arrest, and an army of *yakshas* would be waiting for him wherever he landed. Far off in the distance, fires burned out of control. For the war that had ravaged heaven was nearly over now. There were only a few rebel warriors like Rudradrishti left. That they had lost – or nearly so – was certain, and at the thought, his spirits plunged – for even in heaven, you can carry hell in your breast.

Rudradrishti saw the lake below him and descended, feeling the sudden emptiness of the descent in his belly. When he was young, red bulls had watered here and golden deer had browsed among the silver apples. But that was thousands of years ago. Beside the lake was an old stone shrine. It was hardly more than one low room opening on the water. It was here he came to rest and to re-arm himself from the cache of weapons stored beneath its floor.

But as Rudradrishti went to enter it, he saw that there was someone there. He steeled himself to fight – or fly. But something restrained him, for the figure inside the temple was neither moving nor hiding, but sitting motionless with an air of immense serenity.

A goddess in the light of a celestrial sunset is magnificent – and the being who sat before him now, on a piece of bark whose rare design was more wondrous than any earthly carpet, was indubitably beautiful. Rudradrishti took a seat beside her on a low bench and leaned his back against the stone. For a while, neither of them spoke. They rested, their divine faces suffused by the evening glow. Some night fairies, the size of damselflies, were ferrying the lake on stiff wings, while further off against the glowing sky, they watched the silhouette of a demon plummet and attack something in a far-off valley.

The goddess sighed. 'They're getting bolder every year. When I was young, no self-respecting *rakshasa* would dare appear so close to the palace. The King's grip must be slipping.'

Rudradrishti sadly smiled. 'That's what my father thought.'

'Your father?'

'My father is the King,' he said, 'who seized the throne of heaven some months back.'

'Ah, yes! And almost kept it, as I recall.'

'But was repulsed and exiled.'

'But we all thought it a wonderful show. Nothing so daring had been tried around here for ages. To just seize it like that. How bold, how godly!'

'Some said demonic.'

'The line between the two is thin *I* will concede. So you are his son, you are . . .'

'Rudradrishti.'

'And where is your father now, O Prince?'

'In hell. Soon I may be joining him.' Rudra, in fact, had visited him there and been dismayed to find he was nothing but a disembodied head, floating and screaming in space, surrounded by other screaming heads. Rudradrishti had tried to comfort him, but the rebel lord had not appeared to recognize his son – his maddened eyes had only bulged and rolled at terrors only he could see, like a man imprisoned inside a dream.

The *devi*, easily reading his thoughts, said, 'Heaven, Prince, is a dream, as well. A pleasant one, yes; but a dream all the same.'

'I only wish it was,' Rudradrishti said. 'Then I could awaken and return to the Palace.' But looking out at the twilit pond and garden, he saw quite clearly, it was not a dream. The stone slab against his back was real. The setting suns were real, the aging goddess, the chariot trails, his heavenly memories and hellish future. How could any of it be a dream?

'And what if I told you you had lived before, and will live again?'

Rudradrishti smiled. 'I'm afraid I wouldn't believe you, Goddess.'

She laughed. 'And how do you think we got here then?'

Rudradrishti shrugged. 'Luck, I guess.'

'O Prince! Have you forgotten all your teachers taught you? There is no luck. Our noble conduct on the earth won us this high station, and when those actions have been rewarded fully, we will once again plummet from the sky. Even the mighty

Lord Indra, King of Heaven, shall one day fall when his merit is exhausted. Don't you see? We are prisoners of fortune. The wheel of karma spins and spins us with it, producing a series of magnificent dreams. In some, we are an insect; in others, a god; in another, a human named Philip Higgins. Each dream leads to another and to another and to another in an infinite series without rest or pause. Once a person perceives the truth of this wonder, there arises within him only one desire – to somehow, some way, get off of the wheel.'

But Rudradrishti was hardly listening. He did not want to get off the wheel. He liked heaven. There were too many lovely nymphs to fondle, worlds to conquer, scores to settle; too many carafes of *soma* to drink; too many beautiful *devis* to woo over late, delicious suppers.

In the shadows beyond the pond, something moved and the Prince started. 'What was that?'

'Fairies, *deva*. You are just . . . overtired.' She looked beyond him through a chink in the mortar at the leavings of light on the brink of the sky. 'Gods are so foolish,' she said, chiding them both. 'They've lived a million times, nay, eight times a million. They've tasted every foul excess and sweet thing under heaven, and still they are not satisfied. Still, they want *more*.' Her passion spilt, she said hollowly, almost emptily, 'What did *you* want, Rudradrishti?'

The Prince looked out at the darkling garden. White stars had filled the sky of heaven, and elves had lit their little lanterns. They glimmered and drifted in the leaves and grass. What had he wanted? Fame? He had achieved that. Power? He was a *deva*. Love? If that's what one called what the *devis* gave, the voluptuous *yakshis* and long-limbed *apsaras*. 'I wanted and got,' Rudradrishti said, 'the Queen of Heaven.'

The goddess started and opened her eyes. She stared at him in wonder. 'The *Queen*?'

'We are lovers, yes.'

'Rudradrishti!'

The fairies scattered like sparrows. The somnolent air of the temple was shattered. The goddess jumped to her feet, straightening her *sari* in a sudden fit of modesty, as if she was suddenly conscious of the maniac she entertained. 'It wasn't rape, was it?' she asked unsurely.

'Goddess,' he said, 'do I look like a raptor?'

She quieted herself with a heavenly proverb, ' "Truly, when prosperous, the arrogant become deluded." Prince Rudradrishti! What possessed you?'

That was easy, he thought. A brilliant pair of almond eyes, a teasing wit, and a pair of arms more white and fair than the ninth wave of the sea. Her breasts were large and hung in a luscious animal manner – especially when she was bending over – which was both rare and attractive in a goddess and drove Rudradrishti absolutely mad. And then, of course, there was the challenge of the conquest.

The goddess drew a curtain protectively across the temple's entrance. (The cloth, though weather-stained and threadbare, was a hundred times told lovelier than any earthly shawl.) Several frightened fairy faces peeped in from under the short-fall of the cloth. The goddess lit the stub of a candle. She sat a moment, staring into its flame. 'And do you love the Queen? Or did you simply use her to avenge your father?'

'I do love her,' Rudradrishti said. Though the knowledge of who her husband was had certainly sweetened the prize.

'And your wife. What of her?'

'Ah, Vasanta,' Rudradrishti sighed. 'For her, I am truly sorry.' It was his one real regret.

For a moment he was silent, then casting off his bitter mood, he bent and unearthed the celestial weapons. They glowed with power, and taking one up, a brilliant discus, he gathered it in his arms.

'Where are you going?'

'I don't know. Perhaps I'll flee to another world until this storm blows over.'

'That might not be for quite a while. And anyway, *devas* fare poorly in other worlds. The food and climate never suits them and, after the wonders of heaven, every other plane seems provincial and colorless, I am told. No, Prince. If you're as wise as you are beautiful, you will come with me.'

'Where?'

'To earth. Where we will serve the saints.'

'What?' He was horrified. 'And enter into a human womb? No, thank you,' he said with finality. Some of his old arrogance had returned. 'I am a god. As was my father before me. The saints serve *us*.' And shifting his weapons, he drew back the curtain to go, then softened and said, 'However, Goddess, you must grant me this. If and when your service bears fruit, come to me wherever I am – in hell, on earth, or here in heaven – that I may worship you and give you honor.'

'And you, in turn, must grant *me* a favor.'

He nodded.

'Never forsake the Princess Vasanta.'

From the moment he left the dilapidated temple and stepped into the perennial spring of the heavenly night, he knew that he was being watched. Was it only the myriad fairy people? Or was it devils crouched and waiting in the grasses with blood-smeared lips and long-toothed smiles? Or was it divine lovers trysting in the shadows? Or was it the King's *yakshas*?

A peacock called announcing the hour and Rudradrishti moved away from the lake. He moved the way a *deva* moves – with a surging grace. His instinct was to take refuge in the wilderness. There, in that desolation, even the *yakshas* would not follow, and he could live in exile with Ops, Dius Fidius, Brahma, and Mammi – and all the gods who no one loved or worshipped anymore.

It was then the first *yaksha* leaped from the bushes hitting him so hard he lost his balance. *Yakshas* two and three assaulted him from behind and the four of them tumbled backward into a frenzied ball, from out of which Prince Rudradrishti – The Potent, The Unvanquished – emerged fleeing upward, but was caught head-high and dragged by his lotus feet vertically back downward, pounced upon, manacled, and flung into a chariot waiting in the grass. Thus it is written, 'He was bound and beaten.' And thus was the *deva*, Prince Rudradrishti, captured by *yakshas* and delivered up to the King of Heaven.

Devil Dust

◆

Chapter 26

At the downstairs desk the Doctor signed a paper and received a gun – he had no idea what type or caliber – which fitted in a holster that clipped on to the back of his belt. He was in an anxious state. Every few seconds he would reach beneath his jacket and touch the gun to make sure it was still there. He thought of his friend, Rabon, coming down the mountain on top of the newly built barracks filled with celebrating soldiers. Operation Rorschach would end right there. He thought of what they would do to the girls at the airbase if Puerto Valle was not in rebel hands by morning. In the basement of the police station, their deaths would be slow, cruel, and pornographic.

He looked at his watch. It was nine fifty-seven. He was too excited to eat supper and he still had some time to kill. Restless, he began to wander, hardly aware of where he was going. The troubled night suited his mood: it was wild and blowy, the wind a constant presence. He walked for a while, aimlessly – until he looked up and found himself passing a ruined brownstone.

Higgins was sitting on a blanket on the porch. Beside him sat Sara Devi. The Doctor stopped and greeted them. Since the incident at the hospital and the subsequent recovery of the wounded boy, his feelings toward the *mestiza* girl had shifted – subtly. He still didn't believe in anything she told him – he was still convinced she was totally insane, and that Higgins was crazy along with her – but despite all this, he found he *liked* her, that his heart, despite his head, felt rather warmly toward her.

'So *there* you are,' he called to her. 'Ah ha!' and he bounded up the stairs.

'How goes it, Uncle?' Sara asked, extending her hand, which the Doctor, in a gallant and debonair gesture, kissed.

'I am well, thank you,' the Doctor said. 'I hope I am not interrupting anything.' Though even as he asked, he wondered what he could possibly be interrupting. He supposed they'd been discussing *karma*, or holding a séance or something. They were not engaged in important business like the Doctor. They were not about to liberate a country; they were not about to *kill* someone. Then he realized that Higgins hadn't spoken because Higgins wasn't really there. He was sitting up, his legs folded beneath him, but his eyes were closed, and his chin was resting on his chest. The Doctor presumed that this was meditation. He had never seen anyone meditating before, and he found himself oddly disappointed that it was not a bit more distinguished-looking – that it looked so much like forty winks or passing out on too much gin.

'And how is he doing?' the Doctor said, indicating his oblivious friend.

'He's in heaven,' Sara Devi told him.

Well, the Doctor thought, it was nice to know that someone, at least, was having a good time.

'Your patient is much better.'

'Yes, much.'

'Don't let him get his hands on any more guns, eh?' and the child's eyes strayed to the back of the Doctor's coat where his pistol was hidden.

The Doctor shook his head and laughed. 'In his condition, he is hardly a threat.'

But the child only smiled and cryptically added, 'No one's who you think they are.' Then she reached into the pile of fruit and gifts at her feet and plucked a small white bag cinched with string from among the bunches of plantains, grapes and bananas. 'Here, Uncle,' she said.

'What is it?' the Doctor asked, pleased by the little present.

'Devil dust.' She leaned forward and her eyes flared like flames. 'If ever you encounter a vicious black devil with red eyes and white fangs . . . don't worry! Just reach in your pocket and take a pinch of this, sprinkle it on him, and the fiend will become your friend.'

There was a corpse of a smile on the Doctor's lips where his happiness had died. He had sincerely tried to relate to these people – he really had – but they defeated him at every turn. 'Devil dust?' the Doctor asked. She was kidding, wasn't she? It was all some kind of childish game. But no, she was not smiling. 'Well, yes. Well, thank you.' The Doctor took the bag, laughed, and tucked it in his pocket, getting set to go. For he had to be leaving. It was nice to have met her and so, *so* good – ha, ha, ha – to have seen Higgins again (even if Higgins did not see him.) But now, he was busy, busy – he had *mucho* important business to attend. He had to, he almost said, murder someone. Goodbye, goodbye, and in another moment – O don't bother to get up – the Doctor was headed down the stoop and was walking as fast as his long legs would carry him, away from this cell of religious lunacy, this hive of psychotic and deviate vibrations.

Devil dust! He should have been amused, but he was disgusted. Devil dust, indeed!

The King Of Heaven

◆

Chapter 27

The court of the King of Heaven was in a high meadow surrounded by colorful flags that sung in the wind. Lanterns marked the court's circumference, but as was the custom, lights were kept low, for while light is the friend of ordinary beings, darkness is the friend of things that shine, and the *devas* shone with a fluttering effulgence that made even the least of them wondrous to behold.

It was before this divine assembly that Rudradrishti was now led by the three *yakshas* that had captured him. At the sight of the Prince a cry went through the gathering, a ripple of excitement and dismay. But the Prince, despite his wounds and bonds, was calm and poised as he stood before the court. First, he turned and bowed to the Queen. Then he turned to the King and said, pleasantly enough, 'Your Majesty, I understand you wish to speak with me.'

Some of the celestials laughed aloud at this further piece of insolence. They fell silent, however, as Rudradrishti was confronted with the evidence of his treason.

'King, let's dispatch with talk of treason, shall we? My father is your enemy. Whose side should his son take? It's not treason that's the issue here, but that the Queen and I are lovers.'

A gasp went through the gathering, followed by several lascivious leers. The Queen, whose face was pale and strained, blushed at his confession, becoming in that instant a hundred times more delicious, like a ripening apple, or a lotus bud opening in the sun.

The directness of Rudradrishti's response set the King choking in anger and pain. Attempting to control himself, he turned to the Queen and softly begged, 'Tell me, my Lady, it isn't true. Tell me it is only Rudradrishti attempting to provoke me, and we will speak of it no more.'

The denizens of heaven awaited her answer. But the Queen lowered her eyes and said, 'It is true, my Lord.'

The pain that flashed in Indra's eyes hurt even Rudra's heart to see, and for a moment some of his old arrogance left him. Then the King's face hardened. He commanded the Queen to step down from her throne and to stand beside her lover. Then Lord Indra, King of Heaven, drew himself up and grasped the scepter of his rule. 'The two of you have made your bed in heaven, now you may lie in it in hell. For every night you spent in adulterous embrace, you will spend a year in the nether regions.'

A shudder went through the celestials, then a murmur and a buzz, as the royal wazir leaned over and consulted with the King. The wazir must have had a demon in his family, for his hands were curving yellow claws. It was he who held the power here, though rarely had Rudradrishti heard him speak; always he whispered in the King's left ear, returning to his hookah then with an enigmatic smile and moistened lips.

The King sighed and said, 'My minister beseeches me to lighten your sentence. Hell, he feels, is not a fitting place for gods. So, in deference to him, instead of hell, I charge you be confined to earth.'

'May your mercy be rewarded,' said the Queen. But Rudradrishti only frowned. 'I'm afraid it's not like that, my lady. And the King knows it. In hell, fresh karma is impossible to accrue. You suffer pain and burn off sins. And when those sins are fully paid, your sentence ends. But on earth each action is like the planting of a seed which someday must ripen and bear fruit. A bed in hell would be a blessing in comparison, for if we descend to earth as human beings, we will become so embroiled in human destiny that it will be millennia, if ever, before we return'.

At this, the Queen began to weep. Rudradrishti didn't blame her. At the thought of their misfortune, he felt like weeping too.

'Silence,' the King said, bitterly. 'I am not done. And so that the two of you are not too glad in your earthly exile – for even those on earth taste fleeting joys – I will send you a reminder of my displeasure.' And at his word, in a cloud of smoke, three monstrous *rakshasas* appeared.

The *devis* shrieked and clapped their hands to their faces, for the sight and stench of the devils was enough to make one gag. The first was nothing but a gaping mouth, a huge maw studded with tusks and bristles and filled with slashing teeth and gushing streams of boiling hot saliva.

The second, you could barely see. It was like a wraith, a shadow, a piece of broken glass, a flap of skin viewed sideways, something you hallucinate after drinking poison.

The third looked like a monstrous pup, except it wore a necklace of hearts and heads.

An infernal entourage of imps and goblins accompanied these three, boiling out now from beneath their masters' robes. One imp overturned a beaker of nectar for no other purpose than to watch it spill, while another one gnawed at a *deva*'s supper and, when cuffed for its insolence, gave a hideous squeal and emptied its bowels on the plate of food. A third sort of gnome was winged like a gargoyle.

'Now,' the King said, 'take them away.'

'Wait, my Prince. I am going with you.' It was Rudradrishti's wife, Vasanta, who, thus far, had been looking on in silence. And for the first time since his capture, Rudra felt a miserable shame. 'A wife,' Vasanta said, 'should be with her husband. And I am your wife, O Prince, whether you want me or not.'

'Vasanta, please; don't be a fool,' Rudradrishti said.

'Perhaps, I *was* a fool to marry you. But now that I have, I would be a bigger fool to wait for your return.' She took his arm, proprietorially.

The Queen took Rudra's *other* arm and, stamping her foot in pique, asked, 'Whom do you love? Her or me?'

Rudra looked at the Queen of Heaven. Her impassioned face was more lovely than that of any living creature, and was moist and heated now as at the height of their amours. Her eyes were like drowsing black bees, her breasts were smeared with sandalwood paste, while her navel was a pool in which a man or god could drown his mind.

Then he turned to his beloved wife. She was no less lovely though in a different way, lovely the way the light is lovely, or the first snow; moving as a memory; satisfying as an answer; sweeter than the cider offered to him at the end of every earthly summer. It was impossible to choose. He loved them both in different ways. He had never thought that it would come to this. He had only wanted to have the Queen and never in his wildest dreams had he thought it would lead to their downfall and exile. For Rudradrishti was about to fall, to lose heaven and all that he had gained. He could not choose. 'I love you both,' he said. 'Both of you shall come with me.'

'Then I will go, too,' a voice declaimed, as a tall, comely *deva* with a bristling moustache stepped forth from the crowd.

It was Rudradrishti's brother, Kshemaraja. Though he had played no part in the attempted coup, he had refused to fight against his father, and as a result had fallen into disfavor with the King.

'Go right ahead,' the King rejoined, clearly glad to be rid of the entire treacherous clan. 'Take them away.'

But Rudradrishti did not stir. He said, 'O Lord, you have cursed us most cruelly. I beg you to remove this curse.'

'Begging for mercy, Rudradrishti? Tell me why I should show you mercy.'

'Because you are a great King, O Maharaj. And the greatness of a monarch is measured by his compassion even more than by his strength of arms.'

This answer gave the King a moment's pause. Then he smiled grimly and said, 'You know that even if I wished to,

Prince, I could not do it. Once a curse is voiced, it cannot be removed. Take them away.'

But Kshemaraja's and Vasanta's loyalty had struck a nerve, and incredibly, a small exodus of rebel angels followed. Kshemaraja's wife joined her husband, bearing their infant daughter, as did his loyal *yaksha* servant with his muscular arms and minuscule white moustache. The fairy attendants of the Queen followed suit, scurrying like windblown leaves and taking refuge in the folds of their mistress's *sari*, from out which the three of them peeked at the assembly with faces at once wizened and childish, frightened and bold.

In the end, there were ten who chose to go – plus the three *rakshasas* and innumerable gnomes.

'All right, then,' Rudradrishti insisted, 'if you will not lift this curse from us, then you must at least tell us how it may end.'

The divine sibyl was helped to her feet. As usual, she was drunk on nectar and could hardly stand. 'This curse will end, O Rudradrishti, when beauty poisons ugliness. And the least defeats the first.'

But Rudradrishti only muttered in disgust. As always with these damnable prophecies, it took some work to figure them out. Surely, the most beautiful among them was the Queen of Heaven; the ugliest, the monstrous maw. Similarly, who the first of the *devas* was there was no doubt. They were in his court. But the least of them? Rudradrishti looked around at his band of falling angels. His eyes fell on his brother's wife who held her tiny blonde daughter in her arms – a *devi* barely three years old. Here, perhaps, was the least of their tribe. But the idea that this sweet weak female might someday grow strong and fierce enough to overthrow the Lord of Heaven was absurd. Rudradrishti's father had not succeeded, backed by a full rebel army. And Rudra felt his spirits fail.

Just then, there was the sound of thunder; all of heaven began to tremble and looking up Rudra saw a sight that filled even a god with awe. A fissure had cleft the floor of heaven, and from out of it an army was pouring from the depths of hell into the celestial evening. They were being rescued, saved, by his father's rebel army!

But Rudra's joy was premature, for he saw now that none of them bore arms. A second army of fiends and *Yakshas* was driving them up from the bowels of hell, while a group of *devas* in war chariots, floated overhead blasting with thunderbolts any prisoner mad enough to flee.

Rudra watched the brilliant cloud of rebel gods still forming in the night. Some looked happy; some looked sad; others seemed like animals kept in cages longer than their spirits would allow. And then, even as he watched them rise, they began to fall – not back into hell, as he had feared, but down into empty space. And as the rebel angels fell, Rudra could see the stars and planets far below them like shining bubbles in the cosmic ink, and far below that, like a blue and white pebble, Earth.

Rudra turned and embraced his queens. The Queen seemed terrified; his wife resigned. Then the ground split at his feet and he, too, began to fall into the inky void. And as they fell, a *yaksha* hurled a pail of nectar after him, splashing his face.

The instant he felt the nectar touch, he looked about him – but there was no heaven, no *devas*, no nectar, no queens. He was on a porch somewhere, beneath a starlit night, and for one indescribably disorienting instant, he had no idea who or what or where he was. The fabric of reality had been rent. Was he a man dreaming he was a *deva*, or was he a god dreaming he was a man?

Then he looked at Sara Devi. He touched his face; it was dripping wet. His flight, the court, the Queen of Heaven . . . he had seen them all in the instant it takes a cup of water to travel through the air! He shook his head and wiped his eyes. 'What I saw . . . was it true?'

Sara Devi scrunched her nose. And yet, even as he asked, he could still envision the sky of heaven, and see his brother Kshemaraja's face, which, he realized now, looked remarkably like the Doctor's. Many other *devas* he recognized as well. More importantly, Higgins had seen the faces of his enemies. He knew who they were.

Puerto Valle

♦

Chapter 28

It had not been a happy journey – though at times the trek had had a kind of terrifying beauty. Led by the two *Indio* boys, they had followed a track cut into the face of the hills, a spiral path that was less a trail than a scratch in the rock, a faint blaze in the vegetation. One false step and you slid to your doom down a dim green steep of rain-slicked ferns, below which silvery ropes of water plummeted into lush green valleys, and vultures slid like flying crosses.

Now and then, they came upon an Indian village, and whenever they did, they adopted the strategy Rabon had devised to discourage the Indians from reporting their presence: reaching in their knapsacks, they donned Halloween masks. The Indians' faces – wide, frightened eyes framed by two blue-black falls of hair – reflected their evil appearance better than any mirror, as a hundred armed devils with the faces of Woody Woodpecker, Batman, and Mickey Mouse paraded through their village.

Soon, the villages became deserted, save for a scorched cookpot bubbling over a greenwood fire – a peace offering to the evil ones – as beyond the huts in the tangled forest, savage shapes and copper faces shifted in the sunflecked leaves and watched while the spirits rested, pushing their monstrous faces up upon their brows to reveal beneath them other faces that were even more hideous and bizarre. The spirits ate,

411

smoked, and rested, dipping their spoons into the bubbling pot. And then, leaving behind some pieces of silver, they disappeared into the mountainous night.

Now within a thousand yards of their destination, they had been stopped by planes. All morning the planes had circled the volcano, as though they were searching for something, as though they knew that they were there. There were two of them, Cessna C–40s, sleek silver birds glimmering in the sunlight. After a week in the jungle, their man-made lines seemed to Garcia unnatural and surreal.

Suddenly, a Cobra gunship came over the volcano's cone, flying so low Garcia could almost see the tartar on the gunner's teeth – all of this air activity keeping them pinned to the rim of the jungle, unable to cross the grassy meadow that led to the cliffs above Puerto Valle. Garcia knew they could not stay this way forever, their faces pressed into the earth. Already, some of the men were groaning with cramps and hunger. It was noon time; they had traveled all night. They would attack at four the next morning, and they had not eaten since the previous evening.

Then, mercifully, a cloud appeared and, within minutes, blanketed the summit. Hidden from the planes, the men sat up, stretched, and began lighting fires to cook tea. But no sooner had the *maté* scalded their tongues than their scouts reported several men from a small government lookout at the top of the mountain headed in their direction. Ambushing them would have been easy, except that they could not risk the chance of gunfire exposing their position. Their only recourse, Garcia knew, was to retreat back into the jungle.

So why, he wondered now, was Commander Rabon leading them forward in the opposite direction? Under cover of the cloud, they were moving out across the grassy savannah and up the bare slope of the volcano itself – until they were poised on the very rim of the crater.

Garcia felt extremely uneasy. Their position was untenable. There was no cover here – only a floor of hard, smooth, lichen-covered lava. He could not imagine what Rabon had in mind. At any moment the clouds might lift, leaving them exposed on the top of the mountain at the mercy of the planes and the deadly gunship.

Then, to his amazement, they began to descend – not back down the mountain as he had imagined, but down . . . down into the mouth of the volcano itself!

It was not the descent that Garcia found so difficult, though the inside of the crater was slippery with rivulets and mud. It was the *idea* of the thing that terrified him. The volcano's mouth was clogged with clouds, like a cotton plug in the neck of a bottle, and now as they descended through it, the mist was so thick that for several minutes he could see little more than the disembodied head of the man below him and the legless boots of the man above. Grabbing vines and bushes and finding footholds as best they could, uttering groans and obscenities as their packs and weapons snagged on roots and creepers, the band half crawled, half slipped and fell down into the volcano's depths.

Then they were beneath the cap of clouds and in another world entirely. The weird half-light that filtered down revealed a green, steaming, streaming realm of giant ferns, little pink geckos, and dripping tropical vegetation relieved only by the luminous plumage of long-winged birds soaring through cathedral spaces, and the silver braids of distant streams.

Garcia was instantly drenched in sweat. It was more then the exertion of the descent. The air was a steam bath. He felt like a worm trapped in a terrarium, and half expected, at any moment, some enormous face to peer into the crater and ogle them with curiosity. But the luminous blanket of clouds that hid them, though seething, remained unbroken.

The men pitched camp on a series of narrow ledges. Far below them, the inner walls of the crater fell away, culminating in a group of massive primordial-looking rocks through which steam escaped from the lowest depths.

Then they heard the throbbing *vibrato* of the gunship. They watched its shadow hover above the crater. Garcia wiped the sweat from his eyes and waited. If the damn thing decided to drop through the clouds . . .

The first body almost hit him. He thought at first that one of the men above him had slipped and fallen. But looking up, he saw a second body falling through the clouds and watched as a prisoner, his eyes wide, his hands tied behind his back, fell past him, screaming. For an instant, their eyes locked. Then the man hit the wall and his screaming stopped. He bounced in slow motion, and plunged silently now down into the very center of the earth.

Garcia turned his face away and called upon the Blessed Virgin. He wondered what the man had thought, in his final moments, seeing Garcia clinging to the volcano's inner wall. Garcia waited, staring up through the clouds, but there were no more executions.

Eventually, he fell asleep. When he awoke it was early evening, and the men were already beginning to ascend. Claustrophobic, he clamored after them, anxious to get out.

Back upon the surface, he felt reborn. He was in love with the kissing winds, the shining air, and the sight of the evening sun setting beyond the purple mountains.

He was eating his rations when a scout approached. An Indian woman was following them, he said. She was camped a little ways off, watching their every move.

'See what she wants.'

'I did, my Captain.'

'Well, what does she say?'

The scout seemed tongue-tied, nervous. 'She wants *you*, sir.'

'Me?'

Garcia stood up and looked at the woman across the savannah. She was seated on a blanket about fifty yards away, smoking a pipe. She looked at first like a thousand other Indian women, with her flat leathern face, a black rope of hair flung down her back, and black button eyes – though on a closer look he saw that she was really quite handsome – and vaguely familiar. 'Bring her here.'

The scout hurried off and, in a few minutes' time, returned with the woman. She was at once dignified, excited and shy. She stared at Garcia wonderingly, though when their eyes met, she looked away. She mumbled something in her native tongue. 'She says,' the scout repeated, 'it has been a long, long time. But she knew you would come back to her someday as you promised.'

'I did?'

The woman, growing bolder, looked up at him and said: 'You married me, then deserted me! Why? I loved you so. For twenty years I wore your picture on a locket at my throat, the way other women wear the image of their Saviour.'

'This is incredible!' Garcia said, leaping to his feet. 'I don't believe her. Ask her what proof she has?'

The woman smiled in a way he almost recognized. And opening her locket then, Garcia stared into the face of his youth.

We Meet Again

◆

Chapter 29

Higgins knew now exactly what he had to do and he did it quickly for he didn't have much time. He telephoned Crespi and insisted on their meeting at eleven that evening in the Italian restaurant where they had met before. He overruled the agent's protestations with news the shipment was flying out that very evening, and there were a number of last-minute details to confirm.

Next, Higgins called his Cayman banker. He had to drag the man from a Georgetown dinner party to do it, but the size of the account Higgins opened with his bank must have more than made up for any social embarrassment. Then Higgins phoned a bistro in Nice, and for forty-five minutes argued intensely, in fractured French, with a man who appeared to be both very drunk and stupid. Higgins told the man that he wanted the product shipped out at once – while the man argued with a classical Gallic obstinacy and phlegm, that it was past midnight there, and that he didn't see why, in the name of the Virgin, it couldn't wait until tomorrow evening. In the end, Higgins had to wonder if the man was half as stupid as he seemed, for Higgins had wound up paying him a great deal more than he had expected to – though not before extracting from him a solemn oath, on his mother's grave, that the 'peanuts,' minus a few items which had still not arrived, would be flown out of the Marseilles warehouse before dawn broke above the Rhône.

Then Higgins made a few more phonecalls – to tie up some loose ends – and when he was finished, it was time for the meeting. He walked directly to the restaurant. There was no reason not to. In all his travels, he had not once been followed – and there was no one, he was certain, who was following him now.

Higgins arrived a few minutes early. Crespi was not yet there. He spoke with one of the waiters, instructing him in what he wanted, then took a seat at the bar. It was a glorified service bar with a few highbacked and cushioned barstools around it. The restaurant was busy. The bartender had his hands full drawing beer and mixing drinks for the house. Higgins studied the bottles – but ended up ordering a *cappuchino*. At eleven precisely, a cab pulled up and Crespi entered. He seemed annoyed, at first, by the sudden summons, but Higgins pretended not to notice, plying him instead with half a dozen essential questions which the accelerated timetable required be answered – including where, precisely, he wanted the plane to land. The airport at Puerto Valle was controlled by the Junta; Higgins received the coordinates of another landing strip in a rebel-held province. Then he asked Crespi to meet him again at 5 a.m. the next morning at a private airstrip just outside of Newark.

'What the hell for?'

'I have something to show you.'

Crespi raised his gray eyebrows in alarm. 'You're not thinking of bringing it in *here*, are you? I mean, that would be . . .'

'Look,' Higgins said, acting gravely insulted, 'what do you think, I'm a *complete* asshole?' Then he softened and smiled. 'I got something for you – a little surprise.'

'What surprise?'

'You go shopping, you sometimes run into bargains, don't you? Well, I ran into a doozy. I couldn't resist buying it.' He grinned. 'I think you guys are gonna like it.'

Crespi stared at him. Higgins could almost hear the gears

417

and ratchets whirring behind his eyes as he tried to imagine what it was that Higgins had acquired. Higgins watched him as he mentally chose and discarded a dozen possibilities. Then suddenly, with a look of interest, he whispered, 'Chemical?'

'Jesus!' Higgins said, slumping in his seat, and letting his eyes roll toward the ceiling. 'It's *peanuts*,' he hissed. '*Peanuts*, remember?'

'Philip, is it really you? Philip Higgins?'

Higgins swiveled in his chair.

'Well, I'll be! It's Bradford Buck!' It was the classmate he had talked to on the phone the other day.

'In the flesh.'

'Gee, how the hell are you?' Higgins asked, warmly shaking the stranger's hand. 'My God. How many years has it been?'

'Let's not count them.' Buck laughed, then turned his gaze expectantly to Crespi.

'This is, uh . . . Carlos Castaneda,' Higgins said. Stupid, he thought; but it was the first Spanish name that jumped into his head. '*Doctor* Castaneda.'

'Doctor,' Buck said, and bowed slightly sticking out his hand. 'Is it possible we've met?' There was almost an elderly frailty to his movements; his hair was a cloud of fine spun gold.

Crespi held out a hand, clawed and knobbed with arthritis. 'Never.' They shook.

'So, Brad,' Higgins said, shaking his head. 'It's great to see you. What are you up to?'

'Me? Oh, same old thing I got into after college. Working for the Institute.'

'Institute?'

'Of East-West Studies. Think tank. And you?'

'I'm in business.'

Buck frowned slightly. 'Did you have a book published recently? I thought I read in *The Bulletin* . . .'

'Yeah, Sanskrit poetry,' Higgins said. 'It's not exactly burning up the charts.'

Buck laughed.

'Look,' Higgins said, 'I wish to hell we could stay and chat, but . . .'

'You're not *leaving* are you . . . ?'

'Sorry, Brad. Some other time? I'll give you a ring at your think tank, huh?' And Higgins threw a bill on the bar to pay for the undrunk *cappuchino*.

'Well, then, Philip,' Buck said stiffly, clearly miffed that Higgins was rushing off so fast. He ran a long freckled hand through the cloud of feathery gold. 'Nice to have met you, Doctor Castaneda. Perhaps, some other time.'

Crespi only nodded. 'Friend of yours?' he asked when they'd reached the door.

'Just some guy I went to college with. Haven't seen the dude in fifteen years.'

'Funny you running into him tonight.'

'Funny? What's so funny about it? You know how this town is. Take your honey to some party at Lincoln Center, and the lady who's greeting the guests at the door turns out to be your wife!'

The remark did not have quite the effect he'd intended. It was meant to foster a sense of *macho* pride and male bonding. But Crespi only frowned at Higgins, as if such camaraderie was the last thing on his mind right now. 'You're awfully calm for a man who's about to conclude a five-million-dollar deal.'

'Why not?' Higgins asked with the same cocky air he'd employed all along. 'And it's seven,' he corrected, 'with the new goodies.'

Higgins hailed a cab for Crespi, and gave him the name of the airport where they'd meet in the morning. He waited until the agent's car drove off and his schoolchum, Buck, departed the bar, then went back in to tip the waiter.

Beware Of The Dog

◆

Chapter 30

On the way to La Club, the Doctor stopped at the hospital once more to look in on the wounded boy. The child was sleeping. The Doctor observed the ugly pink scar tissue already forming around the eye, the empty socket puckered and drawn. He sat down on the edge of the bed and rested, immensely weary, though his mission was still before him. Then the boy, in his sleep, did a curious thing: he moaned and curled his arm around the Doctor's waist, snuggling up against him. The Doctor smiled. The boy was probably dreaming of his sweetheart or his mother.

For a long while, afraid of waking the sleeping child, the Doctor sat quietly, gazing out at the colored lights with which the *barrio* was festooned. He wished, at that moment, he had not given up smoking. He would have liked to go somewhere where the lights were low and a sad saxophone was blowing softly, and smoke a cigarette, very slowly, with a glass of rum. He imagined all his cares and worries dissipating into the misty swirls of smoke and sound. He thought of Jane, and of the life they might yet have together. He saw them living in a European city where the men were bearded, the women beautiful and chic. They were sitting on a balcony after dinner, peeling oranges and drinking wine while a breathless saxophone played on the phonograph and the sun sank beneath the sea.

But when the Doctor looked at his watch again, it was already eleven thirty. He shook himself awake; he had forgotten where he was. He disengaged himself from the boy's embrace and left the hospital, rehearsing on his way the lie he'd tell to *El Duende*.

El Duende was sitting in his upholstered throne, receiving a back rub from Jane, when the Doctor called. 'What do you want?' He was clearly annoyed by the interruption.

'General Cereno's retreat is not real. It's a feint. As soon as you let down your guard, he's going to come back and hit you with everything he's got.'

El Duende looked at him warily and said, 'This afternoon you told us just the opposite, Doctor.'

'I was deceived myself. You know Benitez. He is highly secretive.'

'And difficult to kill.'

'Whose fault is that?' the Doctor asked. 'He was sitting at his desk when I left the room, two feet from the damn thing. How was I to know, in the moments it took me to press the trigger, he would be answering the call of nature?'

El Duende looked at the Doctor. 'And so *now* you say the attack is on.'

'I understand,' the Doctor nodded, 'that if it bogs down, it will be supported by warplanes from the USS *Nimitz*!'

'What?'

The Doctor smiled. 'What did you think the Undersecretary and Benitez have been discussing all this time? Baseball?'

El Duende rose to the bait. The Doctor saw it. He came halfway up out of his chair, took the intelligence in, and tasted it. Then, like the big old crafty catfish that had lived in a hole behind the Cuban *finca*, he spat it out before the hook was set. 'Nonsense,' he said. 'The US would never get involved.'

The Doctor shrugged – he would play this one softly. 'I am only reporting to you the intelligence I have overheard. It's up to you, of course, to decide upon its merits.'

Again *El Duende* looked at him long and hard. For a moment the Doctor could almost see scales inside the man weighing his words, could almost hear the ticking of the microchips as the data was taken in, processed and recorded, or perhaps, in *El Duende*'s case, it was more like the whispering beads of an abacus. Then, at last, the computation was completed, and the scales tilted – in disbelief.

'You are a liar, Doctor and, I think, a spy. And so is your little *puta*!' And turning in his chair, *El Duende* grabbed Janie by her ear.

'Owww! Let go of me.'

'You will stop that now,' the Doctor said.

'Stop it?' *El Duende* asked. 'Don't you think I've been watching you two? Don't you think I know where she goes when she leaves me?'

'We are . . . in love,' the Doctor said.

'In love! Ha! With a whore? Mucho will show the two of you love! And then maybe we'll get a few straight answers.'

Mucho, summoned, rose from his chair and grinned.

'All right, gentlemen,' the Doctor sighed. 'That's it. Back off. Let her go, Fatso, or I'll blow your head off.' And cooly, confidently, he reached behind him for his gun.

Only – son of a bitch! – the gun wasn't there! It *had* to be there! He scrabbled at his belt, but the holster remained confoundedly empty.

For a moment, no one knew what to do. Mucho was frozen in mid-stride, while *El Duende* stared at the Doctor in confusion. Then the Doctor, feeling a kind of idiotic crimson shame burning his face and body, feinted to the left, then broke for the back stairwell, tilting the awkward Mucho over on his rear.

The Doctor had a good head start. *El Duende* was too fat to rise unaided from the chair, and as the Doctor fled, he saw Mucho stagger to his feet, only to go down again as Janie tripped him.

The Doctor ran, as fast as he could. He ran for his life, and for the lives of them all – for Benitez, Garcia, Rabon and all the peasant souls and soldiers in Dorado. He fled, blindly, wildly, into the gray maze of cellar rooms, past a sign which read, 'Beware of the Dog!' and another reading, 'Warning! Poison!' He made a left, two rights, another left and right, then ran a hundred yards down a long narrow corridor, turned one last corner and slowed to a halt. He listened, but there was no one behind him. He had lost them. Unfortunately, he had also lost himself. Where were the stairs that led to the street? Panting, the Doctor hurried on, thinking that at any moment he would recognize something, but though he wandered for several minutes he could not seem to get his bearings. A dim room full of broken furniture gave in turn on strange stone arches and a set of locked steel doors which, though the Doctor pried at them until his fingers bled, he could not open.

The Doctor turned back now, beginning to panic, for time was running out. What had he done? He had blown it. He felt fear, yes, but fear mixed with a bitter shame that he had failed Benitez and run away – leaving Jane with *El Duende*.

Frantically, he tried several more doors. One of them opened on a small windowless chamber with a cot and several pin-ups on the wall. He slipped inside and closed the door behind him. He did not feel well at all. He sat down on the cot and almost without warning vomited, twice. No sooner had he emptied his stomach than an eerie singing filled the room and for a moment he had the irrational thought that he was in the presence of an evil spirit. Then he saw the pinscher rising from a corner. The animal's eyes were starving. How long the dog had been imprisoned here, he could only guess. The beast had been lying in its own waste. Strings of dried spittle hung from its jowls. Unsteadily, it approached the vomit and began to feed upon the vile pool, lapping it up in no time at all, all the while crooning in an eerie falsetto from some center deep inside its throat. Then when he was finished, the dog began to sing another song, this one equally mad and bizarre, all about the softness of the Doctor's throat and how the Doctor's blood would taste – squirting salty hot and fresh – as it drank from his neck. The Doctor stood up. 'Good dog, good doggie,' he said. But the beast only crouched, getting ready to spring. The Doctor glanced toward the door, but knew he could never reach it in time. He stretched out a hand and started to back pedal, looking for something to interpose between his throat and the creature's fangs, when suddenly he remembered something, 'If ever you encounter a vicious black devil with red eyes and white fangs . . .' Yes! And fumbling in his jacket pocket, he withdrew the little paper packet given him by Sara Devi, ripped it open, and flung its contents into the air – with a gesture not unlike Tinkerbell.

The effect was instantaneous. The pinscher rose upon its haunches, sniffing at the falling powder. Then as the magic flakes descended, he canceled his plans to eat the Doctor and began to roll upon the floor instead. The Doctor, breathing deeply, stepped from the room, as the dog followed, his stub of a tail wagging, his manner quite reformed. The Doctor gave him another pinch of the magic powder, then reached in his coat and fed him a cough drop, which he devoured. Gingerly, the Doctor patted his sleek black skull, and a moment later he had a friend for life: a vile-smelling, homicidal friend with fangs, but a friend all the same. And at that moment, he knew, the Doctor could use all the friends he could get.

The Doctor commanded the creature by name. 'Satan, come.' But the dog stood motionless, deaf and unheeding. The Doctor had an inspiration. 'Satan, *venca*.' And at once, the animal sprang into motion. The dog wasn't stupid: he understood Spanish, was all!

The Doctor and his new companion moved quickly and quietly back down the hallway. The first couple of doors the dog ignored, but at the third he stopped, sniffed, and pawed with interest. The Doctor gently tried the knob. It opened on a telex machine. An operator with earphones was sending a message. The Doctor could not believe his good fortune. It was the very room he had been looking for! The dog entered first and the Doctor followed, closing the door behind them.

'Who are you?' the operator said.

'I am Dr. Castellano, and this is Satan. We have a message for General Cuzo in Puerto Valle.'

'Sorry, buddy,' the man said. He was an *Anglo*. 'I take my orders from Colonel Schmidt.'

'Schmidt, is it?' The Doctor smiled. 'You see this dog? He has eaten nothing in seventy-two hours. Also, he has been trained to go for the throat. If I command him to attack you and he opens your carotid artery, you will be dead and bloodless in two minutes flat. Though I am a doctor, I will do nothing to save you. Satan, *matalo!*'

The dog's ears flattened and, fixing on the man, it began to hiss like a snake.

'What did you tell it?'

'*Matar*? In your language, "murder!" Now shall we send the message?'

The man, still watching the pinscher, asked unsurely, 'Where's it going?'

'Commander Cuzo, Puerto Valle.'

There was a sound behind them. The Doctor swivelled. Omar stood in the doorway, holding a pistol.

'*Matalo!*' The Doctor ordered.

Satan sprang. Omar fired. Dog and bullet merged in mid-air.

Poison

◆

Chapter 31

'If you don't have something, you yearn for it. Then as soon as you get it, you worry about losing it. I was like a man possessed of an enormous treasure who, just before he gets to cash it in, has to watch his wealth disintegrate before his eyes, his emeralds soften and turn to jelly, his diamonds powder and blow away as dust. This was me and my beauty. Do you know how that feels? Of course, not. You don't look a day over twenty. Why don't you say something?'

'Shut up, Ma, will ya? I'm tryna think.'

Gil got up and went into the bedroom. She'd been listening to the maudlin soliloquy all evening. Her mother-in-law was about to drive her mad. She looked down on her sleeping daughters. And as she did so, she glimpsed herself in the lamp-lit window. Though she was profoundly agitated, she did not show it on the surface. She appeared beautifully collected, marvellously composed. She reminded herself of those tortured souls who decide at last to end their lives. No sooner, they say, is this decision reached, than their torments cease and they become unreachably and inviolately calm.

But Gil's torments hadn't ceased, rather they had peaked at last. She had been abandoned now, or so it felt. Her brother had not been mentally present for months. Then, Garcia had left – for parts unknown. While lately, even Higgins had been absent – she watched him from the window feeding handfuls of change into phonebooths on the corner as though they were slot machines, sometimes for half the morning. And then he would disappear for days at a time, only to return in a rumpled suit, with gifts for the children, a passionate embrace, and absolutely no explanation.

There was the guard, of course, who Benitez had loaned them to replace Garcia – but the man was a loser. His uniform didn't fit him, and he only shaved every few days. Gil had tried to impress upon him the danger and urgency of his duty, explaining that at any moment armed men might storm the house, but the man seemed unaroused by this warning, paying far more attention to the shape of her buttocks and to the cigarettes and coffee she brought him for breakfast. She looked forlornly out the window, but she couldn't even see the joker now.

Gil tied a kerchief round her head, checked her purse and applied some lipstick. Then she looked once more at her sleeping children. She wondered if she would ever see them again. She kissed them all, but couldn't bear to say goodbye. She went back out to the kitchen and opened the door.

Rosita sighed. 'I was a fool. I married young for love.'

'Yeah?'

'Instead of late. For money.'

'Don't wait up for me, Ma, will ya?' Gil said. 'I might be late.' Then she closed the door behind her.

Outside, it was a wild autumn evening with a river wind that toiled in the streets, ceaselessly gathering and scattering, arranging and rearranging the fallen leaves. The dry leaves rasped in the gutters, while windblown trash cans rattled and banged and rolled in the mews and alleyways like tin drums, and you could smell winter in the air, and the musty odor of the powdering leaves and the acrid smoke from carts of coals where chestnut vendors hawked their wares.

Gil wondered where she was going on such a wild and wooly evening. Then she realized she was headed for the Black Hen. And yet even as she walked there, she marveled at her resolution. It reminded her of something Higgins once told her: how man does nothing, God does all. She had not understood that – until this instant. For only a couple of minutes before, some powerful will inside of her had overcome her fear and terror, picked her up from the kitchen table, and pushed her out into the windy street. Though whatever this will was, she certainly wouldn't have called it God.

But then again, it wasn't Gil either. She, Gil, was not that brave. She, Gil, only wanted to sit in the circle of lamplight listening to the wind whip the city, commiserating with Rosita, victimized, sick with dread.

But the one inside her wouldn't let her. It didn't give a shit about wind or lamplight, but was interested only in doing its duty, in doing what it had to do, which was not like it sounded – moralistic and Republican – for its duty was less a mental construct than a burning and visceral urge. And what it wanted now was Dante Guzman.

La Negra Polla, this weekend evening, had reached the summits of buffoonery. Two old men made up as women were dancing with each other, while a real woman danced with a huge, shaggy dog. *La Polla*'s patrons seemed to find this sight enthralling. They laughed and cawed above the music, banging their assorted canes and casts and crutches on the bar.

Gil pushed past the crowd at the door and asked the young bartender for *Señor* Guzman. The boy replied that he had not seen Guzman since early morning. Gil asked the boy to go below to Guzman's quarters and announce that Gilberta Castellano wished to see him. Her tone left little room for refusal. Ordering a tequila, she sat down at the bar to wait.

Gil was acutely conscious of the many eyes upon her. Some were inquisitive, others lecherous, others so acidic they seemed to want to eat her soul. She refused to be intimidated. She forced herself to look into them and to glance about the wretched tavern. She spied the child who waited tables seated at a table with several men. Gil almost didn't recognize her. False lashes and an oversized red mouth made her look at once pathetic and bizarre.

Gil tried to catch the child's eye, but the child looked

428

through her, as if Gil was non-existent. Gil glanced back at the dancing creatures and noted, with horror, that the dog had a glistening lavender erection. That's why *La Pollo*'s patrons were shrieking!

Shuddering, she turned away and looked down at her drink. She was not about to put the unclean vessel to her lips. She tried to think of something else, something that didn't sicken or unnerve her. She thought of Higgins. She liked his temperature, his *Anglo* cool. He wasn't *hot* like a Latin. He didn't brag and shout about whatever it was that he was doing, didn't posture in the kitchen like her brother, who seemed to think he was Che Guevara, or even act like Garcia, who the morning he was leaving her had a foolish light in his eyes, as if he was going on a mission for God.

She was touched, too, by his devotion – not to her, but to some higher power – something she had hardly thought she'd find attractive in a man. Several times, late at night, she had stepped into his room only to find him kneeling before his little altar, not upright like she knelt in church, but seated back upon his haunches. He had not heard her even when she called his name, and she'd been amazed to find him so deeply absorbed.

And now, for some reason, Gil remembered something he had told her once, how one morning, in meditation, a ghostly trap had opened in his palate, and several drops of the most exquisite liquor had fallen on his tongue.

It sounded, she'd told him, like post-nasal drip. Then, realizing she was being a bitch, she'd asked him what he thought it was, and Higgins had said he thought it was nectar.

El nectar. Ah, yes. The drink of the gods. In Spanish and in English it was the same. Not to be confused with ambrosia, what deities eat. 'There lives shee with the blessed Gods in blisse, there drinks shee Nectar with Ambrosia mixt . . .' Shakespeare? No, Spenser. She had known the whole thing once and had recited it to great effect.

The bar boy returned. *Señor* Guzman was not in. His door was locked and no one answered. Gil could leave a message for him if she wished.

Gil was relieved, but the one inside of her was not. No. The one inside of her wanted the key to Guzman's chamber, and said so. The boy reddened and, with an apologetic motion of his his head, demurred.

Gil understood. The one inside did not. The one inside her told the boy to give her the key now and be quick about it or she would have 'his head upon a platter.' The strange, archaic threat surprised her. Where had it come from? She spoke with all the arrogance of royalty. The boy hesitated, then perhaps sensing overhead the whisper of some ghostly pike, fumbled with a ring behind the counter and pressed a key before her on the bar.

Her voice was silk and kisses now. *Gracias*. What a good boy. Why, she was only joking of course. *Un momento*. She wouldn't be long.

Leaving the bar, she wended her way past the dancers, coldly ignoring an obscene proposition and gracefully eluding several lecherous hands. At the top of the stairwell, she looked back once, but no one had followed.

The empty cellar was something of a relief after the madness of the bar. The juke was muted, and in the quiet she could hear the sound of water dripping above the dull pulsations of a walking bass. Soon she came to Guzman's door. Light showed beneath the crack. She knocked and, when no one answered, inserted the key and moved the tumblers. She wondered what she would say if Guzman found her. She didn't have to wonder long.

Guzman was seated in a chair before her. His eyeballs bulged in stupefaction as though Gil's entrance was a monstrous surprise. She cried out and fell back before realizing that he did not see her. His mouth was gagged with flesh, his wrists and ankles nailed to the wooden limbs of the chair. Something slid in her then and she almost fell down. She steadied herself and looked away, holding her breath until the panic passed and the nausea subsided. Horrified, she peeked again at the gruesome crucifixion.

Someone had taken a knife to Guzman's groin. The flesh below his belt was gone. Beneath the chair was a half-coagulated pool of blood and something that looked like links of sausage. Christ!

She gagged again and staggered out the door. This time, nausea flooded her throat and nearly drowned her. Instinctively, she fled down the hall, away from the butchery, but the one inside her stopped her in her tracks. She was forgetting something, wasn't she? For there was something in the room it wanted.

Gil groaned in agony, but returned obediently to the open door. Trying not to look at the body, she scanned the room for the reason she had come. She knew it when she saw it, and the one inside of her was pleased. A glass phial lay on an orange crate just beyond the reach of Guzman's straining fingers. Holding her breath and averting her vision, she crept inside, stretched out an arm and secured the potion. Then she slammed the door and fled.

She did not remember going back up the stairwell. She did remember throwing the key on the bar and pushing her way out the door of the bar. Then she was out on the night street and coughing dryly into the gutter. The nightwind washed her face and body, but the fecal odor remained inside her, in her nose, in her pores, in her mind and memory – gagging her like a finger down her throat.

A car pulled up to the curb beside her. 'Hey, babe. Wanna lift?' It was relentless: the Spanish male libido. Here she was vomiting in the gutter and some guy was actually trying to pick her up.

'I'm sick,' she said. 'Lay off me, will ya?'

'Course you're sick. Anybody be sick drank in there.'

Gil looked up and saw it wasn't a pick-up at all, but a gypsy cabdriver looking for a fare.

'Hop in, babes, and I'll run ya home. Pardon the expression, hon, but you look like shit on toast.'

Gil got in the cab and started to give her brother's address. She was very nauseous and only wanted to lie down. But the one inside her overruled her and gave the address of La Club instead.

La Fiesta Ha Terminada

◆

Chapter 32

The room in which the Doctor would die was a large basement space with a floor of poured concrete. He watched it coming toward him now as Omar walked him down the hall. It seemed to him incredible that *this* was where his life would end, in such a cruddy little basement chamber, with a pool of rusty rainwater on the floor, bad lighting, and some beige folding chairs pushed against the cinderblock wall. For the Doctor knew that when they reached the room, Omar would order him down upon his knees, place the gun behind his head, and blow his brains out. He would do the same to Janie, too. Already, he could see her waiting for them, kneeling in the submissive posture of a victim.

And yet as he walked to the room where he would die, something quite amazing happened. Everything became so *interesting*! The Doctor passed a paperback lying on a footstool, a tawdry western with a cowboy on the cover firing his pistol as he leaped over a stone wall, and though the Doctor had never even deigned to look at such a type of book before (considering it beneath him), suddenly it seemed to him like something he would love to read!

What a silly, silly old man he'd been not to have enjoyed things more, not to have grabbed at life when he'd had the chance – to have considered himself above such delightful and endearing things as dime novels and to have turned his nose up at so many simple pleasures. And the Doctor swore then that if only Life would let him live, he would not be like this any longer.

But it did not seem like Life had heard. For the Doctor was defeated, whipped. He knew it. Omar knew it. Janie did, too, by the way she was kneeling. He was like that dying and dismembered god the world forever murders, munches and adores. Except that in the Doctor's case, he wasn't going to rise again; there wasn't going to be an Easter parade. It would just be, '*Finito*, Love,' and 'Sorry, Charlie,' and, 'Hell, what a sweet and sour symphony, *Señor*!' – and Eternity to forget it in.

They reached the room, and when they did there was almost an embarrassed moment as the three of them regarded each other. What was the protocol for an execution? Who did what first? No one seemed to know.

The Doctor looked at Omar. He was holding the automatic pistol at his side. He seemed embarrassed, pained, nor would he meet the Doctor's anxious eyes. It was so unlike his normal manner that the Doctor knew for certain then that he would kill them.

'I would like a moment with my . . . wife,' the Doctor said as he turned to Jane. Her face was masklike and unreadable. He lifted her up and embraced her strongly, and as he did, she told him something with her eyes. And it was then the Doctor felt the knife being pressed into his hand. It was a fruit knife, like barmen use for slicing limes, with a long thin blade and a small wooden handle. He held it there, blade upward, secreted against the plane of his forearm, the wooden handle balanced in his palm. And as his fingers curled familiarly around the shaft the Doctor had another revelation. All these years he had thought of himself as defenseless and inept – but while it is true he was quite useless with a gun, he was a genius with a scalpel. And as this insight flared inside him, Janie ducked, and the Doctor turned and swung his arm.

The insertion, above the sixth rib and through the fifth intercostal space, was surgically perfect. In fact, it almost seemed as if a little broken line had drawn itself on Omar's shirt, just below his pocket, like an illustration in a surgical textbook, and the Doctor had simply stuck the target. The knife went in without obstruction until he felt it prick the heart.

A look came over Omar's face. It was as though at first he could not comprehend the stabbing pain between his ribs. Then he did. '*Hombre*,' he said, twisted and crashed.

The Doctor bent down and removed the blade, aware he had just destroyed a man, but feeling, too, he had performed a necessary surgery, though he was unprepared for the sudden hot snake of blood that leapt from the wound, soaking his trousers.

Janie gave a cry and jumped back, too.

The Doctor, feeling shaken now, wiped the blade on the sleeve of Omar's coat. He looked at his watch. It was well past midnight. 'C'mon,' he said, 'we have a message to send.'

Just then, however, heavy footsteps approached. The Doctor picked up Omar's automatic pistol. He wondered if it was *El Duende*. But it was only Mucho come for the body.

'Body? What body?' the Doctor said, wondering how they could have known so quickly what he had just done. Then he realized Mucho had come for *his* body.

'Uh, it's right here,' the Doctor said, making a quick substitution.

Mucho looked at Omar's corpse. 'Mr. Valpero says I can have the head.'

'The head? Why, yes. Go right ahead,' the Doctor said awarding the boy the grisly prize.

'I have to take it to New Jersey though.'

'Jersey? What a good idea. I'm sure the head will like it there.'

Mucho looked at Jane with longing. 'Can I have hers, too?'

'One to a customer,' the Doctor said.

Mucho shrugged, disappointed, but bent to the task of dragging Omar's carcass out the door, leaving a bloody smear along the poured concrete

'C'mon,' the Doctor said to Jane.

But now – *goddamnit* – someone *else* was coming. The

434

Doctor froze, listening to the footsteps confidently approach. His blood was hot, and he almost felt that he might shoot whoever entered on the spot. Then the door swung open and the Doctor looked up. Standing before them was Jorge Vazpana.

The Doctor was so profoundly shocked, he dropped the pistol. The girl pounced on it, like a hungry ratter. She hefted it coolly, snapping back the bolt, and pivoted gracefully, covering both men.

'You?' the Doctor said, disbelieving.

But the boy only looked at him – first with surprise, then with bitter hate. Then he turned and said to Jane, 'Paul Pagan, Captain. First Lieutenant. MIRA.'

'You are not Paul Pagan,' the Doctor said.

'Captain,' the young man appealed to the woman. 'As you can see, he is trying to confuse you.'

'What do you mean, "Captain"?' the Doctor asked. He looked at Jane.

'He is your man,' the young man said, pointing at the Doctor. 'Don't you know? It is he who has been spying for *El Duende*.'

The girl turned and questioned the Doctor with her eyes.

'Well, yes, I *have*,' the Doctor said. 'But not how you think. I am, you see, a double agent.'

'Double agent!' the boy sneered.

'It's true! What I am giving is false information.'

'False? Like the rebel column you had destroyed last month? Or the position of our troops in Leon Province?'

'Well, yes, but see, we did that on purpose. We had to make them think . . . that what I said . . . was true,' though even as the Doctor said it, he knew it sounded hopelessly lame. He looked at Jane, but he could not read her.

'And now he is sending intelligence to Dorado that will destroy the entire rebel army. You must stop him!'

The Doctor's confusion was giving way to anger. 'Idiot!' he said. 'You have got it backwards. The message I send will win us the war.' He turned to Jane. 'Give me that,' he said reaching for the pistol.

'Don't,' the girl said, and clearly meant it. She held the gun in both her hands, pointing it steadily at the Doctor's heart.

'Thank God, you believe me,' the young man said, and tried to move behind her.

She jumped and spun. 'Freeze!'

'But, Comrade,' the boy said with a wounded air. 'I am on your side. It's Castellano who's the traitor. It's been him all along.'

The Doctor sighed and looked at his watch. It was 1:47. 'I had a message to send one hour ago. I will send it now. After I send it, we may discuss this matter all you wish.'

'Don't let him go!' the boy declared.

'I am going,' the Doctor said. 'If you wish,' he told Jane, 'you may shoot me in the back.'

'Doc,' the girl said sadly. 'Don't.'

'Shoot him, Captain. Now! Before he gets away.'

'Captain?' the Doctor shrieked. 'Who is this Captain? And you,' the Doctor said, turning on the boy, 'you are not this . . . Paul Whatever. You are . . . Jorge Vazpana!'

The girl's eyes widened; the pistol fired. It was not like in the movies; there was a terrible scream and an immediate stench of shit and blood as the bullet entered belly-level and the young man rolled on the concrete floor, wailing and shrieking in pain.

'C'mon,' Jane said, and stepped coldly over the wounded agent. They ran from the room and out into the hallway. The Doctor couldn't get over her transformation. Her gawky coltlike air was gone; she had the air of a serpent, poisonous and certain.

They paused at the threshold of the telex room, then flung open the door, surprising a man seated with earphones at a console.

'*Buenos días, Señor,*' Jane said in impeccable Spanish. 'We have a message for the Junta.'

The man took off his earphones and looked at Jane, then at the Doctor's blood-stained trousers, then at the gun. 'I don't understand Spanish,' he said.

In answer, Jane touched the gun to his ear. He flinched

and cried out, burned by the hot barrel. 'Ah ha,' she said, 'but pain he understands. Sit down. Go ahead, Doctor. Write it out.'

The Doctor printed in Spanish the message Benitez had given him. Translated, it read: '*Expect full-scale attack on Puerto Valle from western front at 0600 hours. 7,000 troops. Artillery and armor. Air support from USS* Nimitz. *Repeat. All-out rebel attack imminent from western quarter. Respond.*'

'Good,' Jane said. 'That should get their attention.'

The man hunched over the message, and placed his fingers on the keys.

Jane raised the gun and pressed it to his ear. 'Aren't we forgetting something, *hombre*?'

The man was silent for a moment. Then he swallowed and said, 'The safety device.'

'What is it?'

'X for P.'

'Fix it, Doctor.'

'I don't understand.'

'Change every "P" in the message to "X". For Puerto, write Xuerto.'

'*Si, Señorita*, the Doctor said.

Then Jane turned to the operator and warned, 'If there is any problem with this message getting through, or if anyone doubts its authenticity, I'll kill you. It's as simple as that.' She looked at him and smiled. 'Even if it's not your fault. Now send it.'

The man swallowed again and took a deep breath. They watched the operator's fingers on the keys. The telex sent, they awaited its reply. It came within two minutes. '*Message received. Cuzo notified.*'

'Ahh,' Jane said. She pointed to a cable running through the ceiling. 'Cut it.' And she supervised as the man sawed the cable with a knife. The wire cut, the telex went down.

'Now,' she said. 'You come with us.'

'Where?' the operator asked, trembling with dread.

'Behave yourself and you won't get hurt.' And she led the

man back to the room where the boy had been shot, tying him to the pipe.

The Doctor looked down at his dying enemy. He was sprawled upon the cellar floor, crumpled upon a brilliant and expanding shield of blood. His chest heaved – he was still breathing; and though a moment ago the boy had tried to have the Doctor killed, the Doctor felt a sudden pulse of pity. He knelt and felt the young man's pulse. He was in a state of shock and hemorrhaging profusely. 'We must get him to a hospital right away.'

'What?' Jane asked. 'After what he did to our *companero*?'

'You are not *Anglo*,' the Doctor said, noticing that the girl's hillcountry twang had completely disappeared.

'Hell, no, Doc,' she said, the accent reappearing.

'Who are you then?' the Doctor asked.

The woman tucked the pistol in her belt. 'I am Captain Wilhelmina Crespi.'

'Crespi?' the Doctor said in wonder. 'MIRA?'

She nodded.

'Then who is this?' the Doctor asked, turning to the dying boy.

'Don't you know? That is Schmidt. Of AES.'

The Kill

♦

Chapter 33

She was repulsed anew by his monstrous appearance. His hands were so fat they were stiff, like fins. He looked like a sea-turtle tilted up upon its tail, with the white rhombus of the napkin on his belly, his short, pointed arms, beaked nose, and imperious amphibian eye. It was true what they said about him, Gil thought; he was inhuman, surely – as though he had turtle blood coursing through his veins, gallons of green, cold, salty turtle blood sloshing through the fatty chambers of his heart.

Gil sat beside him and *El Duende* put his arm around her, drawing her close. She had invited this, after all. She had offered him *anything* if he would not harm her children, and what he had wanted was exactly what she had thought. But even as she felt his hands and breath upon her, she knew that her decision to submit had been an error. It would earn her nothing but his contempt. None of it would help her children in the least. She must have been crazy to think it would. When he was done with her, he would hand her over to the other men, perhaps even Mucho. And she saw all too clearly now how her head would look on the top of Mucho's mantle. She saw the waxen pallor of her cheeks, the closed lids fringed with their delicate black lashes, like shrunken heads she had seen as a girl. The image did not frighten her. What scared her was the agony and terror she knew she would feel before she died. God help her! And in desperation, her hand clenched in her pocket and closed upon the lethal phial.

Fast as a cat, *El Duende* caught her wrist and drew it out. He pressed it and her fist blossomed like a flower, the little phial sparkling in her palm.

'What is that?'

She looked around her. She waited for a miracle, for an angel to descend from heaven and save her. And then she heard her voice say, 'Nectar.' And that was when Gil realized the angel was inside her.

El Duende raised his eyebrows. He looked intrigued. 'Nectar? And what is . . . nectar?'

'The sweetest thing in this or any world.'

Her answer stopped him cold. It should have; the words were his own. And it dawned on her then that all the work she had done over the course of her long and inglorious theatrical career had been for this one moment, for this squalid little scene.

'Nectar?' *El Duende* asked again. And though he tried to restrain himself, she could feel his excitement growing. 'And where would you get . . . nectar?'

'Higgins.'

He waited for her to go on. But she didn't. (Play it cool, she told herself.) He watched her, searching her eyes for a trick. And Gil had the feeling then he would kill her if he discovered she was lying. 'And where,' he asked carefully at last, 'would Higgins have ever gotten nectar?'

'From his guru. Sara Devi.'

The flat, clear, fantastic answer sounded unexpectedly convincing, so that for one moment, Gil herself believed she held in her palm a fraction of an ounce of that most miraculous liquor, the essence of every earthly joy. Yes. Higgins' guru had given it to him, and he in his love had given it to her, and she, out of fear for her life and love for her children, was offering it up to *El Duende*. It was a perfectly reasonable scenario and quite believable – if life was a fairy tale or you were a brain-damaged child.

'Have you tasted it?'

440

'Nuh unh.'

'Why not?'

'I was saving it for my children.'

'Yes. But how do you know it's really nectar? Don't you think you should taste it and see?'

'All right,' Gil said and raised it to her lips.

'Wait,' *El Duende* said nervously, staying her hand. (She would be dead now if he had not.) 'What did Higgins say again?'

'He said it was sweeter than anything – sweeter than music, sweeter than youth. And that if I tasted it, I would be forever satisfied.' She placed her hand upon his thigh, and sighed in a way calculated to inflame him. But he was no longer interested in food – or sex. His eyes were lit with greater fires. 'This. . . . Sara Devi. She is a powerful enchantress.' He paused, seeming to want her confirmation.

'I wouldn't call her that. No. A saint.'

'And this . . . nectar. Where would *she* have gotten it?'

Gil laughed. 'From heaven? I don't know. Perhaps . . . some spirit gave it to her . . . as a gift.'

He stared at her hard. 'You believe in such things?'

She nodded, cooly.

'Most people don't.'

'Most people are fools.'

El Duende searched her face. It seemed he was discovering in it a thousand hidden virtues. Perhaps he would spare her after all. Perhaps – perish the thought – he would make her his mistress.

'May I?' he asked, and plucked the phial from her fingers. He examined it minutely, with utmost care and fascination. He unstoppered the top and held the amber liquor to the light. He put it to his nose again. And then, the power of his gluttony overruled him. How could it not? He took the phial and put it to his lips.

Gil looked away, afraid that her expression would betray her, and so in fact, she did not actually see him drink it – though when she looked again, the phial was empty. *El Duende* had the strangest look his face. He seemed to be waiting, listening intently, as though some amazing transformation was going on inside.

Then his expression changed. Sweat broke out upon his brow, and, frowning, he rose to his feet. Instantly, he was bathed in sweat, as though someone had turned a hose upon him. He looked at Gil, then looked about him, and then his whole body flexed, as though he'd been electrocuted, and with a crash he fell and lay upon the floor, looking up at Gil, stunned and disbelieving. '*Puta*,' he said, with hate. Then he coughed, spilling an incredible quantity of vomit.

Gil watched in fascination as *El Duende* attempted to rise. In fact, one sick part of her wanted to reach out and help him up. Clutching the throne, he drew himself up and now, incredibly, started toward her. But he had not gone more than several paces, when another electric shock convulsed his body, punching him like a fist. His body reared; his head and heels attempted to touch. He hit the floor, but, this time, he did not get up. His eyes rolled back. He lay there, twitching. Then, very slowly, like a poisoned insect, his whole body trembled, twisted, and froze.

Gil stared in disbelief. She was like a computer programmed to execute a single command, and now that it was over with, she was helpless and could do nothing.

As she left the room, she looked back once. *El Duende* was sprawled upon the tiles. His mouth was open, his blackened tongue protruding, his eyes wide in stupefaction, as though Death was the most astonishing of sights.

Gil, on the other hand, felt next to nothing – neither joy, nor sorrow, nor victory, nor remorse – only a sort of distant satisfaction, as if the whole affair had been the work of someone other than herself.

For Gil had not killed him for personal reasons. She had not killed him out of passion or self-preservation, nor under the influence of any religion, political party, credo, or drug.

She had killed *El Duende* for the very same reason a shebear will attack you if you threaten her cubs.

Descent

◆

Chapter 34

Crouched on the rim of the volcano so that his silhouette could not be seen against the sky, he looked down at Puerto Valle. The first stars were coming out as the capitol's lights winked on below. It was that moment right before dusk when the world glows with an uncanny radiance. All the copper pots in Dorado gleamed at that instant with a lovely heavy light. Through the binoculars, Garcia could see the thin stalks of cooking fires rising into a roseate mist that swathed the city. This mist was turning purple now as the light withdrew from the city in the valley, though in the hills where Garcia lay, the rocks were pink and the air still shining, so that he looked like an angel poised upon the lip of some nether region.

Through the glasses, Garcia could see General Cuzo's army bivouacked along the Rio Negro. Though the river there was only inches deep and hardly a barrier, it afforded the capitol a natural line of defense. The bridges crossing it were heavily defended against a western assault, blockaded at their heads with armored cars.

But Garcia would not fight that battle. His orders were to proceed to the Presidential Palace, to liberate it, and to hold it for Benitez against all would-be heirs and claimants of either side. And thinking of his mission then, of his Indian 'wife,' and looking down once again at his native city, Garcia felt a thrill in his old tired heart, a thrill of blood and moon, of the hunt and hunter. There was a blurring in his brain, as if all the moments of his life were coming together – the way rainwater pours off every mountain, rushing as rivulets into streaming brooks and rivers, only to throw itself headlong off the edge and fall, boil, then pool, collect and resolve itself back into one purling, silver, and unbreachable stream.

In this excited state, Garcia fell asleep and had the most extraordinary dream. In it, he was wandering through a rocky waste which was somehow both the mountains of his youth, and those of Dorado this very evening. Then he heard the thunder crack, and, looking down, he saw a fissure in the dry, red rock and a shaft of golden light gleaming up through the earth. Garcia put his eye to the crevice and there beheld, within the hill, a splendid city more beautiful than Babylon. He gazed upon its Moorish turrets and splashing windwhipped tanks and fountains, the sheen of quiet gold, and the naked forms of adolescent girls bathing in the splashing waters.

And at the sight, Garcia felt a joy in his groin and a mounting exultation, even as he wondered what city it was. And as he wondered, a voice within the cavern answered:

'*Feast your eyes on El Dorado, the rich and immaculate city of gold! Here blooms the lotus and the rose. Here nectar spills and drips and shivers in the crystal pools, and the moon soars in the stars and spires. Here Mozart plays, and Jesus listens, and you are young and loved, and it is always spring.*'

Then Garcia had entered into the shining city and was hurrying through its golden streets. He was searching for his wife, his true wife, the one he had married ages ago, as a crescendo of pleasure arose in his body, and the booming voice continued to sing:

'*And in the deepest heart of this sweet Hell, there is a bed. And there your Bride lies waiting to embrace you. O Hero, why do you resist her? Her breasts are wine. Her lips are honey. Her name is Love. And the mortal man who lies with her rises up forever-young.*'

When Garcia awoke, it was misting softly. He lay on his

back in the dark on the hard-scrabble ground, amazed by the brightness of the city he had seen inside him, reveling in the extreme erotic sweetness of the dream. For a moment he glimpsed again the windwhipped spray of the splashing fountains and the wet thighs of the bathing girls. Then he became conscious of a discomforting wetness about his own and, unbuttoning his fly, was shocked to discover that his underpants were drenched with seed.

Garcia laughed, amazed. He had not had such a dream in half a century! His masculine nature had returned with a vengeance! His erection, in fact, was so relentless that when he went to make water, his stream shot straight up at heaven, then fell in a sparkling, starlit arc.

Always before a battle he had felt afraid. But not tonight. Tonight, he could barely contain his jubilation. Standing there beneath the stars, reveling in the return of his virility and power, he felt the joy the jaguar feels on its midnight perch, waiting for the goats to come to water.

Garcia washed himself, and changed his linen. Then he rechecked his equipment. He looked at his watch, compass, and his pistol, made certain he had a dozen extra clips of ammunition, then dismantled his AK and cleaned it one last time, enjoying the sound of the neat oiled *clinks* and *chocks* the metal made as it was broken down and reassembled.

Half an hour later the band moved out, bringing Garcia's Indian 'wife' along with them. In the dark, they passed a rainfilled barrel full of stars. The reflection of the moon, Garcia knew, would soon be lacquered on its still black surface, like a coin of an indescribable thin brilliance. A wind sprang up and distressed the water, shimmering planets, wrinkling worlds. Somewhere in the valley far below, a dog barked; nearby, palm fronds kissed and clashed in the dark, making a sound like a cymbalist with brushes. Once, he thought he heard the sounds of jubilee rising up from the town below. He stopped and listened, but he could not be certain. It might have been carousing soldiers – or the ceaseless soughing of the mountain wind.

At the head of the path that led down the mountain, there

was an unexpected challenge. 'Announce yourself! Who goes there?' A young sentry stepped forward, pointing his ancient rifle with its bayonet in their direction.

'When on watch, son,' Garcia said, 'never lower your weapon.'

'Who are you?' the boy demanded. Then his eyes widened as he made out in the starlight the rebel army streaming up from behind.

'I am *Capitán* Ambrosio Garcia.'

'*Capitán* Garcia?' the sentry asked unsurely.

'Of *Comandante* Rabon's Liberation Army.'

Whether or not the sentry appreciated this intelligence soon became moot, as at that instant a loop of piano wire bit into his throat. The white cut instantly brimmed with blood, then flowed into a streaming necklace, and the sentry pitched forward, his neck severed to the spine.

Garcia cursed the garroter, Segundo Jimenez. There had been no need for that, Garcia told him – even as the leering corporal pulled the blood-slick wire through his handkerchief and deftly coiled it away.

They found several more soldiers asleep on cots in a nearby tent. They, too, were little more than boys, and Garcia ordered them guarded, along with his long-lost Indian bride. Then they waited.

At 0140 there were several rounds of fire on the western front. Then there was silence.

At 0220 the moon rose above the hills.

At 0300 they started to descend.

The Bliss Of Liberation

Part IV

Surrender

◆

Chapter 1

The Doctor and Jane left the cellar of La Club. On their way, they passed the bloated corpse of *El Duende*. He was lying, belly-up, in the middle of the restaurant, unmourned and unattended.

They hurried through the early autumn morning to Benitez's headquarters. On entering it, however, the Doctor sensed at once that there was something wrong. The front door was unguarded. Inside, it was as quiet as a funeral parlor – while on the Chippendale sideboard, a tuna fish sandwich had been abandoned in mid-bite.

The Doctor imagined a host of tragedies. Benitez was dead – from a heart attack or an assassin's bullet! But there was no sense of violence or hysteria in the air, only an emptiness, the void of deep defeat.

Anxiously, the Doctor and Jane climbed the marble stairwell. At the top, they encountered the Chief of Security lying with his head propped against the banister. The Doctor rushed to his aid – only to discover that the man was clutching a bottle of tequila and wasn't hurt as he had thought, but drunk. 'What are you doing?'

'Ah, shut up, Doc,' the fellow said, not unkindly.

'How dare you abandon your position!'

'This *is* my position. Horizontal.'

'Where is the President?' the Doctor demanded.

'Fuck the President.'

'What did you say?'

'Sleeping,' a third voice interrupted. It was Lieutenant Calderon, Guido's replacement. He was standing in an office doorway in the upstairs hall. He, too, looked wasted, though not by drink. His handsome face was strained and pale.

The Doctor pointed to the drunken guard. 'I want this man charged with insubordination!'

'Fuck you,' the officer cried. 'Hey, *muchacha*,' he asked Jane. 'You wanna drink?'

The Doctor, enraged, kicked the bottle from the guard's hand. As he did, he noticed the stain on his trousers where he had knelt in Schmidt's dark venous blood. It had been a long, difficult, trying evening, and he was in no mood for drunks. 'What the hell is going on here?' he demanded. He pointed at the guard. 'I want this man court-martialed!'

'Come into my office, Doctor,' the Lieutenant soothed.

'Court-martialed?' the sentry laughed. He looked at Jane. 'Who the hell does he think he is? The whole thing is over,' the sentry called after them. 'It's over, Doctor. You understand? You can forget your dreams of power and glory.'

The Doctor ushered Jane into the Lieutenant's office and slammed the door. 'This is . . .'

'Captain Crespi,' the Lieutenant said saluting smoothly. 'Good to see you, Captain.' He turned to the Doctor. 'Did you send your message?'

'Yes. And now what the hell is going on?'

The Lieutenant shook his head and said, 'Commander Rabon got caught. Red-handed.'

'What?'

'Have a drink, Doctor. You look like you could use one.'

'No! When?'

'Shortly after midnight. One of our people in Puerto Valle was arrested and brought to the new military barracks . . .'

'He talked?'

The Lieutenant shook his head. 'But while he was being interrogated, two Indians arrived. They were very drunk and quite excited. They told the soldiers a wondrous tale: the spirits of their dead ancestors were pouring out of the volcano and coming down the mountain.'

'God!' the Doctor said, knowing the feeling that had made someone else abandon their sandwich – a sick pain in the pit of his stomach that took away his appetite, as if someone had kicked him there with a boot. 'And then what?'

'In all the excitement, our man escaped. He urged us to warn Commander Rabon – but that isn't possible. For security reasons, we've been out of radio contact with the Commander for days. And even if we *could* reach him . . .' He shrugged and looked at the clock. It was 3:05. 'The operation has already started.'

'Mother of God,' the Doctor said. For he didn't need to hear any more. The soldiers, forewarned, had only to step outside and train their searchlights on the volcano. There they would find, clinging to the rocks a thousand feet above their heads, an army of spirits, all right – wearing green fatigues and carrying AK–47s.

'There is nowhere for them to run,' the Lieutenant added.

'*Ay, Dios mio,*' Jane said and bit her lip. There was a long bitter silence. So that was that.

'And the President?' the Doctor asked at last.

'He is sleeping. I saw no reason to disturb him.'

The Doctor and his young beloved walked out into the early dawn. It had started to snow. Strangely enough, the Doctor did not feel as bad as he had thought he would. He felt instead a tremendous stillness, a peace like he had never known. The world, the dawn, the flakes of falling snow seemed to happen in a vacuum, in a void that was at once both empty and replete; only round its edges was there any hint of agitation.

He envisioned their troops being picked off the mountain. He watched Rabon take a round in the chest, saw Garcia dying. He heard the shrieks and screams of panicked soldiers, the cries of the wounded and the thunder of cannon impacting the rock – and yet, in the Doctor's mind, it did not seem to mar the silence in the least, as if the silence lived inside the battle, undisturbed and adamantine.

And the Doctor knew then that peace you taste when you've bet your life and soul – and lost; and there is nothing more to do or say, no argument or appeal, no words to wish or think or speak – only the peace of what will be, and the freedom of surrender.

Surrender! Ah, how sweet the word! The rain surrenders to the river, and the river to the sea. The day surrenders to the evening and the morning to the light of noon. A man surrenders to a woman and she in turn surrenders to her man. Truly, he thought, all things on earth are accomplished through surrender.

Peanuts

◆

Chapter 2

The air was already beginning to lighten when a car rolled up on the airport tarmac, the door opened, and the agent got out. He was dressed warmly in an overcoat and an alpine hat. A cigarette fumed in a corner of his mouth, its smoke mixing with his smokey breath.

Higgins left the heated hut where he'd been drinking coffee with the crew and went to meet him. They shook gloved hands, while the crew roused itself, traipsing past them to board the plane.

This morning the agent seemed particularly dour. His gray, unshaven cheeks had the texture and unforgiving tint of sharkskin; he did not appear to have slept. A driver sat behind the wheel of the Lincoln looking equally disgruntled.

'C'mon. I want to show you something,' Higgins said, brightly, and pointed him toward the open door of the jet which sat like a silver cylinder of light, golden rays streaming from its windows.

Inside, save for a couple of seats up front, the cabin was filled from floor to ceiling with dozens of wooden packing crates. The words: 'Huebner's Peanuts' were stencilled on their sides. Even the agent had to smile at the little joke.

Higgins produced a crowbar and handed it to his partner. 'Go ahead. Take a look.' Shrugging off his overcoat, the man grasped the bar and prised open one side of the closest crate.

A river of unshelled peanuts gushed at his feet. 'Very good,' he said, and grinned once more. Then he began to probe the carton, using the bar to feel for something, but the longer he probed, the more peanuts spilled out. Throwing Higgins a questioning look, he speared a second crate. Crushed and broken peanut shells erupted through the wood. The agent poked and prodded vigorously, but the crowbar sunk until it touched bottom. He scowled at Higgins. 'What the hell is this?'

'Peanuts,' Higgins said. 'That's what you asked for, isn't it?'

The man looked at Higgins in disbelief. 'And the parts?'

'Oh, *those*,' Higgins said. 'Don't worry about those. They're in the air. They're on the way.'

The agent appeared to relax a fraction, as if perhaps – just perhaps – this thing with the peanuts had been some sort of benign, if stupid, joke.

'The only thing is,' Higgins said, 'they're not going to land at the coordinates you gave us. And you know why? Because two days ago that airstrip was seized by the Junta. It's no longer in rebel hands.' He smiled. 'But then again, you knew that, didn't you?'

With this final question, the long masquerade ended, and the two old enemies looked upon each other's faces without masks.

'Who *are* you?' the agent hissed.

'The question is,' Higgins said, 'who are *you*?'

'Don't you know?'

'I have my suspicions. I think you're probably Hercules Cordero. What I *do* know for certain is that your name isn't Crespi, and you don't work for MIRA – AES.'

The man looked at Higgins evenly. His eyes were hoods. Then he looked around him, as if suddenly aware of his position. He was standing in the aisle facing the cockpit, crates at his back, Higgins before him, hemmed in by seats on either side. Behind Higgins stood the steward, looking huge and immovable.

With a leisurely air, the agent from AES drew from his

jacket a battered pack of cigarettes, igniting one with a silver lighter which clicked and glimmered, then disappeared once more into the folds of his coat. Having exhaled, he said quite calmly, picking a flake of tobacco from his lip: 'And where are the parts now?'

'On the way to another airstrip. One that's still in rebel hands.'

'I see,' the agent said and frowned. He looked at Higgins. 'Congratulations. Who are you anyway? CIA?'

'Could be,' Higgins said, amused by the notion. 'Then again, what if I told you I was just an ordinary guy who didn't like your filthy attitude?'

'I wouldn't believe you.'

'I didn't think so.'

'And how did you know,' the agent wondered, 'who I was – and wasn't?'

'That you wouldn't believe, either, I'm sure.'

'Why don't you try me?'

'Okay,' Higgins said. 'Let's put it this way. I saw it in a dream . . .'

'A *dream*?' He stared at Higgins, as though attempting to decipher his words – but couldn't. Then, deciding, perhaps, that their business was over and that Higgins was only playing with him now, he parked his cigarette in a corner of his mouth, picked up his overcoat, lowered his head, and tried to pass. But Higgins didn't budge. The steward placed fists the size and shape of Easter hams on the back of the seats and hung his bulk in the aisle to reinforce the message of constraint. Cordero stopped and assessed the situation. 'I am your prisoner?' He raised his gray eyebrows. 'If you know who I am, as you say you do, you must be very stupid, indeed. I have diplomatic immunity. Touch a hair on my head and it will cause quite a problem between our two countries.' He paused for a moment. 'Whatever they are.'

Higgins said nothing. And in the long silence, some of the agent's arrogance departed. 'Like I said,' Higgins said at last, 'I'm not working for any country. I can do whatever the hell I want.'

The agent's eyes flickered nervously, moving momentarily to the face of the steward who, it was obvious now, wasn't really a steward at all, but some sort of hired gun. 'And what do you intend to do with me? Kill me?' He said it quickly, the way people say things they don't want to be true.

'I'm tempted to,' Higgins said. 'I really am. But I'm afraid it wouldn't do much good. If I killed you now, sooner or later, you'd just come back again. You know what I mean?'

'Come back again?'

'This way, if I show you some mercy, maybe this thing can end right here – forever.'

There was a longish pause, while Cordero thought upon these words. He was obviously trying to extract their meaning. 'So,' he said, at last, 'I am free to go?'

'Yes,' Higgins said. 'On this plane. Back to Puerto Valle – with half a ton of peanuts.'

'What for?'

'To make sure that your career is over. When the Junta discovers what you've bought with their money, I don't think they'll pin a medal on you. Do *you*?'

The agent did not seem too disturbed by this prospect. He said, philosophically, 'Such things happen in war. Shipments are destroyed . . . lost. My superiors understand this.'

'Don't make me laugh,' Higgins said. 'You fucked up royally, man.'

Cordero flushed. 'And you, you stole half a million dollars. You're not a patriot – you're a pirate.'

'Oh no,' Higgins said. 'I didn't take a *sou*. Except for my expenses, see?' And he withdrew from his breast pocket for Cordero's review a neatly-typewritten sheet of paper. 'Here,' he said, pointing to a figure. 'This is the cost of the parts and arms. Here's the leasing of the jets and crew. Four thousand dollars – that's for the peanuts. And this $598,000 figure? That's my commission – which I'm returning to you.'

The agent's eyes widened in disbelief.

'Of course,' Higgins said, folding the sheet away, 'I didn't think you'd want to carry all that cash, so I took the liberty of setting up a special bank account in your name. If you check, you'll see that funds were transferred into it this morning from the Institution of East-West Studies. Now, do you know what that is? The Institution, I mean? No? Okay. It's a holding company I created. But, you see, it *sounds* a lot like another company called . . . are you ready for this? . . . the *Institute* For East-West Studies.'

'What the fuck are you talking about?'

'I'm talking about the Institute For East-West Studies. Doesn't that ring any bells? Think. Didn't you meet someone earlier this evening who works there?'

The agents' eyes slid back and forth beneath his lizard lids. 'Your friend. At the restaurant.'

'Good! But even more interesting – do you know what it is? The Institute, I mean.'

Cordero thought. 'A think-tank, he said.'

'Think-tank?' Higgins asked. 'Oh, that's what they *always* say. You didn't believe that, did you? No, the Institute For East-West Studies is a think-tank, yeah – for *the CIA*. My friend, you see, is a very big man in the US intelligence community – despite his modest mien. Even more significantly, he's now your friend, too.'

And Higgins produced from his breast pocket a three by five Polaroid taken at the restaurant. It showed the three of them, Higgins, Cordero and Buck, standing at the bar, while Buck pumped Cordero's hand.

Cordero stared at the photograph in horror.

'Are you beginning to see the picture now? Take a good look, because a copy has already been sent to the Junta – along with the number of your Cayman account. Therefore, when you land with your peanuts, it will look like more than just stupidity. It will look, I'm afraid, very much like treason.

'I mean, look at it from *their* point of view. You were given the assignment to buy seven million dollars' worth of vitally needed parts and arms. Now, not only were these arms delivered to your enemies, but the night they were delivered, there is a picture of you, the dealer, and a senior CIA agent meeting in a New York restaurant. On top of that, there is evidence of a secret bank account in your name into which more than half a million US dollars has been paid by the Institution of East-West Studies. Any difference between it and the CIA-funded *Institute* For East-West Studies will get lost, I think, in the Spanish translation, don't you? All in all, it will look to them, and to everyone else, like you sold out your country for a little more than half a million dollars.'

'You *are* CIA! You and your friend!'

'Don't blame my friend,' Higgins said. 'He doesn't know a thing about this. I just phoned him and asked him to meet me for a drink. It's true I hadn't seen the guy in twenty years – but I'd followed his career. The waiter took the picture.'

The agent opened his mouth to speak.

'Hey, I'm sure you can explain it all. But it will be hard work, don't you think? And somehow I have the feeling that your debriefing won't take place in some posh safehouse tucked away in the suburbs, but in some place more . . . secluded and austere – like the sub-basement of the police station in Puerto Valle. You know it well, though. You used to work there, didn't you? Now you'll get to see the work they do there from a . . . slightly different point of view.'

'They won't believe it – *any* of it.'

'Oh, no? I think they will. And, anyway, in the end, even if they don't, it doesn't matter. Even if you somehow prove you're innocent, you won't be able to prove you're not stupid.

'And that's the worst thing of all. Making them look incompetent, unmanly. Oh, they hate that – even more than treason. And they'll hate you, too, for having done it to them. I promise you that. But, you just wait and see.'

Cordero's eyes widened and his nostrils flared, as though he was just beginning to appreciate the cunning dimensions of the trap he had stumbled into, the fine design of the net that was closing overhead.

Higgins ducked as the crowbar slammed his shoulder. Immediately, the steward had his gun out and was pointing it at Cordero's head. 'That's enough,' Higgins said.

The agent turned his back to them then, like a man who's just been damned to hell. His cigarette had fallen and was smoldering amid the peanut shells. With a mechanical movement, he ground it out. He took a while to catch his breath. Then he said, 'If you're not with anyone, and you don't want the money, then tell me why the fuck you're doing this to me?'

'Don't you know?' Higgins asked. He looked out the window at the blowing snow. And it seemed to him then that the snow had always been blowing like this, was blowing now, and would continue to blow this way forever. He turned to Cordero. 'You killed my wife. My sweet, beautiful, adorable, young wife. In the middle of the street. With a filthy umbrella.'

Cordero cringed, as though burned. He looked away. 'That . . . that was an accident!'

'Yeah, I know,' Higgins said. 'An accident. You were trying to murder my best friend.'

Strength

◆

Chapter 3

It was a beautiful fall morning: the clouds were charcoal gray and rose, the sky a snapping blue, the sun blinding. The snow had stopped and was already melting; runoff sang in the drains and gutters, while the cab left dazzling gold-black tracks on the macadam.

The Doctor and Jane had slept only a few hours when wakened by an urgent phonecall bidding them report to Benitez at once. The Doctor did not want to go. He had no desire to hear the details of the massacre on the mountain, to trade recriminations, or to spend his Sunday thinking up lies to tell the press. God save them. What fools they'd been to think a little sleight of hand and a hundred fighters could wrest a country from the claws of the Junta!

But it was too late now. They were already there. He paid the driver. 'C'mon,' he said, 'we'd better get this over with,' and, climbing up the sanded steps, they opened up the door.

But headquarters ressembled a funeral parlor no longer. Rather, it reminded the Doctor of an Irish wake at which the corpse has just sat up, sung *tooraloo*, and asked for a glass of porter. A wondrous energy rolled through the rooms, secretaries ran about, doors slammed, phones rang, and loud manly laughter spilled through the halls. The same officer who, several hours before, had been drunk and insubordinate, was standing at attention – sober, freshly shaven, in spotless dress whites – while the tuna fish roll on the Chippendale sideboard had been replaced by a vase of fresh gardenias.

It was then the group of men at the top of the stairs sighted the Doctor and broke into cries of welcome and applause.

The Doctor raised his eyes to them, and felt something glorious stir inside him – that same shining light that was reflected in their faces. 'What's going on?' he asked. He looked at Jane. Then, answering his own question, said, 'We won! Didn't we?' But the Doctor did not need any outer affirmation. The rising bubble of joy inside him told him it was so.

'Doctor,' Benitez said, emerging from the little group and raising a glass in salutation. 'To you. To us. To the Republic of Dorado. And to those who made it possible.' And throwing back his head, he drained the long-stemmed flute, then let it fall and smash with a striking brilliance on the parquet marble floor one flight below. Instantly, several aides followed suit; the impact of the breaking crystal sounding like a repeating pistol.

'Your Excellency,' the Doctor called. 'May I have the honor of presenting to you Captain Wilhelmina Crespi.' And Jane, in high-heeled pumps, fresh lipstick, and skin-tight jeans, bowed and received in return a round of cheers laced with wolfish whistles.

Then the Doctor and his beloved were handed champagne and escorted up the marble stairwell. There were many *abrazos*, triple kisses, and pounding embraces. The Captain especially was repeatedly kissed – several officers, the Doctor felt, taking advantage of the situation to sample her charms – but other than that there was nothing but joy abounding.

For they had won a great victory, the Doctor now learned. Benitez's rebels were in full control of Puerto Valle. At 0900, New York time, General Cuzo had surrendered, along with seven thousand government soldiers. The plan had worked perfectly, thanks in part to the Doctor's timely message which had emptied the barracks at the foot of the mountain, allowing Rabon's forces to descend the volcano and infiltrate the city. Cuzo's men, most of whom were already drunk, had panicked when they had found themselves surrounded. In several cases, they had turned on their own officers. In others, they had flung down their weapons and fled into the swamp.

The one pitched battle had occurred at the Presidential Palace. The Palace Guard, armed with machine guns and hunkered down behind several armored cars, had fought to the death keeping Rabon's commandos at bay for more than two and a half hours despite a barrage of mortar, rockets, semi-automatic weapons' fire, and grenades. In the end, the defenders had not so much been defeated as expunged. The Palace had been reduced to rubble. A helicopter rising from the roof had crashed and burned, brought down by a bazooka. It contained the ashes of two of the Junta's ruling generals, plus a suitcase full of melted gold.

'But I thought,' the Doctor protested, 'that the Indians *saw* us.'

'It's true. They did,' Benitez said. 'But,' he laughed, 'no one would believe them. Toltec warriors coming out of the volcano? Would *you* have believed them, Doctor? On the Night of the Dead?

'Maybe not,' the Doctor said. 'But I would, at least, have stepped outside and had a look.'

'Yes.' Benitez frowned. 'In the end, you see, it was their contempt for their own people that sealed their fate.' He looked at the Doctor and then at Jane. 'I want . . . I want to thank you both so much. I heard . . . from Victor here . . . a little bit about last night. It was rough, I know.' He shook his head, and then embraced them warmly. 'I want you both to come with me to Puerto Valle. How does Minister of Health Services sound to you, Doctor? And you, Captain, will be of great assistance in helping to reorganize our intelligence service. For this is not the end. Oh, no. Only the beginning. You will see.'

There were murmurs from the group of aides as the Lieutenant and several other men, overhearing Benitez's words of praise, offered the Doctor and Jane their homage and congratulations.

'Come into my office,' Benitez said.

When they had entered, Benitez's look of victory fled. He sighed; he seemed sincerely grieved. 'Commander Rabon is dead.'

'What?'

'He took a bullet in the chest in the first few minutes of the assault on the Palace. If it's any consolation . . . he died at once.'

The Doctor closed his eyes. He wanted to cry at the unfairness of it all. Only fourteen of their soldiers had been killed or wounded. Why did one of them have to be this man?

The door flew open and the Lieutenant rushed in. 'Excuse me, your Excellency, but we are getting reports that looting has broken out in the slum. Plus a battalion of Wild Boars is holed up in the Military College. Also, several warships and submarines at sea are refusing to recognize your authority and return to port.'

Benitez closed his eyes and waited for a moment, as though praying for this cup to be taken from him. Then he drew a breath and said, 'Declare martial law. Tell the Boars they have' – he looked at his watch – 'exactly seventeen minutes to lay down their arms. If they don't, we will burn the college down. As for the Navy, call Admiral Prado. Tell him he will be shot, no, *hanged*, if his comrades do not return to port at once. Tell him . . . excuse me, Doctor, why don't you show the Captain around? Have some breakfast. And some more champagne. But don't overdo it. There's a press conference at noon.' He turned back to the Lieutenant. 'Tell him if those ships aren't back in port by seven o'clock this evening . . .'

The Doctor and Jane left the suite and stepped out onto the landing. Already, the brownstone was looking like a Presidential Palace. The aides and the military attachés of several nations had begun to throng the lower lobby, waiting to pay their respects to *El Presidente*. The Doctor noticed a fat black man in a dashiki, with purple tribal scars on both his cheeks, talking to a diminutive, blue-suited oriental.

The Doctor, detaching himself from Jane, approached

Lieutenant Calderon. 'When will his Excellency be returning to the capitol?'

The Lieutenant seemed harassed and uncertain. 'We don't know yet. The situation is still unclear. It's not as final as you might have heard. Commander Cereno reports there are still some pockets of resistance. And there appears to be an enemy column marching in from the north. At any rate, the President will not return until everything's secure.'

'And when might that be?'

'By tonight, hopefully. Commander Cereno is busy sterilizing the capitol. He has embarked upon a program of . . . purification.'

'What does that mean?' the Doctor asked, taken aback by the medical imagery.

'All enemy officers from colonel up are being shot.'

'What!' the Doctor said, horrified. 'We can't do that! They *surrendered* to us.'

'The President knows best,' the Lieutenant said impatiently and hurried off.

The Doctor re-entered the President's office.

'What is it, Doctor?'

'I understand you are executing all military personnel above the rank—'

'You understand correctly, Doctor.'

'But your Excellency! I must protest! Such actions violate international law, not to mention all standards of human decency and civilized be—'

'Doctor, Doctor, calm yourself. And please don't lecture me on international law. Where the hell was international law when they were dropping my people into the volcano? Eh?'

'Because they act like devils doesn't mean—'

The Lieutenant interrupted once again. 'Commander Montenegro and the trade syndicalist Matz have just appeared on CBS. They declare our new government a sham. Montenegro's forces have retreated across the southern border, but he says he will be striking at us again as soon as he regroups . . .'

'Damn!' Benitez said. 'I thought Colonel Martinez was taking care of him.'

'Montenegro appears to have taken care of Martinez. We have had no radio contact with the Colonel since yesterday morning.'

Benitez sighed wearily. 'Well, we will deal with Montenegro later. And Lieutenant.'

'Yes, your Excellency?'

'Tell Cereno to arrest the heads of the unions.'

'Yes, sir.'

'Your Excellency . . .' the Doctor protested once again.

'Look, Doctor,' Benitez said patiently, 'I cannot rule a country I don't control. We must be strong. You want this revolution to turn out like Allende's? What did you think I was going to do after victory? Give the generals pensions?'

'I only thought . . .'

Benitez laughed ruefully and shook his head. 'You are naive, Doctor. And that is one luxury I cannot afford. Don't you see? I show these people *any* kind of mercy, and within six months they will be at my throat and plotting against me. They will kill my men, rape my women, starve my children and once again destroy my country. And *that* I will not permit to happen again!'

Then he became thoughtful and quietly said: 'And anyway, we don't need them. We have the support of the people. And of the Indians. Do you know what the Indians are saying about us? That we are the souls of Toltec warriors, reborn of Masaya, Mother of Spirits, to liberate her country. Do you know what we can do with that kind of feeling?'

The Doctor was afraid he could.

The Lieutenant's head reappeared in the doorway: 'Montenegro charges us with shooting Commander Rabon ourselves – because he would not go along with our . . . program of purification.'

Benitez shook his head in anger and dismay. 'Commander Rabon died a patriot's death from hostile fire. He will be buried with full military honors and given a hero's funeral.'

'Montenegro demands that Rabon's body be released for an independent autopsy. He says it will show he was shot in the back.'

President Benitez exploded at last. 'Montenegro has no power to demand anything! Montenegro has *lost*! He is in exile and will soon be dead. *I* am in command!' He thought for a moment. 'Have Montenegro's supporters rounded up and detained. I will *not* countenance treachery and subversion!'

The Blissful Bride

◆

Chapter 4

In the dream, her house was burning, and burning with it, all of her possessions. She tried to save them, but a guardian stood before them, his back to the fire, and motioned her away. Let them go, she told herself. Still, her heart craved some memento of the past, and she tried to get around him. Then she beheld, in each of his hands, a shining, whirling weapon – it was some sort of luminous rotating blade, like a skill saw without a cover – and she jumped back with a new respect for his power. Then, sometime later in the dream, this being had embraced her.

Gil had taken one of the pills they had given her after her accident, and she lay in the sour milk-scented darkness of the children's bedroom reveling in its bliss. She liked the drug: it made her see unsuspected perspectives; it had allowed her to envision the being in the dream, though she did not know who or what he was – unless he was an angel, the angel that had saved her.

Now the door opened slightly, cutting a wedge of light into the room. Higgins entered. She peered at him as though from a great distance. The drug was like looking through the wrong end of binoculars. Higgins was there, sharply defined, but somehow, also, far, far away. He sat down beside her and took her hand. She questioned him with her eyes.

'They're fine. Rosita's taking care of them.'

Then he saw she was silently crying. 'I'm sorry,' Higgins said. 'I know.' And he wondered what reserves of strength and courage she had spent to defeat *El Duende*.

'It's not that.'

'What is it then?'

For the longest time she wouldn't answer.

'Gil?'

'I'm pregnant.'

'What? You sure?'

She narrowed her eyes. 'Of course, I'm sure!'

Higgins thought for a moment. Then he kneeled and squeezed her hand. 'Marry me?'

Life was like this, the poets said. A stranger from another land proposes, and you accept, and going forth from your father's house, you who were two became one flesh, cleaving to each other's breast.

Only Gil knew it wasn't like this in the least – and she wasn't going to fall for it. Life was not some fruity poem by Gibran.

No. The man who opens your clothes in the dark, whispering sweet nothings, making your glands spit fire and cream and filling up your heart with honey, turns out, upon acquaintance, to be a bigamist and a cheat. She knew; it had happened before. She wasn't going to fall for it again – the candlelight, the violins. She would keep her love at arm's length. She didn't want any more . . . complications. She didn't *need* anyone. She was supremely independent. Hadn't she just proved that to anyone's satisfaction?

The drug revealed the cedar scent of pencil shavings across the room, and Gil thought, yes, let him love me like that – from a distance. Let him ache for me – like I once ached for him. She wasn't going to give her heart again only to have it shat upon, mutilated, used as an ashtray.

She began to weep. She was so afraid.

'Yes,' she said.

468

Sacrifice

◆

Chapter 5

'Doctor, there are reliable reports that executions are taking place in and around the capitol. Our sources say that the Military College has been burned to the ground, resulting in a great loss of life. Will you comment?'

'The Military College refused to surrender and to lay down its arms. Of course, there has been loss of life, Mr. Jenkins; after all, this is war. However,' the Doctor lied, 'there have been no executions.'

'Then perhaps you would care to look at these,' a voice declared. And another reporter, a leering young stringer whom the Doctor had never particularly liked, passed him a stack of photographs.

Color snapshots of an impeccable clarity, they showed high-ranking officers of the Junta sprawled in death, their brown khaki uniforms, shoulder patches, and squadron insignia clearly visible. Pools of blood drained into the dust and shone black in the sun beneath a bright blue sky. On the horizon, crooked black towers of smoke – like approaching tornados – arose from burning military vehicles.

The Doctor leafed through the stack of pictures, examining several close-ups. 'This proves nothing,' he said *sotto voce*, handing the pictures back. 'There has been a war. You show me photographs of dead soldiers . . .'

'. . . not soldiers! All colonels and generals. You can see

469

the stars and bars . . . And in this one, look the hands are bound!'

'No, it is quite impossible,' the Doctor insisted, though even as he spoke he heard the hollowness in his voice and wondered if they heard it, too. For perhaps Benitez was right and this *was* the correct political solution. Perhaps, like a boated mako, the army had to be cut and gutted and not just merely stunned or else it might, when you least expected it, come alive and eat them all.

And yet frankly, the Doctor had no stomach for this sort of thing. Even now the memory of the Chilean boy bleeding to death on the cellar floor made him feel guilty, filthy and ill. And he understood at last why war is such dirty business, because no matter how true or righteous your cause, you still ended up with blood on your hands.

'Doctor, when will new elections be held?'

'There have already *been* elections, Mr. Mobuto, and there will be new elections when *El Presidente*'s present term expires. In seven years' time.'

'Seven years!'

'Doctor, Sandy Sheaffer here. *Chicago Sun*. The Administration has just recognized your new government and announced it will be sending nineteen million dollars in emergency humanitarian aid.'

'So soon?' the Doctor said, then bit his tongue. It was amazing they would do so before the ink was dry or, for that matter, the blood.

'Is that your comment?'

'Off the record, of course.'

'What kind of deal did you make with them?'

'Deal?'

'Yes. There are rumors the Administration may be signing an agreement with President Benitez for a naval base at Laguna de Elena capable of supporting nuclear submarines. Will you comment, Doctor?'

'No, I won't,' the Doctor said. For the Doctor, in fact, was too flabbergasted to say anything. A naval base for nuclear subs! And yet, even as he heard the rumor, he knew that it was true. Of course! This is what the Under secretary and Benitez had been negotiating all along. It was nothing so nebulous as 'regional stability.' The Ambassador wanted hardware. And Benitez had given it to him!

The Doctor ended the press conference then and there. Shaken by the photographs and the unexpected news, he left the room and closed the door behind him. Why hadn't Benitez told him what he was up to? For months, he had risked his life and the lives of those he loved. For what? My God! So that Yankees might put nukes in Central America? Furious, the Doctor turned and pushed past the guards into the Presidential suite.

'What's the matter now, Doctor?' Benitez said, barely looking up.

'I was questioned about the naval base. As I never knew of its existence, it was difficult for me to give them an answer.'

'I see.'

'Nuclear submarines? My God. How could you? You sold out!' the Doctor said, with more emotion than he meant to show.

Benitez raised his sad brown eyes. 'I did nothing of the kind. I only did what I had to do to – in order to reclaim my country. If it's any consolation to you, Doctor, I fought them on it – tooth and nail. But . . . they insisted.' He shrugged. 'Sometimes in this business, one is forced to make compromises which are distasteful.'

'But why? *Why?*' the Doctor pleaded.

'The why of it is very simple. Without the Administration's backing, there would have been no coup. And the Administration does not give its backing for nothing. Christ, you're old enough to understand these things. What is that expression? *One hand washes the other?*'

'And if those hands are washed in blood?'

'Then so be it!' Benitez declared. 'If that's what it takes to liberate my country!'

The Doctor sighed, even as he felt his outrage fade. Despite his personal feelings, he could not blame Benitez for what he had done. He understood its political necessity all too clearly.

Nor could he blame himself for the revulsion he felt – that was the way the Doctor was. There would always be hunters, who fired their guns, and there would always be doctors who bound up the wounds of the hunted. And the Doctor was indubitably the latter. The Doctor was . . . a doctor.

And with this insight, for the first time in months, the Doctor's mind returned to his patients. It was funny. As a doctor, he had dreamed of war. Now, a successful warrior, he could hardly wait to resume his practice as a doctor. All that had seemed so pedestrian about it seemed to him suddenly so excellent and good. He wondered how *Señora* Esposito's liver was behaving. And how many teenage girls had become pregnant in the last three months without the Doctor to dispense prophylactics. And it seemed to him then that affixing a bandage to a child's bloodied knee was a far greater act, in the eyes of the angels, than the liberation of any number of Central American countries.

The Doctor sighed. 'I am afraid, your Excellency, I must tender my resignation.' There went his statue in the Square of the Light!

'I won't accept it,' Benitez said. 'Both Dorado and I need you sorely.'

The Doctor thought for a moment, tempted by the flattering words. For an instant he saw his destiny glimmer in the sky above the volcano – but it was only a mirage. Now that the Doctor's private war was over, his place, he knew, was here – with his people. 'I'm afraid not, your Excellency. I am sorry. But I have patients who need me.'

'Doctor, Doctor . . . don't you see what we can do . . .' He stopped short. 'And I cannot persuade you to change your mind?'

The Doctor thought for a moment, then shook his head.

'I see,' Benitez said. He seemed sincerely aggrieved. 'Very well, then.' He sighed, rising sadly. '*Companeros?*' he asked, holding out a hand.

The Doctor took it and Benitez pulled him forward into a full *brazo*. They embraced with real feeling and kissed each

472

other's cheeks with a bittersweet fervor – like lovers who know they are parting forever. 'Always,' the Doctor said.

'Good,' Benitez said, blinking slightly, squeezing hard the Doctor's arm.

Just then the door flew open and Jane came in with a drink in one hand and Lieutenant Victor Calderon in the other. She looked so happy the Doctor did not have the heart to tell her of his resignation. There would be plenty of time to discuss it later, nights beneath a down comforter in the autumn rain . . .

'Your Excellency,' the Lieutenant announced. 'A plane has just landed in Puerto Valle with Colonel Hercules Cordero. He is offering your government half a million dollars, provided that you show him mercy.'

'Colonel Cordero? My God,' Benitez said, with astonished delight, 'what won't happen next? Take him into custody, and tell him we will consider keeping him alive, provided that he spills his guts.'

'Your Excellency, your car is waiting.'

'Ah, my friends. I must leave you now. I must return back home . . . to Puerto Valle!' There were cheers and whistles. 'Doctor, may I have the honor of you and the Captain escorting me to my car?'

'The honor is all ours, your Excellency,' the Doctor said, and meant it.

As the doors to the Presidential office flew open, a crowd of well-wishers tried to surge into the room. They were barely restrained by a human chain of burly gun-toting body-guards.

The crowd was amazing. People were trying to touch the Doctor as though he was the conduit of some victorious power. He and Jane, followed by Lieutenant Calderon and, finally, by *El Presidente* squeezed their way through the people, down the marble stairwell, and out onto the steps above the street. It was mid-afternoon; the snow was gone. A stretch limousine was waiting at the curb. Hundreds of onlookers lined the sidewalks. Some were merely curious and staring, while others – exiles – were cheering wildly. For a minute, Benitez and the Doctor stood on the steps waving grandly to the crowd below. Reporters snapped pictures and some of the crowd began spontaneously to sing the Dorado National Anthem. It was a perfect moment, the zenith of the Doctor's fortune. Then it passed, and they started down the steps.

The Doctor did not see the wretched boy with the pistol until it was too late. 'No,' Jane cried and hurled herself forward. There were two sharp reports, as both Jane and the boy disappeared in the crowd, like bodies falling through the ice. At once, the cheering turned to screams and there was a near-stampede as Benitez was hurriedly whisked down the steps and flung into the back of the waiting limousine.

The Doctor was almost trampled himself as he tried to find Jane among the kicking feet and stampeding people. A hideous energy had invaded his body, like something blind without a mouth screaming inside him. He punched someone hard in the gut and drove his elbow into someone else's knee – before he found Jane's yellow hair spilling down the steps like water.

The red spreading stain on the front of her blouse was the only thing about her that was moving. There was no pulse, no respiration. She had left in the space of a moment or two. 'Jane,' he cried, but she did not see him.

'Call a doctor!' someone shouted.

'I am a doctor,' the Doctor whispered, but he had no medicine against this.

The Eternal Person

$\blacklozenge$

Chapter 6

Gil's eyes fluttered shut at last; her breathing thickened. Higgins waited until he was sure she was sleeping, then kissed her brow, and went out into the hall. He was doubley delighted. He was going to get married and become a father, as well.

Higgins hurried off to Sara Devi's in order to tell her the unexpected good news. To his shock, her house was gone! Bulldozed, flattened, it was impossible to say where once it had stood. All that remained was a field of rubble on which a blue gingham curtain, trapped by some debris, flapped and fluttered in the cold, autumn wind.

Early one morning several weeks later Higgins, Gilberta and the three little girls left the *barrio* for Boston. The Doctor, who had been depressed, had begun to show the night before the first signs of incipient life. In a fit of rage over an under-cooked muffin, he had called his sister a 'Mexican whore' and Higgins a 'demented swami,' before dissolving into rueful tears – a sure sign, they had all agreed, that his recovery was progressing well.

Now, this morning of their departure, a cab had been called and the Doctor was supervising the packing of their luggage. There was too much of it, however, and the Doctor and the cabbie were arguing loudly over the best way to fit it all in the trunk.

Higgins, meanwhile, was trying to load the kids – a move they were resisting. To this end, he gave the littlest one a playful tap on her behind, sending her into paroxysms of tearful self-pity.

Wailing, she appealed to her mother, but Gil with her hands on her hips only said, 'Good. You should listen to your father. He told you to do something and you wouldn't do it. So, now you get whacked. Good.'

The child continued to wail, however. Higgins picked her up and threw her over his shoulder as the Doctor and the cabbie started shouting at each other, and Rosita in her night-dress descended the steps, shawled against the dawn chill. She sidled up to Higgins with a secretive air. 'I had a dream.'

'Really? Maybe you could tell me about it later.'

'You're leaving, aren't you? How could I tell you?'

'You could always write me a letter.'

She appraised him for a moment. 'You're a wise guy. You know that? No. In my dream, I received a message for you.'

'A message from who? From outer space?'

'From your guru, Sara Devi.'

Higgins set down the child, and straightened up at once. 'What message? Where is she?'

'I told you. She was in my dream.'

'*Your* dream. Why didn't she just appear in mine?'

'I imagine your guru knows what she is doing. Don't you?'

'Of course,' Higgins said, chastened once again.

' "*The soul you love is in Gilberta's womb.*" '

'I'm sorry,' Higgins said. 'What was that?'

'That was Sara's message to you.'

For the longest moment, Higgins didn't understand. Then he did. He turned to Gil. The faint swelling of her waist was barely visible, her motherhood was as of yet only a subtle radiance and a heaviness around her belly, breasts, and jowls. She looked at him and smiled. Higgins smiled back, in a daze. He looked away at the dawn-lit ghetto. The buildings were hosannas frozen in stone.

'But what . . . but *how* . . . ?' He fumbled for the words. He knew it had not hit him yet, that it would not hit him fully for another several hours, days, and then its meaning would grow inside of him with every passing month and moment like the child itself. 'I mean . . . are you absolutely certain she said that? Because, you see, she told me once that it couldn't be done. She said, it was *her* destiny. And that even God, try as He might, cannot undo your destiny.'

'That's what Sara said you'd say!' Rosita said smugly, as if the two of them were on the closest terms.

'She did?'

'Yes! And when you did I was to tell you something else. Now, what was it?'

'Please!' Higgins said.

'Oh, yes. "Perhaps *God* cannot change your destiny, *Señor*, but . . ."' Rosita closed her eyes in bliss, happy to pronounce what she'd always known. ' " . . . *Love* can." '

'Idiot!' the Doctor shouted. 'Pack those things more carefully! My consultant and his family are going all the way to Boston!'

The Morning Star

◆

Chapter 7

It was not until one thawing winter morning in early March the deadness left the Doctor's heart. He awoke early feeling rested, and waited for the depression which invariably mugged him upon waking – but this morning, it just wasn't there.

Getting out of bed, he put on his bathrobe and wandered through the house, listening to the ice melting on the rooftops and the water singing in the drains and gutters. It had taken the Doctor some time to get used to the empty apartment, though even now he still missed the kids. He missed Higgins and his sister, too. He even missed Rosita – that lascivious and overstuffed old shrew!

The Doctor retrieved the Sunday paper. On its front page was a picture of Rodolfo Benitez entering Puerto Valle in a wooden-wheeled cart drawn by two oxen, as worshipful citizens waved palm fronds and sang his praises all around. Dorado's Presidential Re-Inauguration had been held only yesterday in the newly restored Presidential Palace, though even in victory, in the midst of the ecstatic throng, Benitez's expression was detached and sober, like the face of a Zen master, or a merchant reviewing his wares.

Beside him in the cart, with his Indian wife, sat the newly appointed Vice President of Dorado, four-star General Ambrosio Garcia. Naming Garcia Vice-President had been a

478

masterstroke on Benitez's part, uniting as it did the Spanish with the Indians, left and right, civilian and military, old and new. A school had even been named in his honor – The General Garcia Academy of Military Strategy – a sort of a military reform school for wealthy, wayward boys.

The Doctor, of course, was a hero, as well. He even had a small medal to prove it. It had arrived in the mail one morning last week. The gold round showed the profile of President Jose D'Aquila. Attached to it via thin silken ribbons were several silver thunderbolts and little gold stars. The Doctor, on opening the box, had thought he was going to remember something – as though these trivial symbols were all that remained of some magnificent conflict, the souvenir of an Olympian battle, reduced by time and forgetfulness to a pitiful handful of tiny metal thunderbolts and stars.

But it was Jane who was the true heroine. The grateful Republic was even erecting a monument in her honor in the Square of the People (as the Plaza of Peace had been renamed). The Doctor had been sent a sketch of the statue. Unfortunately, it did not resemble Jane in the least. Instead of high heel pumps and skin-tight jeans, she was dressed, for some reason, in military fatigues, her oak-blonde hair pinned and hidden beneath a peaked cap. Instead of a drink in one hand and a lipstick-kissed cigarette in the other, she was flaunting a machine pistol and staring off at the volcano with a look of heroic determination.

Only the inscription was moving. It read:

> *Captain Wilhelmina Crespi,*
> *Patriot,*
> *Who stopped a traitor's bullet*
> *With her heart.*

But the real monument to Jane was in the Doctor's heart. The idol of Evangeline had been dismantled and in its place stood Jane, smiling at him now like she had the first night he had met her, her painted lips leaking smoke – her look mocking, insouciant, come-hither. The Doctor had tried to alter this idol, to clean it up, as it were, but it seemed to have a life of its own. And so like a temple priest, the Doctor worshiped it, waved at it the lights of his love, burned before it the incense of his memories, and placed the flowers of his devotion at its lotus toes, shod in Parisian high heel sandals.

He would never marry. No! He would never do anything to violate her precious memory. He would be true to her til the end of his days!

Of course, the Doctor thought, remembering a girl he had seen the other afternoon, he might fool around a little.

The Doctor lay down the paper now and gazed out the window. Though the sun had not yet risen, Venus was already shining in the east, like a farm wife who rises early to prepare her husband's breakfast.

But though the Doctor had been awarded the Jose D'Aquila Medal of Liberation, and had been written up in several national news magazines, no wife had risen early to cook *his* breakfast. He contemplated this irony as he gnawed at a piece of toast moistened with a little muddy coffee, and gazed upon the empty rooms filling up with morning light.

'No one's who you think they are.' These words of the *mestiza* had struck in the flesh of the Doctor's mind, like arrows. He had thought she was talking about other people at the time: Jorge, Jane, Guido, Benitez – and perhaps she was. But mostly, he realized, she was talking about him.

For the Doctor had once considered himself a loser. And yet, through his daring, sacrifice, and courage, he had managed to help liberate an entire country and to free himself from an onerous and oppressive yoke as well. To say that he was happy would have been untrue – but he was happier, surely, then he had been six months ago, and who was to say, if things kept up in this manner, how he would feel in ten years' time? Luminous surely, and as hot and bright as a spear of summer lightning!

Heartened by this hope, the Doctor rose from the table and headed down the hall. On an impulse, he opened the door to the children's old bedroom. He had not been inside it since the day they had left, and it still held their scent of spoiled milk and broken crayons. He looked at their beds, remembering all those summer nights he had lain across them in despair. And it was then that he saw, propped against a pillow, another of those fiendish dolls.

For a moment the Doctor just stared at the thing. Then he began to laugh aloud. In fact, the Doctor laughed so long and hard he grew red in the face and had to sit down on the edge of the bed to catch his breath and keep from falling. Oh, what silly fools they'd been – what silly old fools – to see the children's gifts as curses!

But the Doctor's laughter soon turned into tears. Christ, but he missed Janie so.

And yet the pain of her loss had definitely lifted in the night – even his tears felt sweet. Then again, he thought, drying his eyes, it was about time – more than four months had passed since she had died.

So why, he wondered now, did he have the strangest impression that he had spoken to her only minutes ago?

Because of the dream. Yes! *The dream!* He remembered it now – though the whole thing was so fantastic and bizarre, he knew he could never decipher its meaning.

For in his dream, the Doctor had been traveling in some high, bright country where the people were all beautiful, healthy, and young. A magnificent city glowed in the distance; while all about him, herds of scarlet deer roamed wild. And in this country, as in Dorado, a coronation was taking place.

The Doctor, with a mounting sense of excitement, had pressed forward in order to watch the rite, but all he could see was a pair of hands holding aloft a golden crown. And as he watched, the crown descended and a voice like thunder proclaimed, 'The sacrifice has been accepted. The least has become the first.'

Then the newly crowned Queen arose from her throne and the Doctor saw that it was Jane! She had shed her jeans and was dressed in splendour, the gems and pearls in her little diadem sparkling with a soft blue radiance and luster. And next to her was Sara Devi.

481

Then in the dream, the Doctor had rushed forward, falling at their feet, laughing and weeping with joy and relief, and when he was finished he had felt much better, pounds lighter, like he had as a child after going to Confession. Then Jane had reached down and lifted him up, and with her fair hair had wiped away his tears, going so far as to garland him with flowers and, rising on her tiptoes, to plant a kiss of victory on his cheek. Then all the host had started cheering, crying out the Doctor's name. And in the sky of the Doctor's dream, strange, mustachioed angels had appeared in the clouds chanting his praises, hailing his victory, and raining blossoms and blessings down on their heads.

But the Doctor, even as he reveled in their adulation, could not help thinking there was some mistake. What victory could be so great? 'No es nada,' he'd said, embarrassed. 'It was nothing, really.'

'Nothing?' Jane cried, and her eyes had widened in disbelief. 'You underestimate yourself, my lord. This one called Schmidt was a powerful being, difficult to conquer, impossible to deceive. You have no idea how high he was – or how hard or far he fell.'

And the Doctor recalled his enemy then, lying upon the cold concrete of a *barrio* cellar in the red pond of his own gore. 'I pity him,' the Doctor said.

But Sara Devi shook her head. 'To pity him,' she said, 'is not to understand his true greatness.'

'Greatness? What?' The Doctor smiled. 'After all, he was just a boy.'

'Yes,' Sara said. 'He was just a boy.' And her eyes had gotten distant then and dim, like she was gazing off at fairy realms he could not see. 'But once long ago . . . in a land faraway . . .' She turned to him. Her eyes were suns. 'He was the King of Heaven.'